SWORN TO
SILENCE

SWORN TO
SILENCE

LINDA CASTILLO

MINOTAUR BOOKS ✷ NEW YORK

This is a work of fiction. All of the characters, organizations, and events portrayed
in this novel are either products of the author's imagination or are used fictitiously.

SWORN TO SILENCE. Copyright © 2009 by Linda Castillo. All rights reserved.
Printed in the United States of America. For information, address St. Martin's
Press, 175 Fifth Avenue, New York, N.Y. 10010.

ISBN-13: 978-0-312-37497-6

I'm one of those writers lucky enough to have a strong support system that sustains me in the long, and sometimes difficult, months it takes to write a novel. This book is dedicated to my husband, Ernest, who just happens to be my real-life hero. And to Jack and Debbie, for that wonderful trip to Amish country. I love you guys.

ACKNOWLEDGMENTS

A writer's quest for facts while working on a book is a seemingly endless process. Though the writing itself is a solitary endeavor, writers are rewarded during the research phase of the book with the opportunity to speak with countless interesting individuals and professionals who so generously share their expertise. I have many people to thank for helping me bring *Sworn to Silence* to fruition.

First and foremost, I wish to thank my fabulous agent, Nancy Yost, who saw the possibilities from the start and never faltered along the way. To my wonderful editor, Charlie Spicer, whose enthusiasm for the story and editorial direction shaped the book into a winner. I'd also like to thank the entire St. Martin's/Minotaur team in New York: Sally Richardson, Andrew Martin, Matthew Shear, Matthew Baldacci, Bob Podrasky, Hector DeJean, David Rotstein, Allison Caplin, and Sarah Melnyk. There are many more brilliant individuals who remain unnamed due to space constraints, but I'm blessed to write for such a dynamic and capable group of people.

On the technical side of things I owe huge thanks to Chief Daniel Light of the Arcanum, Ohio, Police Department, for so generously sharing his knowledge and experience of the inner workings of a small town police department. Thank you to A.C. for all of your insights into the Amish culture and for sharing all of those precious details about daily Amish life. To my critique group: Jennifer Archer, Anita Howard, Marcy McKay, and April Redmon, thanks for letting me keep you up late Wednesday nights. To Kurt Shearer of the Ohio Bureau of Criminal Identification and Investigation, for answering all of my crazy questions without blinking an eye. I took much literary license when depicting many of the law enforcement agencies in my book, particularly BCI. It is a top-notch agency administered by consummate professionals who are very good at what they do. Any procedural errors and embellishments are mine.

Forwith the devil did appear,
For name him and he's always near.

—Matthew Prior, "Hans Carvel"

SWORN TO
SILENCE

PROLOGUE

She hadn't believed in monsters since she was six years old, back when her mom would check the closet and look beneath her bed at night. But at the age of twenty-one, bound and brutalized and lying naked on a concrete floor that was as cold as lake ice, she believed.

Enveloped in darkness, she listened to the hard drum of her heart. She couldn't stop shivering. Couldn't keep her teeth from chattering. Every minuscule sound made her body tense in terrible anticipation of the monster's return.

In the beginning, she'd entertained fantasies of escape or convincing her captor to let her go. But she was a realist; she knew this wasn't going to end nicely. There would be no negotiation. No police rescue. No last-minute reprieve. The monster was going to kill her. It was no longer a question of if, but when. The waiting was almost as hellish as death itself.

She didn't know where she was or how long she'd been there. She'd lost all concept of time and place. All she could discern about her surroundings was that the place stank of rotting meat, and every little noise echoed as if she were in a cave.

She was hoarse from screaming. Exhausted from struggling. Demoralized by the horrors he'd inflicted upon her. A small part of her just wanted this terrible struggle for life to end. But dear God how she wanted to live . . .

"Mama," she whispered.

She'd never contemplated death. She had too many dreams. She was too full of hope for the future, and a firm believer in the promise that tomorrow would be better than today. Lying in a cold slick of her own urine, she accepted the fact that there would be no tomorrow. There was no hope. No future. Only the black dread of her impending death and the agony that knowledge brought.

She lay on her side with her knees drawn up to her chest. The wire binding her wrists behind her had tormented her at first, but over the hours the pain had ebbed. She tried not to think of the things he'd done to her. He'd raped her first. But even that outrage was nothing compared to the other depravities she'd endured.

She could still hear the snap of electricity. She felt the hard wrench of it as it jumped through her, jolting her brain inside her skull. She could still hear the animalistic sound of her own screams. The roar of adrenaline-rich blood through her veins. The wild drum of her heart beating out of control. And then there was the knife.

He'd worked with the intense concentration of some macabre artisan. He'd been so close she'd felt the whisper of his breath against her skin. When she screamed, he hit her with the electrical prod. When she lashed out with her feet, he'd hit her again. In the end, she'd lain still and endured the agony in silence. She'd accepted the pain. And for a few brief minutes, her mind had taken her to the beach in Florida where she'd gone with her parents two years ago. White sand hot on her feet. A breeze so moist and warm it was like the breath of God on her soul.

"Help me, Mama . . ."

The sound of boots against concrete jerked her from her reverie. She raised her head and looked around wildly, trying in vain to see past the blindfold. She could hear her breaths rushing between her teeth, like a wild animal that had been hunted down for slaughter. She hated him. She hated what he was, what he'd done to her. If only she could loosen her bonds and run . . .

"Stay away from me, you son of a bitch!" she shouted. *"Stay away!"*

But she knew he wouldn't.

A gloved hand brushed her hip. Twisting, she lashed out with both feet. A fleeting sense of satisfaction unfurled when her tormenter grunted. Then the snap of electricity cracked like lightning. Pain raked down her body as if she were at the end of a bullwhip that had just been snapped.

For an instant, the world went silent and gray. Vaguely, she was aware of hands touching her feet. The distant clink of steel against concrete. Cold seeping into her until her entire body quaked uncontrollably.

A pristine new terror whipped through her when she realized her attacker had wrapped a chain around her ankles. The cold links dug into her skin when it was drawn tight. She tried to kick, tried to free her legs so she could make one last, desperate stand.

But it was too late.

She screamed until she ran out of breath. She floundered, twisting and writhing, but her efforts were futile. Above her, steel rattled against steel. The chain slowly lifted her feet from the floor.

"Why are you doing this?" she cried. *"Why?"*

The chain jangled, pulling her feet upward, higher and higher until she was hanging upside down. All the blood in her body seemed to pool in her head. It pounded in her face, the veins throbbing. She fought to right herself, but gravity tugged her down. "Help me! Someone!"

A mindless panic gripped her when a gloved hand grasped her hair. A scream poured from her lungs when the monster drew her head back. The sudden heat of a razor cut pricked her throat. As if from a great distance she heard the sound of water pouring down, like the spray from a shower echoing off tile walls. Staring into the darkness of the blindfold, she listened to her lifeblood drain away. This could not be happening. Not to her. Not in Painters Mill.

As if someone had flipped a switch, her mind went fuzzy. Her face grew hot, but her body was cold. Terror ebbed into a dull and steady hum. Pain faded into nothingness. Her muscles went slack. Her limbs began to tingle.

He's not going to hurt me after all, she thought.

And she escaped to the white sand beach where slender palms swayed like elegant flamenco dancers. And the bluest water she'd ever seen stretched as far as the eye could see.

CHAPTER 1

The cruiser's strobes cast red and blue light onto winter dead trees. Officer T.J. Banks pulled the car onto the shoulder and flipped on the spotlight, running the beam along the edge of the field where corn stalks shivered in the cold. Twenty yards away, six Jersey cows stood in the bar ditch, chewing their cud.

"Stupid fuckin' cows," he muttered. Besides chickens, they had to be the dumbest animals on earth.

He hit the radio. "Dispatch, this is forty-seven."

"What's up, T.J.?" asked Mona, the night dispatcher.

"I got a 10-54. Stutz's damn cows are out again."

"That's the second time in a week."

"Always on my shift, too."

"So what are you going to do? He ain't got no phone out there."

A glance at the clock on the dash told him it was nearly two A.M. "Well, I'm not going to stand out here in the frickin' cold and round up these stupid shits."

"Maybe you ought to just shoot 'em."

"Don't tempt me." Looking around, he sighed. Livestock on the road at this hour was an accident waiting to happen. If someone came around the curve too fast it could be bad. He thought of all the paperwork an accident would entail and shook his head. "I'll set up some flares then go drag his Amish ass out of bed."

"Let me know if you need backup." She snickered.

Yanking the zipper of his coat up to his chin, he slid his flashlight from its nest beside the seat and got out of the cruiser. It was so cold he could feel his nose hairs freezing. His boots crunched through snow as he made his way to the bar ditch, his breaths puffing out in front of him. He hated the graveyard shift almost as much as he hated winter.

He ran the flashlight beam along the fence line. Sure enough, twenty feet away two strands of barbed wire had come loose from a gnarled locust-wood post. Hoofprints told him several head had discovered the opening and ventured onto the shoulder for some illicit grazing.

"Stupid fuckin' cows."

T.J. went back to the cruiser and popped the trunk. Removing two flares, he set them up on the centerline to warn traffic. He was on his way back to the cruiser when he spotted something in the snow on the opposite side of the road. Curious, he crossed to it. A solitary woman's shoe lay on the shoulder. Judging from its condition and lack of snow cover, it hadn't been there long. Teenagers, probably. This deserted stretch of road was a favorite place to smoke dope and have sex. They were almost as stupid as cows.

Frowning, T.J. nudged the shoe with his foot. That was when he noticed the drag marks, as if something heavy had been hauled through the snow. He traced the path with the flashlight beam, tracking it to the fence and into the field beyond. The hairs at the back of his neck prickled when he spotted blood. A lot of it.

"What the hell?"

He followed the trail into the ditch where yellow grass poked up through the snow. He climbed the fence and found more blood on the other side, stark and black against pristine white. It was enough to give a guy the willies.

The path took him to a stand of bare-branched hedge apple trees at the edge of a cornfield. He could hear himself breathing hard, the dead corn stalks whispering all around. T.J. set his hand on his revolver and swept the beam in a 360-degree circle. That was when he noticed the object in the snow.

At first he thought an animal had been hit and dragged itself there to die. But as he neared, the beam revealed something else. Pale flesh. A shock of darkish hair. A bare foot sticking out of the snow. Adrenaline kicked hard in his gut. "Holy shit."

For an instant he couldn't move. He couldn't stop looking at the dark circle of blood and colorless flesh. Giving himself a hard mental shake, T.J. dropped to his knees beside the body. His first thought was that she might still be alive. Brushing at the snow, he set his hand against a bare shoulder. Her skin was ice cold, but he rolled her over anyway. He saw more blood and pasty flesh and glazed eyes that seemed to stare right at him.

Shaken, he scrambled back. His hand trembled as he grappled for his lapel mike. "Dispatch! This is forty-seven!"

"What now, T.J? One of them cows chase you up a tree?"

"I got a fuckin' body here at Stutz's place."

"What?"

They used the ten-code system in Painters Mill, but for the life of him he couldn't remember the number for a dead body. He'd never had to use it. "I said I got a dead body."

"I heard you the first time." But the words were followed by a stunned pause as realization hit her. "What's your twenty?"

"Dog Leg Road, just south of the covered bridge."

A beat of silence. "Who is it?"

Everyone knew everyone in Painters Mill, but he'd never seen this woman before. "I don't know. A woman. Naked as the day she came into this world and deader than Elvis."

"A wreck or what?"

"This was no accident." Setting his hand on the butt of his .38, T.J. scanned the shadows within the trees. He could feel his heart beating fast in his chest. "You'd better call the chief, Mona. I think we got us a murder."

CHAPTER 2

I dream of death.

As always, I'm in the kitchen of the old farmhouse. Blood shimmers stark and red against the scuffed hardwood floor. The scents of yeast bread and fresh-cut hay mingle with the harsh stench of my own terror, a contrariety my mind cannot reconcile. The curtains billow in the breeze coming through the window above the sink. I see flecks of blood on the yellow fabric. More spatter on the wall. I feel the stickiness of it on my hands.

I crouch in the corner, animal sounds I don't recognize tearing from my throat like stifled screams. I feel death in the room. Darkness all around me. Inside me. And at the age of fourteen, I know evil exists in my safe and sheltered world.

The phone rattles me from sleep. The nightmare slinks back into its hole like some nocturnal creature. Rolling, I grapple with the phone on the nightstand and set the phone against my ear. "Yeah." My voice comes out like a croak.

"Chief. This is Mona. Sorry to wake you, but I think you'd better come in."

Mona is my graveyard dispatcher. She's not prone to hysterics, so the anxiety in her tone garners my full attention. "What happened?"

"T.J.'s out at the Stutz place. He was rounding up cows and found a dead body."

Suddenly, I'm no longer sleepy. Sitting up, I shove the hair from my face. "What?"

"He found a body. Sounds pretty shaken up."

Judging from the tone of her voice, T.J. isn't the only one. I throw my legs over the side of the bed and reach for my robe. A glance at the alarm tells me it's almost two-thirty A.M. "An accident?"

"Just a body. Nude. Female."

Realizing I need my clothes, not the robe, I turn on the lamp. The light hurts my eyes, but I'm fully awake now. I'm still trying to get my mind around the idea of one of my officers finding a body. I ask for the location, and she tells me.

"Call Doc Coblentz," I say. Doc Coblentz is one of six doctors in the town of Painters Mill, Ohio, and acting coroner for Holmes County.

I cross to the closet and reach for my bra, socks and long johns. "Tell T.J. not to touch anything or move the body. I'll be there in ten minutes."

The Stutz farm sits on eighty acres bordered on one side by Dog Leg Road, the other by the north fork of Painters Creek. The location Mona gave me is half a mile from the old covered bridge on a deserted stretch of road that dead ends at the county line.

I crave coffee as I pull up behind T.J.'s cruiser. My headlights reveal his silhouette in the driver's seat. I'm pleased to see he set out flares and left his strobes on. Grabbing my Mag-Lite, I slide out of the Explorer. The cold shocks me, and I huddle deeper into my parka, wishing I'd remembered my hat. T.J. looks shaken as I approach. "What do you have?"

"A body. Female." He's doing his best to maintain his cop persona, but his hand shakes as he points toward the field. I know those tremors aren't from the temperature. "Thirty feet in by those trees."

"You sure she's dead?"

T.J.'s Adam's apple bobs twice. "She's cold. No pulse. There's blood all over the fuckin' place."

"Let's take a look." We start toward the trees. "Did you touch anything? Disturb the scene?"

He drops his head slightly, and I know he did. "I thought maybe she was . . . alive, so I rolled her over, checked."

Not good, but I don't say anything. T.J. Banks has the makings of a good cop. He's diligent and serious about his work. But this is his first job in law enforcement. Having been my officer for only six months, he's green. I'd lay odds this is his first dead body.

We crunch through ankle-deep snow. A sense of dread staggers me when I spot the body. I wish for daylight, but it will be hours before my wish is granted. Nights are long this time of year. The victim is naked. Late teens or early twenties. Dark blonde hair. A slick of blood two feet in diameter surrounds her head. She'd once been pretty, but in death her face is macabre. I can tell she'd originally been lying prone; lividity has set in, leaving one side of her face purple. Her eyes are halfway open and glazed. Her tongue bulges from between swollen lips, and I see ice crystals on it.

I squat next to the body. "Looks like she's been here a few hours."

"Starting to get freezer burn," T.J. notes.

Though I was a patrol officer in Columbus, Ohio, for six years, a homicide detective for two, I feel as if I'm out of my league. Columbus isn't exactly the murder capital of the world, but like every city it has a dark side. I've seen my share of death. Still, the blatant brutality of this crime shocks me. I want to think violent murder doesn't happen in towns like Painters Mill.

But I know it does.

I remind myself this is a crime scene. Rising, I fan my flashlight beam around the perimeter. There are no tracks other than ours. With a sinking sensation, I realize we've contaminated possible evidence. "Call Glock and tell him to get out here."

"He's on va—"

My look cuts his words short.

The Painters Mill PD consists of myself, three full-time officers, two dispatchers and one auxiliary officer. Rupert "Glock" Maddox is a former Marine and my most experienced. He earned his nickname because of his fondness for his side arm. Vacation or not, I need him.

"Tell him to bring crime scene tape." I think about what else we're going to need. "Get an ambulance out here. Alert the hospital in Millersburg. Tell them we'll be transporting a body to the morgue. Oh, and tell Rupert to bring coffee. Lot's of it." I look down at the body. "We're going to be here a while."

Dr. Ludwig Coblentz is a rotund man with a big head, a balding pate and a belly the size of a Volkswagen. I meet him on the shoulder as he slides from his Escalade. "I hear one of your officers had a close encounter with a dead body," he says grimly.

"Not just dead," I say. "Murdered."

He wears khaki trousers and a red plaid pajama top beneath his parka. I watch as he pulls a black bag from the passenger seat. Holding it like a lunchbox, he turns to me, his expression telling me he's ready to get down to business.

I lead him into the bar ditch. It's a short walk to the body, but his breathing is labored by the time we climb the fence. "How the hell did a body get all the way out here?" he mutters.

"Someone dumped her or she dragged herself before she died."

He gives me a look, but I don't elaborate. I don't want him walking into this with preconceived notions. First impressions are important in police work.

We duck under the crime scene tape Glock has strung through the trees like toilet paper at Halloween. T.J. has clipped an AC work light to a branch above the body. It doesn't cast much light, but it's better than flashlights and will free up our hands. I wish for a generator.

"Scene is secure." Glock approaches holding two cups of coffee and shoves one at me. "You look like you could use this."

Taking the Styrofoam cup, I peel back the tab and sip. "God, that's good."

He glances at the body. "You figure someone dumped her?"

"Looks that way."

T.J. joins us, his gaze flicking to the dead woman. "Jeez, Chief, I hate to see her laid out like that."

I hate it, too. From where we stand I can see her breasts and pubic hair. The woman inside me cringes at that. But there's nothing I can do about it; we can't move her or cover her until we process the scene. "Do either of you recognize her?" I ask.

Both men shake their heads.

Sipping my coffee, I study the scene, trying to piece together what might have happened. "Glock, do you still have that old Polaroid?"

"In my trunk."

"Take some photos of the body and the scene." I think of the trampled snow and mentally kick myself for disturbing the area. A boot tread might have been helpful. "I want shots of the drag marks, too." I speak to both men now. "Set up a grid inside the crime scene tape and walk it, starting at the trees. Bag everything you find, even if you think it's not important. Be sure to photograph everything before you touch it. See if you can find a boot tread. Keep your eyes open for clothing or a wallet."

"Will do, Chief." Glock and T.J. start toward the trees.

I turn to Doc Coblentz, who is standing next to the body. "Any idea who she is?" I ask.

"I don't recognize her." The doc removes his mittens, slides his chubby fingers into latex gloves. He grunts as he kneels.

"Any idea how long she's been dead?"

"Hard to tell because of the cold." He lifts her arm. Red grooves mark her wrist. The surrounding flesh is bruised and smeared with blood. "Her hands were bound," he says.

I look at the scored flesh. She'd struggled violently to get free. "With wire?"

"That would be my guess."

Her painted fingernails tell me she's not Amish. I notice two nails on her right hand are broken to the quick. She'd fought back. I make a mental note to get nail scrapings.

"Rigor has set in," the doc says. "She's been dead at least eight hours. Judging from the ice crystals on the mucous membranes, probably closer to ten. Once I get her to the hospital, I'll get a core body temp. Body temp drops a degree to a degree and a half per hour, so a core will narrow down TOD." He releases her hand.

His finger hovers above the purple flesh of her cheek. "Lividity in the face here." He looks up at me. His glasses are fogged. His eyes appear huge behind the thick lenses. "Did someone move her?" he asks.

I nod, but I don't mention who. "What about cause of death?"

Removing a penlight from his inside pocket, the doctor peels back an eyelid and shines it into her eye. "No petechial hemorrhages."

"So she wasn't strangled."

"Right." Gently, he sets his hand beneath her chin and shifts her head to the left. Her lips part, and I notice two of her front teeth are broken to the gum line. He turns her head to the right and the wound on her throat gapes like a bloody mouth.

"Throat was cut," the doc says.

"Any idea what kind of weapon made the wound?"

"Something sharp. With no serration. No obvious sign of tearing. Not a slash or it would be longer and more shallow on the edges. Hard to tell in this light." Gently, he rolls her body to one side.

My eyes skim the corpse. Her left shoulder is covered with bright red abrasions or possibly burns. More of the same appear on her left buttock. Both knees are abraded as well as the tops of her feet. The skin at both ankles is the color of ripe eggplant. The flesh isn't laid open like her wrists, but her feet had definitely been bound.

My heart drops into my stomach when I notice more blood on her abdomen, just above her navel. Obscured within the dark smear is something I've seen before. Something I've imagined a thousand times in my nightmares. "What about that?"

"Good God." The doctor's voice quivers. "It looks like something carved into her flesh."

"Hard to make out what it is." But in that instant I'm certain we both know. Neither of us wants to say it aloud.

The doc leans closer, so that his face is less than a foot from the wound. "Looks like two X's and three I's."

"Or the Roman numeral twenty-three," I finish.

He looks at me and in his eyes I see the same horror and disbelief I feel clenching my chest. "It's been sixteen years since I've seen anything like it," he whispers.

Staring at the bloody carving on this young woman's body, I'm filled with a revulsion so deep I shiver.

After a moment, Doc Coblentz leans back on his heels. Shaking his head, he motions toward the marks on her buttocks, the broken fingernails and teeth. "Someone put her through a lot."

Outrage and a fear I don't want to acknowledge sweep through me. "Was she sexually assaulted?"

My heart pounds as he shines the pen light onto her pubis. I see blood on the insides of her thighs and shudder inwardly.

"Looks like it." He shakes his head. "I'll know more once I get her to the morgue. Hopefully the son of a bitch left us a DNA sample."

The fist twisting my gut warns me it isn't going to be that easy.

Looking down at the body, I wonder what kind of monster could do this to a young woman with so much life ahead. I wonder how many lives will be destroyed by her death. The coffee has gone bitter on my tongue. I'm no longer cold. I'm deeply offended and angered by the brutality of what I see. Worse, I'm afraid.

"Will you bag her hands for me, Doc?"

"Sure."

"How soon can you do an autopsy?"

Coblentz braces his hands on his knees and shoves himself to his feet. "I'll shuffle some appointments and do it today."

We stand in the wind and cold and try in vain not to think about what this woman endured before her death.

"He killed her somewhere else." I glance at the drag marks. "No sign of a struggle. If he'd cut her throat here, there'd be more blood."

The doctor nods. "Hemorrhage ceases when the heart stops. She was probably already dead when he dumped her. More than likely the blood here is residual that leaked from that neck wound."

I think of the people who must have loved her. Parents. Husband. Children. And I am saddened. "This wasn't a crime of passion."

"The person who did this took his time." The doctor's eyes meet mine. "This was calculated. Organized."

I know what he's thinking. I see it in the depths of his eyes. I know because I'm thinking the very same thing.

"Just like before," the doctor finishes.

CHAPTER 3

Snow swirls in the beams of the headlights as I turn the Explorer onto the long and narrow lane that will take us to the Stutz farm. Next to me, T.J. is reticent. He's my youngest officer—just twenty-four years old—and more sensitive than he would ever admit. Not that sensitivity in a cop is a bad thing, but I can tell finding the body has shaken him.

"Hell of a way to start the week." I force a smile.

"Tell me about it."

I want to draw him out, but I'm not great at small talk. "So, are you okay?"

"Me? I'm good." He looks embarrassed by my question and troubled by the images I know are still rolling around inside his head.

"Seeing something like that . . ." I give him my best cop-to-cop look. "It can be tough."

"I've seen shit before," he says defensively. "I was first on the scene when Houseman had that head on and killed that family from Cincinnati."

I wait, hoping he'll open up.

He looks out the window, wipes his palms on his uniform slacks. In my peripheral vision I see him glance my way. "You ever see anything like that, Chief?"

He's asking about the eight years I was a cop in Columbus. "Nothing this bad."

"He broke her teeth. Raped her. Cut her throat." He blows out a breath, like a pressure cooker releasing steam. *"Damn."*

At thirty, I'm not that much older than T.J., but glancing over at his youthful profile, I feel ancient. "You did okay."

He stares out the window and I know he doesn't want me to see his expression. "I screwed up the crime scene."

"It's not like you were expecting to walk up on a dead body."

"Footwear impressions might have been helpful."

"We still might be able to lift something." It's an optimistic offering. "I walked in those drag marks, too. It happens."

"You think Stutz knows something about the murder?" he asks.

Isaac Stutz and his family are Amish. A culture I'm intimately acquainted with because I was born Amish in this very town a lifetime ago.

I make an effort not to let my prejudices and preconceived notions affect my judgment. But I know Isaac personally, and I've always thought of him as a decent, hardworking man. "I don't think he had anything to do with the murder," I say. "But someone in the family might have seen something."

"So we're just going to question him?"

"*I'm* going to question him."

That elicits a smile. "Right," he says.

The lane curves left and a white clapboard farmhouse looms into view. Like most Amish farms in the area, the house is plain but well kept. A split rail fence separates the backyard from a chicken coop and pen. I see a nicely shaped cherry tree that will bear fruit in the spring. Beyond, a large barn, grain silo and windmill stand in silhouette against the predawn sky.

Though it's not yet five A.M., the windows glow yellow with lantern light. I park next to a buggy and kill the engine. The sidewalk has been cleared of snow and we take it to the front door.

The door swings open before we knock. Isaac Stutz is a man of about forty years. Sporting the traditional beard of a married Amish man, he wears a blue work shirt, dark trousers and suspenders. His eyes flick from me to T.J. and back to me.

"I'm sorry to bother you so early, Mr. Stutz," I begin.

"Chief Burkholder." He bows his head slightly and steps back, opening the door wider. "Come in."

I wipe my feet on the rug before entering. The house smells of coffee and frying scrapple, an Amish breakfast staple consisting of cornmeal and pork. The kitchen is dimly lit, but warm. Ahead, a mantel clock and two lanterns rest on a homemade shelf built into the wall. Lower, three straw hats hang on wood dowels. I look beyond Isaac and see his wife, Anna, at the cast-iron stove. She is garbed in the traditional organdy *kapp* and a plain black dress. She glances at me over her shoulder. I make eye contact, but she looks away. Twenty years ago, we played together. This morning, I'm a stranger to her.

The Amish are a close-knit community with a foundation built on worship, hard work and family. Though eighty percent of Amish children join the church when they turn eighteen, I'm one of the few who didn't. As a result, I was put under the *bann*. Contrary to popular belief, shunning is not a type of punishment. In most cases, it's thought to be redemptive. Tough love, if you will. But it didn't bring me back. Because of my defection, many Amish do not wish to associate with me. I accept that because I understand the ideology of the culture, and I don't begrudge them in any way.

T.J. and I enter the house. Always respectful, T.J. removes his hat.

"Would you like coffee or hot tea?" Isaac asks.

I'd give up my side arm for a cup of hot coffee, but decline the offer. "I'd like to ask you a few questions about something that happened last night."

He motions toward the kitchen. "Come sit next to the stove."

Our boots thud hollowly on the hardwood floor as the three of us move into the kitchen. A rectangular wood table covered with a blue-and-white-checkered tablecloth dominates the room. In its center, a glass lantern flickers, casting yellow light onto our faces. The smell of kerosene reminds me of my own childhood home, and for a moment I'm comforted by that.

Wood scrapes against the floor as the three of us pull out chairs and sit. "We received a call last night about some of your livestock," I begin.

"Ah. My milk cows." Isaac shakes his head in self-deprecation, but I can tell by his expression he knows I didn't come here at five A.M. to censure him about a few wayward cattle. "I have been working on the fence."

"This isn't about the livestock," I say.

Isaac looks at me and waits.

"We found the body of a young woman in your field last night."

Across the room, Anna gasps. *"Mein gott."*

I don't look at her. My attention is focused on Isaac. His reaction. His body language. His expression.

"Someone died?" His eyes widen. "In my field? Who?"

"We haven't identified her yet."

I see his mind spinning as he tries to absorb the information. "Was it an accident? Did she succumb to the cold?"

"She was murdered."

He leans back in the chair as if pushed by some invisible force. *"Ach! Yammer."*

I glance toward his wife. She meets my gaze levelly now, her expression alarmed. "Did either of you see anything unusual last night?" I ask.

"No." He answers for both of them.

I almost smile. The Amish are a patriarchal society. The sexes are not necessarily unequal, but their roles are separate and well defined. Usually, this doesn't bother me. This morning, I'm annoyed. The unspoken Amish convention does not apply when it comes to murder, and it's my job to make that clear. I give Anna a direct look. "Anna?"

She approaches, wiping her chapped hands on her apron. She's close to my age and pretty, with large hazel eyes and a sprinkling of freckles on her nose. Plain suits her.

"Is she Amish?" she asks in Pennsylvania Dutch, the Amish dialect.

I know the language because I used to speak it, but I answer in English. "We don't know," I tell her. "Did you see any strangers in the area? Any vehicles or buggies you didn't recognize?"

Anna shakes her head. "I didn't see anything. It gets dark so early this time of year."

It's true. January in northeastern Ohio is a cold and dark month.

"Will you ask your children?"

"Of course."

"You think one of the gentle people is responsible for this sin?" Defensiveness rings in Isaac's voice.

He is referencing the Amish community. They are for the most part a pacifistic culture. Hardworking. Religious. Family oriented. But I know anomalies occur. I, myself, am an anomaly.

"I don't know." I rise and nod at T.J. "Thank you both for your time. We'll see ourselves out."

Isaac follows us through the living room and opens the door for us. As I step onto the porch, he whispers, "Is he back, Katie?"

The question startles me, but I know I'll hear it again in the coming days. It's a question I don't want to ponder. But Isaac remembers what happened sixteen years ago. I was only fourteen at the time, but I remember, too. "I don't know."

But I'm lying. I know the person who killed that girl is not the same man who raped and murdered four young women sixteen years ago.

I know this because I killed him.

Cumulus clouds rimmed with crimson churn on the eastern horizon when I park the Explorer on the shoulder behind T.J.'s cruiser. The crime scene tape is incongruous against the trees, locust posts and barbed wire. The ambulance is gone. So is Doc Coblentz's Escalade. Glock stands at the fence, looking out across the field as if the snow whispering across the jagged peaks of earth holds the answers we all so desperately need.

"Go home and get some sleep," I say to T.J. His shift began at midnight. In light of the murder, sleep is about to become a rare commodity for all of us.

I shut down the engine. The cab seems suddenly quiet without the blast of the heater. He reaches for the door handle, but doesn't open it. "Chief?"

I look at him. His little-brother eyes are troubled. "I want to catch this guy."

"Me, too." I open my door. "I'll call you in a few hours."

He nods and we get out of the Explorer. I start toward Glock, but my mind is still on T.J. I hope he can handle this. I have a terrible feeling the body he found this morning isn't the last.

Behind me I hear T.J. start his cruiser and pull away. Glock glances in my direction. He doesn't even look cold.

"Anything?" I ask without preamble.

"Not much. We bagged a gum wrapper, but it looked old. Found a few hairs in the fence. Long strands, probably hers."

Glock is about my age with military short hair and two-percent body fat on a physique that puts Arnold Schwarzenegger to shame. I hired him two years ago, earning him the honor of becoming Painters Mill's first African-American police officer. A former MP with the Marine Corps, he's a crack shot, possesses a brown belt in karate, and he doesn't take any shit from anyone, including me.

"Find any prints?" I ask. "Tire tracks?"

He shakes his head. "Scene was pretty trampled. I was going to try to lift some impressions, but it doesn't look promising."

Capturing footwear impressions or tire tracks in snow is tricky. Several layers of a special wax must first be sprayed onto the impression to insulate it. That prevents the loss of detail from the exothermic reaction of the hardening dental stone casting material.

"Do you know how to do it?" I ask.

"I need to pick up the supplies at the sheriff's office."

"Go ahead. I'll stay until I can get Skid out here." Chuck "Skid" Skidmore is my other officer.

"Last I heard he was laid out on a pool table with some blonde at McNarie's Bar." Glock smiles. "Probably hungover."

"Probably." Skid is as fond of cheap tequila as Rupert is of his Glock. The moment of levity is short lived. "Once you lift the impressions, get imprints from all the first responders. Send everything over to the BCI lab. Have them run a comparison analysis and see if we have something that stands out."

BCI is the acronym for the Bureau of Criminal Identification and Investigation in London, Ohio, a suburb of Columbus. A state agency run by the attorney general's office, the bureau has a state-of-the-art lab, access to law enforcement databases, and a multitude of other resources that may be utilized by local police agencies.

Glock nods. "Anything else?"

I smile, but it feels unnatural on my face. "Think you could postpone your vacation?"

He smiles back, but it looks strained. If anyone is deserving of some downtime, it's Glock. He hasn't had any measurable time off since I hired him.

"LaShonda and I don't have any big plans," he says, referring to his wife. "Just finishing up the nursery. Doc says any day now."

We study the scene in companionable silence. Even though I'm wearing two pairs of socks inside waterproof boots, my feet ache with cold. I'm tired and discouraged and overwhelmed. The press of time is heavy on my shoulders. Any cop worth his weight knows the first forty-eight hours of a homicide investigation are the most vital in terms of solving it.

"I'd better get those supplies," Glock says after a moment.

I watch him traverse the bar ditch, slide into his cruiser and pull away. I turn back to the field where drifting snow whispers across the frozen earth. From where I stand, I can just make out the bloodstain from the victim, a vivid red circle against pristine white. The crime scene tape flutters in a brisk north wind, the tree branches clicking together like chattering teeth.

"Who are you, you son of a bitch?" I say aloud, my voice sounding strange in the predawn hush.

The only answer I get is the murmur of wind through the trees and the echo of my own voice.

Twenty minutes later Officer Skidmore arrives on the scene. He slinks out of his cruiser toting two coffees, a don't-ask expression, and a half-eaten doughnut clutched between his thumb and forefinger.

"Why the hell can't people get murdered when it's seventy degrees and sunny?" he mutters, shoving one of the coffees at me.

"That'd be way too convenient." I take the coffee, pop the tab and brief him on what we know.

When I'm finished he considers the scene, then looks at me as if expecting me to throw up my hands and tell him the whole thing is a big, ugly prank. "Hell of a thing to find out here in the middle of the night." He slurps coffee. "How's T.J.?"

"I think he'll be okay."

"Fuckin' kid's gonna have nightmares." His eyes are bloodshot and, as Glock had predicted, I realize he's sporting a hangover.

"Late night?" I ask.

He has powdered sugar on his chin. His grin is lopsided. "I like tequila a lot more than she likes me."

It's not the first time I've heard that. Originally from Ann Arbor, Michigan, Skid lost his job with the police department there because of an off-duty DUI. Everyone knows he drinks too much. But he's a good cop. For his sake, I hope he can get a handle on it. I've seen booze ruin a lot of lives, and I'd hate to see him added to the heap. I told him the day I hired him if I caught him drinking on the job I'd fire him on the spot. That was two years ago and so far he's never crossed the line.

"You think it's the same guy from back in the early nineties?" he asks. "What did they call him? The Slaughterhouse Murderer? The case was never closed, was it?"

Hearing the sobriquet spoken aloud raises gooseflesh on my arms. The local police and FBI worked the case for years after the last murder. But as the evidence grew cold and public interest dwindled, their efforts eventually slacked off. "It doesn't feel right," I offer noncommittally. "It's hard to explain a sixteen-year gap in activity."

"Unless the guy changed locales."

I say nothing, not wanting to speculate.

Skid doesn't notice. "Or he could have been sent to prison on some unrelated charge and just got sprung. Saw it happen when I was a rookie."

Hating the speculation and questions, knowing there will be plenty more in the days ahead, I shrug. "Could be a copycat."

He sniffs a runny nose. "That would be odd for a town this size. I mean, Jesus, what are the odds?"

Because he's right, I don't respond. Speculation is a dangerous thing when you know more than you should. I dump my remaining coffee and crumple the cup. "Keep the scene secure until Rupert gets back, will you?"

"Sure thing."

"And give him a hand with the impressions. I'm heading to the station."

I anticipate the heater as I start for the Explorer. My face and ears burn with cold. My fingers are numb. But my mind isn't on my physical discomfort. I can't stop thinking about that young woman. I can't stop thinking about the uncanny parallels of this murder with the ones from sixteen years ago.

22

As I put the Explorer in gear and pull onto the road, a dark foreboding deep in my gut tells me this killer isn't finished.

Downtown Painters Mill is composed of one major thoroughfare—aptly named Main Street—lined with a dozen or so businesses, half of which are Amish tourist shops selling everything from wind chimes and bird houses to intricate, handmade quilts. A traffic circle punctuates the north end of the street. A big Lutheran church marks the southernmost section of town. To the east lies the brand-new high school, an up-and-coming housing development called Maple Crest and a smattering of bed-and-breakfasts that have sprung up over the last couple of years to accommodate the town's fastest growing industry: tourism. On the west side of town, just past the railroad tracks and mobile home park, is the slaughterhouse and rendering plant, the farmer's mercantile and a massive grain elevator.

Since its inception in 1815, Painters Mill's population has remained steady at about 5,300 people, a third of whom are Amish. Though the Amish keep to themselves for the most part, no one is really a stranger, and everyone knows everyone else's business. It's a wholesome town. A nice place to live and a raise a family. It's a good place to be the chief of police. Unless, of course, you have a vicious, unsolved murder on your hands.

Sandwiched between Kidwell's Pharmacy and the volunteer fire department, the police station is a drafty cave carved into a century-old brick building that had once been a dance hall. I'm greeted by Mona Kurtz, my third-shift dispatcher, as I push open the door and enter the reception area. She looks up from her computer, flashes an over-the-counter white smile and waves. "Hey, Chief."

She's twentysomething with a mane of wild red hair and a vivacity that makes the Energizer Bunny seem lazy. She talks so fast I understand only half of what she says, which isn't necessarily a bad thing since she usually relays more information than I need to hear. But she enjoys her job. Unmarried and childless, she doesn't mind working the graveyard shift and has a genuine interest in police work. Even if that interest derives from watching *CSI*, it was enough for me to hire her last year. She hasn't missed a day since.

Seeing the pink message slips in her hand and the fervor in her eyes, I wish

I'd waited until her shift was over before arriving. I enjoy Mona and appreciate her enthusiasm, but I don't have the patience this morning. I don't pause on the way to my office.

Undeterred, she crosses to me and shoves a dozen or so messages into my hand. "The phones are ringing off the hook. Folks are wondering about the murder, Chief. Mrs. Finkbine wants to know if it's the same killer from sixteen years ago."

I groan inwardly at the power and speed of the Painters Mill rumor mill. If it could be harnessed to generate electricity, no one would ever have to pay another utility bill again.

She frowns when she glances down at the next slip. "Phyllis Combs says her cat is missing, and she thinks it might be the same guy." She looks at me with wide brown eyes. "Ricky McBride told me the vic was . . . decapitated. Is it true?"

I resist the urge to rub at the ache behind my eyes. "No. I'd appreciate it if you'd do your best to nip any rumors in the bud. There are going to be a lot flying around in the next few days."

"Absolutely."

I look down at the pink slips and decide to put her enthusiasm to good use. "Call these people back. Tell them the Painters Mill PD is investigating the crime aggressively, and I'll have a statement in the next edition of the *Advocate*." The *Advocate* is Painters Mill's weekly newspaper, circulation four thousand. "If you get any media inquiries, tell them you'll fax a press release this afternoon. Everything else is 'no comment,' you got that?"

She hangs on to every word, looking a little too excited, a little too intense. "I got it, Chief. No comment. Anything else?"

"I could use some coffee."

"I got just the thing."

I envision one of her soy-espresso-chocolate concoctions and shudder. "Just coffee, Mona. And some aspirin if you have it." I start toward the sanctuary of my office.

"Oh. Sure. Milk. No sugar. Is Tylenol okay?"

A question occurs to me just as I reach my office. I stop and turn to her. "Has anyone filed a missing person report for a young female in the last few days?"

"I haven't seen anything come across the wire."

But it's still early. I know the call will come. "Check with the State Highway Patrol and the Holmes County sheriff's office, will you? Female. Caucasian. Blue. Dark blonde. Fifteen to thirty years of age."

"I'm on it."

I walk into my office, close the door behind me and resist the urge to lock it. It's a small room crowded with a beat-up metal desk, an antique file cabinet speckled with rust, and a desktop computer that grinds like a coffee mill. A single window offers a not-so-stunning view of the pickup trucks and cars parked along Main Street.

Working off my coat, I drape it over the back of my chair, hit the power button on the computer and head directly to the file cabinet. While the computer boots, I unlock the cabinet, tug out the bottom drawer and page through several case files. Domestic disputes. Simple assault. Vandalism. The kinds of crimes you expect in a town like Painters Mill. The file I'm looking for is at the back. My fingers pause before touching it. I've been the chief of police for two years, but I've never been able to bring myself to look at the file. This morning, I don't have a choice.

The folder is fat and brown with frayed edges and metal clasps that are broken from use. The peeling label reads: *Slaughterhouse Murders, Holmes County, January 1992.* I take the file to my desk and open it.

My predecessor, Delbert McCoy, was a stickler for detail and it shows in his record-keeping. A typed police report with dates, times and locations stares up at me. I see witness names replete with contact information and background checks. It appears every facet of the investigation was carefully documented. Except for one incident that was never reported to the police . . .

I page through the file, taking in the highlights. Sixteen years ago a killer stalked the quiet streets and back roads of Painters Mill. Over a two-year period he murdered four women with indiscriminate savagery. Because of the killer's MO, exsanguination, which is similar to the "bleeding" of livestock during slaughter, some headline-grabbing reporter dubbed him "The Slaughterhouse Killer" and the name stuck.

The first victim, seventeen-year-old Patty Lynn Thorpe, was raped and tortured, her throat slashed. Her body was dumped on Shady Grove Road—just two miles from where T.J. discovered the body this morning. A chill hovers at the base of my spine as I read the autopsy report.

ANATOMICAL SUMMARY:
I. Incised wound of neck: Transection of left common carotid artery.

I skim the Notes and Procedures, External Examination and other details until I find what I'm looking for.

DESCRIPTION OF INCISED NECK WOUND:
The incised wound of the neck measures eight centimeters in length. Said wound is transversely oriented from the midline and upwardly angulated toward the left earlobe. The left common carotid artery is transected with hemorrhage in the surrounding carotid sheath. Fresh hemorrhage and bruising is present along the entire wound path.

OPINION:
This is a fatal incised wound or sharp force injury associated with the transection of the left carotid artery with exsanguinating hemorrhage.

It is strikingly similar to the wound on the body discovered this morning. I continue reading.

DESCRIPTION OF SECONDARY STAB WOUND:
A secondary abdominal wound located above the navel is noteworthy. The wound is irregular in shape, measuring 5 centimeters by 4 centimeters in height and width, respectively, with minimal depth of penetration at 1.5 centimeters. Fresh hemorrhage is noted along the wound path, which goes through the skin and subcutaneous tissue, though the penetration did not breach muscle. The wound was ante mortem.

OPINION:
This is a superficial cutting wound and is found to be non-life-threatening.

Again, very similar to the wound carved into the abdomen of the victim found this morning.

I turn to the police report where Chief McCoy scribbled a footnote.

The abdominal wound appears to be the capital letters V and I or perhaps the Roman numeral VI. The laceration on the victim's neck was not the wild slash of a crazed killer, but the calculated incision of someone who knew what he was doing and wanted a specific end result. The perpetrator used a knife with a nonserrated blade. The carving on the victim's abdomen was not made public.

Below, the report notes that the victim sustained vaginal and rectal trauma, but smears sent to the lab didn't return foreign DNA.

I flip through several more pages, stopping at Chief McCoy's handwritten notes.

No fingerprints. No DNA. No witnesses. Not much to go on. We continue to work the case and follow up on every lead. But I believe the murder was an isolated incident. A drifter passing through on the railroad.

His words would come back to haunt him.

Four months later sixteen-year-old Loretta Barnett's body was discovered by fishermen on the muddy bank of Painters Creek. She'd been accosted in her home, sexually assaulted, taken to an unknown location where her throat was cut. It was later ascertained that her body had been thrown from a covered bridge west of town.

At that point, McCoy called the FBI to assist. Forensics suggested the killer used a stun gun to subdue his victims. Both victims sustained genital trauma, but no DNA was found, which, according to Special Agent Frederick Milkowski, indicated the killer had had either worn a condom or resorted to foreign object rape. The killer may have shaved his body hair.

Bruising at the victim's ankles indicated she had been hung upside down by some type of chain until she bled out. Most disturbing was the discovery of the Roman numeral VII carved into the flesh of her abdomen.

At that point it became evident the police had a serial murderer on their hands. Because the victims were murdered via exsanguination, a practice associated with many slaughterhouses, McCoy and Milkowski turned to the local slaughterhouse for clues.

I read McCoy's investigative notes:

In an informal interview, J.R. Purdue of Honey Cut–Purdue Enterprises, the corporate entity that owns and operates the Honey Cut Meat Packing plant, states, "The wounds are consistent with the type of incision used to bleed livestock, but on a smaller scale . . ."

Every person who'd ever worked for the Honey Cut Meat Packing plant was questioned and fingerprinted. Male employees were asked to give DNA samples. Nothing ever came to fruition. And the killing continued . . .

By the end of the following year, four women were dead. Each died via exsanguination. Each suffered unspeakable torture. And each had a successive Roman numeral carved into her abdomen, as if the killer were keeping some twisted tally of his carnage.

Sweat breaks out on the back of my neck when I look at the crime scene and autopsy photos. The similarities to the murder this morning are undeniable. I know what the citizens of Painters Mill will think. That the Slaughterhouse Killer is back. There are only three people on this earth who know that is impossible, and one of them is me.

A knock on the door makes me jump. "It's open."

Mona walks in and sets a cup of coffee and a Sam's Club–size bottle of Tylenol on my desk. Her eyes flick to the folder. "There's a woman from Coshocton County on line one. Her daughter didn't come home last night. Norm Johnston is on line two."

Norm Johnston is one of six town councilmen. He's a pushy, self-serving bastard and all-around pain in the ass. He hasn't liked me since I busted him for a DUI last spring and dashed his hopes of climbing Painters Mill's political ladder all the way to mayor. "Tell Norm I'll call him back," I say and hit line one.

"This is Belinda Horner. I haven't heard from my daughter, Amanda, since she left to go out with her girlfriend Saturday night." The woman is talking too fast. Her voice is breathless and raw with nerves. "I assumed she'd spent the night with Connie. She does that sometimes. But I didn't hear from her this morning. I called and found out no one has seen her since Saturday night. I'm really getting worried."

Today is Monday. I close my eyes, praying the body lying on a slab in the Millersburg morgue isn't her daughter. But I have a bad feeling in my gut. "Has she stayed gone this long before, ma'am? Is this unusual behavior for her?"

"She always calls to let me know if she's staying out."

"When's the last time her friend saw her?"

"Saturday night. Connie can be incredibly irresponsible."

"Have you contacted the State Highway Patrol?"

"They told me to check with the local police department. I'm afraid she's been in a car accident or something. I'm going to start calling hospitals next."

I grab a pad and pen. "How old is your daughter?"

"Twenty-one."

"What does she look like?"

She describes a pretty young woman who fits the description of the victim. "Do you have a photo?" I ask.

"I have several."

"Can you fax the most recent one to me?"

"Um . . . I don't have a fax machine, but my neighbor has a computer and scanner."

"That'll work. Scan the photo and e-mail it as an attachment. Can you do that?"

"I think so."

As I jot her contact information, my phone beeps. I look down and see all four lines blinking wildly. I ignore them and give her my e-mail address.

My stomach is in knots by the time I hang up, but I have a sinking suspicion Belinda Horner is going to have a much worse day than me.

Mona knocks and peeks in. "I got the state highway patrol on one. Channel Seven in Columbus is on line two. Doc Coblentz is on three."

I answer line three with a curt utterance of my name.

"I'm about to start the autopsy," the doc says. "I thought you might want a heads-up."

"I'll be there in fifteen minutes."

"You get an ID yet?"

"I'm working on something now."

"God help the family."

God help us all, I silently add.

I spend ten minutes returning calls and then open my e-mail program. When I hit Send/Receive, an e-mail with an attachment from J. Miller appears in my in-box.

I open the attachment and find myself staring at the image of a young woman with pretty blue eyes, dark blonde hair and a dazzling smile. The likeness is unmistakable. And I know Amanda Horner will never smile like that again.

Hitting Doc Coblentz's direct number, I wait impatiently until he picks up. "Hold off on the autopsy."

"I assumed you wanted a rush."

I tap the Print key on my computer. "I do, but I think her parents will want to see her before you start cutting."

Coblentz makes a sound of sympathy. "I don't envy you your job."

At this moment I hate my job with a passion I cannot describe. "I'm going to drive down to Coshocton County and pay the mother a visit. Can you give the chaplain at the hospital a call? Ask him to meet us at the morgue. We're going to need him."

CHAPTER 4

The Horners live in the Sherwood Forest mobile home park on Highway 83 between Keene and Clark. The sky is as hard and gray as concrete as I turn onto the gravel street. Next to me, Glock studies the map I printed before leaving.

"There's Sebring Lane," he says, pointing.

I make a right and see a dozen mobile homes lined up like Matchbox cars on either side of the street. "What's the lot number?"

"Thirty-five, there at the end."

I park the Explorer in front of a blue and white 12 by 60 Liberty mobile home circa 1980. A living room extension juts from the side, giving it a haphazard look. But the lot is well kept. A newish Ford F-150 pickup sits in the driveway. I see green curtains at the kitchen window. Residual Christmas lights encircle the storm door. An aluminum trash can overflows at the curb. An ordinary home about to be shattered.

I'd rather cut off my hand than look into Belinda Horner's eyes and ask her to identify a body I'm certain is her daughter. But this is my job, and I don't have a choice.

I get out and start toward the trailer. The wind penetrates my parka, icy spears driving into my skin. I shiver as I climb the steps and knock. Beside me, Glock curses the cold. The storm door swings open as if someone is expecting us. I find myself looking at a middle-aged woman with bottle-blonde hair and tired, bruised eyes. She looks like she hasn't slept for a week.

"Mrs. Horner?" I flash my badge. "I'm Kate Burkholder, chief of police in Painters Mill."

Her eyes dart from me to Glock, lingering on our badges. I see hope in her eyes, but that hope is tempered with fear. She knows a personal visit from the cops isn't a good sign. "Is this about Amanda? Have you found her? Has she been hurt?"

"May we come in?" I ask.

She steps back and opens the door wider. "Where is she? Is she in some kind of trouble? Was there an accident?"

The trailer is too warm and cramped with a dozen pieces of mismatched furniture. I smell this morning's bacon, last night's meatloaf and the lingering remnants of hair spray. The television is tuned to a game show where some lucky contestant is bidding on a jukebox. "Are you alone, ma'am?"

She blinks at me. "My husband is at work." Her eyes flick from me to Glock and back to me. "What's this about? Why are you here?"

"Ma'am, I'm afraid I have some bad news."

Something wild leaps into her eyes. Some terrible precursor to grief. She knows what I'm going to say next. I see the awful anticipation as clearly as I've felt it in my own heart.

"We may have found your daughter, ma'am. A young woman matching her description—"

"Found her?" A hysterical laugh squeezes from her throat. "What do you mean *found* her? Why isn't she here?"

"I'm sorry, ma'am, but the woman we found is deceased."

"No." She raises a hand as if to fend me off. Her expression is fierce enough to stop a train. "You're wrong. That's not true. Someone made a mistake."

"We'll need for you to come down to the hospital in Millersburg and identify her."

"No." She chokes out a sound that is part sob, part moan. "It's not her. It can't be."

I drop my gaze to the floor to give her a moment. I take those precious seconds to rein in my own emotions and try not to think about how impossible it is to stand here and fracture this woman's world. "Is there someone we can call to be here with you, ma'am? Your husband or a family member?"

"I don't need anyone. Amanda's not dead." Gasping for breath, she presses a hand against her stomach. "She's not."

"I'm sorry." My words ring hollow even to me.

Her hands curl into fists and she puts them against her temples. "She's not dead. I would have known." Her ravaged eyes meet mine. "The police made a mistake. This is a small town. Mistakes happen all the time."

"There was no identification, but we believe it's her," I say. "I'm very sorry."

She turns away from us and paces to the other side of the room. I glance at Glock. He looks the way I feel; like he'd rather be anywhere in the world than this hot and cramped trailer, tearing this woman's life apart. His gaze meets mine. His nod bolsters me, and I wonder if he knows how badly I need that small sign of support at this moment.

He speaks up for the first time. "Mrs. Horner, I know this is difficult, but we need to ask you some questions."

She turns to Glock and looks at him as if seeing him for the first time. Tears shimmer in her eyes. "How did she . . ."

She knows there's more coming; I see it in her eyes. Some people have a sixth sense when it comes to impending tragedy. She has that look. The mental brace. The ancient eyes. And I know she has received her share of blows.

"The woman we found was murdered," I reply.

Belinda Horner makes a sound that is part scream, part groan. She glares at me as if she wants to attack me, the messenger of unbearable news. I brace, but she doesn't move. For several interminable seconds, it's as if she's frozen. Then her face turns deep red. *"No!"* Her mouth quivers. "You're lying." Her gaze flicks to Glock. "Both of you!"

Unable to meet her ravaged eyes, I focus on a stain in the carpet. After a moment, an animalistic sound erupts from her throat, startling me. I look up to see her bend at the waist, as if someone gut-punched her. When she looks at me, her face is wet with tears. "Please tell me it's not true."

This isn't the first time I've had to deliver bad news. Two years ago, when I'd been on the job for less than a week, I was forced to tell Jim and Marilyn Stettler that their sixteen-year-old son wrapped his brand-new Mustang around a telephone pole, killing himself and his fourteen-year-old sister in the process. It was one of the hardest things I've ever had to do in the course of my law enforcement career. It was the first time in my life I drank alone. But it wasn't the last.

I go to Belinda Horner, set my hand on her shoulder and squeeze. "I'm very sorry."

She shakes off my hand and turns on me. She looks like she wants to tear me apart. "How could this happen?" She is screaming now. Overcome with grief and an impotent rage that is about to burgeon out of control. "How could someone hurt her?"

"We don't know, ma'am, but I promise you we're doing everything we can to find out."

She stares at me a moment longer, then clenches her fists in her hair as if to pull it out. "Oh, dear God. Harold. I have to call Harold. How am I going to tell him our baby is gone?"

Spotting a phone on the counter, I cross to it and pick it up. "Mrs. Horner, let me call him for you. What's his number?"

She wipes her eyes with the back of her hand, leaving a smear of mascara. Her voice trembles as she recites the number from memory. I dial, hating it that Harold Horner's life is about to be torn apart, too. But I don't want this woman left alone. I have a crime to solve and I can't do that from here.

Horner answers on the first ring. I identify myself and tell him there's an emergency at home. He asks about his wife first, and I tell him she's all right. When he asks about his daughter, I ask him to come home and hang up.

Belinda Horner stands at the window, her arms wrapped around herself. Glock stands near the door looking out at the bleak landscape beyond. His forehead is slicked with sweat. I feel that same terrible sweat between my shoulder blades.

"Mrs. Horner, when's the last time you saw Amanda?" I ask.

The question elicits a look that gives me a chill. "I want to see her," she says hollowly. "Where is she? Where's my baby?"

Before I can answer, her knees buckle. I rush toward her, but Glock is faster and catches her beneath the arms just as her knees hit the floor. "Easy, ma'am," he says.

Glock and I help her to the sofa. "I know this is hard, Mrs. Horner," I say. "Please try to calm down."

She turns tear-bright eyes on me. "Where is she?"

"The hospital in Millersburg. The chaplain is waiting for you there if you need him."

"I'm not very religious." She struggles to her feet, glances around the room, but she doesn't move. She seems confused, not sure where she is or what to do next. "I really want to see her."

"That won't be a problem." I try again to get the information I need. "Mrs. Horner, when's the last time you saw your daughter?"

"Two days ago. She was . . . going out. She'd just gotten her hair cut. Bought a new sweater at the mall. It was brown with sequins at the collar. She looked so pretty."

"Was she with someone?"

"Her friend Connie. They were going to that new club."

"What club?"

"The Brass Rail."

My officers have been called there on several occasions. The place draws a young crowd high on hormones and booze and God only knows what else. "What's Connie's last name?"

"Spencer."

I pull a pad from my pocket and jot. "What time did Amanda leave here?"

"Seven-thirty or so. She was always running late. Waited till the last minute to do everything." She squeezes her eyes closed and chokes back a sob. "I can't believe this is happening."

"Did Amanda have a boyfriend?"

"No. She was such a good girl. So young and pretty. Smart, too. Smarter than me and her daddy put together." She looks at me, her mouth trembling. "She was going back to college this fall."

I have no words to console her.

"Do you mind if we take a look at her room?" I ask.

She gives me a thousand-yard stare.

"Could you show us her room, ma'am?" Glock asks quietly.

Keening softly, she shuffles toward the hall. I follow close behind. We pass a tiny bathroom. I see pink towels with lace and a matching shower curtain. She stops at the next door, pushes it open. "This is her room. Her things." Her body convulses with sobs. "Oh, my baby. My poor, sweet baby girl."

I step past her and try to assess what I see with the unbiased eye of a cop. Not easy to do when the grief in the room is so palpable you can't breathe.

The bed is a twin. Unmade. With lacy pink sheets and a matching comforter. Little-girl bedclothes, I think. Probably had them since she was a kid.

A lamp, alarm clock and several framed photographs sit atop the single night table. I cross to it and pick up a photo of Amanda and a young man. "Who's this?"

Belinda blinks back tears. "Donny Beck."

"Boyfriend?"

She nods. "Ex. He was crazy about Amanda."

"Was she serious about him?"

"She liked him, but not as much as he liked her."

I exchange looks with Glock. Another photo depicts Amanda atop a sorrel horse, grinning as if she'd just won the Kentucky Derby.

"She loves horses." Belinda Horner looks as if she's aged ten years in five minutes. Her eyes and cheeks are sunken, her makeup streaked down her face like that of a sad clown. "Harold and I bought her riding lessons for her high school graduation. We couldn't really afford it. But she loved it so much."

I replace the photo. "Did she keep a diary, ma'am? Journal? Anything like that?"

"Not that I know of." She picks up a ratty-looking stuffed bear and smells it. Hugging the bear, she bursts into tears. *"I want her back."*

I look around, hoping to spot something—anything—that will tell me more about Amanda Horner. Being as unobtrusive as possible, I look through the night table. Finding nothing, I move to the dresser and quickly rifle through T-shirts and jeans, socks and underwear.

The sound of a car door slamming outside alerts me that Harold Horner has arrived home. Without speaking, Belinda rushes from the room. "Harold! *Harold!*"

I look at Glock. "Jesus."

He shakes his head. "Yeah."

I enter the living room as the front door bursts open.

"I got here as fast as I could." Harold Horner is a large man. Wearing a red flannel shirt and denim jacket, he looks like a lumberjack. He is bald with the rough hands of a workingman. I notice his eyes are the same color as his daughter's. He scans the faces in the room. "Where's Amanda?"

Showing him my badge, I identify myself. "I'm afraid we have some bad news about your daughter, sir."

"Aw, Jesus. Aw, God. What happened? What's going on?"

"She's dead," Belinda Horner blurts. "Our baby is dead. Oh Harold, dear God." He goes to her and she collapses in his arms. *"Our sweet little girl is gone, and she's never coming back."*

I drop Glock at the station with instructions to head over to the Brass Rail. I'd rather do that myself; I've never been good at delegating. But I need to speak with Doc Coblentz. Revisiting the dead is one responsibility I won't put on my officers.

Earlier, Glock completed the tedious task of lifting tire tread and footwear impressions at the crime scene. Mona couriered everything to the Bureau of Criminal Investigation and Identification lab in London, Ohio, which is over a hundred miles away. A courier fee isn't in the budget, but I can't spare an officer. I'll pay for it out of my own pocket if necessary.

The lab will scan each impression and imprint into a computer and run a comparison analysis, matching impressions at the scene against the imprints of the first responders. It's a long shot, but I'm hoping one impression will stand out and give us our first clue as to the identity of the killer.

It's almost noon by the time I park adjacent the main entrance of Pomerene Hospital in Millersburg. I pass the information desk and take the elevator to the basement. A yellow and black biohazard sign glares at me as I go through the swinging doors. Doc Coblentz sits at a desk inside a glassed-in office where the miniblinds are open. He spots me and rises. Wearing a white lab coat and baggy tan trousers, he looks like an aging Pillsbury doughboy.

"Chief." He extends his hand and we shake. "The parents were here a few minutes ago and identified her." He shakes his head. "Nice family. Sad as hell to see something like this happen."

"They see the chaplain?"

"Father Zimmerman took them to the chapel." With a nod, he's ready to get down to business. "I haven't done the autopsy yet. All I have for you is a prelim."

"I'll take whatever you have." The thought of seeing Amanda Horner's body fills me with dread. But my need for hard facts overrides that human frailty. Right now, information is my most powerful tool. I want to catch the son of a bitch who did this. There is a part of me that wants to pull out my sidearm and fire a round into his face so he can't put anyone else through the hell he's putting the Horners through.

That need drives me forward when the doctor motions to a small alcove. "Grab a gown and shoe covers on the shelf there," he says. "I'll take your coat."

Reluctantly, I relinquish my parka. He hangs it on a hook outside the door. Quickly, I don a sterile gown, slip the disposable shoe covers over my boots and leave the alcove.

Doc Coblentz motions toward the adjoining room labeled with a larger biohazard sign. "It's not pretty," he says.

"Murder never is."

We go through another set of swinging doors and enter the autopsy room. Though it's equipped with a separate ventilation system from the rest of the building, I discern the smell of formalin and an array of other, darker odors I don't want to identify. Four stainless steel gurneys are parked against the far wall. A huge scale used for weighing bodies stands in the center. A smaller scale used for weighing individual organs squats on the stainless steel counter along with an assortment of trays, bottles and instruments.

The doc snags a clipboard from a shelf and takes me to the fifth gurney, the only one in use. He pulls down the sheet and Amanda Horner's face comes into view. Her skin is gray now. Someone closed her eyes, but the left lid has come back up. A sticky-looking film coats the eyeball.

Sighing, Doc Coblentz shakes his head. "This poor child endured a horrible death, Kate."

"Torture?"

"Yes."

I steel myself against a slow rise of outrage. "Do you know the cause of death?"

"Exsanguination more than likely."

"Any idea what kind of knife he used?"

"Something damn sharp. No serration. Probably short-bladed." Using a long wooden swab with a cotton tip, he indicates the cut on her neck. "This is the fatal wound. Sharp force injury is clearly visible. You can see that the wound path is relatively short." He glances at the clipboard. "Eight point one centimeters."

"Is that significant?"

"It tells me he knew where to cut to hit the artery."

"Medical training?"

"Or maybe he's done it before."

Because I don't want to address that, I go to my next question. "How did he initially subdue her? Drugs? What?"

"I'll run a tox screen." He looks at me over the tops of his glasses. "But I think he may have used a stun gun."

"How can you tell?"

Slipping his chubby hands into disposable gloves, he tugs the sheet down to her abdomen.

I've been a cop for almost ten years. I've seen shootings. Bloody domestic disputes. Horrific traffic accidents. It still disturbs me to see the dead up close and personal. Fear of death is a primal response built into all of us to varying degrees. No matter how much I've seen, I'll never get used to it.

"See these red marks?" he asks.

My eyes follow the swab. Sure enough, two small round abrasion-like dots mar the skin at her left shoulder. Two more appear on her chest, above her right breast. Another stands out on her left bicep. If I wasn't looking at the body of a murder victim, I could almost convince myself I was looking at a cluster of chicken pox, or some other benign blemish. But as a cop I know these marks are much more sinister.

"Abrasions?" I look closer. "Burns?"

"Burns."

"Most stun guns don't leave marks."

"You're right," he concedes. "That's particularly true if it's applied through clothing."

"So he hit her with it when she was nude?"

He lifts his shoulders. "Probably. But these marks are not consistent with what I've seen in the past."

"What are you getting at?"

"These burns are more substantial. I think the voltage or amperage of the stun gun was tampered with."

I look at the marks and try not to shudder. Ten years ago I attended the police academy in Columbus. As part of our training, any cadet brave enough to volunteer was hit with a stun gun. Because I was curious, I volunteered. Even though the amperage was set low, it knocked me on my ass. It incapacitated me for a full minute. And it hurt like hell. I couldn't imagine being at the mercy of some psychopath with a souped-up stunner.

"You think the stun gun is some kind of homemade job?" I ask.

"Or modified." He nods. "Whatever the case, she was hit with it multiple times."

I look at the scored flesh on her wrists. A quiver runs through my stomach when I see the white of bone. "What the hell did he bind her with?"

"Some type of wire. For quite some time, evidently." He shakes his head so vigorously his jowls jiggle. "She struggled."

Painters Mill is located in the heart of farm country. Many farmers grow and cut hay, so there's plenty of baling wire around. Even if we identified the type, it would be impossible to trace.

The doctor lifts the sheet. "He used some type of chain on her ankles. Large links with some rust present. Judging from these bruises, he strung her up when she was still alive."

The image my mind conjures is too horrific to contemplate. All I can think is that we're not dealing with a human being. We're not even dealing with an animal. Only true evil could inflict these kinds of horrors.

With the impersonal enthusiasm of the scientist he is, the doc removes the sheet completely. I mentally brace as Amanda Horner's body comes into view. I see multiple burns and abrasions on gray flesh. I'm not squeamish, but my stomach feels jittery. I'm aware of my heart beating too fast. Saliva pooling in my mouth. I know what the doc is going to say next, and my eyes are drawn to the carving on her abdomen, above her navel.

The wound has been cleaned. The XXIII carved into her flesh is unmistakable. Realizing I'm holding my breath, I exhale.

"You need water, Kate?"

The question annoys me, but I resist the urge to snap. "Did you get photos?"

"Yes."

My eyes go to the faint bruising on the insides of her thighs. "She was sexually assaulted?"

"There was minute vaginal tearing. Some anal tearing as well. I also found evidence of burns around the anus, probably from some type of electrical charge. I took swabs, but I don't think there was any semen left behind."

"What about hair or fibers?"

"No and no."

"So he wore a condom."

"A *lubricated* condom, actually. I found traces of glycerin and methylparaben inside her vagina and around the anus."

I consider that. "How can a guy get close enough to rape and not leave hair behind?"

"I have two hypotheses on that."

"Lay them on me."

"He could have shaved his body hair. Wouldn't be the first time a serial rapist has gone to those lengths to avoid the risk of leaving DNA behind."

"And the second?"

"He could have raped her using some type of foreign object. I may know more when I get my swabs back from the lab."

"So, our guy might know something about forensics and evidence."

"Who doesn't these days?" He shrugs. "People watch *CSI*. Everyone's an expert."

"Put a rush on the lab, will you?"

"You bet I will."

Some of the tension leaves me when the doc drapes the sheet over the body. "What about time of death?"

"I took a core body temp as soon as I got her here, which was at three-fifty-three this morning." The doc looks at the clipboard. "Liver temp was 83.6 degrees Fahrenheit. My best estimate on time of death is going to be between four and seven P.M. yesterday afternoon."

Belinda Horner told me the last time she saw Amanda was around seven-thirty P.M. Saturday, so she was abducted at some point after that. "If he abducted her sometime Saturday night, he had her for quite a while before he killed her." The thought sickens me. Makes me want to get my hands on the sick bastard responsible and forget I'm a cop.

"I'm afraid so." He gestures toward the body. "Whoever did this took his time with her, Kate. He wasn't in a hurry and kept her alive for a while."

I try to keep my voice level. "So, he probably took her to a place where he felt safe. A place where he knew he wouldn't be overheard." There are a lot of places like that in farm country, where houses are often more than a mile apart.

I look at the doc. "Was she gagged?"

"Not that I can tell. No sign of tape residue. No visible fibers in her mouth." He grimaces. "She bit her tongue."

He listened to her scream, I think. "So he has a place that's private. A place he can come and go as he pleases. A place that's desolate where no one could hear her."

"Or a house with a basement or soundproof room."

The need to move, to work this case, pumps through me with an intensity that's almost manic. My mind whirls with all the things I need to do. The people I need to question. I must decide which tasks to delegate and which to take on myself. I'm going to need the help of all my officers. I'll need to call in my auxiliary officer, too. My exhaustion from earlier is gone. In its place is the steel resolve to find a monster.

As if realizing I'm finished here, the doctor snaps off his latex gloves. "I'll call you as soon as I finish."

"Thanks, Doc. You've been a huge help."

I'm midway to the door when I remember I have one more question. "Do you have the complete autopsy reports on the vics from before? I've only got the summaries."

"I believe they're in archive, but I can get them."

"I'd appreciate it if you'd pull everything you have and send copies to my office ASAP."

He holds my gaze, and his expression darkens. "I was just out of my residency back then, Kate. I assisted Dr. Kours on all four autopsies." He laughs, but it's a humorless sound. "I swear to God I almost went into dentistry after seeing those bodies."

I don't want to hear what he's going to say next, but I don't turn away.

"You see something like that and it sticks with you." He crosses to me. "Amanda Horner died *exactly* the same way as those girls."

Though I'd anticipated this moment, his words send a chill through me.

"I'm sure you noticed that the number carved into the victim's abdomen jumps from nine to twenty-three," the doctor says. "That concerns me."

"We're not even sure if we're dealing with the same killer," I reply. "Could be a copycat."

He tosses his gloves into the biohazard receptacle. "I don't want to believe there is one man, let alone two, who are capable of this kind of evil. I sure as hell don't want to believe they sprang from this town."

He removes his glasses and wipes the bridge of his nose with a handkerchief, and I realize this veteran doctor is upset by the things he's seen today.

"It's his signature," he says. "I'll stake my career on it."

I stare at him, telling myself he's wrong. But for the first time, a tiny grain of doubt assails me. Some little voice in the back of my mind demands to know if, in the hysteria and horror of that dreadful day sixteen years ago, the shotgun blast failed to do the job.

For half of my life I've believed I took a man's life. I've forgiven myself and asked God to do the same. I rationalized my actions, my silence, the silence of my family. Somehow, I learned to live with it. This murder makes me question all of it.

"Kate?" The doc's bushy white brows knit in concern.

"I'm okay," I say quickly and start toward the door. I feel the doctor's eyes on me as I yank it open. By the time I step into the hall I'm sweating beneath my uniform.

There's only one way to find out if the man I shot all those years ago is dead. To do that I need to talk to two people I've spoken to only a handful of times since. Two people who were there the day my life was irrevocably changed by violence. The day a fourteen-year-old Amish girl picked up her father's shotgun and killed a man.

Or did I?

CHAPTER 5

I sit in the Explorer in the hospital parking lot for five minutes before I'm able to function. My hands are still shaking when I hit the speed dial for dispatch. Mona picks up on the first ring.

"I want you to compile a list of abandoned homes, properties and businesses in and around Painters Mill," I say without preamble. "Say within a fifty-mile radius."

"Anything in particular you're looking for?"

"Just make the list. I'll fill you in on the details when I get back to the station." Putting the SUV in gear, I head for the highway and try not to think too hard about what I have to do next.

My brother, Jacob, his wife, Irene, and my two nephews, Elam and James, live on a sixty-five-acre farm on a dirt road nine miles east of town. The place has been in the Burkholder family for eighty years. In keeping with the Amish tradition, Jacob, the eldest and only male child in our family, inherited the farm when my mother passed away two years ago.

At the mouth of the gravel lane, I jam the Explorer into four-wheel drive and muscle the vehicle through foot-deep snow, praying I don't get stuck. The familiarity of the farm strikes me as I barrel closer at a too-fast clip. A small apple orchard lies to my right. The bare-branched trees seem to glare at me in stern judgment from their white winter blanket.

I'm an outsider here, a foreigner trespassing on sacred ground. That fact has never been more evident as I enter the world of my past. I'm a stranger to the people I once knew intimately. I rarely visit. I barely know my two young nephews. It hurts knowing they'll grow up and never know me. As much as I want to make things right, some chasms are simply too treacherous to traverse.

To my left, six milk cows huddle around a feeder mounded with snow-crusted hay. Ahead, the lane veers right where ruler-straight rows of cut corn usher my eyes to the farmhouse beyond. It makes for a pretty picture in the snow, and for a brief moment I'm reminded of a simpler time. A time when my sister and brother and I ran barefoot and carefree through wheat fields and played hide-and-seek among tall rows of corn. I recall winter days filled with hours of ice hockey with our cousins on Miller's pond. I remember a time when our only responsibilities were milking the cows and goats, feeding the chickens, helping *Mamm* snap beans and, of course, worship.

That childhood bliss ended abruptly in the summer of my fourteenth year. The day a man by the name of Daniel Lapp came to our house with murder on his mind. I lost my innocence that day. I lost my ability to trust. My capacity to forgive. My faith in both God and family. I nearly lost my life, and in the weeks following many times I wished I had.

I haven't been here since *Mamm*'s funeral two years ago. Most Amish probably think avoiding my siblings the way I do is shameful. But I have my reasons.

I never would have returned to Painters Mill at all if it hadn't been for my mother's diagnosis of breast cancer three years ago. But *Mamm* and I had always shared a special bond. She'd been supportive of me when others had not—especially when I informed my parents that I wouldn't be joining the church. I wasn't baptized after my *rumspringa* or "running around" period. *Mamm* disapproved, but she never judged. And she never stopped loving me.

At the age of eighteen, I moved to Columbus and spent the next year broke and miserable and more lost than I'd ever been in my life. An unlikely friendship and, eventually, an even more unlikely job saved me. Gina Colorosa taught me how to not be Amish and gave me a crash course in all the wicked ways of the "English," or non-Amish. Ravenous for new experiences, I was a quick study. Within a month of knowing her, we were roommates living on fast food, Heineken and Marlboro Lights 100's. She was a dispatcher with the Columbus PD and helped me land a job answering phones at a police substation near downtown. In the following weeks that minimum-wage position became my world—and my salvation.

Gina and I enrolled in the community college, our collective sights set on criminal justice degrees. It was one of the most satisfying and exciting times of my life. *Mamm* took the bus to Columbus for my graduation. Riding in a motorized vehicle was a direct violation of the *Ordnung,* the rules of our church district, but my mother did it anyway. For that, I'll always be thankful to her. I introduced her to Gina, and told her we were going to enroll in the police academy. *Mamm* didn't understand, but she never condemned me. It was the last time I saw her before her diagnosis of cancer. *Datt* passed suddenly of a stroke six months after I graduated. I didn't return for his funeral. But I came back for *Mamm.* To be with her during her final days. To help with the farm. That's what I told myself, anyway.

But in all honesty, my roots had been calling to me for quite some time. Looking back, I realize it was more than my mother's impending death that brought me back. Deep inside I knew the time had come for me to face my family—and a past I'd been running away from for over a decade.

A week after *Mamm's* death, as my sister Sarah and I went through her things, two town councilmen drove out to the farm. Norm Johnston and Neil Stubblefield informed me that chief of police Delbert McCoy would be retiring in a month. They wanted to know if I was interested in replacing him.

I was floored that they would ask me: formerly Amish and female to boot. But I was also flattered. A hell of a lot more than I should have been. Only later, after I'd had time to put things into perspective, did I realize the offer had more to do with small town politics than me or my law enforcement experience. Painters Mill is an idyllic town, but it's not perfect. Serious cultural issues exist between the Amish and the English. With tourism being a big chunk of the economy, the town council wanted someone who was good at smoothing ruffled feathers, whether those feathers were Amish or English.

I was the perfect candidate. I had eight years of law enforcement experience and a degree in criminal justice. I'd been born and raised in this town. Best of all, I'd once been Amish. I was fluent in Pennsylvania Dutch. I understood the culture. I was sympathetic to the Amish way of life.

A week later I accepted the job. I quit the force in Columbus, bought a house, loaded everything I owned into a U-Haul trailer and moved back to my hometown. That was just over two years ago and I've never regretted my decision. Until today.

The house where I grew up is white and plain with a big front porch and windows that look like long, sorrowful eyes. Beyond, the barn stands bold and red as if in testament to its centrality. Next to it, a grain silo juts high into the misty winter sky.

I park in the driveway and shut down the engine. The backyard is visible from where I sit. The maple tree my father and I planted when I was twelve is taller than the house now. It always amazes me at how little the place has changed when my own life has shifted so dramatically.

Of all the things I've had to do this morning, this is the most difficult. That I can look at the tortured corpse of a young woman more easily than I can face my own family is not a comforting thought. I don't want to ponder what that says about me as a person. It shames me to admit I could live the rest of my life quite contentedly if I never saw either of my siblings again.

I force myself to leave the Explorer. Like the Stutz house, the sidewalk has been shoveled. Not the work of a motorized snow blower, but shoveled by hand, the Amish way. My legs tremble as I step onto the porch and cross to the front door. I want to blame my shaky state on too much coffee or stress or the cold. But the tremors rippling through me have nothing to do with the temperature or caffeine—and everything to do with the man I'm about to face and the secrets that bind us.

I knock and wait. Footfalls sound, then the door swings open. My sister-in-law, Irene, is younger than me by several years. She has pretty skin and clear, hazel eyes. Her hair is drawn into a bun at her nape, and she wears the traditional *kapp*. Dressed in a green print dress and white apron, she is the kind of woman I might have been had Fate not stepped in and changed everything.

"Good afternoon, Katie." She speaks in Pennsylvania Dutch. Her tone is friendly, but in her eyes I see a caution she cannot hide. Stepping aside, she swings open the door. *"Wie geht's?"* How are you?

The smells of baking lard crust and rhubarb greet me as I step into the living room. The house feels warm and cozy, but I know the rooms get drafty when the temperature dips to below zero.

I don't waste time on niceties. "Is Jacob here?"

Irene doesn't understand my inability to interact with my family. I've only met her a handful of times, but I always get the impression she thinks my brusqueness stems from my being under the *bann*. Reality couldn't be further from the truth. I have great respect for the Amish and their way of life. I do not begrudge them for trying to bring me back. But I have no desire to enlighten Irene.

"He's in the barn, working on the tractor," she says.

I almost smile at the mention of the tractor. My father used only horse-drawn plows. Jacob, considered a liberal by many of the old order, bought a steel-wheeled tractor just last year.

"Would you like me to fetch him for you?"

"I'll meet him out there." I want to ask about my nephews, but I can't bring myself to do it. I tell myself I don't have time, but the truth of the matter is I don't know how to reach out.

Straightening her apron, Irene starts toward the kitchen. "I was just making rhubarb pies. Would you like a piece, Katie? Would you like a cup of hot tea?"

"No." My stomach burns with hunger, but I have no appetite as I enter the kitchen. The room is hot from the stove. The walls are a different color than the last time I was here. New floor-to-ceiling shelves filled with canning jars and dried beans line the wall to my right. But none of the cosmetic changes can erase the memories that haunt this room.

Those memories press into me like rude, insistent fingers as I walk toward the back door. My chest tightens as I pass by the sink. In my mind's eye I see blood, stark and red against the white porcelain. More on the floor. On my hands. Sticky between my fingers . . .

I try to draw a breath, but can't. My lips and cheeks begin to tingle. Vaguely, I'm aware of Irene speaking, but I'm so immersed in my thoughts I don't respond. I fumble with the knob, yank open the door. The cold snaps me from the dark tunnel of my past. The memories recede as I make my way down the sidewalk. By the time I reach the barn, the shakes are gone. I'm thankful because I'm going to need every scrap of strength I can muster to deal with my brother.

The barn door opens to a clean and well-maintained workshop. My brother's booted feet protrude from beneath the undercarriage of a tractor, which is supported by two old-fashioned hand jacks.

"Jacob?"

He slides out and sits up. His eyes meet mine as he rises and brushes the dirt from his trousers and coat. He's surprised to see me. His expression isn't hostile, but it's not friendly.

"Katie. Hello."

At the age of thirty-six, my brother's full beard is already shot with gray. A mouth that had once smiled at me with genuine affection is now permanently lined and turned down into a perpetual frown.

"What are you doing here?" Removing his work gloves, he tosses them onto the tractor seat.

In the back of my mind I wonder if he already knows about the murder. The Amish strive to believe they are a separate society from the English, but I know that isn't wholly true. My sister works in the Carriage Stop Country Store in town. Most of the customers are English tourists and townspeople. A healthy grapevine runs the length of this town. If you have ears, you hear things. Even if you're Amish.

Shoving my hands into my pockets, I walk deeper into the shadows of the barn, taking a moment to get my thoughts in order. The earthy smells of animal dung and hay remind me of childhood days spent in this barn. Ahead, four jersey cows, their pink udders swollen with milk, stand head-in. To my right, a dozen red and white mailboxes fashioned to look like farmhouses line shelves built from pine and cinder block. I see intricately built birdhouses and rocking horses with genuine horsehair manes, and I realize Jacob is as good with his hands as our father was.

I hear Jacob behind me and turn to him. "A girl was murdered in Painters Mill last night," I begin.

He stands a few feet away, his head cocked, his expression circumspect. "Murdered? Who?"

"A young woman by the name of Amanda Horner."

"Is she Amish?"

It annoys me that it matters to him. But I don't voice my feelings. There are too many boiling inside me. Once I open that Pandora's box, I'm afraid I won't be able to close it. "No."

"What does this murder have to do with me and my family?"

I give my brother a hard look. "The woman was murdered exactly the same way those girls were killed in the early 1990s."

His quick intake of breath is but a whisper in the silence of the barn. He stares at me as if I'm some outsider who's come here to wreck his world.

"How can that be?" he says after a moment.

The same question roils inside me like a storm. Because I have no answer, I stare back at him and try desperately not to tremble. "I think it might be the same guy."

I see Jacob's mind dragging him back to that terrible day. A day that devastated everyone in our family, but most of all me. He shakes his head. "That's impossible. Daniel Lapp is dead."

I close my eyes against words I've believed for sixteen years. Words that have caused me insurmountable pain and guilt for half of my life. When I open my eyes and meet my brother's gaze, I can tell he knows what I'm thinking. "I have to be sure," I say. "I need to see the body."

He looks at me as if I've asked him to renounce God.

It wasn't until weeks after the incident that I found out Jacob and my father buried the body. Horrific nightmares had been plaguing me. One night I woke screaming in my bed, certain the man who'd tried to kill me was in my bedroom. But my big brother came to my side. Jacob held me, and in the warm comfort of his arms, he revealed that *Datt* had buried the body in a defunct grain elevator in the next county, and he would never hurt anyone again.

"You know where he is buried," Jacob says. "I told you."

I know the place. The old grain elevator has been abandoned for twenty years. I've driven by it hundreds of times. But I've never stopped. I've never looked too closely. I rarely let myself think of the secrets buried there. "I need your help."

"I cannot help you."

"Come with me. Tonight. Show me where."

His eyes widen. I see fear in their depths. My brother is a stoic man, which makes his reaction even more profound. "Katie, *Datt* did not take me inside. I do not know where—"

"I can't do it alone. The elevator is a big place, Jacob. I don't know where to look."

"Daniel Lapp could not have done this terrible thing," he says.

"*Someone* killed that girl. Someone who knew details about the murders that were never released to the public. How do you explain that?"

"I cannot. But I saw . . . his body. There was blood . . . too much for him to have survived."

"Was he still bleeding when *Datt* buried him?" Dead men don't bleed. If Lapp was still bleeding at that point, he was alive. He could have dug his way out of a shallow grave and survived . . .

"I do not know. I do not wish to be part of this."

"You already are." I step closer to my brother, invading his space. This surprises him, and he steps back, looking at me as if I'm a dog with contagious mange. I raise my finger, shove it to within an inch of his nose. "I need your help, goddamn it. I need to find the remains. There's no other way."

He stares at me, as stoic and silent as a statue.

"If I don't stop this son of a bitch, he'll kill again."

Jacob winces at my language, and a small, twisted sense of satisfaction ripples through me. "Do not bring your English ways into my home."

"This has nothing to do with Amish or English," I snap. "This has to do with saving lives. You stick your head in the sand and more people could die. Is that what you want?"

My brother drops his gaze to the dirt floor, the muscles in his jaws clenching. When he raises his eyes to mine, they seem ancient. "For sixteen years, I have asked God for His forgiveness. I have tried to forget what we did."

"You mean what *I* did, don't you?"

"What all of us did."

The barn falls silent, as if in reverence to the secret that's been revealed. I knew he would be reluctant, that I would have to push. But I hadn't anticipated a refusal.

Words I need to say stick in my throat like a dull razor blade. I can feel the veins pulsing in my neck. My cheeks growing hot. I remind myself that I'm a cop working a case. But deep inside, I'm still a child cowering from unfathomable brutality. A girl crushed by secrets no one should have to bear. A teenager shocked by her own capacity for violence.

"If you go to hell it won't be because of what you did that day." My voice quivers. "But because of what you didn't do today."

"I will be judged only by God, not you."

A hot rush of anger propels me to him. I can hear my teeth grinding, the blood roaring like a freight train in my head. "If he kills again, you'll have another death on your conscience. An innocent woman will suffer unspeakable torture before her throat is cut. Think about that tonight when you're trying to sleep."

Dark emotions thrash inside me as I spin and start toward the door. I want to crush the pretty mailboxes and birdhouses my brother has so painstakingly built. I want to lash out and hurt him, the same way he is hurting me. I cling to control, telling myself I can do this on my own.

I hit the barn door with the heels of both palms and send it flying open. I'm midway down the path when I hear Jacob's voice behind me.

"Katie."

Under any other circumstance, I'd keep going. Or revile him with a few choice words that would illuminate just how far I've strayed from my Amish roots. I stop and turn only because I'm desperate. Because I'm scared. Because I don't want anyone else to die.

"I will do it." He utters the words, but his eyes tell me it is with profound reluctance. "I will help you."

The words bring hot tears to my eyes. Emotions I don't want to feel rise inside me. Because I don't want him to see those vulnerabilities, I turn away and continue on toward my vehicle in the driveway.

"I'll pick you up after dark," I say over my shoulder, and leave him staring after me.

CHAPTER 6

The curtains at the kitchen window part as I slide into the Explorer. I see Irene in her plain dress and *kapp*, standing in her overheated kitchen. I think of my nephews, and I suddenly feel depressed. Irene waves, but I pull away without responding. Not because I don't want to, but because I can't.

I can breathe again as I zip down the lane at a too-fast clip. Only then does the breadth and width of the situation grip me. I'm frightened of my secrets and the lengths I'll go to keep them. I'm afraid of what my brother and I will or will not find in the grain elevator tonight. But, it is the thought that I won't be able to stop this killer before he strikes again that fills me with terror.

I call T.J. on my way to Connie Spencer's apartment. He answers with a rough. " 'Lo?"

"It's me," I say, realizing I woke him. "Did you sleep?"

"A little. What's up?"

"Doc Coblentz says our killer wore a condom. Lubricated. I want you to hit the grocery stores, pharmacies and that carryout on Highway 82 and see if the clerks remember anyone buying lubricated condoms."

"Why do I get all the fun assignments?" T.J. sounds less than thrilled.

It surprises me that I can smile. But it reminds me I'm a cop, not a helpless fourteen-year-old. "See if the person used a credit card." There are two grocery stores, two pharmacies and one carryout in and around Painters Mill. "I think the carryout has a security camera. If they sold any condoms in the past week, get a copy of the video."

"I'm on it, Chief."

"I'll see you at the station," I say and disconnect.

Connie Spencer lives in an apartment above a furniture store on Main Street. My boots thud dully against the ancient steps as I ascend to the second floor. I knock, but no one answers. I stand in the dank hall, the smell of old wood and stale air filling my nostrils, and I realize she's probably at work.

Back at the Explorer, I dial Glock. "Any luck at the bar?"

"I found Amanda Horner's Mustang in the parking lot."

My heart jigs. "You take a look inside?"

"Yup, but we got nada."

"Shit." Frustrated, I rap the steering wheel with the heel of my palm. "Process the car. See if you can get some latents."

"Okay."

"You talk to the bartender?"

"He remembers serving her cosmos."

"Does he remember if she was with someone?"

"Says they were busy." Glock sighs. "Any luck with the friend?"

"I'm at her place now, but she's not home."

"You might try the diner. Last time I was there she burned my hash browns."

I call the station as I head toward LaDonna's Diner. My first shift dispatcher, Lois, answers on the second ring and puts me on hold before I can stop her. When she finally comes back on, I'm steamed.

"Sorry, Chief, but the phones have been nuts." She sounds rattled.

Nothing burns up the phone lines like a murder, I think darkly. "Any messages?"

"Lots of folks calling about the murder."

I remember I was supposed to type a statement this afternoon. I'm running out of time. I wish I could stop the clock. "Tell anyone who asks I'll have a statement later today."

"Norm Johnston has called three times. He sounds pissed."

"Tell him I'll touch base with him later. I'm pretty tied up right now."

"Will do."

I disconnect, knowing I won't be able to put off Norm much longer.

The clock on my dash tells me it's three P.M. when I park outside the diner. Though it's well after the lunch rush, the place is packed. The heart of the Painters Mill grapevine.

The smells of old grease and burned toast assail me when I enter. Dishes clatter over the din of conversation. From a radio next to the cash register, George Strait laments about desperation. I feel the stares as I walk to the counter. A woman in a pink waitress uniform and big hair smiles as I approach. "Hiya, Chief. Can I get ya a cuppa joe?"

I've met her before, but only to say hello. "That'd be great."

"Wanna menu or you gonna have the special?"

I'm starved, but I know if I eat here these people will descend on me like hyenas on a fresh kill. "Just coffee."

I slide onto a stool and watch her pour, hoping the coffee is fresh. "Is Connie Spencer around?"

She slides the cup in front of me. "She's on her break. Poor thing's been a basket case all morning. Amanda's murder really freaked her out. You guys know who did it yet?"

I shake my head. "Where is she?"

"Out back. Been smoking like a chimney all day."

"Thanks." Leaving the coffee, I head into the kitchen area. The cook looks at me through the steam coming off his grill. A boy with a bad case of acne eyes me from his place in front of the industrial-size dishwasher, then glances quickly away. I spy the door at the back and start toward it.

I find Connie Spencer sitting on a concrete step outside. She's a thin woman with narrow shoulders and small, quick hands. Her eyes are the color of barn muck and rimmed with blue liner. Pink blush streaks nonexistent cheekbones. Her mouth is bare of lipstick, revealing a cold sore in the corner. Huddled in a faux fur coat, she sucks on a long brown cigarette.

The door slams behind me. Turning, she gives me the evil eye, her expression defiant. A tactic I've seen more than once, usually when some tough guy is trying to cover nerves. I wonder what she's nervous about.

"I was wondering when you were going to show up." She glances at her watch. "Took you a while."

Already I don't like her attitude. "What made you think I would want to talk to you?"

"Because I was with Amanda Saturday night and now she's dead."

"You don't seem too broken up about it."

She tongues the cold sore. "I guess I'm still in shock. Amanda was so . . . *alive*, you know? I can't believe it."

"When's the last time you saw her?"

"Saturday night. We went out. Had a few drinks."

"Where?"

"The Brass Rail."

"Anyplace else?"

"No."

"Anything unusual happen while you were there?"

"Unusual like what?"

"A guy showing too much interest in her. Someone she didn't know buying her a drink. Did she have an argument with anyone?"

"Not that I remember." She gives me a hard laugh. "But I was pretty wasted."

"Do you know of anyone who might have wanted to hurt Amanda? Did she have any enemies?"

For the first time she gives me her full attention. Some of the attitude drops away and I get a glimpse of the young woman beneath all the trashy brawn. "That's what I don't get," she says. "Everyone liked Amanda. She was like . . . a nice person, always up. Laughed a lot, you know?" A smile that's much too worldly for a twenty-one-year-old twists her mouth. "I'm the one people usually don't like."

I consider telling her she might contemplate an attitude adjustment, but I'm not here to enlighten some smart-assed punk. I'm here to find out who killed Amanda Horner. "What about a boyfriend?"

She lifts a shoulder, lets it fall. "She went out with Donny Beck some, but they broke up a couple of months ago."

My cop's radar goes on alert. This is the second time Beck's name has come up. "How bad was the breakup?"

"Amanda didn't put up with any of that me-Tarzan-you-Jane shit. She laid down the law and he listened."

"Tell me about Donny Beck."

"Not much to tell. He's a clerk at Quality Implement. Likes Copenhagen and Bud and blondes with big tits. His biggest goal in life is to manage the store. Amanda's too smart to get tangled up with someone like that. She knows there's more to life than cow shit and corn."

I notice she's speaking of Amanda in the present tense. "Any messy breakups in the past?"

"Don't think so."

"Can you think of anyone who might be holding a grudge for some reason?"

"Not that I know of."

I'm chasing my tail and we both know it. A gust of wind snakes around the building, bringing with it a swirl of snow. "What time did you last see Amanda?"

Her overplucked brows knit. "Eleven-thirty. Maybe twelve."

"Did you leave the bar together?"

Exhaling smoke, she shakes her head. "Separate cars. I don't like having to rely on other people for transportation, you know? If I want to leave and they want to stay . . ." Shrugging, she lets the words hang. "Could be a pain in the ass."

Her lack of emotion bothers me. Amanda was allegedly a good friend. Why isn't this young woman more upset?

She rises and brushes at the back of her coat. "I gotta get back to work."

"I'm not finished."

"You going to pay me for this, or what?" She motions toward the door. "They're sure as hell not if I don't get back in there."

"We can do this here and now or we can do it at the police station," I say. "Your call."

She frowns like a petulant teenager, then plops down hard. "This is a bunch of shit."

"I need you to tell me everything that happened Saturday night. Don't leave anything out."

Sarcasm laces her voice as she recaps a night of drinking, dancing and flirting. "We ordered a pizza and pitcher of beer and talked." She sucks hard on the cigarette and I notice her hand shaking. "After that we played some eight ball and talked to some people we know. A few guys hit on us. I wanted to get laid, but they were a bunch of fuckin' losers."

"What do you mean 'losers'?" I picture a group of hard-drinking, drug-dealing types looking for trouble.

She looks at me as if I'm dense. "Farmers. A bunch of go-nowhere, I'm-going-to-live-in-bum-fuck-the-rest-of-my-life good ole boys. I could prac-tically smell the pig shit on their boots."

"Then what happened?"

"I left."

"I need the names of everyone you and Amanda talked to."

Sighing, she recites several names.

I pull out my notebook and jot them down. "What time did you leave?"

"I told you. Eleven-thirty or twelve." Her smile is hard-edged. "What are you trying to do? Trip me up?"

"The only time people trip up is when they're lying. Are you lying about something, Connie?"

"I don't have any reason to lie."

"Then stop being an asshole and answer my questions."

She rolls her eyes. "For an Amish chick you sure can cuss."

Under different circumstances I might have laughed, but I don't like this young woman. I'm cold and tired and desperately want something, anything that will put me on the trail of the killer. "Was Amanda still at the bar when you left?"

"I looked for her to tell her I was leaving, but couldn't find her. I figured she was in the shitter or talking to someone outside. The pizza didn't agree with me so I went home early."

"Did you see her with anyone before you left?"

"Last time I saw her she was at the pool table, playing with a chick and two guys."

"They on the list?"

"Yup." She rattles off three names.

I circle them with fingers stiff from the cold. "Is there anything else you can tell me that might be important?"

She shakes her head. "It was just a regular, boring night, like always." Taking a drag off the cigarette, she flicks it onto the step and crushes it beneath her shoe. "How did she die?"

Ignoring the question, I shove the notebook into my jacket pocket and give Connie Spencer a hard look. "Don't leave town."

"Why? I told you everything I know." For the first time, she looks upset. I don't like her and she knows it. She rises as I turn toward the door. "I'm not a suspect, am I?" she calls out to my back.

I slam the door without answering.

Snow greets me when I walk out of the diner. The sky is dark and low, a parallel to my mood. I know better than to let Spencer's lack of concern annoy me, but my temper is pumping as I head toward the Explorer. I don't think she's involved, but I want to wipe that sneer off her face.

I work my cell phone from my pocket as I climb behind the wheel and call Lois at the station. "I need a favor," I begin, knowing I'll get a higher level of cooperation if I ask nicely. Lois isn't the most obliging person working for me, but she's got a good work ethic, strong organizational skills, and she can type like a bat out of hell.

"Glock just handed me a year's worth of typing and these phones just won't shut up." Her sigh hisses through the line. "What's up?"

"I need a central meeting room where I can meet with my officers while we're working this case. I thought that file room next to my office might work. What do you think?"

"It's cluttered and kinda small." But I can tell by her tone she's pleased to be in on the decision-making.

"Do you think you could get someone to help you clear it out and put that folding table and chairs in there?" When she hesitates, I add, "Call Pickles. Tell him he's on active duty effective immediately. He can help you with that old file cabinet."

Roland "Pickles" Shumaker is seventy-four years old and my only auxiliary officer. The town council tried to force me to fire him two years ago when he shot Mrs. Offenheimer's prize bantam rooster after the thing attacked him. But Pickles has been a cop in Painters Mill for going on fifty years. Back in the eighties, he single-handedly busted one of the largest meth labs in the state. I couldn't see ending his career over a dead chicken. So I asked him to accept auxiliary duty and, knowing the alternative, he agreed. He's a grouchy old goat, smokes like a teenager on a binge, colors his hair a weird shade of brown, and lies incessantly about his age. But he's a good cop. With a murder to solve and the clock ticking, I need him.

"Pickles'll be glad to get the call, Chief. He still checks in every day. Been driving Clarice nuts since he got the axe. She don't like him hanging around the house all day."

"We'll put him to good use." I think of some of the things I need for the meeting room. "Order a dry-erase board, flip chart and corkboard, will you?"

"Anything else?"

I hear her phone ringing. "That's it for now. I'll be in to brief everyone in ten minutes. Hold down the fort, will you?"

"Kinda like trying to hold down a leaf in a tornado, but I'll try."

Next, I call Glock and ask him to run a background check on Connie Spencer. In typical Glock fashion, he's already on it.

"She got a DUI in Westerville last year and an arrest for possession of a controlled substance, but no conviction."

"What was the controlled substance?"

"Hydrocodone. Her mom's. Judge let her off."

"Keep digging, see what else you can find." I tell him about Donny Beck and pass along the list of names Spencer gave me. "I want checks on all of them."

"Logging in now."

I disconnect and hit the speed dial for T.J. to see how he's doing on the condom front. "How's the search going?"

"I feel like a frickin' pervert." He sounds as if his day is shaping up like mine.

"You're a cop with a badge working a murder case."

Assuaged, he gets down to business. "The cash register at Super Value Grocery uses SKU numbers for inventory. Manager went through the tape. They sold two boxes of lubricated condoms on Friday. Another on Saturday."

"Do they have the customers' names?"

"One guy paid with cash. The other two with checks, so I have two names. I'm on my way to talk to one of them now."

"Nice work." I think about the guy who paid with cash. "Did any of the clerks recognize the cash guy?"

"Nope."

"Does the store have security cameras?"

"Grocery has two cams. One above the office inside and one in the parking lot. The one inside isn't positioned to capture customer faces, but the one in the parking lot is worth a shot."

"Do we know when the cash guy bought the condoms?"

Paper rustles through the line. "Eight P.M. Friday."

The timing is right; the murder happened Sunday. "Get the film. Let's see if we can ID him."

"You got it."

"I'm on my way to the station. Can you swing by for a quick meeting?"

"I can be there in ten minutes."

"See you then." I hit End and toss the phone onto the passenger seat. The clock on my dash flicks to four P.M. The passage of time taunts me. Fourteen hours have passed since Amanda Horner's body was found and I'm no closer to knowing who did it than I was at the start.

As I speed toward the station, I try not to think about my brother and our plans for tonight. I honestly don't know whether to hope that we find a body buried in that old grain elevator. Or pray that we don't.

CHAPTER 7

John Tomasetti knew he was in serious shit the instant he walked into Special Agent Supervisor Denny McNinch's office and saw Deputy Superintendent Jason Rummel standing at the window. The last time he'd seen Rummel was when Field Agent Bryan Gant was shot and killed while executing a search warrant in Toledo six months ago. Word among the agents was that Rummel only ventured from his corner office for hirings, firings or deaths. John didn't have to wonder which of the three had warranted this personal visit.

Seated at the conference table with her requisite Kasper suit and Starbucks mug, Human Resources Director Ruth Bogart paged through a brown expandable file. A file that was too thick from too many forms being shoved into it, and worn from too many bureaucratic fingers paging through. A file John was pretty sure had his name printed on the label.

He should have been worried for his job. At the very least he should have been concerned that he was about to lose his salary and health insurance. Not to mention bear witness to the end of a law enforcement career that had taken him twenty years to build.

The problem was, John didn't give a damn. In fact, he didn't give a good damn about a whole hell of a lot these days. Self-destructive, he knew; not a first for that, either. But at the moment all he felt was mild annoyance that he'd been pulled away from his cranberry muffin and dark roast.

"You wanted to see me?" he said to no one in particular.

"Have a seat." Denny McNinch motioned toward one of four sleek leather chairs surrounding the table. He was a large man who wore his suits too tight and never removed his jacket, probably because his armpits were invariably wet with sweat. John wondered if he knew that the field agents and administrative assistants called him Swamp Ass behind his back.

Two years ago, when John had first come on board with the Ohio Bureau of Criminal Identification and Investigation, Denny had been a field agent. He'd been a weight lifter and could run a five-minute mile with a fifty-pound pack strapped to his back. He'd been a decent marksman and a black belt in karate. Nobody fucked with Denny McNinch. Back in the day, he'd been a real ass-kicker. Then he'd begun the arduous climb up the political ladder. Somewhere along the way he'd become more figurehead than principal. He stopped shooting. Stopped running. Too much deskwork turned brawn to flab, respect from his peers to mild disdain. John didn't have any sympathy; Denny had made his choices. There were worse fates for a man.

Rummel, on the other hand, was a paper-pusher from the word go. He was small in stature with a wiry build and a Hitleresque mustache that had made more than one field agent crack a smile at an inappropriate moment. But it was usually the last time they smiled at Jason Rummel. Rummel made up for his physical shortcomings by being a mean son of a bitch. A real corporate sociopath. The man with the hatchet. At fifty, he was at the top of the Bureau's political food chain. He was a predator with big fangs and sharp claws and a proclivity for using both. He fucked up careers for the sheer entertainment value.

As John pulled out a chair, he figured he was about to be on the receiving end of those claws. "What's the occasion?" he asked. "Someone's birthday?"

McNinch took the chair beside him without speaking, without making eye contact. Not a good sign. None of this was.

"Don't be a smart-ass," he muttered.

Rummel chose to stand. The short man striving to be tall. He walked to the table and looked down at John. "Agent Tomasetti, you've had a remarkable law enforcement career."

"Remarkable isn't the adjective most people use," John said.

"You came to BCI with the highest of recommendations."

"A day I'll bet you've regretted ever since."

Rummel smiled. "That's not true."

John scanned the three faces. "Look, I think everyone in this room knows you didn't call me in here to slap me on the back and tell me how remarkable I am."

McNinch sighed. "You didn't pass the drug test, John."

"I'm on medication. You know that." It was the truth; he had prescriptions. Several, in fact. Too goddamn many if he wanted to be honest about it. He didn't feel inclined to be honest.

Ruth Bogart spoke for the first time. "Why didn't you write it down on the form when you gave your urine sample?"

John shot her a dark look. "Because the drugs I take are nobody's goddamn business."

Bogart's face reddened through her Estée Lauder makeup.

McNinch shifted uncomfortably. "Look, John, can your doctor verify the script?" he asked reasonably. The peacekeeper. The man in the middle. The man who used to be just like John until too much paperwork turned him into another fat guy in a suit who didn't count for shit.

"I'm sure he can." Another lie, but it would buy him some time. John figured it was the best he could hope for at this juncture.

Bogart piped up again, angry now because John had embarrassed her in front of her colleagues. "I'll need the name and number of your physician."

"Which one? I have several."

"The one who prescribed the pills."

"They've all prescribed pills."

Bogart shook her head. "Give me the names, John."

He could tell by her expression she'd wanted to call him asshole, but she didn't have the balls. Ruth Bogart was far too politically correct to say what she really thought. She'd wait until your back was turned, then sink the knife in good and deep.

John recited the names of three doctors and gave her the phone numbers. There were more doctors—he'd done quite a bit of shopping around—but he stopped there since prescription shopping was illegal in most states.

John leaned back in his chair. "If you guys are after my ass, you should have called me in here about my performance or attendance instead of this drug test thing. Considering my history with BCI and the Cleveland Division of Police, termination based on a urinalysis could be tricky." He lowered his voice. "People hate it when the good guy gets the shaft. I don't think you need that kind of negative PR. Hell, if this were to go to litigation . . ." He shrugged.

McNinch looked alarmed. "John, no one's after your ass."

"We don't expect this to go to litigation," Bogart added.

John didn't believe either of them.

Rummel set a leather-bound notebook on the table and sat. "Is there a correlation between the drugs and your attendance?"

John couldn't help it; he laughed. But with his career in the toilet, his life already down the drain, there wasn't anything remotely funny about any of this. Except for maybe Rummel's ridiculous mustache.

The deputy superintendent shot Bogart a look. She passed him a sheet of paper. Rummel set the papers down without looking at them. "You've missed ten days of work this year and it's only January."

"I had the flu."

"For ten days?"

"It was bad."

In his peripheral vision, John saw Bogart roll her eyes.

Rummel frowned. "John, you're bound by the employee handbook just like everyone else."

Bogart chimed in. "You'll need to provide us with a note from your doctor."

"I went to a clinic."

"An invoice will do," she said. "For documentation."

John scanned their faces, his heart rate kicking up. Two years ago he'd had high hopes for the field agent position with BCI. He'd hoped a new job in a new city would provide him a fresh start. He'd hoped it would save him from the black hole that had sucked him down since the fiasco in Cleveland. Or maybe save him from himself. BCI was a top-notch agency. The field agent position was a far cry from working narcotics. His duties were more diverse. He spent less time on the street. There was less stress. The people were decent. Well, except for Rummel.

But like a hiker with a backpack full of stones, John had brought his problems to Columbus with him. The rage. The grief. The outrage at the unfairness of life. His reputation and the stigma. Once in Columbus, cut off from what few friends he had left, he became even more isolated. The fresh start he'd hoped for became a whole new nightmare rife with all the trimmings. Different doctors. Same problems. Same drugs. Same bottle of Chivas. The new job became a new failure. The names had changed, but the move hadn't changed a thing.

Now, the brass at BCI wanted him gone, and at the age of forty-two, John was facing early retirement. Or maybe a security officer position at the local Kroger. But John wasn't ready to call it quits. The sad truth was there wasn't much out there for a former detective with a psych sheet, a reputation as a rogue cop, and the work record of a stoned college student. The grand jury in Cleveland might have returned a no bill, but the stigma would follow him the rest of his life.

Rummel gazed steadily at John. "Have you considered early retirement? Taking into account your service with the Cleveland Division of Police, we could wrangle you a deal."

John knew he should jump at the opportunity. Shoot the horse and put it out of its misery. But God, he didn't want to give up on his career. If he did that he might as well be dead. Even that option had crossed his mind a time or two, but he didn't have the guts.

"What kind of deal?" he asked.

Rummel came forward in his chair, his rodent eyes gleaming. "In case you're not reading between the lines here, John, this is not a request."

"Take the deal," McNinch said quietly.

"It's more than fair," Bogart put in. "Full bennies. Company car."

John's temper writhed. Contempt for these people was like a serpent beneath his skin, twisting, ready to slither out and strike. "Fair probably isn't quite the right word, is it?"

"We know what you've been through," Bogart soothed.

"I seriously doubt it." John said the words through teeth clenched so tightly his jaws ached.

"We sympathize with your . . . situation." This from Rummel.

John looked at him, wondering how many times the man had said those hollow words to other agents who'd lost partners or loved ones. Insincere son of a bitch; he was probably enjoying this. He envisioned himself lunging over the table, grabbing the other man's collar and slamming his face into the rosewood surface until his nose was a bloody pulp. He could feel his pulse throbbing at his temples. The blood roaring in his ears.

Silently, he counted to ten, the way Doc Pop-a-pill had instructed. It didn't help. "I'll take it under advisement," he ground out.

Denny groaned aloud. "John, for chrissake . . ."

Shoving away from the table, John rose abruptly. "If you people want me gone, I suggest you get your cards in order and grow some balls." Not waiting for a reply, he started toward the door.

"John!" McNinch called out.

John didn't stop. He didn't look back.

"Let him go," Rummel said quietly.

John hit the door with both hands, sent it flying open. It banged against the wall hard enough to rattle the framed picture of the attorney general in the hall. Keyboards fell silent. Heads swung his way. Pretty administrative assistants. A field agent holding a Krispy Kreme doughnut. The mail guy with his cart piled high with envelopes. Their expressions were wary, as if they expected John to pull out his sidearm and go postal. A little afternoon entertainment to go with their lattes and Diet Cokes. High drama on the fourteenth floor. Break out the fucking popcorn.

John felt the eyes burning into him as he strode toward his office and yanked open the door. Inside, he looked around, wondering what the hell he was doing. He should have taken the offer. He should have stayed calm. Now, if Rummel had his way, they were going to fire him. God knows he'd given them cause. Liquid lunches. Lost afternoons. That was when he bothered to show up at all. His penchant for prescription drugs was just the icing on the cake.

But God help him, he didn't know what he'd do without the drugs. Didn't know how he'd get through the day or God forbid a whole goddamn night. Talk about a clusterfuck.

He crossed to the window behind his desk and stared out at the traffic on Broad Street fourteen stories below. Not for the first time, the thought of ending it all flitted through his mind. He could go home. Have a couple of drinks.

Work up the courage. Be done with it. But while John was squarely at the bottom of the barrel, he wasn't so far gone that he could blow his brains out.

Not yet, anyway.

Sighing, he turned from the window and slid into the chair behind his desk. He thought about Nancy and Donna and Kelly, and shame for what he'd become cut him. The urge to pull out the photos was strong, but he resisted. Seeing their faces didn't make him feel any better. He couldn't remember them the way they'd been. When he thought of his wife and two little girls, he saw them the way they'd been on the dreadful night he'd found them . . .

A soft rap on the door drew him from dark thoughts. "It's open."

McNinch stepped into his office, his expression contrite. "Sorry about what happened in there."

"Par for the course."

"Rummel knows you're a good agent."

"Rummel doesn't know shit about me."

McNinch slid into the visitor chair and pretended to be interested in the plaques, commendations and framed diploma on the wall. "It was a good deal," he said after a moment.

"I'm not ready to retire."

"There are a lot of things you could do, John. Things with less stress."

The smile felt brittle on his face. "You mean like a rent-a-cop?"

McNinch frowned. "Hell, I don't know. Private detective. Friend of mine from Houston, a former cop, went into corporate security for a major pizza company chain. Draws a decent salary. Another guy I know is now a Justice of the Peace."

"Good for them."

"You gotta do something, man. Rummel wants you gone. He's like a dog and you're the fucking bone. At the moment, you have a choice as to how you walk out that door. In six months, you may not have that luxury."

John gave him a hard look. "I wouldn't call any of this a luxury."

"Hey, man, I know you got a tough break—"

"I didn't have a tough break," he snapped. "For chrissake, just say it. Stop with the fucking euphemisms."

Grimacing, Denny looked down at his hands. "I'm on your side."

"You're on whatever side is convenient. But I get it, Denny. I've been around long enough to know how it works."

"I'm sorry you feel that way."

"Yeah, me, too."

Rising, the other man started toward the door.

John leaned back in his chair and watched him go. When the door clicked shut, he opened his pencil drawer and pulled out the flask, the silver finish tarnished from use. The irony that it had been a gift from his wife never ceased to give him pause every time he took a drink.

Snagging his briefcase, he set it on his lap and snapped it open. He dug into the side pocket. Relief swept through him when his fingers closed around the prescription bottle. John hated what he'd become. A sick parody of the man he'd once been. A fucking junkie. Everything he despised. Weak. Dependent. Pathetic. He wanted to blame it on the doctors. After all, it was they who'd so eagerly prescribed. But two years ago, John had been a basket case. A man truly at the end of his rope. Flirting with thoughts of suicide. Going so far as to put the gun in his mouth. He'd tasted the gun oil and his own fear, felt the cold steel rattle against his teeth.

Popping the cap, he tapped out two Xanax and one Valium. He wasn't supposed to take them together, but he'd experimented and discovered through trial and error a cocktail of pills that provided what he needed to get through the day.

He pulled out the framed photograph and blew off the paper dust and pencil shavings. His late wife, Nancy, and his two little girls, Donna and Kelly, smiled at him as if they didn't have a care in the world. Looking at them never got any easier. He should have been able to protect them.

Propping the frame on his desk, he tossed the pills into his mouth and raised the flask. "Here's to you, Nancy," he whispered and washed them down with eighty-proof whiskey.

CHAPTER 8

I arrive at the station to find all six parking spaces taken, including mine. I'm tempted to ticket the driver, but luckily for them I have other priorities. A Crown Vic with all the trimmings tells me the Holmes County Sheriff's Department has arrived on the scene. I need all the help I can get, but I don't want to get into a pissing contest over jurisdiction because Sheriff Nathan Detrick has his mind set on winning reelection next fall.

I park next to a fire hydrant and start for the front door. The noise level inside rivals a high school cafeteria at lunchtime. At the dispatch station, Lois looks as frazzled as her overprocessed hair. Hovering over her is a middle-aged woman in a pink parka and big pearl earrings. I silently groan when, upon closer scrutiny, I realize the woman is Janine Fourman.

Janine is the president of the Painters Mill Ladies Club, owner of Carriage Stop Country Store on the traffic circle and the Tea and Candle Shop on Sixth Street. She's a member of the town council, a founding member of the Historical Society, a professional busybody and instigator of all that is rumor.

Glock and a muscle-bound Holmes County Sheriff's deputy glance up from their conversation. Glock gives me a covert wink, and I know he's relayed the message I want to the deputy: Help us, but don't try to steal the show.

The deputy gives me a once-over—as if expecting a plain woman in a *kapp* and practical shoes—and extends his hand as I approach. "I'm Deputy Hicks."

He's a stout chap with beefy arms and a neck as thick as a telephone pole. I've met him at some point, but for the life of me I can't remember the circumstance. I shake his hand, noticing the sweaty palm and overtight grip. "Thanks for coming."

"Sheriff Detrick wanted me to let you know we're here to assist if you need us."

"I appreciate the offer."

He looks at Glock as if they're best buds. "Officer Rupert was just filling me in on the case. Hell of a damn thing."

I think of Belinda Horner. "Tough on the family."

"You got a suspect yet?"

"We're running some background checks. Waiting for the autopsy and the lab results."

"Do you think it's the same guy as before?"

I look around, aware that the reception area has fallen silent. People are listening, watching, their eyes alight with the anticipation of news. Details to titillate the dark side of their imaginations. Reassurances to calm their fears so they can get on with their lives without worrying about a madman running amok in their town.

I shake my head. "We don't have anything concrete to substantiate that."

"Has to be, though, don't it?" He looks genuinely curious, a cop who likes a good murder mystery with a twist. "I mean, what are the odds of two killers with the same MO in a town this size?"

I don't answer. Instead, I look him square in the eye, the way I might a suspect who'd ventured too close. Hicks gets my message and backs off.

Not wanting to ruffle feathers just yet, I tell him about the briefing I'm about to hold. "You're welcome to sit in on it."

His expression tells me this pleases him. He's in the loop. One of the guys. "I gotta get back. Sheriff just wanted you to know we're available if you need manpower."

If this had been any other case, I would have jumped on the offer. I would have formed a multi-jurisdictional task force and included not only the sheriff's office, but the State Highway Patrol and the Ohio Bureau of Criminal Identification and Investigation. I can't do that with this case. The last thing I need is a half dozen overzealous cops breathing down my neck.

I make a mental note to call Detrick later to thank him personally and stave off any questions about my lack of action. "Let me see where we're at on this thing and I'll give you guys a call. We're going to need all the help we can get."

"Good enough." He jerks his head, then heads toward the door.

I smile at Glock. "Thanks."

"Don't mention it."

"Briefing in two minutes." I start toward dispatch to collect my messages. "My office. Let everyone know about it, will you?"

Glock gives me a mock salute and hustles to his cubicle.

I'm midway to the dispatch desk when Janine Fourman blocks my path. "Chief Burkholder, I'd like a word with you."

The urge to push past her is strong, but I don't. She's a substantial woman, both in physical stature and her standing in the community. I've been around long enough to know any mishandling on my part will come back to bite me. Janine ran for mayor last election and lost, but only because a few people figured out a clawed creature exists beneath that favorite-aunt façade. I've seen those claws extended a time or two myself, and I have no desire to get verbally mauled when I have a murder to solve.

"Janine, I'm about to meet with my officers."

She is a woman of about fifty-five with dyed black hair, small brown eyes, and a body as short and round as a milk-fed beef cow. "Then I'll get right to the point. This whole town is abuzz about the murder. The rumors are flying that it's the serial killer from the early nineties. Is that true? Is it the same guy?"

"I'm not going to speculate."

"Do you have a suspect?"

"Not at this time." It doesn't elude me that she doesn't ask about the victim.

"Why on earth did you turn down Sheriff Detrick's offer to help? You're not going to try to handle this on your own, are you?"

I'm usually pretty good at handling pushy numbskulls like Janine. But the things I've seen so far on this seemingly endless day, coupled with fatigue, the weight of my responsibility to this town—and my own secrets—have squashed my patience.

"I did not turn down Detrick's offer for help," I snap. "I told that deputy

I'd give the sheriff's office a call after I meet with my officers and figure out where we are." Her eyes widen when I take a step toward her. An edgy sense of satisfaction ripples through me when she gives up ground and steps back. "And if you're going to quote me, you'd better make damn sure you get it right."

"As a member of the town council, and I'm entitled to some answers," she huffs.

"You're entitled to a lot of things, but you are *not* entitled to embellishing upon information you overhear. That includes misquoting me. Are we clear?"

Her mouth tightens into a thin, unpleasant line. Pink spreads up her neck all the way to her cheeks. "It would benefit you greatly, Chief Burkholder, if you were more cooperative with the people who sign your paycheck."

"I'll try to remember that." Pulling myself back from a place I don't want to go, I glance toward my office. "If you'll excuse me, I have to get to work."

I push past her and don't stop until I reach dispatch. "Messages?"

Lois shoves a stack of pink slips at me and puts her hand over the mouthpiece of the phone. "Nicely done, Chief," she whispers in a conspiratorial tone.

"If she tries to get into my office, shoot her."

Snorting, Lois returns to her phone call.

I start toward my office.

"Chief Burkholder!"

I turn to see Steve Ressler, publisher of the *Advocate,* jog up to me. He is tall and wiry with a ruddy complexion and a head full of bright red hair.

I stop because he's probably the only friendly media I'll see in the coming days. "Make it quick, Steve."

"You promised a press release this afternoon."

"You'll get it."

He glances at his watch. "Presses start at five."

The *Advocate* usually comes out on Friday. Today is Monday, which tells me a special edition is going to press. "Give me an hour, will you?"

His grimace tells me he's not happy about the delay, but he's perceptive enough to realize I'm not going to put the case on hold to accommodate his schedule. Steve might look like an older version of Opie from the *Andy Griffith Show,* but he's a type A personality from the word go.

He checks his watch again. "Can you fax it to me? Say by six?"

It will be fully dark by six. I find myself dreading the darkness. "I have some safety tips for citizens I want printed, too."

"That's good." I can tell by his expression he's going to ask about the murder, but I turn away before he can.

An odd sense of relief flutters through me when I enter my office and turn on the light. The familiarity of this cramped little space comforts me. Working off my coat, I hang it on the hook and close the door. I need a few minutes to regroup. The energy that's been driving me since the wee hours of the morning drains from my muscles, and I collapse into my chair. Closing my eyes, I put my face in my hands and massage my temples. I want coffee and food. For a few precious minutes, I want a reprieve from questions I have no idea how to answer, and the nightmare of this case.

But when I close my eyes, I see Amanda Horner's brutalized body. I see the bruises at her ankles. The black gleam of blood in the snow. Ligature marks that cut all the way to the bone. I see the anguish in her parents' eyes. I feel a different kind of anguish in my own heart.

Turning on my computer, I pull the "Slaughterhouse Murders" file from my drawer and set it in front of me. I grab a legal pad and as the computer boots, I jot the things I want to review with my officers.

Assignments. T.J.—condoms? Glock—footwear imprints? Tire-tread imprints? Mona—abandoned properties. Me—similar crimes. Background checks— Connie Spencer. Donny Beck. People at the bar. Suspect list.

My hand pauses. I think of the killer. I ponder his mind-set, and I write.

Motive. Means. Opportunity. Why does he kill? Sexual gratification. Sexual sadist. Where does he kill? A place he feels safe—remote, i.e., no gag. Not worried about victim's screams. Basement? Soundproof room? Abandoned property?

I think of opportunity and wonder if he has a job, and I write:

Does he work?

A knock interrupts my thoughts. "It's open."

The door opens a few inches and a hand clutching a paper bag from Ellis's Burger Palace appears.

"I come bearing gifts."

"In that case come in."

T.J. enters and approaches my desk. "Hamburger with pickles, hold the onions. Large fries and a Diet Coke."

The aroma elicits a grumble from my stomach. I smile as I reach for the bag. "If you weren't already engaged, I'd ask you to marry me."

"Sustenance, Chief. You gotta eat." But he blushes.

Behind him, Glock appears holding four biggie coffees in a cardboard carrying tray. "I got the caffeine."

I unpack my lunch as Skid drags in a folding chair. I steal a few bites of the hamburger as the men take their seats. "We've gotta catch this guy," I begin.

Glock sets his coffee on the edge of my desk. "So is it the same guy from before or not?"

I shake my head. "We can't operate under that assumption."

"Why not?"

"We don't want to limit ourselves." I don't believe that. But I can't reveal that the murderer from the early nineties is dead—if that is the case. I hate it, but I have no choice but to lie to my team. "We could have a copycat."

"That'd be pretty fuckin' strange," Skid says between bites.

"The one thing we can assume is that we probably have a serial murderer on our hands. This was no crime of passion. He was organized. Deliberate."

The room goes so quiet I hear the buzz of the fluorescent lights overhead.

"So you think he's going to kill again?" T.J. asks.

"That's what he does. He kills. He's good at it. He likes it." I sip my Coke. "And it'll happen right here in Painters Mill unless he moves on to another town."

"Or we get him first," Glock adds.

I set my drink on my desk. "We've got to pull out all the stops, guys. That means mandatory overtime."

Three heads nod, and it's reassuring to know I have the support of my small force. I look down at my hastily scratched notes. "I've got Mona working on a list of abandoned properties in the two-county area. T.J., where are you on the condoms?"

"Manager of the Super Value gave me the names of the two guys who paid with checks." He glances at his palm-size notebook. "Justin Myers and Greg Milhauser. As soon as we finish up here I'm going to talk to them."

"Good. What about the cash guy?"

"Manager is going to get me copies of video first thing in the morning."

"We need it now."

T.J.'s expression turns sheepish. "His daughter is having some kind of birthday party tonight."

"Call him. Tell him you need that tape yesterday. If he balks, tell him we'll get a search warrant and he'll be scraping produce off the floor for a month."

"Got it."

"Once you get the tape, I need the cash guy identified. This is a small town. It shouldn't be too hard." I turn my attention to Glock. "What about the tire tread and footwear imprints?"

"I had them couriered to BCI. I'm still working on getting imprints of city vehicles and footwear. Probably be another courier fee, Chief."

"Don't worry about the budget. How soon can you finish?"

"Today. If you guys give me a shoe imprint before you leave this meeting, that would be great."

"You got a kit?"

"I'll just use an ink roller and put them on paper if that's all right."

"Should be good enough for a comparison analysis." I think about that for a moment. "Did BCI give you a time frame?"

"Two days. Three max."

"Tell them we want priority or I'll call the attorney general and have him light a fire."

Glock nods. "Okay."

My mind jumps to the next subject. "You getting background checks on those people at the bar?"

"A few have come back." Glock opens a tattered folder. "Aside from Connie

Spencer, the only other hit that came back is for a guy by the name of Scott Brower."

"Tell me about him."

"Thirty-two years old. High school dropout. Worked at the oil filter factory down in Millersburg, but he got into some kind of altercation with his boss, threatened to cut her throat."

"Nice guy," T.J. says.

"I bet he didn't get the raise," Skid comments.

Glock meets my gaze. "Boss was female. Anyway, he's been working as a mechanic over at the Mr. Lube."

"Did the factory press charges for the threats?" I ask.

"Fired him, but there were no charges filed."

"Any arrests?"

"Four. Two were domestics. One for slugging a guy in a bar in Columbus. The other he pulled a knife on a guy in a bar in Kingsport, Tennessee."

"Sounds like Mr. Brower has a penchant for knives."

"And bars," Skid interjects.

"Not to mention a problem with women," Glock adds.

I nod. "You got a current address?"

Glock rattles off the address of a downtrodden apartment complex on the west side of town.

"He ever work at the slaughterhouse?" I ask.

"HR says no."

"See if he's got a juvie rec. I'll pay him a visit."

Glock looks mildly concerned. "Alone?"

"We don't have the manpower to work in teams."

"Chief, with all due respect, this guy seems to have problems with women in places of authority."

"Yeah, well, I have my .38 to back me up in case he mistakes me for the weaker sex."

Skid gives a raucous laugh.

Impatient, I tap my pen against my notes. "What about Donny Beck?" I ask Glock.

"Squeaky clean."

"Go talk to his friends and family. I'll rattle his cage a little. See if he has an alibi."

He gives me a thumbs-up.

I transfer my attention to Skid, who's slumped in his chair like a sleep-deprived tenth grader in study hall. His eyes are bloodshot. His hair looks like it hasn't been washed for a couple of days. He hasn't shaved. He straightens when I address him. "I want you to finish interviewing the rest of the people at the bar. And I want background reports on the Horners."

"You think they—"

"No," I cut in. "But we leave no stone unturned."

Skid nods.

"Lois and Mona can help you guys type up your reports," I say. "Document everything."

I contemplate my team. All three men are good cops, but only two are experienced. I have a good bit of experience myself. But mine is mostly limited to patrol. I worked a total of four homicides during my stint in Columbus. *God help us* is all I can think.

"Recap." I lean back in my chair. "People of interest?"

"Scott Brower," Glock says.

"The three condom guys," Skid adds.

"Donny Beck," I say.

T.J. pipes up. "The Slaughterhouse Killer."

If I totally dismiss the old case, I risk appearing incompetent. "I pulled the file," I say. "Doc Coblentz is sending the complete autopsy reports. I'd like for each of you to familiarize yourself with the details of the case."

Glock nibbles the cap of his pen. "Let's say it is the Slaughterhouse guy. What's up with the lapse in activity? And wasn't the Roman numeral IX carved into the last victim?"

"So what happened to ten through twenty-two?" Skid asks no one in particular.

"Maybe he's been a busy boy somewhere else," Glock surmises.

"Or he wants the cops to think that," T.J. offers.

I cut in before the conversation takes a turn I don't want it to take. "I've got some database queries going for similar crimes. If he changed locales and used the same signature, we'll get a hit."

"He could have been arrested on some unrelated charge," Skid puts in. "Went to jail, did his time, and was recently released."

I meet his gaze. "Follow up on that. Check with DRC." DRC is the Ohio Department of Rehabilitation and Corrections. I hate wasting his time on a ruse, but I have no choice. "Get a list of names for all male inmates released in the last six months, between the ages of twenty-five and forty-five years of age."

Skid looks like a gas pain hit him. "That's a lot of names."

"Ask DRC to narrow it down for you. They keep statistical information on parolees. Check males with two or more violent offenses, especially sex crimes and stalking. Start with the five surrounding counties, then expand from there. Include Columbus, Cleveland and Wheeling, West Virginia. I'll call Sheriff Detrick about getting you some help. In the interim, I'll okay Mona and Lois for overtime."

He nods, but looks overwhelmed by the task I've put before him.

I scan the room. "The victim's clothes were not found at the scene. That means he either discarded them, left them at the murder scene or he's keeping them."

"You mean like a trophy?" T.J. asks.

"Maybe," I reply. "Something to keep in mind."

I glance at my notes, realize I've covered everything I wrote down. "Mona and Lois are working on getting the old file room set up as our command center. It might be a while before all of us are here at the same time again. We may have to do most of our communicating via phone. As always, mine will be on 24/7. Until we catch this son of a bitch, I expect the same from you."

All nod in agreement.

"Does anyone have anything they want to discuss before we adjourn?"

T.J. is the first to speak. "Do you think at some point you'll call BCI or FBI for help, Chief?" All eyes land on him, and he flushes. "I'm not saying we aren't capable of doing this on our own, but our resources are limited here in Painters Mill."

"Yeah, who's going to round up all those loose fuckin' cows while we work the case?" Skid offers with a smirk.

T.J. holds his ground. "There are only four of us."

The last thing I want to do is involve another agency. But law enforcement protocol dictates I do. My team expects it. I must have their respect to be effective. My credibility depends on my doing the smart thing.

But I can't ask for help at this stage. As much as I despise lying to them, I can't risk some deputy or field agent figuring out that sixteen years ago I shot and killed a man, that my family hid the crime from the police and swept the entire sordid mess under the rug.

"I'll make some calls," I say, being purposefully vague. "In the interim, I've activated auxiliary officer Roland Shumaker."

"Ain't seen Pickles since he shot that rooster," Glock says.

"He still dye his hair Cocoa-Puff brown?" Skid wonders aloud.

"I expect you to treat Officer Shumaker with respect," I say. "We need him."

The men's expressions indicate that for now they're satisfied with the way I'm handling the case. Two years ago that wouldn't have happened. I'm Painters Mill's first female chief of police. Initially, not everyone was happy about it. The first few months were tough, but we've come a long way since then. I've earned their respect.

I know from experience cops tend to be territorial. These men do not want some other agency horning in on the investigation. On the other hand, if the killer strikes again, I'll have another death on my conscience because I didn't do my job the way I should have. It's an unbearable dilemma.

I think of the press release I'm about to write and fight a slow rise of dread. Steve Ressler isn't the only media I'll be dealing with in the coming days. As soon as word of this murder hits the airwaves, I'll have reporters from as far away as Columbus skulking around town, looking for photo ops.

"Let's go get this animal," I say.

As the men file from my office, I can only hope none of them look hard enough to find the whole truth.

CHAPTER 9

Denny McNinch entered the deputy superintendent's office to find Jason Rummel leaning back in his leather executive chair like a king presiding over his adoring court. Human Resources Director Ruth Bogart sat adjacent his desk. Denny hoped this wouldn't take long; he was supposed to meet his wife for dinner in fifteen minutes.

"Denny." Rummel motioned toward the vacant visitor chair. "Sorry for the short notice."

Short notice was a stretch. Car keys in hand, Denny had been on his way out the door when Rummel called. "No problem."

"We received an RFA this afternoon from the town of Painters Mill," Rummel said. RFA was BCI-speak for "Request for Assistance."

Denny shifted, glanced at his watch, waited.

"The town council believes they have a serial murderer on their hands."

Denny stopped fidgeting. "Serial murder?"

"Apparently, there's a history of a killer working the area. It's been a while, fifteen or sixteen years. The councilwoman I spoke with said the general consensus is that the killer is back."

Dinner forgotten, Denny leaned forward.

Rummel continued. "Painters Mill is mostly rural with a population just over five thousand. Amish country, I'm told. The small police force is overwhelmed. The chief is small town. Female. Inexperienced."

Usually, it was Denny who was contacted by local law enforcement. It was, after all, his responsibility to assign RFAs to agents. On the outside chance the RFA found its way to Rummel's desk, he would normally reroute it back to Denny. He wondered why Rummel was handling this one. He wondered why Ruth Bogart was there, since field cases didn't fall within her realm of responsibility. He wondered why the hell *he* was here when this could have been handled over the phone.

"I'm assigning the case to John Tomasetti," Rummel said.

That was the last thing Denny expected him to say. "Tomasetti's not ready for field work."

"He's a field agent drawing a paycheck every week."

"With all due respect to John, he's a fucking train wreck."

"This isn't a day care. We've offered him a sweet retirement deal and he turned it down. If he's going to continue working here, he's going to have to pull his weight."

"To be perfectly honest, I have some concerns about his emotional stability."

"He's been given a clean bill of health."

Denny wondered if he should point out the drug use issue or, more importantly, John Tomasetti's reputation. The Cuyahoga County grand jury might have given him a free pass, but Denny had been a cop long enough to know how to read between the lines. He'd heard the rumors about what Tomasetti did in Cleveland. Nothing had been proven, but it was the general consensus within the Division of Police that after the murder of his partner and family, Tomasetti had taken the law into his own hands and gone rogue.

"He spent two weeks in a psycho ward," Denny said. "I don't think you want to turn him loose on the public."

Rummel got up and closed the door. "John Tomasetti is dead weight. He's a liability to the agency. A liability to this office. A liability to me. The only reason he's still around is because of the threat of litigation if I fire him."

Denny was starting to connect the dots. He didn't like the picture they made. "Tomasetti can't handle a case right now."

Rummel leaned forward. "I'm speaking to you off the record here, Denny. If any of what I'm about to say leaves this room, I'll have your ass in a bag. Are you clear on that?"

Heat crept up Denny's neck. "I understand."

Rummel gave Ruth Bogart a pointed look. "Ruth?"

Crossing her legs, she glanced down at her notes. "We're well aware of what John went through," she began. "Our hearts go out to him. As you know, we offered him a deal, including full medical benefits. He turned it down. If we terminate him, he'll sue us, and he'll probably win."

Rummel cut in. "We want him gone, Denny. We've tried reasoning with him. We've been more than fair. This is the only way."

Denny almost couldn't believe what he was hearing. Almost. But he'd known Rummel for three years now. He knew the man played dirty to get what he wanted. If you were on Rummel's hit list, you may as well hang it up because you were going down.

"If you play it this way, there's a chance you're going to have collateral damage." Denny looked from Rummel to Ruth Bogart. "Tomasetti isn't going to be much help to this town. If there's a serial murderer operating there, I don't have to tell you more people could die."

Bogart spoke up. "Best-case scenario, the RFA alone will compel him to reconsider the retirement deal. On the outside chance he accepts the assignment, he won't last. We'll get complaints from local law enforcement. That will give us grounds to terminate him with no repercussions."

"Everyone wins," Rummel added.

Everyone but John Tomasetti and the citizens of Painters Mill, Denny thought.

"I want you to get him dispatched ASAP," Rummel said. "I want everything done by the book. You understand?"

Denny couldn't imagine assigning John Tomasetti a major case. The man was teetering on a precipitous edge. One shove and he'd tumble into an abyss he might not be able to climb out of. "If we assign Tomasetti this case, it'll push him right over the edge."

Bogart looked down at her notes.

Stone-faced, Rummel held his gaze. "We're counting on it."

Full darkness has fallen by the time I leave the police station. The night sky is so clear I can see the Big Dipper. The weatherman promised temperatures would plummet to below zero by morning. Not a good night to be prowling an old grain elevator looking for a corpse.

I finished the press release and handed it off to Lois on my way out. She was gracious enough to stay late for some final editing, and agreed to fax it to Steve Ressler before heading home to her husband and children and the kind of normal life I can only imagine.

I need a shower and a few hours of sleep. I should have already questioned Donny Beck. Those things are going to have to wait until Jacob and I search the grain elevator fifteen miles away in Coshocton County. If we find Daniel Lapp's remains, I'll know without a doubt I've got a copycat on my hands. If we do not find any remains, I'll know Lapp survived. The focus of my investigation will shift, and I'll begin working the case from that perspective.

I turn into the gravel lane of Jacob's farm to find the windows dark. Parking in the same spot I did earlier in the day, I start toward the door. I'm midway there when I see Jacob striding toward me, holding a lantern of all things.

"I've got flashlights," I say.

"Quiet," he snaps in Pennsylvania Dutch, then douses the lantern and sets it in the snow.

I wonder if he's sneaking out of the house. "You didn't tell Irene?"

His head jerks toward me, and I realize he's not sure of the meaning behind my question. "She knows nothing about this."

I ruminate on that as we start toward the Explorer. I've always wondered if he told her what happened all those years ago. The way she looks at me sometimes . . .

We climb into the Explorer. Tension fills the cab as I start the engine and head down the driveway. I sense an array of emotions radiating from my brother, the most powerful being resentment. He shouldn't be riding in the car with me, especially since I'm under the *bann*. But I sense that isn't the main source of his discontent. He doesn't want to help and begrudges me asking him for it. I don't understand that. Once upon a time we were close. He was loving and protective and would have done anything for me. All of that changed the day I shot Daniel Lapp.

"I saw Sarah today," he says after a moment.

Sarah is our sister, the middle child. Married with a baby on the way, she lives on a farm a few miles away. "How is she?" I ask.

"Frightened." He gives me a pointed look.

"You told her about Lapp?"

"She heard the talk in town. She is afraid, Katie. She believes Lapp is alive and angry with us for what we did."

I'd wanted to be the one to tell her. I knew the murders would frighten Sarah. But I haven't had time to pay her a visit. "I'll talk to her."

"She is afraid he will harm us. She is afraid for her unborn child." He grimaces. "For you."

I'd known she would worry about me. Sixteen years ago, she watched me come very close to unraveling. "You know I'm fine," I say.

Jacob nods. "She wants you to tell your English police what happened."

I nearly drive into the ditch. "No."

"They do not need to know all of it. Just that Lapp could be alive and killing."

"No, Jacob. We don't tell anyone."

"She is frightened, Katie."

"I'll talk to her."

He looks out the window, then back at me. "I do not believe Daniel is alive. But if he is . . ." Shrugging, he lets the words trail. "Maybe Sarah is right."

"I'll handle this," I snap.

"How can you when you do not know where he is?"

"Hopefully, in a few hours we'll know exactly where he is."

Half an hour later I stop on a desolate stretch of road where railroad tracks bisect the snow-covered asphalt. Fifty yards to my left, the massive grain elevator juts from the earth like some primordial rock formation. I see triple concrete silos. A water tower tilts at a precarious angle. The original wooden structure flanks the rear and is slowly being devoured by the encroachment of the skeletal forest beyond. Front and center, the corrugated steel main building stands three stories tall, impossibly narrow at the top. The lack of proportion gives it the gangly appearance of some ugly waterfowl.

The Wilbur Seed Company elevator and silos were built in 1926, but fell to ruin in the early seventies when the new railroad came through Painters Mill. A few years later a more modern grain elevator was built on the west side of town and the Wilbur Seed Company closed its doors. The old structure is a landmark, an eyesore of historical significance, a favorite place for people to dump trash, and an attractive spot for teenagers to drink beer and make out. It is also the perfect place to hide a body . . .

For a moment, the only sound comes from the hum of the engine and the hiss of the heater. I glance at my brother to find him staring out the passenger window. I should thank him for agreeing to do this, but something inside me won't allow it. After a lot of years of blaming myself, I finally realized I wasn't the only one who did something wrong that day. My parents' refusal to report the crime—my siblings' tacit assent—tainted me for life, drove me in directions I never would have imagined. As far as I'm concerned, Jacob owes me.

Jamming the Explorer into four-wheel drive, I turn in to the entrance, using the telephone poles to guide me toward the rear.

Jacob grips the armrest. "You will get stuck in the snow."

"I know what I'm doing." I muscle the truck through deep drifts. The tires spin and grab alternately. The engine revs as we bounce past the steel building. I cut the wheel and we slide around to the rear where the vehicle will be out of sight from the road. The last thing I need is for some well-meaning cop—one of my own or a deputy from the sheriff's office—driving by and finding us. A logical explanation would be hard to fabricate.

Cutting the engine, I pull on my gloves and get out. The frigid air stings my face, slithers down my collar as I pass beneath the massive overhead door. Inside the behemoth structure, the wind whines like an injured dog. A stained mattress and two fifty-gallon drums riddled with jagged holes from a shotgun lay scattered haphazardly. Half a dozen trash bags have been piled against the far wall of the truck aisle, several torn open by roaming dogs or raccoons.

A few yards away a padlock hangs on the office door. The concrete walkway is cracked as if by some massive earthquake. Winter-brown grass juts from between the crumbling gaps, nature trying to reclaim what had once been hers. The weigh platform has sunk a foot into the ground. At the end of the truck aisle, a second overhead door, knocked off its track by vandals or the wind, hangs at a precarious angle. Beyond, steel piping that had once fed grain from the silos to waiting trucks transects the night sky.

The task before us is overwhelming and macabre. I don't know where to start. I wonder what will be left of the corpse. Bones? Clothing? Will we even be able to find the makeshift grave? Looking down, I stomp the ground, find it frozen solid, and I'm glad I thought to bring the pickax.

Standing next to me, Jacob huddles more deeply into his coat. "I have not been to this place since that night."

I've driven past the elevator a thousand times, but never stopped. Just driving by was enough to give me the creeps. Every time the PD received a call about activity out here, I dispatched someone else.

Hands on his hips, my brother looks around as if trying to get his bearings. "Where do we dig?" I prompt.

"I am not certain."

"What do you mean you're not certain?"

"I stayed outside with the buggy that night. *Datt* dug the grave, not me."

Frustration churns inside me, but I hold my tongue. Leaving him, I walk to the Explorer. I open the rear door and pull out two shovels, bolt cutters and the pickax, and lean the tools against the quarter panel.

Jacob walks the length of the building, studying the ground, his head moving from side to side as if he's lost something.

I leave the tools and cross to him. "We have to find the grave," I say.

He shrugs. "Perhaps we can look for disturbed earth."

I suspect any earth that was disturbed sixteen years ago has long since settled. Staving off a terrible sense of hopelessness, I look around, searching for anything that might offer a clue. "Where did you enter the building that night?"

Jacob motions toward the wrecked overhead door at the far end. "It was in working order back then. I stayed with the buggy. *Datt* dragged the body . . ." He lets the sentence dangle. "It was dark. Raining. The horse was skittish. We were soaked to the skin. Scared. For ourselves." His eyes land on me. "For you. I'd never seen *Datt* so . . . distraught. He was muttering to himself. Praying for God to forgive us."

I've never heard Jacob speak of that night. His words conjure memories I've spent half my life trying to forget. My sister on her knees in the kitchen, mopping blood off the floor. *Mamm* washing the curtains in water tinged pink. Me sitting in a bathtub filled with scalding water, my body scrubbed raw but not clean. A small, hated part of me wishing I was dead, too.

Shoving the past aside, I approach Jacob, reminding myself I'm a grown woman now. A cop with the resolve to see this through no matter how difficult. "Let's spread out."

I don't wait for his response. I've already decided I can only give this grisly excursion a few hours. I need to work on the more pressing aspects of the case. If we can't find the grave tonight, I'll have to come back.

Jacob wanders toward the overhead door at the far end of the aisle. I look around, trying to put myself in my father's head. It was summertime. Storming. Dark. He was upset. Horrified by what had happened to his daughter, perhaps even more horrified by what she had done. He had a body to dispose of. A family to protect. Where would he bury the evidence?

I find myself studying the weigh platform. The wood planks are covered with decades of dirt, oily grime and gravel. The smell of creosote mingles with the breathtaking cold. Setting down the Mag-Lite, I pick up one of the shovels and wedge the blade between the steel frame and the edge of the platform. I put my weight into it and lean. The platform emits a groan, but doesn't budge.

"Katie! Over here."

I look up to see my brother standing near the rear door, looking down at a small mound of earth. "I found something."

Snagging the pickax, I approach and hand it to him. "Dig."

Without looking at me, Jacob sets down his flashlight, raises the pickax above his head and begins to whack away at the frozen ground, grunting with every swing.

I shine the beam of my Mag-Lite on the deepening hole and watch frozen chunks fly.

"Mein gott." Jacob falls to his knees, digging with his gloved hands. "This must be it."

Hope jumps through me. I go to my knees beside him and dig like a dog. My stomach lurches when I see a thatch of dark hair.

He sits back on his heels, his brows knit. "This is very shallow."

"Gotta be it." I continue digging, too caught up in the moment to consider his words. "Ground could have shifted. There sure as hell aren't *two* bodies buried here."

"Katie . . ."

Only then do I realize we've unearthed a dead animal. I see matted fur. The dull white of old bone. The glint of a choke collar tells me it's a dog. Disappointment spreads through me. I stare at the carcass, denial rising. I look at my brother and choke back angry words. "Damn it, Jacob, we've got to find those remains."

"Do not speak to me with your English tongue."

I grapple for patience that has long since worn thin. "Can you stop thinking about Amish versus English? This killer makes no distinction! It could just as easily be an Amish girl next!"

"I am trying."

"Try harder!" In some small corner of my mind I'm aware that I'm not helping the situation by losing my temper, but I can't stop myself. "Damn it, Jacob, you owe me this."

My brother blinks, his eyes owlish in the dim light from my flashlight. "I have no debt to you."

"Oh, come on! A crime was committed that day! *Datt* swept the entire, sordid mess under the rug. That wasn't the way it should have been handled, and you know it."

"*Datt* did what he thought was right."

"Right for whom?"

"The family."

"What about justice for me?" I smack my chest with my open hand. "I had to go the rest of my life unable to speak of it because *Datt* decided everyone in our family should pretend it never happened! What do you think that did to me?"

His eyes blaze. "You were not the only one affected by the sin we committed that night."

"I was the only one who was raped and nearly killed! I was the only one who was forced to take a life!" The rage behind my words shocks me. A voice I don't recognize echoes within the confines of the building, harmonizing weirdly with the howl of the wind.

"All of us have blood on our hands!" Jacob hisses. "We share the same sin."

"It was different for me! You haven't looked at me the same since." I run out of breath. I don't know where this is coming from. Some emotional pressure cooker that's been simmering unacknowledged inside me. I try to stop the words, but they gush like blood from a wound. "You didn't stand by me. You didn't support me when I made the decision to leave the church."

"I still do not condone your decision." He stares at me, his complexion strangely pale against his full beard. "But I will tell you this. If I had held the gun in my hand that day I would have killed for you. I would have gone against God's will and taken a life because it would have been worse to not have you in this world. This is my sin, too, Katie."

Tears threaten, but I fight them back. My own breaths billow before my face as I grapple for control. "Then why do you hate me?"

"I do not hate you."

"You blame me. How can you hold what happened against me?"

My brother says nothing.

"Why?" I shout.

His gaze burns into mine. "I saw you smile at Daniel Lapp."

My blood freezes in my veins. I feel myself go still as my mind tries to comprehend the meaning behind his words. *"What?"*

"We were in the pasture. Daniel and I were digging postholes for the fence. It was hot. You brought us lemonade. He looked at you the way a man looks at a woman. Katie, you smiled at him."

My reaction is physical, like a fist slamming into my gut. Staring into my brother's eyes, knowing what he is thinking—what he has believed about me all these years—and I feel sick. The old shame churns inside me, a cauldron of acid eating away at my very foundation. "How dare you insinuate what happened was my fault."

"I am not laying blame. But I cannot change what I saw."

"For God's sake, Jacob, I was a kid."

My brother's expression closes, and I realize he doesn't want to talk about this. He doesn't want to hear my explanations. That I feel the need to defend myself shames me. I did what I had to do that day to save my life. But ingrained beliefs are difficult to exorcise no matter how valiant the attempt. I've always considered myself an enlightened woman. But I was raised Amish and some of those old values will always be a part of me.

I look around, fighting my way back to the present and the situation at hand. Once again I remind myself that I'm a police officer, that I have a murder to solve. Slowly, the dark emotions slink back into their hidey-hole.

Bowing my head, I rub at the ache between my eyes. "I can't talk about this right now. I need to find Lapp's body."

He stares at me for a long while, saying nothing, then turns and walks away.

My feet throb with cold. My fingers are numb. I'm not sure if the tremors ripping through me are from the temperature or the emotions freezing me from the inside out. The one thing I am certain of is that I've lost my brother. Another shattering truth piled on top of a dozen others. I feel like crying, but I pick up the shovel instead. Propping my flashlight against a broken cinder block, I set the blade to the frozen earth and dig.

CHAPTER 10

John knew better than to go to the bar. He knew if he did he'd end up getting shitfaced. He'd lose track of time and the bartender would end up pushing him out the door when they closed at two A.M. But like all the other nights he'd ended up at the Avalon Bar and Grill, it was better than drinking alone.

The place was a dive. The bartender was a rude asshole. The glasses weren't quite clean. The management watered down the booze. But the burgers were decent. And even drunk out of his mind, John could always find his way home. He'd learned to appreciate the little things in life.

He ordered a double shot of Chivas and a dark beer, then played a game of eight ball. One game led to six. One double led to too many to count. John Tomasetti, drunk again. What was the world coming to?

Standing at the bar, he watched the bartender pour another shot. He downed it in a single gulp. The alcohol scalded his esophagus and landed like a fireball in his belly. He'd never developed a taste for even the top-shelf whiskies, but this wasn't about pleasure. It was about getting through another day without blowing his brains out.

At some point he'd lost track of the man he'd been playing pool with. A couple of college kids had taken over the pool table. Time to kick it up a notch, John thought, and headed toward the men's room. Locking himself in a stall, he fished a Xanax from his pocket, chewed it and swallowed. He savored the bitter chalkiness of the pill, then washed the taste from his mouth with beer.

He knew mixing prescription drugs with alcohol was stupid and pathetic and that some day Fate would make him pay. Sooner or later, she always got her due. But he didn't think that cruel bitch could do anything worse than what she'd already done. In some sick way, it was a comforting thought.

Two years ago, he would have laughed his ass off if someone had predicted this future for him. That his family would be taken from him and he would be left alone to mourn them. That he would kill a man in cold blood and feel nothing more than a fleeting sense of satisfaction. That he would use his law enforcement know-how to frame another man for the crime. That he would have to rely on booze and a cocktail of pills just to make it through the day.

For the thousandth time John wished it had been him instead of his family. He would have given his own life a thousand times over to save them. But that was another quirky thing about Fate; she never bargained, and she never gave second chances.

Back at the bar, he ordered another double and watched some weird game show he didn't understand on the TV above the bar. He drank the beer and tried not to think about anything but the alcohol running like nitro through his veins. The Xanax just starting to kick in . . .

"John."

The familiarity of the voice yanked him from his mental fog. Turning, he was surprised to see Denny McNinch beside him, looking like he'd just come from a funeral.

"Nice suit."

"Nordstrom's," Denny said. "Had 'em on sale."

Around him, the room dipped and curved, but John maintained eye contact, hoping he didn't look as fucked up as he felt. "I'd ask if this is a social call, but judging from the look on your face, it isn't."

"It's not." The bartender set a beer on the bar and Denny took a long drink.

"You here to fire me or what?"

"Worse."

John couldn't help it; he laughed.

Denny reached into the breast pocket of his suit jacket and laid the RFA on the bar. "Rummel wants you on it."

"You're kidding?" John slid the RFA closer and skimmed the particulars.

DESCRIPTION OF CRIME:
Possible serial murder. Local law enforcement overwhelmed.

LOCATION:
Painters Mill, Ohio.

CONTACT:
Janine Fourman, town councilwoman. Norm Johnston. Mayor Auggie Brock.

"Not exactly my area of expertise," John said.

"Like you have an area of expertise these days."

"I'm pretty good at fucking up."

Denny raised his glass. "That doesn't count."

John squinted at the form, unable to believe they were assigning him a case. He wasn't exactly in the running for agent of the year. "Why me?"

"Maybe you drew the short straw."

They both knew Rummel never did anything without a reason. He was a man with an agenda, and that agenda never served anyone but himself.

Denny shrugged. "Maybe he thinks it's time you got off your ass and earned your keep."

"Or maybe that sneaky little fucker wants to watch me unravel."

"So prove him wrong. You were a cop. You've got the mojo."

Even through the lavender haze of inebriation, John noticed the other man's misery, and he thought he knew why. Denny might be just another figurehead in an ocean of figureheads. But he was a straight shooter. Something wasn't right about this, and they both knew it.

"You could retire," Denny offered.

John folded the RFA and tucked it into the inside pocket of his jacket. "I'll take the case."

"You sure?"

John nodded. "Just do one thing for me, will you?"

"You got it."

"Tell Rummel he can kiss my ass."

Laughing, Denny picked up his glass. "I'll drink to that."

CHAPTER 11

Midnight descends with the cold stealth of a nocturnal predator. Freezing and discouraged, I pack our tools into the rear of the Explorer. In five hours time, we dug eight holes at various positions, but found no trace of human remains. I'm left not knowing if the man I shot survived to haunt this town again, or if we were simply unable to find the grave.

Jacob and I don't speak during the drive to his farm. He offers no apology for his inability to find the remains—or his accusation—but I don't expect one. I want to ask him to help me again tomorrow, but I don't. Finding Lapp's body is on my shoulders and mine alone.

The case is almost twenty-four hours old. I've raced against the clock all day, but accomplished little. My back and shoulders ache from the physical exertion of digging. The confrontation with my brother has drained the last traces of optimism from my psyche. Still, the need to hunt down this killer consumes me.

After dropping Jacob, I head for home. Around me, Painters Mill sleeps with the sweet innocence of a child. The shops are closed, their pretty storefronts dark and locked down tight. An expectant hush has fallen over the town. I think of Amanda Horner's death, and I cannot reconcile such utter brutality with this postcard-perfect place I've come to love.

I stop the Explorer in front of my house, but I don't turn in. I should call it a night and get some rest. Tomorrow promises to be even longer than today. But though my body is beyond exhaustion, my mind is wound tight. If Daniel Lapp survived all those years ago, where would he go for help?

In a time of need, an Amish man would turn to family.

Cutting the wheel, I hit the gas and head out of town. I know better than to approach Benjamin Lapp at this hour. Cops have protocol and rules of conduct they are bound to follow, one of them being you don't knock on doors at one o'clock in the morning. But if anyone knows the whereabouts of Daniel Lapp, it's his brother. Because he's Amish, I feel reasonably certain he won't run screaming "police brutality" to the town council in the morning.

East of town I turn onto Miller-Grove Road. The Lapp place is midway to the dead end and down a long and winding lane. Unlike most Amish farms, this one is unkempt. The moon illuminates a barn with a swayback roof. Grass as high as a man's hips pokes out through the snow. I park adjacent to the workshop, remove my Mag-Lite and head toward the front door.

I don't feel as if I'm in danger, but I thumb the snap off my holster. A cop can never be too cautious, even among pacifists. I open the storm door, knock loudly and wait. When that doesn't rouse Lapp, I use the flashlight against the wood. The sound is thunderous in the stark silence.

A few minutes later, a yellow light flickers inside. I step back and aside, my hand resting on my .38. The door swings open. Holding a lantern, Benjamin Lapp squints at me as if I just beamed down from another planet.

"Katie Burkholder?"

Even in the dim light, the likeness of the two brothers gives me pause. A chill chases gooseflesh down my arms. I see light blue eyes. Brown hair shorn into a jagged cut. The same thin mouth and jutting chin. A flash of memory almost sends me back a step, but I will away the slow rise of revulsion.

"I need to ask you some questions, Benjamin."

Because he is unmarried, Benjamin is clean-shaven. He wears trousers with suspenders hanging down and a shirt that's only partially tucked. Wool socks cover his feet.

"Is there a problem? It is very late."

I shove my badge at him. He stares at it as if he's suddenly lost his ability to read. "This won't wait."

He blinks at me. "What is this about?"

"Your brother."

"Daniel?" His eyes widen. "Do you have news of him?"

"Do you?" I push past him.

Stepping back, he watches me as if I'm some dangerous animal that's ventured out of the woods. The house smells of wet dog and cow shit. The darkened kitchen is straight ahead. A shadowy hall beckons to my right. Beyond, stairs lead to the second floor.

"When's the last time you saw Daniel?" I ask.

Another blink, owlish and sleepy. "A very long time."

"How long?"

"I haven't seen him since the summer he disappeared. Over fifteen years, I think."

I stare hard at him. "You sure about that? He hasn't been here or in town?"

"I am certain of it."

"Has he contacted you?"

"No."

"Have you sent him money?"

His brows knit.

"Don't lie to me, Benjamin. I can check."

"Why do you ask these things? Do you have news of Daniel?"

Ignoring his question, I step closer, letting some attitude slip into my voice. "You know better than to lie to the police, don't you?"

"I do not lie."

"Where's your brother?"

"I do not know."

"Tell me about the last time you saw him."

"I told the English police—"

"Tell it again," I snap.

He scratches his temple with two fingers. "He did work for your *datt* that summer. He helped Dwayne Bargerhauser put up a fence for his cattle. He left in the morning and never came back."

"Do you know what happened to him?"

"I do not. *Datt* and I talked to everyone Daniel worked for, but no one saw him after that day. We do not know where he went or why he left."

I stride to the kitchen and shine my light around the room. I see one cup on the counter. One flat-brimmed hat on the wood dowel. One coat on the rack. The place is a mess, but there's no sign more than one person has been here. I walk down the hall, do a quick search of the bathroom and downstairs bedroom, checking the closet and under the bed.

Benjamin follows me to the foot of the stairs as I take them two at a time to the top. "Why are you doing this?" he calls out.

Using my flashlight, I quickly clear the top level of the house. The first bedroom I pass is totally vacant. No clothes in the closet. No suitcases. The second bedroom is almost as sparse, with a single twin bed, a night table and dresser. The closet holds plain clothes for a single man. In the bathroom the single towel is damp. One toothbrush sits on the sink.

I descend the stairs to find Benjamin holding the lantern up and squinting into the semidarkness. "What are you looking for?"

I shine my flashlight in his face. I'm so close I see his pupils contract. "If I find out you're lying, it won't matter that you're Amish. I'll come down on you so hard you'll wish you were in prison."

"I have no reason to lie." He looks offended.

"Then tell me about your brother! Why did he leave? Where did he go?"

My rapid-fire tactics work. For the first time Benjamin's composure falters. "Perhaps Daniel wanted to leave the simple life."

"Why would he do that?"

His gaze drops. "Perhaps he could not abide by *Gelassenheit*."

Gelassenheit is a German word that encompasses the Amish spirit and ideals: yielding to God, putting others before yourself, and leading a content and modest life.

I don't want to believe him; nothing would please me more than for Daniel Lapp to jump out of a closet so I could pump a round into his forehead. But my instincts tell me this man is telling the truth. Another dead end.

I knew coming here was a long shot, but my disappointment is keen. "If Daniel was in trouble, is there somewhere else he would go?" I ask. "Did he have other friends or family he trusted?"

Benjamin shakes his head, his gaze meeting mine. "Why are you asking these questions?"

"I'm following up on some information I received."

He doesn't believe me. I see suspicion in his eyes. There's nothing I can do about it. "If he shows up, Benjamin, you come get me. Day or night. It's important."

He nods.

I start toward the door.

"Is my brother in trouble?" he calls out.

Yanking open the door, I step onto the porch. "We're all in trouble," I whisper, and start toward the Explorer.

The scents of vanilla potpourri and yesterday's garbage greet me when I arrive home. I'm not the world's greatest housekeeper, but my place is clean and comfortable. After enduring the day from hell I'm unduly glad to be home.

Flipping on the living room light, I toe off my boots and leave them by the door. I shed my coat and toss it on the sofa as I head toward my bedroom. In the hall I unbuckle my holster, setting it and my .38 on the console table. In the bedroom, I kick off my uniform trousers and unbutton my shirt, letting both drop to the floor. The bra comes next and I fling it onto the bed as I pass.

Shrugging into my robe, I shove my feet into slippers and head toward the second bedroom, which is my office. My laptop is ancient, the dial-up painfully slow, but it will get me to OHLEG, the Ohio Law Enforcement Gateway system. Created by the Ohio attorney general, OHLEG is an information network that provides local police agencies access to nine law enforcement databases.

While the computer boots, I go to the kitchen. I should eat something, but food isn't what I crave. I find the bottle of Absolut in the cabinet above the refrigerator and set it on the table. I toss ice into a tumbler and pour. I know better than to drink alone when my mood is so dark, but I take that first dangerous sip anyway.

The alcohol burns all the way down, but I drain the glass and pour again. The things I saw today hover in the forefront of my mind. Amanda Horner's savaged body. The agony in her mother's eyes. Jacob and I digging for the remains of a man I spent half of my life believing I'd killed. I know alcohol won't solve my problems, but if I'm lucky, it will get me through the night.

Back in my office, I log in to OHLEG. I'm not familiar with the system, but I stumble around until I find what I'm looking for. The search engine is capable of querying numerous data sources from a single interface. I type in the name: Lapp, Daniel, enter the county and hit Return. I know it's a long shot, but if he's been arrested, convicted, fingerprinted or added to a sexual predator list anywhere in the state, I'll get a hit by morning.

I'm in the kitchen topping off my glass when a scratch at the window startles me. Spinning, I reach for my sidearm only to realize I left it on the console table. A laugh escapes me when I see the orange tabby on the brick sill. I'm no fan of cats, particularly scraggly-looking strays. But this particular cat has skillfully appropriated my compassion. He's pushy, vocal and has no idea he's the ugliest thing to hit Painters Mill since Norm Johnston's mug shot. The cat has been coming around since Christmas. Because he was so damn skinny, I began putting out the occasional bowl of milk. That, of course, led to the occasional bowl of cat food. Tonight, with the temperature hovering around zero, I'm no doubt obligated to bring him inside.

I pad to the back door and open it. The tabby darts in with a burst of cold and looks at me as if to ask "what took you so long?"

"Don't get used to it," I mutter.

The cat purrs at the sound of my voice, and I wonder how he can still trust human beings when he's evidently spent the brunt of his life being neglected and abused by them.

Bending, I pick him up. The animal makes a halfhearted attempt to bite me. I manage to avoid his teeth. Slowly, his body relaxes. He's little more than skin and bone wrapped in a ratty coat. Making eye contact with me, he meows loudly.

"You're going to have to settle for milk, pal."

His ears are jagged from old fight wounds. A scar bisects his mottled nose. The whiskers are missing on one side of his face. A survivor who keeps going despite life's tribulations. There's a lesson in there somewhere.

I pour milk into a bowl and refill my tumbler with Absolut. Setting the cat on the floor, I raise my glass. "Here's to getting through the night."

CHAPTER 12

Birds chatter like children outside the kitchen window. I'm lost in the chore of baking bread. Above the sink, yellow curtains billow in the breeze. Beyond, the leaves of the maple tree tremble and hiss, revealing their underside, and I know it will storm later. The smells of fresh-cut hay, kerosene from the stove, and warm yeast fill the air. I want to go outside, but as always there's work to be done.

I push my hands into warm dough. Bored with bread making, I wish for a radio, but Datt *has expressly forbidden it. Instead, I hum a tune I heard in the Carriage Shop in town. A song about New York, and I wonder what the world is like beyond the cornfields and pastures of Painters Mill. They are dreams I shouldn't have, but they are mine and they are secret.*

I sense someone behind me. When I turn, I see Daniel Lapp at the door. He wears dark trousers with suspenders and a gray work shirt. A flat-brimmed straw hat covers his head. He looks at me the way a man looks at a woman. I know I shouldn't, but I smile.

"God will not forgive you," he says.

That's when I notice the burgeoning red stain on his shirt. Blood, I realize. I want to run, but my feet are frozen. When I look down, I'm standing in a lake of blood. I see flecks of red on the curtains. Handprints on the counter. Smears on my dress.

Outside the window, a crow caws and takes flight. I feel Daniel's breath against my ear. I hear vile words I do not understand.

"Murderer," he whispers. "Murderer."

I wake in a cold sweat. For an instant, I'm fourteen years old, helpless, terrified and ashamed. Throwing off the covers, I sit up and put my feet on the floor. My breaths echo in the silence of my bedroom. Nausea climbs up my throat, but I swallow it and slowly the dream recedes.

Sitting on the side of the bed, I put my face in my hands. I hate the nightmare. I hate even more that it still wields the power to reduce me to a frightened adolescent. I breathe deeply and remind myself who I am. A grown woman. A police officer.

As the sweat cools on my body and I rise to dress, I swear to the God I have forsaken—the God who has forsaken me—I will never be helpless or ashamed again.

Farmers begin their day early in Painters Mill. At seven o'clock sharp I stand outside the double glass doors of Quality Implement and Farm Supply and think about the conversation I'm about to have with Donny Beck. The sign on the door tells me the store opens for business at seven A.M. Monday through Saturday. Someone is running late this morning. Peering through the glass, I tap with my keys.

A short woman wearing a red smock and a nametag that reads "Dora" smiles at me through the glass. The keys in her hand jingle as she twists the lock. "Morning," she says. "You're the first customer of the day."

I flash my badge. "I need to talk to Donny Beck. Is he here?"

Her smile falters. "He's in the break room getting coffee."

"Where?"

"It's at the back of the store." She points. "Want me to take you?"

"I'll find it." I start toward the rear of the store. I shop here every so often. It's a nice place to pick up yard stuff like flowers, pots, hand tools. The police department buys tires for city vehicles here. But Quality Implement mostly sells farm supplies. Plowshares. Tractor tires. Fencing. Augers.

The rubber smell of new tires fills my nostrils as I approach the back of the store. I make a left, walking between massive, floor-to-ceiling shelves stacked with tires of every shape and size. Ahead, I hear laughter. A door stands open at the end of the aisle. I purposefully arrived at the start of the business day to catch Beck off guard. I want him unprepared so I can gauge his unrehearsed reactions when I ask him about Amanda Horner.

I find Donny in the break room wolfing down a breakfast sandwich from the diner. A petite blonde wearing a Quality Implement smock sits across from him, slurping Coke through a straw. Both young people look up when I enter. The sandwich stops midway to Beck's mouth. He knows why I'm here.

I give the girl a pointed look. "Can you excuse us?"

" 'Kay." She grabs her Coke and leaves the room.

Closing the door behind her, I face Donny Beck.

He swallows hard. "I guess you want to talk to me about Amanda."

I nod. "I'm Kate Burkholder, Chief of Police."

"I know who you are. You gave my dad a speeding ticket once." Rising, he leans over the table and extends his hand. "I'm Donny Beck. You already know that, though."

I shake his hand. His grip is firm, but his palm is slick with sweat. He seems like a decent young man. A farm boy. Probably uses the money he earns here to fix up his muscle car and raise hell on Saturday night. "When's the last time you saw Amanda?" I begin.

"The night we broke up. About six weeks ago."

"How long had you two been seeing each other?"

"Seven months."

"Was it serious?"

"I thought so."

"Who broke up with whom?"

"She broke up with me."

"Why'd she do that?"

"She was going back to college. She didn't want to be tied down." He grimaces. "She said she didn't love me."

"You get pissed off when she dumped you?"

"No. I mean, I was upset, but I didn't get mad."

"Really? Why not?"

He chokes out a sound of denial. "I'm not like that."

"Did you love her?"

Emotion flashes in his eyes, and he looks down at his half-eaten breakfast sandwich. "Yeah, I guess I did."

"Were you sleeping with her?"

To my surprise, his face reddens. He gives me a nod.

"She sleep around with anyone else?"

"I don't think so."

"Did you two fight?"

"No." As if catching himself, his gaze snaps to mine. "I mean we did. Sometimes. But not often. She was pretty easygoing." He shrugs. "I was crazy about her."

"Did she have any enemies?"

He shakes his head. "Everyone liked Amanda. She was sweet. Fun to be with."

"Where were you Saturday night?"

"I went to Columbus with my dad and little brother."

"What were you doing in Columbus?"

"We went to a basketball game. Special Olympics. My brother's handicapped."

"You spend the night?"

"Yeah."

"Where did you stay?"

"Holiday Inn off of Interstate 23."

"You know I'm going to check." I jot everything down.

"It's okay. We were there."

"When Amanda told you she didn't want to be tied down, did you get jealous?"

"No. I mean, a little. Like, when I imagined her going out with other guys. But not like that."

"What do you mean?"

"I'd never hurt Amanda. Jesus Christ, not like that." A quiver runs through the last word.

"Like what?"

"I heard . . . what he did to her."

"Who'd you hear it from?"

"Waitress at the diner said he . . . you know." Sweat beads on his forehead and upper lip. Wrapping the sandwich in a napkin, he tosses it into the trash. "Makes me sick."

"I need you to think hard about this, Donny. Is it possible Amanda was seeing someone else?"

He shakes his head. "I don't think so. She wasn't guy crazy or anything. Amanda had a level head."

"So you think she was being straight with you?"

"She said she wanted to stay friends." He lifts a shoulder, lets it drop. "I figured that was a lot better than never seeing her again." His eyes mist. "Doesn't matter now. I'm never going to see her again, anyway, am I?"

I shove my notepad into my coat pocket. "Don't leave town, okay?"

His gaze meets mine. In his eyes I see the kind of pain a twenty-two-year-old farm kid probably can't fake, and I feel an uncharacteristic need to reassure him.

"You guys think I did it?" he asks.

"I just want you to be available in case I have more questions."

Leaning back in the chair, he swipes at his eyes with the back of his hand. "I don't have any plans to go anywhere, anyway."

I offer my card. "If you think of anything else, call me."

He looks at the card. "I hope you guys catch the lowlife who did that to her. Amanda didn't deserve to die."

"No, she didn't." As I make my exit, I mentally cross Donny Beck off my list of suspects.

It's not yet eight A.M. when I arrive at the station. Glock's cruiser is parked in its usual spot. Next to it, Mona's Ford Escort is covered with a thin coating of snow. I wonder what new catastrophe waits for me inside.

Mona looks up from her phone when I enter. "Hey, Chief. You've got messages."

"Now there's a surprise." I take a dozen slips from her.

Her hair is piled on top of her head with little ringlets spiraling down. Her lipstick is almost as black as her nail polish. Maroon eyeliner makes her look like she's got a bad case of pinkeye. "Norm Johnston is getting pissed about having to leave messages, Chief. He's like, you know, taking it out on me."

"Did he say what he wants?"

"Your head on a platter, probably."

I give her a look.

"Just a wild guess."

I laugh. "Where's Glock?"

She glances down at the switchboard where a single red light stands out. "On the phone."

"When he gets off, tell him to call me." I walk to the coffee station and fill the biggest mug I can find. In my office I turn on my computer, then drape my coat over the back of my chair. I'm anxious to see if OHLEG came back with a hit on Daniel Lapp.

My hopes are dashed when I log in. If he's alive, he's being careful. Probably using an alias. Maybe even a stolen identity or false social security number. Under normal circumstances, I'd start flashing his photo around town. But I can't risk raising questions. People will want to know why I'm asking about a man who hasn't been seen for sixteen years. They'll put two and two together, and Daniel Lapp will rise out of obscurity like some Amish version of Jack the Ripper.

I dial Norm Johnston's number. Miller's pond would do the job. It's a good size body of water with a muddy bottom.

Johnston answers on the first ring. "I've been trying to reach you for almost two days, Chief Burkholder."

"I'm tied up with this murder, Norm. What can I do for you?"

"The town council and mayor want to meet with you. Today."

"Norm, look, I need to work—"

"With all due respect, Kate, you are obligated to keep us informed. We want an update on how the investigation is progressing."

"We're working on a couple of leads."

"Do you have a suspect?"

"I put out a press release—"

"That doesn't say squat."

I sigh. "To be perfectly honest, I don't know much."

"Then a meeting won't take long. I'll have everyone in the city room at noon. We'll have you out of there in twenty minutes."

He hangs up without waiting for a response and without thanking me. He's still pissed about that DUI. Self-serving bastard.

"Chief?" I'm so immersed in my thoughts I didn't hear Mona approach. "There's someone here to see you."

Something in her eyes puts me on alert. *Now what?* I think. A moment later my sister appears in my doorway. I've been the chief of police for over two years. In all that time, neither Sarah nor my brother have visited me here. For a moment I almost can't believe what I'm seeing. Then I remember my conversation with Jacob the night before.

"Hello, Katie." Sarah wears a navy dress with a black apron and a heavy winter cape. Her blonde hair is parted severely at the center and drawn into a bun at her nape, all of which is covered by the traditional Amish *kapp*. She's two years older than me, pretty and expecting her first child in just over a month.

Rising, I round my desk, pull out the visitor chair for her and close the door. "Have a seat." After an awkward moment, I ask, "How are you feeling?"

It's an uncomfortable question. This isn't the first time Sarah has been pregnant. There have been three times that I know of. Each time she's miscarried late in the second trimester.

She smiles. "I think it is God's will that I have this baby."

I return her smile. She'll be a good mother; I hope she gets the chance. "Did you drive the buggy into town all by yourself?"

She nods, her gaze flicking away briefly, and I know she's here against her husband's wishes. "William is at the horse auction in Keene."

"I see." Waiting, I watch her struggle with some internal conflict I can't quite identify.

"I talked to Jacob," she says after a moment. "He told me you went to the grain elevator. That Daniel Lapp may be alive."

"It's only a theory." I can't keep my eyes from sliding to the door to make sure we're not overheard.

She continues as if she didn't hear me. "All these years we believed he was with God."

God. The word burns away the last of my patience. I want to tell her the son of a bitch who raped me is burning in hell where he belongs. "Even if he's dead, I doubt he's with God."

"Katie." Her eyes meet mine. "Someone was in the barn. Three days ago."

The hairs at my nape prickle. "Who?"

"I do not know."

"Tell me what happened."

"I was milking and heard the hay chute door slam. When I looked, no one was there. But I saw footprints in the snow."

"Were the tracks made by a man?"

"I think so. The shoes were large."

"Why didn't you tell me this sooner?"

"At the time I did not think it important. But now . . ." She averts her gaze, then looks back at me with nervous eyes. "Do you think it could be Daniel? Is he back and killing?"

To consider the possibility that Lapp is not only alive but a possible threat to my family adds an edgy new dimension to the situation. "I don't know."

"What if he is angry with us for what we did and seeking revenge?" She lowers her voice. "Katie, I do not wish to burden you with my fears, but I believe the time has come for you to tell your English police about Lapp."

I flinch. "No."

"You do not have to tell them . . . all of it."

"No." The word comes out more harshly than I intend, but I don't take it back. "Don't ask me to do that."

Sarah's gaze remains steadfast on mine. "What if Daniel returns? What if he tries to hurt me or William?" She sets her hand on her swollen abdomen. "I have this child to think of now."

Dread curdles like sour milk in my gut. I try to think of some way to reassure her. But I have no words. Leaning forward, I take her hand and lower my voice. "Sarah, listen to me. Jacob believes Daniel died that day. I think so, too."

"Then why were you looking for his body?"

My brain scrambles for answers that aren't there. "All I can tell you is that I'm good at what I do. Please. Trust me. Let me handle this my way."

My phone rings again. I look down to find three lines blinking in discord, but my attention stays focused on my sister. "You know I'll do everything I can to keep you safe."

"How can you keep us safe when you don't even know where he is?"

I hate it that I don't have the answers she needs. A knock on the door draws my attention. "Sarah, I'm sorry." I release her hand. "I have to get to work. We'll talk more about this later."

"I do not think this will wait."

"Please, just give me some time."

The door opens. Mona steps in. "Sorry, Chief, I just wanted to let you know the sheriff called." She passes pink slips to me.

"Would you ask T.J. to escort Sarah home?" I ask Mona.

Sarah tosses me a sheepish look. "That is not necessary."

"I'd feel better if he did. The roads are slick in spots."

Mona offers Sarah a grin. "Come on, Sister Sarah. Let's find T.J."

Watching my sister walk away, I try not to be troubled, but I am. Who was in her barn and why? Is she right about Lapp? Has he targeted my family? Are they in danger? The questions taunt me with terrible possibilities.

. . . *the time has come for you to tell your English police about Lapp.*

Sarah's words echo inside my head like a hammer strike against steel. I tell myself she doesn't understand the implications of a confession on my part. That it would irrevocably harm my career. My reputation. My credibility. This case. Maybe even land me in jail. That's not to mention the damage that would be done to my family. If Lapp is dead, it would all be for nothing.

There's no way dredging up the past will help.

No way at all.

Ten minutes later I find Glock in his office, the phone stuck to his ear. He looks at me when I peek in and raises his finger, telling me to hold on. After a moment, he hangs up and shakes his head. "That was the BCI lab in London."

"Any luck with the tread or footwear imprints?"

"They got a partial tread that doesn't match any of the first responders."

My heart rolls into a staccato. "Can they match it with a manufacturer?"

"Their tire guy is working on it." He shrugs. "Fifty-fifty chance of IDing the tread."

The news isn't great, but I'll take anything positive at this point. "I'm

going to talk to Scott Brower." Brower was at the Brass Rail the night Amanda
Horner disappeared. He's of particular interest because he's got an arrest record,
one of which involved a knife. "Wanna come?"

"Wouldn't miss it. You buying breakfast?"

"As long as it's fast."

Ten minutes later we're in my Explorer heading toward Mr. Lube, where
Brower works as a mechanic. Next to me, Glock finishes his breakfast burrito
and stuffs the napkin into the bag.

"Any luck with Donny Beck?" he asks.

Shaking my head, I tell him about my conversation with the kid. "I don't
think he did it."

"He got an alibi?"

"I still need to verify, but I think it'll pan out."

"Maybe we'll have better luck with Brower."

Mr. Lube operates out of a ramshackle garage located in the industrial district near the railroad tracks. The parking lot is part asphalt, part gravel and
covered with dirty snow, most of which hasn't been cleared. A blue Nova, circa
1969, sits on concrete blocks. Next to it, a man in brown coveralls has his head
stuck beneath the hood of a truck.

I park near the overhead door and we exit the vehicle. Glock huddles more
deeply into his uniform jacket. "I hate snow," he mutters.

A buzzer sounds when we open the door. Behind the counter, a heavyset man
with a bad case of rosacea looks up from a box of doughnuts. "Hep ya?"

"I'm looking for Scott Brower." I show him my badge and try not to notice
the goop in the corner of his mouth.

"What'd he do now?"

"I just want to talk to him. Where is he?"

"Garage out back."

Glock and I turn simultaneously.

"If he did somethin' I wanna know about it!" the man yells.

I close the door behind us without responding. We follow trampled snow
to the rear. The steel building looks as if it survived a tornado—barely. A
piece of sheet metal has torn loose and flaps noisily in the wind. I hear the

drone of a power tool inside. Hoping Brower is alone, I shove open the door and step inside.

An electric heater blows hot air that stinks of motor oil and diesel fuel. Light filters down from an overhead shop light. Steel shelves line three walls. Pinned above the workbench, a 1999 calendar depicts two nude women engaging in oral sex. Every square inch of space is taken up with either tools or junk. Standing at the table saw in the center of the room, Brower muscles a blade through steel. Sparks fly and scatter.

I wait until he finishes the cut before speaking. "Scott Brower?"

He looks up. To my surprise he's a nice-looking man. He has a baby face. Puppy-dog eyes. A child's nose. A bow mouth that's surprisingly feminine. He's thirty-two years old but looks younger. His eyes flick from me to Glock and back to me. "Who's askin'?"

"The cops." I show my badge. "I need to ask you some questions."

"About what?"

"Were you at the Brass Rail Saturday night?"

"So were a couple hundred other people. Last time I checked that wasn't a crime."

I grind my molars, but keep my voice level. "Did you talk to a woman by the name of Amanda Horner?"

"I talked to a lot of chicks. Don't recall no Amanda."

"Let me refresh your memory." Never taking my eyes from his, I pull out a photo of a dead Amanda Horner lying on a gurney. "Now do you remember?"

He doesn't flinch at the sight of the dead woman. "So that's what this is about. The chick who got herself killed."

"What did you two talk about?"

"I don't recall."

"You think a trip to the police department would help your memory?"

His gaze darts to the door. "Hey, man—"

"I'm not a man," I snap. "I'm a police officer, so stop being a dipshit and answer my questions."

"Okay." He raises his hands. "Look, I hit on her. We flirted. I swear, that's all."

I'm aware of Glock moving around the garage, looking in the trash barrel, opening a toolbox. I'm thankful I have him here to back me up. I don't like Scott Brower. I don't trust him. And I'll bet behind that baby-face façade he's a nasty son of a bitch.

"You got a temper, Scotty?"

His gaze goes wary. "Sometimes. If someone fucks with me."

"Did Amanda fuck with you?"

"No."

"Did your boss at Agri-Flo fuck with you?"

His face darkens. "I don't know what you're talking about."

"You threatened to cut her throat. Ring a bell?"

"I didn't do that, man."

"I told you not to call me that."

His grimace is more like a snarl. The baby face is breaking down, giving way to the real deal. He's getting agitated. That's exactly where I want him. "What do you want with me?" he asks.

"What time did you leave the Brass Rail Saturday night?"

"I don't know. Midnight. Maybe one A.M."

"Do you own a knife?"

He looks around, a fox about to be mauled by hounds. "I think so."

"What do you mean you think so? You don't know? You don't remember? How can you not be sure if you own a knife?"

Glock passes close behind him. "You might try some of that gingko shit, buddy. I hear it's good for the memory."

Brower sneers. "Look, I just . . . ain't seen it in a while."

"Did you lose it? Maybe you disposed of it."

"Look, it's probably layin' around my house somewhere."

I glance Glock's way. "Sounds like we might need a warrant."

"I think so," he responds.

Brower looks from me to Glock and back to me. "Why are you guys fuckin' with me like this?"

"Because I can. Because you smell bad. Because I think you're a lying piece of shit. All of the above."

He stares at me, his face turning a deep shade of red. "You can't talk to me like that."

I glance over my shoulder at Glock. "Did you hear me say anything inappropriate?"

"Maybe he's sensitive, Chief."

"Fuck you," Brower spits in Glock's direction. "Goddamn nigger cop."

Glock laughs outright.

My temper ignites. There's nothing I hate more than a bigot. Even if this man is innocent of murdering Amanda Horner, he's a rude pig. I'm going to ruin his day. His week. His entire month if I can manage. "You got any weapons on you, Scotty?"

"No." He shoves his hands into his pockets.

"Keep your hands where I can see them."

He doesn't obey. Instead, he takes a step back, putting space between us. I set my hand on the expandable baton at my belt. I'd like to taze him, but they weren't part of the Painters Mill budget. "I'm not going to ask you again."

My heart begins to race when I realize he's not going to comply. Adrenaline burns my midsection and spreads like an arterial injection to my limbs with enough force to make me shake. I step toward him, and he bolts.

Glock and I tear out after him simultaneously, two sprinters out of their blocks and running. Brower is agile and fast. He jets through the back door, upends a shelf to block our way, and heads toward the alley.

I hurdle debris and blast through the door after him. In my peripheral vision I see Glock trip and go down. My vision tunnels on Brower. Blue coveralls. Arms pumping. Occasional look over his shoulder. The ground is slick with snow. My boots slide, but I recover quickly and keep running. I hear a shout behind me, but I'm too focused to make out the words.

To my surprise, I'm gaining on him. I visualize taking him down, kneeing him in the small of his back, sliding the cuffs onto his wrists. But I've been in enough foot chases to know nothing ever goes by the book.

Fifty feet in, the alley tees. Brower veers left. I crash through trash cans and gain ten feet on him. "Stop!" I shout.

He keeps running.

Four more strides and I'll be close enough to take him down. My heart thunders. Adrenaline is a jet engine in my ears. His left foot slides, slowing him. I dive, wrap my arms around his hips, throw my shoulder into him.

An indistinguishable sound bursts from his mouth. He twists in midair. His hands slam down on my shoulders hard enough to bruise. His fingers squeeze like vise grips. "Get the fuck off me, you Amish bitch!"

We hit the ground hard and slide. The impact knocks the breath from my lungs. Snow sprays into my eyes, in my mouth. Blind, operating on instinct, I get my knees beneath me. Sliding the baton from its holster, I snap it out. But I'm not fast enough. The blow comes out of nowhere. His fist is like a sledge-hammer making nice with the bridge of my nose. The force rattles my brain all the way to my sinuses. My head snaps back, and I lose my grip on Brower.

Air whistles as I bring the baton down on his thigh. He snarls like a beast. "Bitch cop!" He draws back to hit me again. I try to get the baton in position, brace for the blow.

Glock moves in from the side, a Mack truck mowing down a VW. I scramble back. Snow flies. A single unmanly scream rents the air. Glock muscles Brower onto his stomach with the skill of a heavyweight wrestler. Climbing on top of him, Glock grinds his knee into the other man's back and grapples for his wrists.

"Stop resisting!" Glock shouts.

Blinking back residual tears from the blow, I grab my cuffs and scramble toward the men. I snap the cuffs onto Brower's wrists, cranking them down tight.

I see blood on the back of his coveralls, realize belatedly it's coming from me. I wipe my nose with my sleeve and am dismayed to find it leaking like a sieve.

"You okay, Chief?"

I look down. Blood spatters the snow. I use my sleeve again, but I'm only making a mess. "I'll let you know as soon as I find my eyeballs."

"I've got him if you want to take care of that nosebleed."

Because my eyes are watering and I don't want him getting the wrong idea, I trudge toward the garage. Behind me, I hear Glock order Brower to his feet.

Blood drips into my mouth, and I spit before entering the garage. Inside, I glance around for something with which to stanch the flow. Blue workshop paper towels stick out of a dispenser mounted above the workbench. I yank out a handful and pinch my nostrils together.

"Jeez, Chief, you look like you just had a close encounter with Mike Tyson."

I look up to see T.J. standing in the doorway. "Yeah, well, you should see the other guy," I mutter. "What are you doing here?"

"Glock put out a call for assistance on the radio." Pulling a handkerchief from his pocket, T.J. approaches and hands it to me. "Here you go."

"Gonna ruin it."

"I got more. My mom buys them for me every Christmas."

Tossing the soaked towels into a trash can, I put the handkerchief to my nose. "Thanks."

Glock and Brower enter through the back door. An abrasion the size of a pear mars Brower's forehead. His hair is wet with melting snow. He looks like a pit bull that just had its ass kicked by a roving band of Chihuahuas.

Glock muscles him inside. "Didn't anyone teach you not to hit girls?"

The man with the rosacea stands at the door, craning his neck to get a better look. "Damn, that dumb sumbitch hit a cop?"

Gathering my composure, I cross to the two men and look Brower in the eye. "You want to tell us why you ran?"

"I ain't telling you shit."

"Either way you're going to jail." I look at T.J. "Pat him down and transport him, will you?"

"My pleasure." T.J. is usually pretty laid back, but he looks pissed as he approaches Brower.

Quickly, T.J. frisks him, then checks his pockets. His hand emerges with a Baggie. "Looks like meth." T.J. holds up the bag.

I look Brower in the eye. "If you'd just answered our questions instead of acting like an idiot, we probably never would have found this stuff."

"I wanna call my lawyer," he says.

"It's going to take more than a lawyer to get you out of this one." I look down at the handkerchief, relieved that the bleeding has stopped. I glance at Glock. "Read him his rights. Book him in. Possession. Intent to sell. Assaulting a police officer. Evading arrest. I'll call you if I think of anything else."

"Bitch," Brower hisses.

Glock smacks the back of his head. "Shut up, loser."

I smile. "Oh, and let him make his call."

"Probably wants to call his mommy," Glock mutters.

T.J. approaches me, his eyes taking in the blood on the front of my jacket. I'm not sure why, but the concern on his face embarrasses me. "I'm fine," I snap.

"It's just that your . . . um . . ." His face reddens.

I look down to see my shirt gaping. My bra is showing. The red, lacy job I ordered on a whim. Quickly, I rebutton my uniform shirt and zip my coat up to my chin. "Thanks."

T.J. looks at the Baggie. "I'll swing by the station, log this in and send it to BCI."

"Any luck on the condoms?"

"Got a name on the guy who paid with cash." Settling back into cop mode, he pulls a spiral notebook from his coat pocket. "Patrick Ewell. Lives out on Parkersburg Road."

"That's not far from where Amanda Horner's body was found."

"I was thinking the same thing."

My heart rate picks up, adrenaline of a different nature. "Get back to the station. See if he has a sheet. See if you can find a connection between Ewell and Amanda Horner. See if he was at the Brass Rail Saturday night." That's a lot for T.J., but I have more pressing things to take care of and time is of the essence.

"You got it, Chief." He starts toward the door.

That's when I spot Pickles standing by the window, smoking a cigarette, taking in the scene with the blasé expression of a seasoned cop who's seen it all. I wonder how more than half of my small department arrived on the scene so quickly.

I start toward him. He makes eye contact with me and waits. He is a short man—not much taller than five feet—with grizzled hair and a day's growth of whiskers. His eyes are the color of a robin's egg and bracketed with lines as deep as a man's finger. Wearing an old-fashioned trench and pointy-toed cowboy boots, he looks like a cross between *Columbo* and Gus of *Lonesome Dove* fame.

I extend my hand and we shake. "Welcome back, Pickles."

He sucks hard on the cigarette and flicks it onto the floor, but not before I see the flash of emotion in his eyes. "Retirement's for goddamn old people."

"You up to speed on the murder?"

He nods solemnly. "Hell of a thing to happen to a young girl. Just like before. Hard to believe."

"You do much work on the case back in the nineties?"

"Some. Seen one of the crime scenes. Gruesome shit, I'll tell ya. I never puked so hard in my life."

"What was the general consensus?" Pickles is smart enough to know I'm looking for information that wasn't necessarily written in any report. Unfounded hunches or suspicions. You never know where something like that might lead.

"McCoy always thought the guy worked at the slaughterhouse. You know, right under our noses. Those girls were butchered like a side of beef."

Pain creeps up my nose, but I resist the urge to touch it. "Call J.R. Purdue over at Honey Cut Meat and get a list of employees. People who work in the slaughterhouse as well as the office. I want you to sit down with Glock and cross-reference with the people who were at the Brass Rail on Saturday night."

For the first time Pickles looks excited. Like an old dog that had been replaced by a new puppy finally getting to play with his ball again. Opening his coat, he hikes his trousers, exposing his sidearm. "I'll get right on it."

I touch his shoulder. "Thanks, Pickles."

"Where you gonna be, Chief?"

"City hall. Probably getting my ass raked over the coals."

Pickles gives me a grumpy old man frown. "Give 'em hell."

As I head toward the Explorer, I suspect I'm going to be on the receiving end of any bureaucratic brimstone and fire.

CHAPTER 13

Ronnie Stedt woke with one thing on his mind: losing his virginity. Today was the day. After seventeen years he would finally know the secret of the universe. His girlfriend, Jess, wasn't a virgin. She'd confessed to having done it with Mike Sassenhagen last year when she was a sophomore. She claimed they'd only done it once, but Robbie didn't believe her. Word around Painters Mill High was that Jess and Sassenhagen had been fucking like a couple of rabbits on speed.

Ronnie didn't care. He didn't care that his mom didn't like her or that his dad thought she was a loose woman. He didn't care about Jess's reputation. He didn't even care that he would miss a chemistry test today. He was in love with her, and being with her was all that mattered.

Instead of catching the bus to school, Ronnie had arranged to borrow his brother's truck so he could pick up Jess at her house. From there they would drive out to the old Huffman place on Thigpen Road. They were going to make love, then go to the mall in Millersburg to hang out and catch the matinee.

Ronnie rushed through his morning chores. Feeding the horses and cows and slopping the hogs. He showered, being generous with his father's Polo aftershave, and put on his best shirt and jeans. He picked up Jess at eight-fifteen. She was wearing the jeans he liked. The ones that rode low on her hips. He knew if he raised her sweater the gold hoop in her belly button would wink at him.

She climbed into the truck, the familiar smells of Obsession and cigarettes tantalizing him. "Hey."

"God, you smell good," he said.

She grinned. "Have any problems getting away?"

"Piece of cake." Leaning close, he kissed her, using his tongue. "What about you?"

"Nope." She extricated her mouth from his. "You bring beer?"

"A joint, too." He dug the pot from his pocket, checked the rearview mirror and pulled away from the curb.

"This is going to be great," she said, and produced a lighter.

They were midway through the joint when he turned the pickup into the driveway of the Huffman farm. The house had been vacant since the old man died a year ago. There was no electricity. No running water. No one around for miles. The perfect place for a Tuesday morning tryst.

Parking at the back of the house, Ronnie gathered the blanket and heater and climbed out. Jess grabbed the beer and radio, and slid from the seat. "You sure no one will bother us?"

"Are you kidding?" He took her hand. "Look at this place."

They took the concrete steps to the back door and let themselves inside. The kitchen offered dingy white walls, chipped tile counters and a peeling linoleum floor. A rusty hot water heater squatted in the corner.

"No wonder nobody comes here," Jess said. "This place is spooky." Flipping on the radio, she popped the tab on a beer and walked into the living room. Tall windows dressed in dirty lace looked out over a bleak and snowy landscape. "What's that *smell*?" she asked, wrinkling her nose.

Ronnie came up behind her and wrapped his arms around her. "Not me, babe. I showered." He nibbled her earlobe. "C'mere."

Turning, Jess raised her mouth to his. Ronnie kissed her deeply. Fever rose in his body. Working his hand beneath her coat, he squeezed her breast. All he could think was that there were too many layers of clothing separating them.

"Let's go to the bedroom," he whispered.

They crossed the living room to the hall. Ronnie wondered if he should

Linda Castillo
tell her he loved her before or afterward. He wondered if she'd think he was an idiot, or if she'd say the same words . . .
Four doors with old-fashioned knobs lined the narrow hall. The stench was worse here. "Smells like a dead rat," Ronnie said.
"Or a dead skunk." Jess chugged her beer.
He was keenly aware of her hand in his. The marijuana buzz mellow in his head. His erection pressing against his fly. Squeezing her hand, he shoved open the door.
Jess's scream rattled his brain. She scrambled back. "Ohmigod!" Her beer clattered to the floor, spewing foam. Turning, she clawed past him like a cat fighting its way out of a bag.
Ronnie looked in. Something vaguely human hung suspended from the ceiling. He saw greenish-brown skin. A horribly bloated abdomen. Blonde hair hanging down. An ocean of black blood. In the back of his mind he remembered his dad talking about a murder. Ronnie hadn't paid attention. Now, he wished he had.
"Oh God!" Jess gripped his arm, her fingers digging into his skin right through his coat. "Let's get out of here!"
Ronnie stumbled back. The beer he'd drunk rushed into his mouth and he vomited. Wiping his mouth, he tugged his cell phone from its case.
"Wh-what are you doing?" Jess whimpered.
"Calling the cops," he said. "Something really bad happened here."
The Painters Mill City Building is located on South Street just off the traffic circle. The two-story brick structure was built in 1901 and has been renovated a dozen times since. It housed the post office back in the 1950s. The elementary school in the 1960s. The town council moved in after the fire in 1985. You can get city permits here, attend council meetings and pay for traffic tickets. One-stop shopping.
I'm hopelessly disheveled from my tussle with Scott Brower, and ten minutes late because of the paperwork involved with his arrest. I brush at the bloodstains on my uniform as I go through the double doors. The bridge of my nose aches as I take the elevator to the second level and make my way to the town council meeting room. Taking a deep breath, I push open the door.

Seven people sit at a cherry wood conference table. All eyes sweep to me when I enter. The elder councilman, Norm Johnston, sits at the head of the table like a king feeding biscuits to his group of lapdogs. Beside him, Mayor Auggie Brock loads cream cheese onto a bagel. The other faces are familiar, too. Dick Blankenship farms soybeans and corn. Bruce Jackson owns a tree nursery on the edge of town. Ron Zelinski is a retired factory worker. Neil Stubblefield teaches high school algebra and coaches the football team. Janine Fourman is the only woman, but from my perspective she's more dangerous to me than all the men combined. The owner of several tourist shops, she's persuasive, pushy, and has a mouth as big as her hair. In Janine's world, it's all about Janine and everyone else be damned.

Sighing, I glance out the frosted window where the bare branches of the sycamore tree shiver in the cold. I find myself wishing I were outside where it's warmer.

"Chief Burkholder." Norm Johnston stands.

Everyone in the room is staring at me. Probably more interested in how I got a black eye and bloodstains on my coat than the business at hand.

Auggie Brock pulls out the only empty chair. "Are you all right, Kate?"

"I'm fine." My eyes find Norm. "I don't have much time so you might want to get things rolling."

The senior councilman looks around as if to say, *See? I told you she's not very cooperative.* "First of all, we'd like a report on how the murder investigation is progressing."

I hold his gaze. "All departmental resources are focused on this case. My officers are on mandatory overtime. We're working around the clock. We're also utilizing the BCI lab and several law enforcement databases."

Janine interjects. "Do you have a suspect?"

"No." I give her my full attention. "We're only thirty-two hours into the case."

"I heard you arrested Scott Brower," Norm says.

Once again I'm amazed at the speed of the grapevine in this town. "He's a person of interest."

Norm Johnson rolls his eyes. "Does that mean he's a suspect?"

With as little fanfare as possible, I relay the details of Brower's arrest.

123

Janine Fourman stands. "Chief Burkholder. This town can't afford to lose its tourists. If people don't shop here, they'll go to Lancaster County. Do you realize how long and hard we've worked to get Painters Mill on the tourism map?" She looks around for the support of her counterparts, all of whom are nodding like mindless bobbleheads. "Protecting the citizens of Painters Mill also extends to providing them with a stable economy."

Norm Johnston raises both hands, a symphony conductor quieting his orchestra. "Kate, we know your resources are limited due to budget and manpower constraints. Frankly, we're not convinced you have the . . . experience to deal with such a difficult case."

The words vibrate inside me like a tuning fork against a broken bone. I'd known this moment was coming. Still, the punch of shock is powerful enough to tie my stomach into knots.

Janine's eyes glint like a rat that's just stolen the cheese without getting crushed. "Don't take this personally, but we've brought in outside help."

I stand there, my heart pounding, sweat pooling beneath my arms. Dread is a block of ice in my gut. All I can think is that I've lost control of the case. "What are you talking about?"

As if on cue I hear the door behind me click open. I turn to see a tall, dark-haired man enter the room. The long, black coat tells me he's not from around here. I wonder briefly if he's press, but when I look into his eyes, I know he's a cop.

For a moment I feel stripped bare, as if every emotion banging around inside me is visible. Vaguely, I wonder which agency he's with. The conservative suit hints at FBI, but I know he could also be with the state. Neither is good news.

"Kate." The mayor pushes away from his bagel and rises. "This is Agent John Tomasetti with BCI."

I make no move to approach him or shake his hand.

Flushing, the mayor turns his attention to the man. "Agent Tomasetti, this is our Chief of Police Kate Burkholder."

His gaze is level as he crosses to me. I notice several things about him at once. His eyes are as dark and hard as black granite, beneath heavy brows. He's got a poker face; his expression is impossible to read. I guess him to be about forty years old. He's looking at me as if I'm some stand-up comic whose jokes are falling flat. I don't want him here and he knows it. But there's not a damn thing I can do about it, and that lack of control brings a hard rush of anxiety.

"Chief Burkholder." He extends his hand. "It sounds like you have your hands full."

I accept the handshake. His palm is warm, dry and slightly rough. His grip is substantial, but not too tight. "It's been a tough case," I hear myself say.

He's got a black carry-on slung over his shoulder, and I realize he's just arrived in town. At this point, I should thank him for being here and offer to drive him to the station. Once there I would introduce him to the team and brief him on the case. Afterward, in keeping with cop etiquette, I'd probably take him out for dinner, some politically incorrect jokes and war stories, and a few too many drinks. I know it's petty, unprofessional and self-defeating, but I'm not going to do any of those things.

"I'm here to assist any way I can," he offers.

"I'm sure the council appreciates that."

A ghost of a smile whispers across his face.

"I've got to get back to work." Extricating my hand from his, I turn and start toward the door. My heart pounds like a piston as I yank it open. I can't quiet the little voice telling me I handled that all wrong. I should have been more diplomatic. More professional. I should have kept my cool.

Someone calls out to me, but I don't stop. I'm too angry to be reasonable. Most of that anger is directed at myself. I shouldn't have let this happen. The truth of the matter is I should have already requested assistance from another agency.

In the hall, I stride to the elevator and slam my fist down on the button. I don't wait for the car to arrive. I'm heading toward the stairs when I hear my name. I turn to see Auggie striding toward me. "Kate! Wait!"

I don't want to talk to him, but I can't run away from this. I stop and watch him approach.

"I'm sorry about what happened in there." His expression reminds me of a little dog that has just pissed on the floor and knows he's about to be punished.

"Were you part of it?" My statement requires no explanation.

"Look, I know you didn't want to call in BCI just yet, but—"

"A heads-up would have been nice, Auggie."

He flushes darkly. "Kate, it was out of my hands."

My temper is lit, but this isn't the time or place for a political coup. The damage has been done. Besides, I have a much more dangerous beast to slay.

Glancing toward the chambers, he lowers his voice. "Watch Norm," he says. "He's after you."

My cell phone trills, but I ignore it. "Maybe that's because I caught him driving drunk and arrested him."

"He's going to get the sheriff's office involved, too, Kate."

Bastard, I think and tug the phone from my belt. "What?"

"Chief!" Mona's voice is high and tight. "I just got a call from Bob Stedt's boy. Him and his girlfriend found a dead body out at the old Huffman place."

The words turn my blood to ice water. I look at Auggie, who's staring at me with an odd mix of concern and alarm on his face.

"Call Glock." I turn away from Auggie, wishing I'd run from the building when I had the chance. "Tell him to meet me there. Tell those kids to get in their vehicle and lock the doors. Tell them not to touch anything. Tell them not to leave the scene, unless they're in danger. Get ahold of Doc Coblentz and tell him to stand by. I'm on my way."

My hand shakes as I shove the cell into its nest. I look at Auggie. I feel sick inside, like I've done something terrible.

"What happened?" The pale cast to his complexion tells me he already knows.

"We've got another body." Yanking open the stairwell door, I rush down the steps.

CHAPTER 14

Death is a terrible thing, but murder is worse. No matter how many times I see it, the ugliness and senselessness of it frighten me on some primal level. My speedometer hits eighty miles per hour on the highway, but I slow to a reasonable speed once I reach Thigpen Road because it's slick with snow. The Huffman place is down a short lane and surrounded by skeletal trees, like bony fingers holding the place together.

I turn the Explorer in to the driveway and follow the tire tracks to the rear of the house. Ronnie Stedt and a teenaged girl I don't recognize huddle inside a pickup truck.

Jamming the Explorer into Park, I swing open the door. The kids disembark and rush toward me.

"What happened?" I ask.

Stedt's face is the color of paste. His eyes are glassy. He stops a couple of feet away and I smell vomit. "There's a dead person inside."

I look at the female. Her cheeks are bright red and streaked with mascara. She looks a lot tougher than Ronnie Stedt. "What's your name?" I ask.

"J-Jess Hardiman."

"Is there anyone else in the house?" I slide my .38 from its holster.

"Just the . . . body."

"Where?"

"B-bedroom."

"Stay here. If you see something or get scared, get in the truck and hit the horn, okay?"

Both heads bob.

I jog to the back door and shove it open. The house smells of death and marijuana. An old Led Zeppelin song blares from a radio on the counter. My nerves crawl like worms beneath my skin. Fear runs thick in my veins as I enter the living room. I don't think there's anyone in the house. But I'm afraid of what waits ahead.

I move into the hall. It's narrow and dark. The smell is stronger here. Blood and feces laced with the underlying stench of putrefaction. I sidestep a puddle of vomit. To my left, the bedroom door stands open. I don't want to look, but I can't stop. I see a horribly bloated corpse. Brown skin stretched impossibly tight. Hair matted and hanging down. Breasts drooping like wrinkled fruit. Ankles bound and chained to a beam in the ceiling. Black feet. A wet, black tongue protruding between swollen lips.

A sound escapes me as I stumble backward into the hall. My breaths come shallow and fast. My stomach roils, and my mouth fills with bile. Footsteps sound behind me. I swing around, my gun rising.

Glock halts, his hands come up. "Jesus Christ, it's me."

"Goddamnit." I lower my weapon. "I almost plugged you."

His gaze flicks down the hall. "Scene clear?"

I shake my head because I can't find my voice. I'm dangerously close to throwing up.

He moves past me and peers into the bedroom. "Holy hell."

While Glock clears the rest of the house, I struggle to pull myself together. By the time he meets me in the hall, I have my cop's coat of armor back in place.

"It's clear," he says.

I don't like the way he's looking at me, as if he thinks I'm going to lose it. "Damn it, Glock, I should have asked Detrick to assist," I manage. "I should have formed a task force."

"Even if you had, it wouldn't have prevented this. She's been there a while. Fuckin' hindsight."

I walk into the living room. Behind me I hear him speaking into his radio. Through the kitchen window, I see Ronnie Stedt and his girlfriend standing where I left them.

Glock comes up beside me. "Pickles and Skid are on the way."

I nod toward the teenagers. "We need to talk to them. I'll take the Stedt boy."

"Chick looks tough."

"You're tougher."

"I'm a Marine," he says, as if that explains everything.

I go through the back door and approach Ronnie Stedt. The air smells incredibly clean and I gulp it like water. He looks at me, then quickly glances away. "Come here," I say.

Glock ushers the girl toward his cruiser. Ronnie watches them walk away and gets a scared-little-boy look on his face.

"You okay?" I ask.

He shakes his head. "I never seen anything like that in my life."

I motion toward the Explorer. "Let's get out of the cold."

Casting a final glance at his girlfriend, he trails me to the Explorer. I put him in the passenger seat, then climb behind the wheel. "You need a smoke?" I ask.

"I don't smoke." He heaves a sigh. "Cigarettes, anyway."

"I'm going to let you slide on the pot."

"Thanks."

I start the engine and turn on the heater. "What were you doing here?"

"Nothin'."

I make eye contact, but he looks away. "You're not in any trouble," I say. "I just need to know how you found that body."

Looking thoroughly busted, he shakes his head. "We skipped school. We were just going to hang out." He shrugs. "I can't believe this happened."

"Was there anyone here when you arrived?" I ask.

"No."

"Did you touch anything? Move anything?"

"We just walked in. Drank a beer. Then we saw that . . . *thing* in the bedroom. Jesus . . ."

Their level of shock and genuine fear indicates these kids had nothing to do with what happened. "Do your folks know you're here?"

He shakes his head. "My dad's going to kill me."

"I'll leave the explaining up to you." I see a cell phone clipped to his belt. "You need to call them right now."

Sighing, he reaches for his phone.

I dial Doc Coblentz's number from memory. "We need you out at the Huffman place on Thigpen Road," I say.

"Tell me this is about a car accident or heart attack."

"I wish I could."

"Good God." A heavy sigh hisses through the line. "I'll be there in ten minutes."

I stand in the bedroom of the old house with Doc Coblentz and Glock, and we try not to stare at what's left of the woman hanging from the rafter. Doc digs into his field kit, pulls out a foil packet of mentholated petroleum jelly and hands it to me. "This'll help."

I tear open the packet and dab it below my nostrils. I offer it to Glock, but he shakes his head. "My mom gave me that stuff when I was a kid. Can't stand the smell."

Under different circumstances I might have laughed. This morning, I merely fold down the top of the packet and put it in my coat pocket.

We've donned shoe covers and plastic gowns, not only to preserve the scene but to protect us from biohazard. "Judging from the amount of blood," the doc begins, "I'd say he killed her here."

"Why change his MO?" I wonder aloud.

Glock jumps in with a theory. "Maximum effect."

The doc and I both look at him. I'm no expert on serial killers; my experience is limited to a handful of murders I worked in Columbus. But I agree with Glock's hypothesis. Whoever did this wanted to terrify. He wanted to show us the carnage he's capable of. I've read that many serial murderers *want* to be caught. Not because they want to go to jail, but so they can claim ownership of their handiwork.

"He knew he wouldn't be disturbed here," I say.

"The closest neighbor is a mile away," Glock adds.

I don't want to look at the victim, but my eyes are drawn to her. Putrefaction has set in. Gases have built up inside the body, bloating it to nearly beyond recognition. The skin is mostly black with small patches tinted green. It's the face that bothers me most. The eyes are gone completely. The wet-looking, black tongue sticks out between broken teeth.

I address Glock. "We need photos before we move her."

"I'll grab the Polaroid." He leaves with a little too much enthusiasm.

Ten minutes ago, the parents of the teenagers arrived to pick up their children. Ronnie Stedt's father tried to force his way into the house. Luckily, Glock was there to stop him. I explained to him that the area was a crime scene and the most helpful thing he could do was take his son to the police station where T.J. was waiting to take statements and fingerprints. On the outside chance we find latents here at the scene, we'll be able to rule them out.

Frightened parents and traumatized teenagers are the least of my worries. Fifteen minutes ago, I called the Holmes County Sheriff's Office and officially asked for assistance. I'm sure the suit from Columbus will be arriving soon. Already, I feel control of the case careening from my grasp.

Skid and Pickles are outside, setting up a perimeter. Once the crime scene tape is in place, they'll conduct a search of the barns and outbuildings. They'll also look for footprints and tire tracks. But with the snow coming down in earnest now, chances are slim that they'll find anything useful.

Glock returns with the Polaroid. A mixture of snow and sleet patters against the windows as he begins snapping photos. The whir of the tiny motor seems unduly loud in the silence. The house is freezing cold. I wear several layers of clothing and long johns beneath my slacks, but I'm chilled to my bones.

"How long do you think she's been here?" I ask.

Doc Coblentz shakes his head. "Hard to tell, Kate. Temperature is going to be a factor."

"She looks frozen solid."

"She is now. But if you'll recall, two weeks ago we had a few days that were well above freezing."

I remember; the temperature rose into the low fifties for almost a week before an arctic cold front blasted through. "So she's been here a while."

"I would venture to say that this body is in stage three decomposition. There's quite a bit of bloating. The greenish hue of early putrefaction is giving way to black putrefaction. That stage usually takes four to ten days." He shrugs. "But in these temperatures, that time frame would have been lengthened substantially. This time of year there's little or no insect activity, which also plays a huge role in the decomposition process."

"What's your best guess?"

"Two weeks, maybe three."

Two women in three weeks is all I can think. That this killer has come out of obscurity and escalated to this level so quickly is rare. What triggered the escalation?

I step closer to the corpse. I see hair matted with dried blood. Her bowels had released at some point and feces dribbled down her back to puddle on the floor. I can feel my heart hammering, a low buzz inside my head. "Was she alive when he hung her up?"

"Judging from the amount of blood on the floor, I would say her heart was still beating."

"What about the wound?" I ask.

The doc looks at Glock. "Did you get a shot of the blood on the floor?"

Glock nods. "Got it."

Coblentz steps into the biohazard, leaving a footprint. Though he wears two pairs of latex gloves, I cringe when he touches the body at the jawline to expose the wound. "I'll have a better idea once I get her to the morgue, but upon preliminary inspection the wound looks very similar to that of the first victim. See here? It's short. Deep with smooth edges. Doesn't look like the blade was serrated."

I try to look at the body with the unaffected eye of a cop. I owe that to this young woman. To this town. I owe it to myself. But my emotions and the revulsion inside me are like a beast pounding its cage door.

For an hour, we work the scene in grim silence. I'm in the process of bagging the victim's hands when movement at the door snags my attention. I look up to see Sheriff Nathan Detrick standing just inside the room, looking like a man who's just been struck by lightning.

"Holy God almighty," he says, his gaze fastened to the corpse.

I met him once, briefly, in the two years I've been chief. He's a beefy man of about fifty years. A weight lifter, I'm sure. Maybe a runner. But his age is beginning to take a toll on a body that was once the envy of every over-forty male in some testosterone-laden gym. His head is bald, but it suits him. I find myself wondering if he shaves his scalp to hide male pattern baldness or if it's a natural state.

He doesn't give me time to ponder. "Looks like you got one hell of a mess on your hands."

I snap off my latex gloves as he crosses to me. He sticks out his hand. Though the task I'd been doing is macabre, he doesn't hesitate when we shake. "Nathan Detrick at your service."

His grip is firm, but not bone-crunching and I give him points for that. His eyes are electric blue, his stare level and direct. His presence is surprisingly reassuring, and for the first time I realize I don't want to shoulder the weight of this case alone.

"Thanks for coming." I see intelligence in his eyes, and I know he's summing me up, making judgments. Touché.

"We've met." He stops pumping, but doesn't let go of my hand.

"The Fairlawn Retirement Home benefit, last Christmas," I say.

"Of course. I remember now. Prime rib. Tough as hell."

"And Santa got juiced."

He counters with a belly laugh. "We raised some money for a good cause, though, didn't we?"

I nod, but our small talk is minimized by what we face at this moment.

He releases my hand and turns his attention to the body. "I read your press release. I can't believe that slaughterhouse son of a bitch is back."

"It's been a tough couple of days."

"We're glad you called us." He lowers his voice. "Just so you know, I'm not big on jurisdictional bullshit. This is your baby."

I wonder if he means it. I wonder if the suit from BCI will feel the same way. "I appreciate that."

It's evident why this man won his bid for office by a landslide. Straightforward and charismatic, he possesses leadership qualities I admire. A big teddy bear here to save all of us from our own incompetence. But I've known a lot of law enforcement types over the years. And I know the teddy bear could easily transform into a man-eating grizzly if someone rubs him the wrong way. T.J. told me just last week that Detrick is in the midst of an ugly divorce. Rumor has it he's got a nasty temper.

"I'm going to need help getting her down," the doc says.

To avoid excessive contamination of the scene, I've limited the number of people inside the house to Glock, myself, the coroner, and now Detrick. It's up to us to help the doctor lower and bag the body.

Doc Coblentz steps away from the body, leaving thick, oil-like tracks on the floor. I pick up the three-rung aluminum stepladder Glock brought in earlier. Though the booties will protect my shoes from biohazard, I cringe as I step into the pool to set up the ladder.

"I've got it." Glock scoots the ladder closer to the body and steps onto it. "If you guys lift her and put some slack in the chain, I'll unhook it."

"Be careful," Doc Coblentz says quickly. "The flesh may slough off so make sure you've got a good grip."

I jolt when Detrick puts his hand on my shoulder. "She's going to be heavy. Let me do it."

I want to be annoyed with him, but I'm more annoyed with myself. For the first time in a long time, I want to step aside and let someone else handle my job.

Doc Coblentz directs Detrick to the extra biohazard gear. He dons shoe covers and ties an apron around his parka. Slipping on latex gloves, the sheriff nods. With the doctor spotting one side of the body and Detrick on the other, Glock steps onto the top rung of the ladder and reaches for the hook end of the chain. "Lift her," he says.

The two men lift simultaneously. Working quickly, Glock unhooks the chain. All three men gently lower the body to the floor. The woman's head shifts and black fluid spreads over the wood planks. I want to close my eyes to escape the sight. Instead, I cross to where Glock left the camera, pick it up and begin taking photos. Somehow the lens gives me the distance I need. I snap shots of the rafter and chain.

I lower the camera. No one speaks. All eyes are fastened on the corpse. I'm cold, but I feel sweat on my back. "We need to bag the chain." The normalcy of my voice surprises everyone, including me.

I cross to the box of garbage bags I'd brought in and snap one open. Glock carries the chain to me and places it inside the bag. "If we can figure out who manufactured the chain," I say, "we might be able to find out where he bought it."

"Probably be best to send it off to BCI," Detrick offers.

"I agree."

On the other side of the room, the doc unzips the body bag and opens it wide. He then approaches the body, squats beside it, his expression deeply troubled. "She's got superficial cutting on her abdomen. Like the others."

My feet take me closer. I lift the camera and snap four shots in quick succession.

"Looks like the Roman numeral XXII," Glock says.

"It's him," Detrick whispers. "He's back. After all this time."

I want to scream and rail that it's not possible. *I shot him! He's fucking dead!*

The doc sighs. "Help me roll her over."

Glock kneels beside the doc, sets both gloved hands gently, almost reverently on the woman's hip. The doc takes her shoulder and the men roll her onto her stomach. I snap several more shots.

"God in heaven."

The shock in the doctor's voice pulls me from my thoughts. I lower the camera. That's when I notice the small object protruding from between her buttocks.

Detrick steps back. "Good Lord."

Glock rises to his full height.

The doctor touches the small protrusion that hadn't been visible before, but does not remove it from her body. "Some type of foreign object."

Revulsion shudders through me.

"Let's get this poor child zipped in." He places the bag next to the body and smoothes it with gloved hands. With Glock's help, the two men roll her onto it.

As the black vinyl is zipped, something inside me breaks loose. I'm not usually squeamish, but my stomach roils. I feel eyes on me as I snap off my gloves. I remove my shoe covers, yank off the gown and toss all of it into the biohazard bag someone hung on the doorknob. I sense Detrick staring at me, but I don't look at him as I brush past him and rush from the room.

My vision dims as I stagger down the hall and into the kitchen. I curse when I see John Tomasetti standing on the back porch in his long black coat and city slicker shoes. He looks at me oddly as I push open the door. He says something as I pass by him, but I'm too upset to comprehend the words.

Cold air bites through the sweat on my face. Vaguely, I'm aware of the ambulance parked in the driveway, the engine rumbling. At the end of the lane a ProNews 16 van idles, exhaust billowing into the frigid air. I see a Holmes County cruiser parked next to Glock's city car. I'm not sure where I'm going until I yank open the door of the Explorer and slide behind the wheel. I hear my ragged breaths tearing from my throat. I feel like crying, but I've deprived myself that outlet for so many years I can't. I haven't eaten yet today, but stomach acid rushes hotly to my mouth. I swing open the door and throw up in the snow.

After a moment, the nausea passes. Slamming the door, I put my hands on the wheel and lay my forehead on them. A tap on my window nearly sends me out of my skin. I open my eyes to see the suit from BCI standing outside the Explorer, his expression as inscrutable as stone. He's the last person I want to talk to, but as has been the case as of late, I don't have a choice.

Instead of rolling down the window, I swing open the door, forcing him back a step.

"You okay?" he asks.

"Peachy. I enjoy throwing up." I slide out and slam the door. "What the hell do you think?"

He's amused, and that's pissing me off. For a moment the only sound comes from the tinkle of sleet against the ground. I'm cold and shivering and it takes some effort to keep my teeth from chattering.

"They're taking the body to the morgue," he says. "Thought you might want to know."

I nod, get my temper under control. "Thanks."

He glances over his shoulder toward the news van. "Vultures smell blood."

"Once word of this second murder hits the airwaves, we'll be seeing a lot more of them."

"You might consider holding a press conference. That way you can deal with them on your terms. Nip any rumors in the bud."

It's a good idea. I've been so immersed in the case, I hadn't considered the media end of it. "I'll get something going."

He stares hard at me, a bad-cop look that has probably convinced more than one recalcitrant suspect to spill his guts. "Look, I know you don't want me here—"

"This has nothing to do with you personally," I cut in.

"That's the same thing they said about you." He looks amused again. "Politics sucks, huh?"

"Something like that."

He's still staring at me. A stare so intense I grow uncomfortable beneath it. "I'm a pretty good cop," he says. "I'm here. You may as well use me. I might even be able to help."

He's right, of course. But the thought of this man poking around in this case sends a shiver through me. My ensuing silence is all the answer he needs.

Giving me a final look, Tomasetti turns and starts toward a black Tahoe parked near the road. I watch him walk away, his words echoing in my ears. *I'm a pretty good cop.* I find myself wondering if he's good enough to crack a sixteen-year-old case and all the secrets buried beneath it.

CHAPTER 15

It's nearly three P.M. when I leave the Huffman place. I feel like I've spent the morning in hell. Three hours at the scene have wrung me out until there's nothing left. On the outskirts of Millersburg, I call Lois. I can tell by her voice she's stressed. "We got media here, Chief. I swear to God these people are curling my hair."

I don't tell her there are probably more on the way. "I need you to set up a press conference."

"You're going to invite *more* of them?"

"You know what they say about keeping your enemies close."

"You are a glutton for punishment."

"Let's do it at the high school auditorium. Six o'clock."

"You got it."

"Call all of my officers and tell them we're meeting at four o'clock. The room you set up. That's going to be our command center." I name each member of my small force, including Mona. "Notify Detrick and Tomasetti, too."

"Tomasetti that Mafia-looking guy?"

Her description elicits a smile. "And check to see if there have been any missing persons reports filed. White female. Twenty to thirty years old. Blonde. Start with the five-county area. If you don't find anything there, go to Columbus, Wheeling, Massillon, Canton, Newark, Zanesville—"

"Slow down."

"Steubenville. Check with county and city agencies."

"Okay, I got it."

"Patch me through to T.J., will you?"

The line clicks. T.J. picks up an instant later. "Hey, Chief."

"Did you get the statements from the teenagers?"

"Lois is typing them now."

"Anything on Patrick Ewell?" Ewell was the man who paid cash for a box of condoms at the Super Value Grocery.

"I ran a background." Paper rattles. "Ewell, Patrick Henry. Thirty-six years old. Lives on Parkersburg Road with his wife, Marsha, and two teenage kids. No record. No arrests. Not even a frickin' speeding ticket." The pitch of T.J.'s voice changes. "Get this, Chief. He works at the slaughterhouse."

It's a tenuous connection, but I'm just desperate enough to follow up. "Find out what he does there. And find out if he was at the Brass Rail on Saturday."

"You got it."

I'd rather talk to Ewell myself, but I need to get the second victim identified first. "See if there's a connection between Ewell and Amanda Horner."

"Okay."

I consider everything we know about Ewell. "Why would a married man with two grown kids buy a box of condoms?"

"Uh, birth control?"

"You'd think for a couple married that long, they'd have a better method."

T.J. clears his throat. That a man of twenty-four years is embarrassed by such talk fills me with hope that the world is not as bleak as it feels at the moment. "Thanks, T.J."

"Don't mention it, Chief."

I feel slightly more human as I pull into the parking lot of Pomerene Hospital. I double-park near the entrance. Sleet patters my head and shoulders as I jog toward the revolving doors. The redhead at the information desk eyes me with a little too much interest as I pass. I send her a passable smile, but she turns her attention back to her computer.

The hospital basement is hushed and not as well lit as the upper floors. My boots thud dully against tile as I pass the yellow and black biohazard sign. I push through the set of swinging doors and see Doc Coblentz in his office, sitting at his desk. "Doc?"

"Ah, Chief Burkholder. I've been expecting you." Wearing a white lab coat and navy slacks, he rises and crosses to me. "Any ID on the victim yet?"

"We're checking missing persons reports." I take a deep breath, trying to prepare for what comes next. "Do you have a prelim?"

He shakes his head. "I've got her cleaned up. I did the initial exam. If you'd like to take a look."

That's the last thing I want to do, but I need to identify this young woman. Somewhere out there, loved ones are worried. She may have children. People whose lives will be irrevocably changed by her death.

I go directly to the alcove. Hanging up my coat, I quickly don a gown and booties. The doc is waiting for me when I emerge. "The cuts on her abdomen do appear to be the Roman numeral XXII."

"Postmortem?"

"Antemortem." He starts toward the second set of swinging doors, and we enter the gray tiled room I've come to despise.

Three stainless steel gurneys are shoved against the far wall. A fourth gleams beneath a huge overhead light. I see the outline of the body beneath a blue sheet and brace.

Doc Coblentz snags a clipboard off the counter. Sliding a pen from the breast pocket of his lab coat, he looks through his bifocals and jots something on the form, then returns the clipboard to the counter. "I've been a doctor for the better part of twenty years. I've been coroner for nearly eight. This is the most disturbing thing I've ever seen."

Gently, he pulls down the sheet. Revulsion sends me back a step as I take in the brownish-green hued skin. Her mouth sags open; I see her tongue tucked inside. The wound at her neck is a black, gaping mouth.

My eyes are drawn to the Roman numerals on her abdomen. The carving is crude, but the similarities to the wounds on Amanda Horner's body are unmistakable. "Cause of death?"

"The same. Exsanguination. He cut her throat and she bled to death."

I need to get a better look at her. I want to see her hair, her nails, her toes—anything that might help me identify her, but my feet refuse to take me closer.

"He raped her. Sodomized her."

"DNA?"

"I took swabs, but there wasn't any fluid."

"He wore a condom?"

"Probably. I'll know more when I get the results back." The doc sighed. "He tortured this girl, Kate. Look at this."

Rounding the gurney, he crosses to the counter and picks up a stainless steel tray about the size of a cookie sheet. "This was inside her rectum."

I can't bring myself to look at the object. I can't even meet the doctor's eyes. Instead, I lower my head slightly and rub at the ache between my eyes. "Postmortem?"

"Ante."

Taking a deep breath, I force my gaze to the tray. The object is a steel rod, about half an inch in diameter and ten inches long. There's a tiny eyehook on one end. The other is tapered. It looks homemade; I can see where whoever made it used some type of grinder to shape it.

"Foreign object rape?" I ask. In the back of my mind, I wonder if the killer is impotent. If maybe he's gone to a urologist for erectile dysfunction treatment. I make a mental note to check it out.

"I don't think that's how or why he used this object."

"What do you mean?"

"I think it's some type of homemade electrode." He picks up the object. "There's copper here. See?" The doc runs a gloved finger along the length of the steel. "I worked for an electrician part-time when I was in high school. Copper is one of the best conductors of electricity."

I don't know much about the dynamics of electricity. I do know it can be used for torture. While in the academy, I remember reading about the Mexican drug cartels using those kinds of tactics when they wanted to make an example of someone.

I look at the doc. I see the same outrage and disbelief in his eyes that I feel clenching my chest. "So this killer may have some electrical experience. At the very least, he tinkers." It's much too benign a word for a person who designed an instrument of torture. Tinkering is the kind of thing your dad does on Sunday afternoons in the garage. Monsters don't tinker.

"This explains the burns Amanda Horner sustained."

"Yes."

"Why would he leave it?" I wonder aloud. But in the back of my mind, I know. He's proud of this vile device. He *wanted* us to find it.

The doc shakes his head. "That's your area, Kate, not mine. I can definitively tell you he tortured her with this, probably with an electrical charge."

For the span of a full minute, the only sound comes from the buzz of the fluorescent lights and the hum of the refrigeration units. I try to rally my thoughts, get my questions in order, but my mind doesn't cooperate. "I'll add that to the profile we're building."

I stare at the deep grooves cut into her wrists. The bloated abdomen. Her hands and feet. I try to see her as she must have been when she was alive. That's when it strikes me that neither her nails or toenails are painted. This woman is totally unadorned. No highlights in her hair. Her earlobes aren't pierced. No jewelry.

She is plain.

A dozen vehicles jam the street in front of the police station when I pull up. I see a ProNews 16 van parked in my reserved space and I'm forced to park half a block away. I slap a citation beneath his wiper on my way in.

Inside, the place is a madhouse. Both Lois and Mona stand at the dispatch station, manning a switchboard gone wild. T.J. sits at his cube, the phone to his ear, his back to the room. Glock slouches in his chair in his cubicle, his fingers pecking at the keyboard. I wonder where Skid and Pickles are, and realize they're probably still at the Huffman place.

Steve Ressler spots me. His cheeks glow red as he rushes toward me. "Is it true there was a second murder?"

"Yes." I don't stop walking.

He keeps pace with me. "Who's the victim? Has she been identified? Has the family been notified? Is it the same killer?"

"I gotta work, Steve," I say. "Press conference at six."

He tosses a dozen more questions at me, but I push past him and head to my office.

"Chief!" Mona's hair is wilder than usual. Heavy on the eyeliner. Pink shadow. Clashing red lipstick. She's ready for the cameras.

"How long has it been like this?" I ask.

"A few hours. I stayed to help Lois."

"I appreciate that." Across the room, Steve Ressler gives me the evil eye. "Everyone behaving?"

"Ressler's a pushy asshole. Norm Johnston's off the chart."

"Tell anyone who asks there's a press conference at six in the high school auditorium."

"Gotcha."

In my office, I flip on my computer and grab a cup of coffee while it boots. My phone rings. I look at it to see all four lines blinking in discord. Ignoring all of them, I dial Lois.

"Did you check missing persons reports?" I ask.

"Nothing, Chief."

I think about the young woman at the morgue. I should be surprised no one has reported her missing. But I'm not. "Remind everyone of the meeting at four."

"You mean the one that was supposed to start ten minutes ago?"

"And send Glock in, will you?"

"Sure."

I'm still thinking about the second victim when Glock walks in. "What's up?"

"Close the door."

He reaches behind him and the door clicks shut.

"I need you to drop everything," I begin.

He moves to the visitor chair and sits. "All right."

"This is just between you and me, Glock. No one can know what you're doing or why. And I can't tell you everything."

"Tell me what you can and I'll run with it."

Relief flits through me that he trusts me enough to work blind. "I want you to dig up everything you can on a man by the name of Daniel Lapp."

"Who is he?"

"He's local. Amish. No one has seen him in sixteen years."

The time frame doesn't elude Glock, and for the first time he looks surprised. "He's *Amish*?"

"People assumed he fled the lifestyle."

"He got family here?"

I nod. "A brother. I've already talked to him."

"He give you anything?"

"No."

Glock studies me a little too closely. "You going to tell me why we're looking at this guy?"

"I can't. I just need you to trust me, okay?"

He nods. "Okay. I'll see what I can dig up."

Just like that. No questions. No objections at being left in the dark. I feel a pang of guilt. Like maybe I don't deserve that kind of trust.

"This a priority?" he asks after a moment.

"The highest," I answer, and hope to God he can find what I could not.

CHAPTER 16

The storage room down the hall from my office has undergone an extreme transformation from catchall to command center. An eight-foot folding table surrounded by mismatched chairs sits in the center of the room. At the front, a half-podium squats atop a rickety card table. Next to the podium is an easel affixed with a pad. Someone nailed a dry-erase board to the wall. A single telephone sits on the floor next to the wall jack, and I realize the cabling won't reach all the way to the table.

Glock and I are the first to arrive. I'm glad because I need a few minutes to gather my thoughts and mentally prepare. It's important for me to appear competent and in control, particularly since the investigation has become multi-jurisdictional.

"Not bad," Glock comments, referring to Mona's and Lois's ingenuity.

"It'll do in a pinch." I muster a halfhearted smile. "How bad is my eye?"

"It's in full bloom, Chief. Purple's not a bad color on you, though."

A flurry of activity at the door snags my attention. I glance over to see Detrick and two uniformed deputies enter. I motion to the table and chairs. "It's every man for himself."

Detrick crosses to me and extends a beefy hand. "ME give you anything on the vic?"

His grip is firm and dry and I find myself wishing I were so calm. "Cause of death is the same as the first vic. I'll go over everything in the briefing."

He nods and motions to his two deputies. "I brought some manpower for you. This is Deputy Jerry Hunnaker."

Hunnaker is slightly overweight with a cocky smirk that rubs me the wrong way. When we shake he grinds my knuckles, and I wonder if Detrick is lending me his dead weight.

The second deputy is tall and angular and looks more like a high school pole-vaulter than a cop. But his eyes are level, his expression natural and though I've already pegged him as inexperienced, I know he'll be more of a help to me than the cocky shit with the grip.

"Deputy Darrel Barton." Detrick sets his hand on the deputy's shoulder, a proud papa introducing his favorite son.

In the few minutes I've spent with Detrick, the room has filled. I see Steve Ressler standing at the door and cross to him. "The press conference is at six," I say.

"I'd like to sit in on this to see what the police are doing."

"This is a task force meeting, Steve. Some of what we'll be discussing is not for public consumption."

"Or maybe you don't want the public to know you don't have squat on this guy."

He looks pleased by his own audacity. I wonder how he would feel if I acted on the impulses running through me and coldcocked him. I nod toward the door. "You can voice your concerns at the press conference."

Turning on his heel, Ressler stalks out.

I take my place at the podium and scan the group. Detrick sits at the table, flanked by his two deputies. Glock and T.J. sit opposite him, segregated by agency and loyalties. Skid and Pickles take chairs at the back of the room. Mayor Auggie Brock sits alone, looking like a new kid on the first day of school. Mona stands near the door, her arms folded at her chest. Behind her, John Tomasetti leans against the doorjamb, his overnight bag at his feet. The gang's all here.

Pulling in a deep breath, I begin. "We are now a multi-jurisdictional task force set up by the mayor and town council."

A hushed stir goes around the room, and I know my team is wondering why I didn't brief them beforehand about the formation of the task force.

I fix my eyes on Auggie and continue. "We will be working in conjunction with the Holmes County Sheriff, Nathan Detrick."

The sheriff stands briefly, then takes his seat.

"And Agent John Tomasetti with the Bureau of Criminal Identification and Investigation out of Columbus," I say.

Heads turn. From his place at the door, the agent nods, and I can't help but think he really does look sort of Mafia-like.

I spend the next ten minutes summarizing the details of both murders. When I finish, I cross to the dry-erase board mounted on the wall. I write the words *Persons of Interest* and underline it. Everyone is expecting me to write the words *Slaughterhouse Killer,* but I begin with another name. *Scott Brower.* "He was at the Brass Rail on Saturday night. A witness reported seeing him with Amanda Horner." I relay details about his record and his arrest just that morning, then go to my next suspect.

"Patrick Ewell." I write the name on the board. "T.J.?"

The young officer looks down at his notes. "To recap . . . Ewell bought uh . . . rubbers at the Super Value Grocery in Painters Mill on Friday. Uh, the lubricated kind which is what the perpetrator used. Ewell paid cash, but we were able to identify him using the surveillance camera. He works at the slaughterhouse. Payroll department. I've since questioned him. Wife alibied him."

I break in. "Wives have been known to lie to protect their husbands. He remains a person of interest." I give T.J. a pointed look. "What about the other two condom guys?"

"They've been identified. Willie Stegmeyer and Bo Gibbas."

"Have you talked to them?"

"Ran out of time, Chief, but they're next on my list."

I jot the names on the board. I feel myself hesitate before I write *Slaughterhouse Killer.* "I don't like the label, but since most of you are familiar with it, we'll go with it." I scan the room. "As all of you know, the killings we're dealing with now are similar to four murders that occurred in the early nineties. I'm not convinced we're dealing with the same killer, and I caution you not to make assumptions this early in the game. We could have a copycat. I base that possibility on the hiatus between killings."

I see divergence on the faces of my audience and add, "The possibility that the killer was incarcerated or injured or even changed locales exists. But keep an open mind and don't be afraid to think outside the box."

I glance down at my assignment sheet. "Here's where we are in terms of investigation. Officer Skidmore is working with DRC to get the names of convicts incarcerated during that sixteen-year period." I glance at Skid. "Report?"

He sits up straighter, but it doesn't help his disheveled appearance. From where I stand, I can see his eyes are bloodshot. His hands aren't quite steady when he picks up a sheet of paper. "I entered official inquiries yesterday." He names several Ohio counties and cities. "DRC gave me priority, so we should hear back this afternoon or first thing tomorrow."

Tomasetti pipes up from his place at the door. "I can expedite your inquiries with DRC."

Skid nods. "That'd be great."

I continue, "Expand your search to hospitals, both medical and mental. I want to know if there were any males between the ages of twenty and forty hospitalized with debilitating injuries, such as from a car accident or serious psychological problems that required institutionalization."

Skid whistles. "Might take awhile. Lotta crazy people out there."

A few snickers erupt.

I turn back to the dry-erase board. "Similar crimes." I write the words on the board. "Pickles, I've got queries going with OHLEG, but I know sometimes for whatever reason data doesn't get entered. I want you to make some calls to local police departments. Look for murders involving a knife, the cutting of the throat, carving on the abdomen, and sex crimes involving a knife. Start with the surrounding eight-county area. Hit the bigger cities, too, including Columbus, Massillon, Newark, Zanesville and Cambridge."

Pickles looks at me as if I've just told him he won the lottery. "You got it, Chief."

I glance at Detrick's cocky deputy. "Hunnaker, Doc Coblentz says foreign-object rape was involved with both victims. There's a possibility this suspect is impotent. I want you to check with area urologists and get a list of men treated for erectile dysfunction."

Hunnaker shifts in his chair and tries not to look embarrassed.

The second deputy, Barton, whispers, "Don't worry, Hun, you can leave yourself off the list."

Laughter rumbles through the room. I don't join them, but the humor eases some of the tension.

Sheriff Detrick nods as if he approves. "What about doctor/patient confidentiality? Won't that be a problem?"

"Not if we can get a warrant." I look at Auggie Brock, purposefully putting him on the spot. "Don't you play golf with Judge Seibenthaler?"

Auggie can't hold my gaze. "Judge doesn't know a damn four iron from a putter," he says.

That earns him a few laughs, but the mood remains somber. "Call him," I say. "See if you can get warrants if we need them."

I address Barton. "I want a list of all registered sex offenders for the same counties and towns I mentioned earlier. Most police departments have lists online."

Nodding, he jots in a small notebook. "Pedophiles, too?"

"That, too." I turn my attention to Glock. "Tread and footwear imprints."

The former Marine leans back and addresses everyone with the cool competence of a CEO talking to a group of high school seniors. "I just got off the phone with BCI. Second batch of evidence has arrived at the lab and is being processed as we speak. We've got priority." He gives Tomasetti a pointed look, telling everyone Super Agent raised his magic wand and lit a fire. "With regard to the first batch of tire imprints and footwear impressions, they ran a comparison analysis and we got a partial tread. They're trying to match it up with a manufacturer now. If they can do that, they'll work on finding the retailer."

"Retailer might be able to get us a name." Detrick states the obvious.

"Especially if he paid by check or credit card," Glock adds.

"Or surveillance cameras." I look at Mona at the back of the room. She's fiddling with the buttons on her sweater. "Mona?"

Her attention jerks to me. She looks excited, pleased to be called upon. She's not a cop, but for the first time, that doesn't matter. I've got the perfect assignment for her.

"I want you to put together a list of evidence," I begin. "I also want a photo log made. You can look online for examples of how they're typically done."

"I saw it on an episode of *Murder Files.*" A murmur of chuckles goes around the room and she bites her lip.

I give her a smile. "How are you coming along on the abandoned properties list?"

"I've got twelve homes and two businesses so far," she replies.

Auggie speaks up. "You might check with the county tax collector on that. Maybe bankruptcy court."

"Okay." Sliding into a chair, she scribbles furiously. "Got it."

"This is a priority." I address Mona. "Give what you have to Sheriff Detrick." I glance at the sheriff. "Can the sheriff's office start checking these properties?"

"Absolutely," he replies.

T.J. starts to raise his hand, realizes the gesture is juvenile and quickly lowers it. "Chief, have you thought about bringing in a profiler?"

I look at Tomasetti. His poker face reveals nothing about what he is thinking or feeling. I find myself wishing I could read him.

"I'm working on a profile now," he responds. "I should have something by the end of the day."

I glance down at my notes. Throats are cleared and boots shuffle restlessly against the floor as I describe the instrument of torture Doc Coblentz found inside the second victim.

"There's a photo of it in the file. It looked homemade. Like maybe this guy made it in his garage or shop. He may have some electrical knowledge."

Detrick leans back in his chair, his arms crossed over his broad chest, watching me intently. "We gotta get this sick son of a bitch, people. I think everyone in this room knows he ain't going to stop now that he's got a taste for it."

I look at Detrick. "We could use extra patrols in the area."

"You got it."

I turn my attention back to the group. "I've called a press conference for this evening," I say. "Six o'clock at the school auditorium. You should be there."

I scan the faces. "One more thing I want to impress upon everyone in this room. We are not releasing the fact that this killer carved Roman numerals onto the abdomens of both victims. Do not discuss anything we've talked about today. Not with your wife or girlfriend or boyfriend or your dog. Is everyone clear on that?"

I see vigorous nods from all in the room. Satisfied I got my point across, I step away from the podium. "Let's go to work."

CHAPTER 17

I arrive at the high school with two minutes to spare. I'd hoped to avoid the media, but I'm too late. Several news vehicles are camped out in the rear lot near the bus-loading zone. Even in the dim light of the sodium vapor street-lamp, I recognize the ProNews 16 van.

I park in a faculty space and head toward a lesser-used side door. To my relief, it's unlocked. The hallway is warm and smells of paper dust and some industrial-strength cleaner that's supposed to smell like pine but doesn't. The auditorium lies straight ahead. I hear the crowd before I see it. Trepidation presses into me when I spot the television crew from Columbus dragging in reflective lights and camera gear.

I duck into a secondary hall that will take me to the rear of the auditorium. I see Detrick standing outside the stage doors, staring down at a small spiral notebook. An actor memorizing his lines minutes before curtain on opening night.

He spots me and lowers the notebook. "You like cutting it close, don't you?"

"This is not my cup of tea." It's an understatement; I'd rather shoot off my little toe than deal with the media.

"Lots of cameras," he comments. "Couple of radio stations, too."

All I can think is, *Shit*. Detrick, on the other hand, looks like some day-time superstar about to accept an Emmy. I see a sparkle of face powder on his bald head and pin lights of anticipation in his eyes, and I remind myself he is a politician first, a lawman second.

He gives me a sage look. "I've been a cop for a long time, and I'm good at it. But I'm a good politician, too, and I've never met a camera that didn't like me." He smiles in a self-deprecating way. "If you want me to handle the media side of this for you, I'm up to the job. I know you've got your hands full, and you can't be in two places at once."

It crosses my mind that this is his first step in hijacking my case. I know that sounds paranoid. But in the public eye, perceptions are everything. When it comes to television cameras, Detrick will outshine me like the sun outshining the moon. But he's right. I need to work the case, not make nice with some twenty-something journalist looking for his big break.

Those thoughts go by the wayside when I see Norm Johnston and Auggie Brock approach. Detrick sticks out his hand and the men shake. Auggie glances in my direction, but his eyes skitter quickly away. Norm doesn't acknowledge me. Taking off my coat, I drape it over a folding chair and try to settle my nerves.

"We're on," Norm says.

We enter the stage as a single, cohesive unit. I blink against the camera flashes and lights, and I wonder how long this fragile sense of accord will last. This is the kind of case that can tear even the most solid of relationships apart. My relationship with the mayor and town council is far from solid.

We stop at a table set up behind the podium. The lights raining down are bright and hot, a stark contrast to the cold outside. Auggie crosses to the podium and taps the mike. "Can everyone hear me?"

Nods and shouts of "yes" emit from the crowd.

Turning slightly, he introduces me. "Chief of Police Kate Burkholder."

I step up to the podium and look out over the sea of faces. I feel a sense of responsibility to the people I've sworn to protect and serve. I hope I can honor my oath of office without dishonoring my family or destroying my own life in the process.

Quickly, I recap the basic information about the case, barring the carvings on the victims' abdomens. "I want to assure all of you that the Holmes County Sheriff's office, the Bureau of Criminal Identification and Investigation and the Painters Mill PD are working around the clock to catch the person responsible. In the interim, I'm calling on every citizen for help. I want you to keep your doors locked. Keep your security alarms turned on. Report any unusual or suspicious activity to the police, no matter how trivial. I also ask you to form neighborhood watch groups. Keep a watchful eye on your neighbors. Your family members. Your friends. If you are female, be vigilant with regard to your personal safety. Don't go out alone."

A barrage of questions erupt when I pause.

"Is it the Slaughterhouse Killer?"

"Do you have a suspect?"

"How were the women killed?"

The pushiness of the crowd annoys me. "One at a time," I snap.

No one pays attention to my request. I spot Steve Ressler in the first row and call him by name. In the back of my mind I hope this makes up for my brusqueness back at the station. The last thing I want to do is alienate the media right off the bat.

"Chief Burkholder, have you contacted the FBI?" he asks.

"No."

Disapproving murmurs ripple through the crowd.

"Why not?"

"Because we're already working with the Bureau of Criminal Identification and Investigation out of Columbus."

A dozen hands shoot up. I point to a thin man wearing glasses with heavy black frames. "Can you tell us how the victims were killed?" he asks.

"Preliminary results from the coroner concludes both victims had their throats cut. Cause of death is exsanguination."

A hush that is part shock, part fear, falls over the crowd. I point to a man wearing a Cincinnati Reds ball cap. "That's exactly how the Slaughterhouse Killer from the early nineties murdered his victims," he begins. "Is it the same guy?"

"We do not know that to be a fact, but we are looking at old case files." Ignoring the buzz that follows, I call on a woman I've seen on the news.

The questions are brutal and pummel me like stones. The answers are hard to come by. I do my best, but after twenty minutes I feel embattled and wrung out. Hands wave madly, but I don't call upon them. "If you'll excuse me I've got to get back to work." Stepping back from the podium, I turn to Detrick. "Sheriff Detrick?"

At this point I'm expected to take my place beside Auggie and Norm and listen to Detrick's spiel. But I've never been a fan of political cabaret so I head toward the rear stage door.

Behind me, Detrick's voice booms from the sound system. Competence and charisma practically ooze from his pores, and I know that in minutes, he'll have this hostile audience eating out of his hand. It shouldn't bother me, but it does. In the public eye, perceptions are everything, even if those perceptions are skewed.

I mentally kick myself for having not done a better job at the podium. I should have been more patient, more forthright. I should have been a stronger leader. But I'm a cop, not a public speaker. Snagging my parka off the chair, I resolve to go back to the station where I can at least be effective.

Detrick's voice is the backdrop to my thoughts as I enter a hall lined with lockers. Even from this distance, I discern the confidence in his voice. And I know he is the one who will make the citizens of Painters Mill feel safe tonight, not me.

"Chief!"

I turn to see Glock stride toward me. Next to him, John Tomasetti's expression is grim. An Amish man with blunt-cut hair, blue eyes and a full red beard follows them. He wears a black wool jacket that doesn't look nearly warm enough. A plump woman wearing a black coat over a wool jumper and leather ankle boots trails the men.

"This is Ezra and Bonnie Augspurger," Glock begins.

It's been fifteen years since I've seen or spoken to them, but I know the Augspurgers. As a child, I spent many a Sunday at their home with my parents for worship. I remember playing with their daughter, Ellen, and a brother by the name of Urie, who liked to make a game of pulling my *kapp*. He didn't tattle when I pushed him into a pile of horse shit. The youngest Augspurger child, Mark, suffered with Ellis–van Creveld syndrome, a form of dwarfism found all too often in the Amish population. Of course, as a kid, all I knew was that Mark was short. But Ellen had once told me he had an extra toe and a hole in his heart. Looking at Ezra and Bonnie, I wonder if Little Markie is still alive.

I extend my hand first to Ezra. His eyes meet mine, and I see fear in their depths. I feel that same fear hammering on the door of my own psyche. I know why they're here, and I know how this meeting will end.

"Ellen is missing." Ezra's voice shakes as he speaks in Pennsylvania Dutch.

"We heard about the murdered English girl and became worried," Bonnie adds. "We want you to help us find Ellen."

I think of the partially decomposed body lying on the gurney at the hospital morgue—the unadorned fingernails and toenails—and I'm filled with a sadness so profound that for a moment I can't speak. I don't want that woman to be Ellen, but I know it is. Guilt spreads through me because I didn't recognize her. Though it's been fifteen years since I saw her, I feel as if I should have known.

Before I realize it, I'm speaking in Pennsylvania Dutch. "How long has she been missing?"

Ezra looks away, but not before I discern the shame in his expression.

"Two and a half weeks." Bonnie's hands twist nervously.

I give Ezra a hard look. "Why didn't you come to me sooner?"

"This was an Amish matter to be dealt with by us."

The awful familiarity of the words make the hairs at my nape stand on end.

"We assumed she had run away," Ezra says. "In the last few months, Ellen had become . . . difficult and rebellious."

"She had told us she would be taking the bus to Columbus to see her cousin Ruth," Bonnie says. "When she disappeared, we assumed that was where she had gone. Last night, we heard from Ruth. Ellen never arrived in Columbus."

I want to take them to the police station where we can speak privately. There are too many people, too many cameras here. I glance down the hall and spy an open classroom door. "Let's go where it's quiet."

Leaving the Augspurgers, I cross to Glock and Tomasetti. "Find a fax machine," I say quietly. "Ask Mona to fax the best photo she can find of the second vic."

When I pull back, both men's eyes are filled with knowledge. They know where this is going. Glock turns and jogs toward the auditorium in search of a school official.

I wish I could handle this without Tomasetti. A salient distrust exists between the Amish and the English police, particularly the conservative Amish, such as the Augspurgers. But protocol dictates I include him. Whether I like it or not, he's part of the investigation.

I go back to Bonnie and Ezra and we start toward the classroom. Tomasetti falls in behind us. I flip on the lights to see student desks, a green chalkboard where someone wrote the word *shit,* and a teacher's desk covered with papers. I pull out a few plastic chairs and we sit.

"Do you know something about Ellen?" Ezra asks in Pennsylvania Dutch.

"Do you have a recent photograph of her?" I ask, but I already know the answer. Most Amish do not believe in having their photographs taken, citing images as evidence of pride. Some believe photos and even paintings depicting faces violate the Biblical commandment, *Thou shalt not make unto thyself a graven image.* Some of the old order still believe a photo steals the soul.

"We do not have a photo," Ezra says.

I take out my notebook. "When's the last time you saw her?"

"The day she disappeared. I caught her smoking cigarettes in the barn. We had an argument . . ." Ezra shrugs. "She said she was going to see her cousin, Ruth."

"Back when Ellen first disappeared, did you notice any strangers in the area? Maybe a car or buggy?"

Ezra's thick brows snap together. "I remember seeing footprints in the snow. I did not know who made them."

"Where?" My heart beats faster. This could be our first clue. Yet this man had taken it upon himself not to contact the police.

"Leading to the road."

There's no doubt any footprints are long gone by now. Still, if the killer was there, he may have left something behind. I glance at Tomasetti. "Get Pickles and Skid out there."

"What's the address?" he asks.

Bonnie recites a rural address. "Do you think someone took her?" she asks.

Rising, Tomasetti unclips his cell phone and goes to the back of the room to make the call.

I turn my attention back to Ezra. "Can you give me a description of Ellen?"

The man is at a loss, so I look at Bonnie and the words tumble out of her in a rush. "She is twenty-seven years old. Blue eyes. Dark blonde hair."

"Height? Weight?"

"She's about five feet three inches. One hundred and twenty-five pounds."

The description matches that of the second victim. "Any distinguishing marks? Scars?"

"She's got a birthmark on her left ankle. A brown mole."

I write everything down, aware that Tomasetti watches my every move. My phone rings. I look down to see Glock's name on the display and I snatch it up.

"I'm outside the door with the photo," he says.

Rising, I look at Bonnie and Ezra. "I'll be right back."

In the hall, Glock is pacing. I click the door closed and cross to him. He hands me the fax. I stare down at the black and white image. The photo was taken at the morgue. I'm sure that in life Ellen looked nothing like the corpse lying on the gurney. But I think there's enough of her left so that her parents will recognize her.

"You think it's their daughter?" he asks.

"I think so." I pull out my phone and hit the speed dial for Doc Coblentz. I get voice mail at his office, so I dial his home number. His wife picks up on the first ring. I wait impatiently for him to come on the line.

"I think we're about to identify the second vic," I say. "I need to know if you recall a brown mole on her left ankle."

The doc sighs. "I recall a large mole on the inside of her left ankle and made a notation of it."

I close my eyes briefly and tell him about the Augspurgers.

"God help them," he says.

"They're going to want to see her, take her home. Have you finished the autopsy?"

"I'm typing my report now."

"Can you meet me?"

"Sure. Give me half an hour."

I hit End and stand there for a moment looking down at my phone. I know it's selfish, but I don't want to go back in that classroom and break the news to the Ezra and Bonnie Augspurger.

"It's her," I say to Glock.

"Damn." He looks around, then back at me. "You want me to go back in with you?"

I shake my head. "Head out to the Augspurger place. See what you can find. Pickles and Skid should already be there."

"What about the suit?"

I almost smile when I realize he's referring to Tomasetti. "I'll take him with me."

"Keep an eye on him. That fucker's got shifty eyes."

"I will." Taking a deep breath, I start toward the classroom.

CHAPTER 18

I enter the classroom to find the Augspurgers huddled at the back window, staring at me as if I hold the secret of the universe in the palm of my hand. Tomasetti stands a few feet away, looking expectantly at me.

Ezra's eyes beseech mine as I cross to them. As if forgetting her place, Bonnie pushes past him. Within the pale depths of her gaze, I see a tangle of desperation and hope laced with the kind of fear a mother should never have to feel.

"The body of a young woman was discovered this morning." I pass the faxed photo to Ezra. "She has a mole on her left ankle."

His hand shakes as he reaches for it. Bonnie puts her hand over her mouth, but it doesn't smother the sound of anguish. Ezra stares at the photo, the paper rattling violently.

Murder is rare in the Amish community. Most often, death is from natural causes. It's viewed as a final surrender to God and is received gracefully. Grief is a quiet and private event. The sound that erupts from Ezra Augspurger's mouth reminds me that not all Amish are stoic. They are human beings, and the loss of a child begets unbearable pain. His cry of outrage and grief goes through me like cold steel. Bowing his head, he presses the photo to his cheek.

"I'm sorry." I touch Ezra's shoulder, but he doesn't acknowledge me.

Bonnie sinks into a chair and puts her face in her hands. Feeling my own emotions winding up, I turn away to find Tomasetti staring intently at me. His expression is grave, but he's not moved the way I am. But then he doesn't know the kindness that was inside Ellen Augspurger's heart. He doesn't know this community. He doesn't know the innate goodness of the Amish the way I do.

I think of the trip this grieving couple must make to the morgue. I think of the questions they'll ask and how unbearably painful it will be to answer. They'll want to take Ellen's body home, dress her in white and place her in a simple hardwood coffin. I'll inform them beforehand that an autopsy was performed. The procedure clashes with basic Amish values, but they won't complain.

"How did she pass?" Ezra's ravaged eyes bore into mine.

"She was murdered," I reply.

Bonnie gasps. *"Mein gott."*

Ezra stares at me as if I'm lying. I've known him most of my life. He's a decent, hardworking man who's had more than his share of hardship. But I know he's got a temper.

"I do not accept that." Though the room is cold, I see sweat on his forehead. Red blotches climbing up his neck.

"I'm sorry," I offer.

He bows his head, places his fingers against his forehead and presses, as if he's trying to shove his nails beneath the skin.

"Ezra, who is the bishop of your district?" I ask.

"David Troyers."

A church district is made up of about twenty to thirty families. A bishop, two or three preachers and a deacon share leadership roles within each district. I know David Troyers. And I know he's one of the few Amish who has a telephone.

Ezra raises his head and struggles to compose himself. "We want to bring Ellen home."

"Of course," I say in Pennsylvania Dutch.

"Where is she?"

"The hospital in Millersburg."

"I want to bring her home." A sob escapes him even as he struggles to square shoulders bowed beneath the weight of unbearable grief.

"Let me drive you to the hospital," I say.

"No."

"Ezra, Millersburg is nearly ten miles away."

"No!" He shakes his head. "Bonnie and I will take the buggy."

He is so immersed in grief, I doubt he realizes the round-trip will take hours. I look at Bonnie for help; she stares back. Unshed tears glitter in her eyes. She has her hand over her mouth as if trying to hold in the screams that echo inside her.

"It's twenty degrees outside," I say. "These are special circumstances, Ezra. Please, let me drive you."

Bonnie rises abruptly. "We will go with you."

"No!" The Amish man slams his fist down on the desktop. "We take the buggy!"

I've had plenty of bad days in my life. For the most part, I take the bad with the good and hold close the belief that in the end it all balances out. It's going to take a lot of good days to zero out today.

I couldn't convince Ezra to let me drive them to the morgue. So I did the only thing I could and followed them in the Explorer. The trip and the identification of Ellen's body took over three hours. It's after midnight now. I'm tired and discouraged and so cold I can't imagine ever being warm again. I should go home and try to get some sleep, but my mind is wound tight. I have no desire to waste precious hours tossing and turning.

"Notifying next of kin is always the worst."

I glance at Tomasetti in the passenger seat and frown.

He doesn't notice. "When you see some dipshit gangbanger lying in pieces on a gurney, you think the world's a better place. But something like this . . ."

"That's cynical," I reply.

"Yeah, but it's the truth."

"I don't share your view."

"You just haven't been a cop long enough."

Tomasetti has been my shadow tonight. A quiet presence I resent more than I should. The irony that I will be the one to bring him up to speed on the case doesn't escape me.

"You going to follow them home, too?" he asks.

"The roads are bad. I don't want them out on a night like this."

He turns his attention back to the window where winter-dead cornfields crowd the road. The night is clear and still, with the temperature falling to near zero. The stars play peekaboo as high clouds skid across the sky.

I called David Troyers, the Augspurgers' bishop, on the way to the hospital. One of the things I loved about being Amish was the support families receive from their neighbors, especially when tragedy strikes. It comforts me knowing there will be a family waiting for Ezra and Bonnie when they arrive home. Tomorrow, that family will assume the farm and household chores, feeding the livestock and cooking meals and helping to plan the funeral.

Ezra's horse maintains a steady clip all the way to the Augspurger farm. When the buggy turns into the long lane, I flash my headlights in farewell and head toward town.

"Where to now, Chief?"

I glance over to see Tomasetti looking at me with those dark, intense eyes. Eyes that are difficult to meet, but once you do it's even more difficult to look away. I see damage in those eyes, and I wonder briefly about its source. I wonder if mine reveal the same thing. It's tough to be a cop without sustaining some kind of damage.

I'm certain I've never met him before tonight, but his face is familiar. "I can take you to your motel or back to the station," I say. "Your choice."

"The station's fine."

"You a night bird?"

His mouth twists. "Insomniac."

I'm used to dealing with all sorts of people, but Tomasetti makes me vaguely uneasy. I want to think I'm immune to his weird thousand-yard stare, but I'm not. Not tonight, when my secrets are in the forefront of my mind.

"So who called you in?" I ask after a moment.

He answers with the nonchalance of a man discussing the weather on a sunny day. "Norm Johnston. The mayor. And the woman with the big mouth."

Janine Fourman. I nearly smile at his apt description. "The Three Musketeers."

"They gunning for your job?"

"They want the murders to go away."

"Is that why they left you out of the loop?"

I cut him a hard look. "They left me out of the loop because they don't want these murders scaring away the tourists."

"I'm glad you cleared that up for me," he says.

The sarcastic sneer in his voice pisses me off. I've known a lot of cops like him over the years. Veterans, usually. Older. They have experience, but they lack the humanity that would otherwise define them as good cops. The more they see, the less they feel. The less they care. They become cynical and bitter and apathetic. They give all cops a bad rap.

"So how long have you been chief?" he asks.

"Two years."

"You a cop before that?"

I resist the urge to roll my eyes. "I didn't work at the Cut and Curl, if that's what you're asking."

One side of his mouth curves up. "This your first murder?"

"Norm Johnston tell you that, too?"

"He said you were inexperienced."

His candor surprises me. "What else did he tell you?"

He looks amused. "Are you pumping me for information?"

"Just the truth."

"Telling the truth usually gets me into trouble."

"I get the feeling you don't mind."

He looks out the window for a moment, then turns his attention back to me. "So what's your experience?"

I lift a shoulder, let it drop. "I was a cop in Columbus. Six years in patrol. Two as a detective. Homicide."

Even in the dim light from the dash, I see his brow arch. "They didn't mention that."

"Didn't think so. What about you?"

"Narcotics, mostly."

"Detective?"

"Yeah."

"How long?"

"Since dinosaurs roamed the earth. In case you haven't noticed, I'm one of them." He smiles.

<footer>164

I resist the urge to smile back. "You look familiar."

"I was wondering when you were going to get around to that."

I'm not sure what he means. "Get around to what?"

"You're not up on your pseudo-celebrities, are you?"

A vague memory tickles the back of my brain. A newspaper or television story out of Cleveland or Toledo about the murder of a cop's family. Home invasion. A decorated cop going rogue . . .

I can't hide my surprise when I look at Tomasetti.

"Yeah, I'm him." He looks amused. "Lucky you, huh?"

Unable to meet his penetrating stare, I look back at the road. "Toledo? Last year?"

"Cleveland," he corrects. "Two years ago."

"I followed the story some."

"You and half the state."

I want to ask him if he did it, but I don't. The general consensus among law enforcement was that John Tomasetti had snapped. He'd gone after the man responsible for the murder of his family and exacted revenge. No one could prove it, but that hadn't kept the DA from putting him in front of a grand jury.

"How did you end up at BCI?" I ask after a moment.

"The commander wanted me gone, gave me a recommendation. The saps at BCI didn't know what they were getting." He gives me a dry smile. "Do you want to get drunk and talk about it?"

"You need to drink to talk?"

"Most of the time."

We drive for a while in silence, and then he asks, "It's not easy to pass that detective's exam, Chief. What made you give up all that glory for small town police work?"

I shrug, feeling self conscious. "I was born here."

He nods as if he understands. "How is it that you're fluent in German?"

He's referring to my conversation with the Augspurgers. "It's Pennsylvania Dutch."

"Obscure language."

"The Amish speak it."

"Plenty of Amish in this part of Ohio." I sense him studying me, wondering.

"There are more Amish in Ohio than Pennsylvania now." A statistic he probably doesn't give a good damn about.

"They offer Pennsylvania Dutch at the community college here or what?"

"My parents taught me."

I see his mind combing through that. He's not sure what to make of it. What to make of me. Had the circumstances been different, I might have enjoyed the moment. He doesn't want to ask. But a man like John Tomasetti doesn't necessarily give a damn about political correctness. He earns points with me when he finally asks, "You Amish, or what?"

"Was."

"Huh. Johnston mentioned you were a pacifist."

"In case you're not reading between the lines, Johnston is full of shit."

"I got that." He whistles. "A gun-toting, cursing, former Amish *female* chief of police. I'll be damned."

The parking spaces in front of the police station are blissfully vacant when we arrive. I walk in to see Mona reclined at the dispatch station, her high-heeled boots propped on the desk. She's holding a half-eaten apple in one hand, a forensic science book with a *CSI*-esque cover in the other. She's tapping her foot to a Pink Floyd remix she has turned up too loud. She doesn't hear us come in.

"I guess working graveyard has its benefits," I say.

She fumbles the book and drops the apple. Her boots slide off the desk. "Hey Chief." To my surprise, she blushes. "Damn book's giving me the heebie-jeebies." She whips out the messages. "Phone was ringing off the hook until about twenty minutes ago."

"I guess people gotta sleep."

"Thank God. The crazies are starting to call. Psychic from Omaha claims she was a victim of the Slaughterhouse Killer in her first life. Oh, and some whack job from Columbus called to tell you Amish women shouldn't be police officers." She crumples the pink slip and shoots it into the wastebasket. "I set him straight."

"Thanks." I take the messages. "Will you do me a favor and make some coffee?"

"I could use some myself." Her eyes fall on Tomasetti—and stick. I know the look of feminine interest when I see it, and I'm surprised. He doesn't exactly fall into the nice-looking category. His eyes are too intense. His mouth is thin and snarlish. His nose is slightly hooked. He's probably not much over forty, but his face sports the lines of a man who's lived hard and long.

What is it about young women being attracted to men old enough to be their fathers? "Mona, this is John Tomasetti with BCI out of Columbus."

He extends his hand to Mona. "Nice to meet you."

Her smile widens as they shake. "We're glad to have you on board."

Rolling my eyes, I start toward my office. Once inside, I shed my coat and flip on my computer. While it boots, I dial Glock. "Anything on Lapp?" I ask.

"Nada. Either he keeps his nose clean or he's dead."

"Keep digging." I reassure myself it was an offhand comment; Glock can't possibly know Lapp is dead. *If* he's dead. "Did you guys find anything at the Augspurger farm?"

"There were some old tracks, but they were almost totally obscured by new snowfall and drifting."

"Were you able to get impressions?"

"No impressions. No prints. Either he's lucky or he knows all of our tricks." He pauses. "We canvassed, but no one saw anything. This guy's a fuckin' ghost."

Tomasetti enters my office holding two cups. I motion for him to sit. "Thanks for the update, Glock. Get some rest."

"You, too."

I disconnect. Tomasetti sets one of the cups in front of me and takes the chair adjacent to my desk. "If you're trying to win over my undying admiration with coffee," I say, "you just scored a few points."

"I could make another pot."

I give him a passable smile.

He doesn't smile back. "They turn up anything?"

I recap my conversation with Glock.

He rubs his hands together like a man preparing for a meal. "You have time to show me what you have so far?"

"It's not much." I hand him the old Slaughterhouse Killer file. "This is the file from the early nineties."

Pulling reading glasses from his breast pocket, he opens the folder. While he reads, I rise and cross to the fax machine. Sure enough, Doc Coblentz has sent the preliminary autopsy report for Ellen Augspurger. I scan the particulars as I take it to the copy room.

Death is attributed to a deep incised wound of the neck severing the carotid artery. Cause of death: exsanguination.

No photos were faxed, but I don't need them. I see it all when I close my eyes. Her partially decomposed body hanging from the ceiling beam at the Huffman farm. The grief-ravaged faces of Bonnie and Ezra Augspurger as they try to absorb news of their daughter's death.

I think of my own secrets and what might have happened all those years ago had I not picked up my father's shotgun and defended myself. I could have been Ellen Augspurger or Amanda Horner, my butchered body reduced to a cold piece of evidence. Staring down at the report, I think about Daniel Lapp and I wish to God I'd shot him in the head instead of the torso.

Tomasetti looks up from the file when I return to my desk. He's scribbled notes on a legal pad. "What's your theory on this?" he asks.

"It's either the killer from before, or we have a copycat on our hands."

"This is no copycat."

"How can you be so sure?"

"The Roman numerals carved into the torsos of the vics was never made public." He looks at me over the tops of his glasses, his expression telling me that should be obvious.

"The information could have leaked."

"If that was the case, you would have seen it in the news."

He's right, but I say nothing.

He shakes his head. "The similarities are too striking. This is the same guy."

"How do you explain the hiatus?"

"He changed locales. Look at the gap in numbering." He studies me with those intense eyes. "Have you plugged any of this into VICAP?"

VICAP is the acronym for the FBI's Violent Criminal Apprehension Program. It's a database that matches major crimes by detecting similar signature aspects and patterns of modus operandi. We both know I should have already done this. Tomasetti's wondering why I didn't.

"I was hoping you could help with that," I say.

"I'll get this signature plugged in right away."

"I've got queries going in OHLEG as well," I add.

"While we're on the subject of resources, is there a specific reason why you didn't contact the FBI?"

There's no recrimination in the question. Just simple curiosity. As if I might have a good reason for not doing what I should have. Of course, I don't. He's backed me into a corner I can't get out of unless I lie. "Some of the town council members were concerned about tourism. They didn't want the national media involved."

"You don't seem like the kind of cop to buckle under that kind of pressure."

Because I don't want to dig this particular hole any deeper, I look down at the file. But my heart is pounding. I feel his eyes on me and I know he's making judgments. About my competence. About me. "You got a theory on the hiatus?" I ask after a moment.

"The numbering suggests there are other victims we don't know about." He taps the folder with his finger. "This guy isn't fucking with the cops, and I don't believe he stopped killing. He doesn't have that kind of control. I think for the last sixteen years, he's killed somewhere else. Unless he was somehow incapacitated. Jail time. Hospitalization."

I glance at the papers in front of him. He's already filled two pages of the pad. His handwriting is slanted and small. "Have you begun a profile?"

"Preliminary." He recites from memory. "He's a white male between the age of thirty-five and fifty. He works full-time, but his schedule is flexible. He's considered successful and is probably in a position of authority. He's controlling and impulsive, but he controls his impulses to a degree. He's married, but his relationship is troubled. May have teenaged or grown children. He's considered a good father. His wife may or may not know he's got a dark side. If she does, she doesn't know the degree. She doesn't know he kills. No one suspects him. He may be impotent and may take medication. Violence excites him a lot more than sex. He derives sexual gratification from inflicting pain.

Torture is the overriding source of his compulsion. Killing is a secondary end result. It's those final moments of life that really get him off.

"As a kid, he may have been cruel to animals, or he may have gotten into trouble for killing them. As a young man or teen, he may have had some psychological problems. Those problems may or may not have been diagnosed. He has an addictive personality, but he's good at hiding his compulsion. He's a classic psychopath. He's egocentric. He probably has a large collection of pornography, particularly S&M-type stuff. He's probably into bondage and may have movies or video on his computer. He spends a great deal of time fantasizing before he actually commits the act. He enjoys the planning stage. Once he's done the murder, he spends a good bit of time reliving it."

If we were dealing with any other case, I might agree with the profile. I might even be impressed. But none of his profile points describe Daniel Lapp.

Tomasetti hands me the pages. "It's all preliminary and subject to change."

Nodding, I turn my attention to the profile. A chill passes through me as I read the particulars.

- Subject is physically strong. He may have a job that requires strength or he may work out regularly.

- He has a controlling personality and may act out in anger when things are out of his control.

- He wants to be seen as attractive. He is meticulous with regard to his appearance and makes an effort to appeal to women.

- He presents himself as charming and nonthreatening.

- He is comfortable around women. He interacts with women and was probably raised with females in his home e.g. mother and/or sisters.

- He is in a stable relationship, but the relationship is troubled. He is angry about the failing relationship, but feels as if saving it is out of his control.

• He can be spontaneous if an opportunity presents itself, but prefers planning.

• He is a newshound and follows the case closely. He enjoys media attention.

Once again I find myself thinking of Daniel Lapp. "I don't think we should limit the investigation by excluding possible suspects who don't meet this criteria."

"Usually this is where people tell me I'm pretty good at what I do."

"I didn't mean to offend you." I hand him the sheet.

"You didn't." He takes the paper. "What don't you agree with?"

"I just don't think we should exclude anyone this early in the game."

He gives me an odd look, as if he's trying to figure me out. I avoid his eyes by looking down at my notes. "This guy is obviously in a period of escalation," I say. "Do you think there was some kind of trigger?"

"I would guess something difficult for him has happened in his personal life. Possibly involving a woman. A wife or girlfriend. He doesn't deal well with rejection and could be retaliating."

"He hates women?"

"He hates them, but he desires them. In deviant ways."

"How does he choose his victims?" I say.

"A woman catches his eye. He spends some time watching her. A few days. A week, maybe. He learns her routine. He figures out when she's vulnerable. When he can get to her."

"I've limited the questioning of witnesses to the hours before the victims' disappearances. If this guy stalked his victims for *days* before abducting them, we would be better served talking to everyone who had contact with Amanda Horner and Ellen Augspurger four or five days before they disappeared."

"I agree."

"Does a particular kind of woman appeal to him?"

"Both victims have been young, in their early to midtwenties. Attractive. Petite."

"Applies to a lot of women in this town."

He nods. "Keep going."

"Where does he kill?" I'm thinking aloud now. Random thoughts. Questions. Brainstorming.

"He needs privacy," he says. "A place where no one can hear him."

"Basement."

"Deserted home or building."

"Soundproof room."

He throws up a roadblock. "If he has a wife, she would know about the room or basement."

"Unless he has property somewhere else. Off-premises. Rental property." I think about that a moment. "Why do you think the wife isn't involved?"

"If she has a dependent personality and he controls her, she could be," he concedes. "But it's not likely. These murders are too brutal. This guy doesn't hold back. He's alone. Uninhibited. Living out his fantasy in absolute privacy."

Silence falls. We look at each other. Tomasetti appears excited. A bloodhound that's caught a scent.

"Assignments," he says after a moment. "I need to know who's doing what. Your officers. Sheriff's office. So we don't waste manpower repeating ourselves."

I flip through my notebook, locate the page where I've jotted assignments. "I'll have Mona type this for you."

"I'll finish this profile tonight."

I nod. "Hand it off to Mona in the morning, and she'll disperse it."

He picks up the Slaughterhouse Killer file. "Can I take this?"

"As long as you bring it back in the morning." I don't ask him when he plans to sleep.

He rises. I catch a glimpse of a pistol in a shoulder holster when he stretches. A Sig Sauer semiauto. It strikes me that, for a cop, he knows how to dress. Pinpoint oxford shirt. Expensive tie. Nicely cut suit. Details I shouldn't be noticing.

"See you in the morning." He starts toward the door.

I watch him disappear down the hall. We didn't accomplish much, but the profile is a start. I think I'll be able to work with him. He'll be an asset to the team. I hope it's enough.

I look out the darkened window at the deserted street beyond where snow sparkles beneath the streetlights. I think about the killer and wonder if his dark hunger torments him tonight. I wonder if he's out there, looking for his next victim. I wonder if he's already picked her out.

CHAPTER 19

The Willowdell Motel was a dump, but then John hadn't expected much.
The management made an attempt to capture the quaint atmosphere of an
Amish tourist shop, but only achieved Midwestern tacky. Second-rate carpet.
Ugly bedspread. Peeling wallpaper in the bathroom. A heater that blew tepid
air smelling of cigarette smoke and mildew. But the place was clean; a bed
and a shower were all he needed. The TV worked, so he tuned it to the Fox
News Channel and broke the seal on the bottle of Chivas.

He poured three fingers into a plastic glass and chugged half while his laptop booted. It was too late to call Harry Graves, his contact at CASMIRC, the
FBI's Child Abduction and Serial Murder Investigative Resources Center, so
he drafted an e-mail instead and made a mental note to touch base with him
first thing in the morning. He poured a second glass of Chivas as he navigated
the FBI's Web site. VICAP wasn't web-based, but he could access the forty-
six page questionnaire online. Finding a signature match was a long shot, but
sometimes long shots paid off. If a similar crime had occurred anywhere in the
United States—and had been entered into VICAP—they might catch a break.

It took him an hour to fill out the form. Once the inquiry was sent, he
opened the Slaughterhouse Killer file and began to read. He scribbled notes
and tried to lose himself in his work, something that used to come with the
ease of breathing. No more. Some days there was no escape from the dark
places his mind chose to dwell.

John didn't take in the details of the murders with the keen and unbiased
eye of the cop he'd once been, but with the abject horror of a man intimately

acquainted with violent death. His past wasn't the only thing on his mind to-night. More than once he found his thoughts straying to Kate Burkholder. He'd worked with a lot of cops over the years. A female chief of police was rare, especially in a small town. An Amish cop was unheard of. Maybe that was why he found her so damn interesting.

She was low-key—a trait he'd learned to appreciate when it came to women cops. She was attractive in a girl-next-door kind of way. Dark brown hair cut short. Eyes the color of a mink coat. A pale complexion that made for a striking contrast. An athletic build. A nice mouth. John didn't have anything against female cops, but he'd known enough of them over the years to know that, like their male counterparts, most were bad relationship material. Not that he was in the market. He was as fucked up as a man could be and still be walking around. From all appearances, Kate was too smart to get tangled up with a head case.

He'd just shut down the laptop when the phone rang. He caught it on the second ring with a rough, "Yeah."

"Agent Tomasetti?"

Surprise rolled through him when he recognized the mayor's voice. "What can I do for you?"

"I'm sorry to be calling so late. Did I wake you?"

"No."

"Good. Good." He cleared his throat. "There's been a development I wanted to discuss."

"I'm listening."

"I had a very . . . disturbing meeting with David Troyers this evening. He's the elder Amish bishop."

John wondered what the hell this had to do with him. "Go on."

"Apparently, someone left an anonymous note on the bishop's door."

"What kind of note?"

"Well, it's about Chief Burkholder. And it's quite troubling." Paper rattled on the other end of the line. "I have it right here. It says: 'Chief Katie Burkholder knows who the murderer is.' "

John let the words run through his head a couple of times. "That certainly qualifies as troubling. What do you want me to do about it?"

"I'm not sure. I thought I should tell someone in law enforcement." He paused. "Why would someone send a note like this?"

"Maybe it's a hoax."

"Maybe." The mayor paused. "I was wondering if you could look into it. You know, anonymously."

Tomasetti considered that, felt his cop's curiosity stir. "I'm not exactly on her list of favorite people. She's not going to talk to me."

"Perhaps you could just . . . observe, make an assessment over the next few days."

"Have you discussed the note with anyone else?"

"No."

"Keep it that way. I'll see what I can do." John glanced at the clock. After two A.M. Too late to do anything tonight. "How many people have handled the note?"

"Bishop Troyer. Me."

"Put it in a brown paper bag and seal it. I'll check it for prints."

"I'll get it to you first thing tomorrow."

They said their good-byes and John hung up, troubled by this new development. The case was complicated enough without the cops keeping secrets. Who would send a note like that and why? Did Burkholder know more about the case than she was letting on? Or had some idiot decided it might be fun to play head games with the cops?

What bothered Tomasetti about the latter scenario was that the note had been sent to an Amish bishop. The Amish weren't known for their practical jokes. Painters Mill was a small town where everyone knew everyone else. Was it possible Kate Burkholder knew the killer? Was he Amish? Was she protecting him because of that? John couldn't see her risking lives to protect some psycho. But he knew from experience some loyalties supplanted even the most fundamental ethics.

That was when he realized that wasn't the only thing bothering him about Kate Burkholder. Faced with a difficult, high-profile case, she should have turned to outside resources right off the bat. Initially, he'd assumed she didn't want some outsider encroaching on her case. But after meeting her, he'd realized she wasn't the territorial type. Why hadn't she asked for help? The question niggled at him like a migraine digging into his brain.

The mayor had dropped this in his lap. John figured he didn't have a choice but to look into it. This case was his last chance. He didn't need some cop with loyalty issues sabotaging it. If Burkholder was keeping secrets, he was going to make damn sure he knew what they were.

The trill of a phone jolts me awake. I bolt upright and an ice pick jab of pain shoots down my neck. For a second, I don't know where I am, then realize I'm in my office at the police station. I fell asleep at my desk. . . .

The phone rings again and I snatch it up. "Yeah."

"Sorry to wake you, Chief."

Mona. She must have found me sleeping and turned off the light . . .

"I just took a 911. Driver says there's a loose cow out on Dog Leg Road, out by the covered bridge."

Groaning inwardly, I look at the wall clock. Nearly three A.M. "Tell T.J. to get out there, will you?"

"He's over at Nell Ramsom's place with a 10-14." She pauses. "We've had six prowler calls tonight."

People are nervous about the murders, I realize. Wishing I'd gone home for a few hours of decent sleep, I rise and shrug into my parka. I've been lenient with Isaac Stutz, letting him off with warnings. With my resources stretched to the limit, I resolve to cite him this time. I don't have time to chase cows. Dreading the cold, I head for the door.

In the Explorer, I turn the heat on high and drive through town well over the speed limit. Around me Painters Mill sleeps. Tonight, I sense it is the uneasy slumber of a child prone to nightmares.

Dog Leg Road is a narrow road lined by a forest on the north side and a plowed field to the south. The hundred-year-old covered bridge that spans Painters Creek is a tourist attraction during the summer. I pass through the wood structure doing fifty.

On the other side of the bridge, I spot the cow in the bar ditch, a Jersey munching on the tall grass poking up through the snow. Grabbing my Mag-

Lite, I shine the beam along the fence until I find the place where the stupid beast pushed through.

Hitting my emergency lights, I hail Mona. "I'm 10-23."

"Roger that, Chief. You find the cows?"

"One cow." I run the beam along the fence. A dozen yards beyond is the spot where Amanda Horner's body was found. I can see a few scraps of the crime scene tape fluttering in the breeze. "I'm going to put the damn thing back in the pasture and call it a night."

"10-4."

The blast of cold takes my breath away as I disembark. A few feet away, the cow rolls her eyes at me and pulls another tuft of yellow grass into her mouth. I grew up around cattle, but I'm not a fan. They're brutish and contrary for the most part. I spent many a cold winter morning pulling teats, and I got kicked more times than I like to recall.

Opening the trunk, I pull out a length of rope and approach the cow. "Come on, you cud-chewing T-bone."

The animal turns away, but I cut her off. She grabs a few more dry blades of grass, and I make my move, tossing the rope from a yard and a half away. The loop sails over her head and settles around her neck. The cow can do one of two things at this point. She can drag me around and make a fool of me or she can cooperate and let me lead her back into the pasture. Much to my relief, she acquiesces when I tug the rope.

I tromp through a snowdrift and reach the fence. Peeling back the wire where the cow escaped, I lead her through and release her. I'm in the process of repairing the fence when a flash of light in my peripheral vision snags my attention. At first I think Isaac Stutz saw my light and is coming over to help. Then I realize the flicker of light originated near the crime scene, not the Stutz house. What the hell is someone doing out here in the middle of the night?

I jog to the Explorer, cut the lights and hail Mona. "I've got a 10-88. Send T.J. Expedite. No lights or siren."

"Roger that. Be careful, Chief, will you?"

"I always am." Grabbing my Mag-Lite, I quietly close the car door. Keeping low, I traverse the ditch and scale the fence. The darkness thickens when I enter the woods, but I don't turn on the flashlight. My eyes have adjusted to the darkness. My feet are silent on the snow as I wend through trees and over deadfall. Overhead, a milky half moon casts just enough light for me to see my shadow. Cold stings my face. The steel Mag-Lite makes my fingers ache with cold. But those minor discomforts are nullified by my need to know who's out there and why.

Twenty yards from the crime scene, I stop and listen. Around me, the wind sighs. In the distance, a dog barks his outrage at being left outside on such a cold night. The snap of a breaking branch sounds behind me. Startled, I spin. I see movement within the trees and flip on the Mag-Lite. I set my other hand on my sidearm and thumb off the leather catch.

"Stop!" I call out. "Police. Stop right there!"

Holding the flashlight steady, I break into a run. My quickened breaths puff out in front of me as my adrenaline surges. I glance down, see footprints in the snow and follow them. Trees whiz by. I'm almost to the crime scene. The cornfield is to my left; I hear the hiss of dry stalks. The beam of my flashlight illuminates movement ahead. The silhouette of a man. It's gone in an instant, but for the first time I know without a doubt I'm not pursuing a deer.

"Stop now! Police!" I rush forward, my revolver leading the way. "Halt!"

I have a good sense of direction, and I'm well aware that I'm being led away from my vehicle. I don't feel threatened; it doesn't even cross my mind to be scared. Tonight, I'm the predator.

I run semiblind through the darkness, my every sense focused on my quarry. I hear his heavy footsteps crashing through brush and deep snow. He has ten yards on me, but I'm gaining. I'm faster than he is, and he knows it.

"Halt! Police!" I fire a warning shot into the ground. He doesn't stop. If I wasn't afraid of shooting some brainless teenager, I'd plug him in the back.

The ground breaks away. I lose sight of him as I plunge down a creek bank. My boots slide as I cross the span of ice and muscle my way up the other side. I'm almost to the top when a heavy body plows into me. The impact knocks me off me feet. I land hard on my side and roll. I see the black silhouette of a man. Something in his hand. I bring up my gun. I hear the *whoosh* of air, then something slams into my wrist. Electric pain streaks up my arm. The .38 flies from my hand. I get my knees under me, swing the heavy Mag-Lite as hard as I can, feel the steel make contact.

"Fucking bitch!"

I throw myself at my fallen weapon. Hands in the snow. Fingers curling around steel. I twist. Bring up the gun. Decide on a body shot when the blow comes out of nowhere, crown of my head, hard enough to daze. A second blow lands above my right ear. A loud *crunch!* inside my head. My vision dims. The next thing I know I'm lying on my side. Snow cold against my face.

I don't know if I've lost seconds or minutes. Afraid my attacker might want to go another round, I raise my head, look around. But the son of a bitch is gone.

"Chief! *Chief!*"

I barely hear T.J.'s voice over the ringing in my right ear. An involuntary groan escapes me as I get to my hands and knees.

He kneels beside me. "What happened?"

"Some crazy shit ambushed me."

He jumps to his feet and pulls his sidearm. "How long ago? Did you get a look at him?"

"A minute ago." I get to my feet, hoping my legs hold. "Male. Six feet. One ninety."

"Armed?"

"With a frickin' club."

Studying me a little too closely, T.J. hits his lapel mike. "Mona, I'm 10-23. We got a 10-88 out here on Dog Leg Road." He repeats my vague description of the assailant. "We need an ambulance."

"No ambulance," I cut in, loud enough for Mona to hear. "I'm fine. Tell her to call the sheriff's office and get a unit to the dirt road by the covered bridge. That's probably where the son of a bitch parked."

T.J. repeats my instructions and ends with, "We're going to look around."

I spot my Mag-Lite lying in the snow and pick it up. "Did you see anything when you walked up?" I ask.

"Just you. Lying in the snow." He grimaces. "Jeez, Chief, this is the second time in two days you've gotten clobbered."

"I don't think we need to keep a tally." I run the flashlight beam in a 360-degree circle.

"What are you looking for?"

SWORN TO SILENCE

"My gun. Tracks." I find my weapon lying in the snow a few feet away and pick it up.

"Look there." T.J. shines his beam on footprints.

"Let's go." We follow them for several yards where they form a T. "He must have parked on the dirt road and walked to the crime scene."

"Crime scene? You think it was some morbidly curious punk—" His eyes widen as realization dawns. "Do you think it's him? The killer?"

"I don't know." I squat for a closer look at the tracks. "He left us a nice tread."

"Size ten or eleven."

"Get Glock out here to get some impressions, will you?"

He hits his lapel mike and relays the request to Mona. I rise to my full height and run my flashlight beam along the tracks.

"Why would he return to the scene?" T.J. asks.

I scan the layers of shadows surrounding us. The forest is monochrome in the pale light of the moon. "I was just wondering the same thing."

CHAPTER 20

"Either he's reliving the kill, or he left something behind and was trying to retrieve it."

For a man who spent the night in a warm hotel room with a bed and shower, John Tomasetti looks more than a little rough around the edges. He wears creased black Dockers, a white button-down shirt and a paisley tie the color of dirty snow. But the conservative image ends with the clothes. His eyes are bloodshot beneath heavy brows. If he shaved at all, he didn't do a very good job. From where I sit I can see his beard is heavy and dark and makes a stark contrast to his pallid complexion. I wonder if he's coming down with something.

I'm probably looking a little rough around the edges myself this morning. I feel a new bruise blooming high on my forehead and hope it doesn't clash with the remnants of my black eye. I didn't make it home last night. Working on my second day without sleep, I'm feeling downright cranky.

T.J., Glock, one of Detrick's deputies and I spent three hours in the woods in subzero temperatures, searching for clues. The perp was long gone, but we found fresh snowmobile tracks. Glock was able to lift a few footwear impressions and one decent imprint from the snowmobile skis. If we're lucky, BCI will match it and give us the make and model of the snowmobile.

Exhaustion tugs at me as I stare down at the hastily typed incident report I threw together. My head pounds from the blows I sustained. My wrist is swollen where he hit me with the club. I can move it, but I'm worried because I'm not ambidextrous when it comes to handling my weapon.

"Chief?"

Tomasetti addressed me, but I have no earthly idea what he said. "You want to bring us up to speed on what you've got going?" he asks.

It's barely seven A.M. on Wednesday morning, but the gang's all here. Glock sits next to me, his fingers pecking at his laptop. Sheriff Detrick leans back in his chair with his arms crossed over his chest. Pickles stares at me as if he wants to help me speak. T.J. and Skid seem fascinated by their coffee mugs.

Quickly, I relay the details of the ambush. "We believe the perp was on a snowmobile. Glock took footwear and track impressions. They look promising."

"Lots of snowmobiles this time of year," Detrick points out.

"I thought it was worth a shot." I shrug. "We couriered everything to the lab and should hear back in a few days."

"I'll see if I can expedite that," Tomasetti offers.

"It's nearly full light," I say. "We need to get back out there and look around."

Detrick clears his throat. "I'll put together a party and get out there as soon as we finish up."

Tomasetti looks up from his notebook. "If this guy was reliving the kill or fantasizing about it, there's a possibility he left behind DNA."

"Semen?" I ask.

"It's all about sexual gratification for him."

"Kinda cold for that," Skid puts in. "Talk about shrinkage."

A few chuckles erupt, but end quickly.

"Speaking of, did we comb the Hoffman place for that kind of DNA?" I ask.

"I can get a CSU out there with a light," Tomasetti offers.

I nod and glance at Skid. "Did you hear back from DRC?"

"I got one interesting hit." He opens a manila folder. "Local guy by the name of Dwayne Starkey. Did fourteen years for sexual assault. Went in a few months after the last murder in 1993. Released nine months ago."

Interest flares inside me. "You got an address on him?"

"Rents a farmhouse off the highway." He recites the address.

"I went to school with Starkey," Glock puts in.

I look at him. "What do you think?"

"Could be. Got a streak of mean in him. He's a bully, a bigot and all-around fuckhead."

"You got details on the sexual assault?" Tomasetti asks.

Skid refers to the report. "Twelve-year-old girl. He was eighteen. Pled not guilty. Got twenty years. Early release for good behavior."

"Where?"

"Mansfield Correctional Institution." Skid lets out a laugh. "Get this: he works at the slaughterhouse."

"Bingo," Tomasetti says.

I rise so quickly, everyone looks at me. "I'm going to pay him a visit." I address Detrick. "You have enough men to search the woods around the crime scene?"

He nods, but doesn't look happy about being relegated to an old crime scene while I talk to our newest person of interest. "We'll canvass the surrounding farms, too."

I grab my coat off the back of my chair and nearly run into Tomasetti. "I'll go with you," he says.

He's the one person I don't want tagging along. I need some time with Glock to see if he was able to unearth anything on Daniel Lapp. "I've got it covered."

He stares at me, his expression inscrutable. "You don't like me much, do you?"

"Like has nothing to do with anything."

"Then it must be your aversion to accepting help from outside police agencies."

The urge to jump down his throat is strong, but there are too many people around. "Glock knows Starkey. I'm taking Glock."

"I profiled him. I know what we're looking for. If you're serious about stopping him, I suggest you start using me as a resource."

There's enough tension in the air to strangle a snake. I don't need to look around to know all eyes are on us. Personality conflicts during high-stress cases are expected, particularly when more than one agency is involved. But I don't want to be perceived as a cop who would jeopardize a case because of territoriality issues. I learned a long time ago the value of choosing my battles. This is a battle I'm probably better off not fighting.

"You drive," I say, and start toward the door.

Dwayne Starkey lives on a small farm surrounded by rolling hills and tall, winter-dead trees. At one time the house had been nice, but as Tomasetti drives down the lane I notice the peeling siding and sagging roof. An old blue pickup is parked behind the house.

"Looks like he's home," Tomasetti says.

"Keep an eye on the doors."

He parks the Tahoe a few yards behind the pickup, blocking the driveway should Starkey try to make a quick exit.

"Do you think we should get a warrant first?" I ask.

"Don't need a warrant to talk to someone."

"If I like him as a suspect, I'll want to search the place." I look past the house where a dilapidated barn lists like a ship trapped in arctic ice. "I don't want to screw this up. If he's our guy, he could be doing the murders here."

"If we like him, we'll get the warrant."

I glance at the back door in time to see the curtains part, then quickly fall back into place. "He spotted us."

"I'll take the front," Tomasetti says.

Cold assaults me when I exit the vehicle. The sidewalk isn't shoveled and my feet crunch through ankle-deep snow. In my peripheral vision, I see Tomasetti continue around to the front. I thumb the snap off my holster when I reach the back door. The top half of the door is glass. A crack runs through it and some-one repaired it with duct tape. Dirty blue curtains gape about an inch. Through the gap I see an old freezer and circa 1970s cabinets.

I rattle the glass with my knuckles. "Dwayne Starkey! This is Kate Burk-holder with the Painters Mill PD! Open up."

I wait thirty seconds and knock again, harder. "Come on, Dwayne, I know you're in there. Open the door!"

The door swings open. I catch a whiff of something vaguely unpleasant and find myself facing a small man with greasy hair, a receding hairline and a mustache the color of spicy mustard.

"Dwayne Starkey?"

"Who wants to know?"

"Kate Burkholder. Painters Mill PD." Keeping my right hand close to my weapon, I pull out my badge with my left and hold it up. He stares at it long enough to make me wonder if he knows how to read. "I need to ask you some questions."

"This about those kilt women?"

"What makes you think that?"

A hard laugh rattles from a cigarette-rough throat. "I know how you cops think. Somethin' bad goes down and you want to hang it on the first con you see."

"I just want to ask you a few questions."

He looks undecided. "You got a warrant?"

"I can have one in ten minutes if you want to do it that way. It'd be a lot faster if you just open the door and talk to me."

"I probably shouldn't without my lawyer."

A familiar baritone voice comes from behind Starkey. "If you didn't do anything wrong, you don't need a lawyer."

I look past Starkey and see Tomasetti standing in the mudroom. I want to ask him what the hell he's doing in Starkey's house, but Starkey beats me to the punch.

"Who the fuck're you? What're you doin' in my house?"

"I'm the good cop, Dwayne. I suggest you stop being a shithead and co-operate with Chief Burkholder. Believe me, you don't want to piss her off."

Starkey looks at me. "How the fuck did he get in my house?"

I'm wondering the same thing, so I don't even try to answer. "Dwayne," I begin, "we just need a few minutes of your time."

Starkey steps back. He wears grungy jeans. A shirt with old sweat stains. He looks like he wants to run. I glance down at his feet and see dirty white socks. If he breaks for the door, he won't get far.

I push open the door and step into a mudroom that smells the way Starkey looks, an unpleasant fusion of cat shit, body odor and cigarette smoke.

Starkey looks from me to Tomasetti and back to me. "I know my rights so don't try any shit."

"You have the right to sit the fuck down." Taking the man by the scruff, Tomasetti muscles him into the kitchen and shoves him into a chair.

"Hey!" Starkey complains. "You can't do that."

"I just want to show you how much we appreciate your cooperation."

I step into the kitchen. The stench of rotting food and animal feces punches me like a fist. An obese cat watches me from atop a 1970s refrigerator. I watch my step when I cross to Starkey.

"You still work at the slaughterhouse, Dwayne?" I ask.

"I ain't missed a day since I started."

"What do you do there?"

"Look, I got a clean record there." He points at Tomasetti. "I don't want you cops fuckin' things up for me."

Tomasetti slaps his hand away. "Answer the question."

"I'm the sticker."

"What's a sticker?" I ask.

"I stick the steer in the neck after he's stunned."

"You cut its throat?"

"I guess you could put it that way."

"You like doing that?" Tomasetti asks.

"It pays the bills."

Something crunches beneath Tomasetti's shoe as he steps into the living room. "You gotta go to school for that?"

Starkey glares at him. "Fuck you."

"Dwayne," I snap. "Cut it out."

He looks at me as if I'm dense. "That guy's an asshole."

"I know." I'm aware of Tomasetti moving around the living room, but I never take my eyes off of Starkey. "Where were you Saturday night?"

"I don't remember." His attention is on Tomasetti, and I wonder if Starkey has something to hide.

For the first time anger stirs. Two women are dead and this filthy little man is doing his utmost to make our job as difficult as possible. Leaning over, I smack the side of his head with my open hand, forcing his attention to me.

"You can't hit me like that," he says.

"Then pay attention. Where were you were Saturday night?"

"I was here. Rebuilt the transmission on the El Camino."

"Was anyone with you?"

"No."

"Were you here all night?"

"Yeah."

"You ever been to the Brass Rail?"

"Everyone's been to the Rail, man."

"When's the last time you were there?"

"I dunno. A week ago." His brows knit. "A week ago Sunday."

"How well did you know Amanda Horner?"

"I don't know no Amanda Horner." He's starting to look nervous, like he's finally taking this seriously. "You guys can't pin no murder on me. I didn't do it."

"You raped a woman fourteen years ago."

"The little bitch lied, man."

A burst of anger goes through me. Before I even realize my intent, my hand shoots out and I slap him open-handed. "Watch your mouth."

He rubs his cheek. "That chick was a tease. Drunk. Fucked up on coke. She wanted it."

"She was twelve."

"I didn't know that! I swear. She looked like a grown-up woman. Tits out to fuckin' here." He makes a slashing sign a foot from his chest. "And she wadn't no virgin like she claimed."

Disgust ripples through me. My temper hammers at the door, but I don't let it out. "How well did you know Ellen Augspurger?"

"Don't know her neither."

"If I find out you're lying, I'll come down on you so hard you'll wish you were back in prison."

"I swear I don't know her. Either of them."

"You on probation?"

"What do you think?"

"You like porn?" Tomasetti breaks in.

Starkey cranks his head around. "What the hell kind of question is that?"

"Kiddie porn? You keep it in the house?"

"I don't do that shit."

"No, I'll bet you're an S&M kind of guy, aren't you?"

"This is bullshit. You can't talk to me that way."

"Dwayne," I cut in, "do you keep knives in the house?"

He blinks again, as if he's having a difficult time keeping up with our questions. "Everyone has knives."

"You hunt?"

He leans back in the chair, balancing himself on two legs. A laugh rattles from his throat. "Can't stand the sight of blood."

"You think that's funny?" I ask.

"Kinda, me being the sticker and all."

My molars grind. I lunge, slap my hands down on his shoulders, and shove hard. He tries to come forward in the chair to regain his balance, but he's not fast enough. The chair tips back and he lands hard on his back.

"You fuckin' cunt!" He snarls the word as he scrambles to his feet. "You can't—"

I set my hand on my baton. "One step and you're going back to Mansfield."

The words freeze him in place. But he's pissed. His face is the color of raw meat. A vein pulses at his left temple. He wants to hit me; I see it in his eyes. Part of me wishes he would try.

"Kate."

I barely hear John's voice over the drum of my heart. I know losing my temper is counterproductive. I tell myself I'm pushing Starkey because I want him rattled. The problem is that while Dwayne Starkey is a lowlife piece of scum, I don't think he's the man we're looking for.

I jolt when Tomasetti's hands come down on my shoulders. I know he can feel the tremors running through me. I don't look at him. "Easy, Chief," he says quietly, then steps up beside me and holds a computer disk out for Starkey to see. "Nice desktop you've got, Dwayne. Big-ass monitor. I'll bet the graphics are killer. How much memory you got in that thing?"

"What're you doing in my bedroom, man?" Starkey whines like a schoolboy who's just been told he's going to be paddled. "He's not allowed to look through my shit."

I shrug, but I want to punch Tomasetti. One badly behaved cop is enough.

"It was in plain sight." Tomasetti looks up from the disk. "*Delilah's Double Date*. Huh. I think I missed that one."

"Ain't no law against X-rated movies," Starkey says.

"That depends on how old the stars are." I look at the disk. "Delilah looks kind of young."

"Just a kid," Tomasetti agrees.

Starkey jabs a finger at the disk. I see grime beneath his nails. "I bought that good and legal."

"What else do you have on your computer?" I ask.

"I ain't got nothin' I shouldn't have. I'm fuckin' rehabilitated."

Tomasetti shakes his head. "We just want to know about the women."

"Don't know those kilt women, man."

I jab my finger in his face. "Put your coat on."

Starkey's eyes go wide. "You can't take me to jail! I ain't done nothin'!"

"You're going to show us your barn, Dwayne," Tomasetti snaps. "Put on your coat or I'll drag you out there without it."

The barn is a dilapidated structure one windy day away from becoming a pile of rubble. Starkey takes Tomasetti and me down the unshoveled sidewalk. I notice footprints in the snow and I wonder why he goes to the barn when he doesn't own livestock.

I get my answer when he slides open the door and we step inside. A yellow El Camino, its paint as glossy as the day it was driven off the showroom floor, sits on cinder blocks with its hood open. Four aluminum wheels lean against a support beam. Beyond, a lawn chair squats next to a rusty fifty-gallon drum. From atop the drum, a radio blasts an old Eagles song. An aluminum pie tin overflows with cigarette butts.

"Nice place," Tomasetti says.

"This is where I was Saturday night." Starkey points at the El Camino. "That there's the car I been working on."

"You into junkers?" Tomasetti asks.

"That ain't no junker, man. She's a classic."

I move deeper into the barn, find myself looking for a snowmobile. I check the dirt floor for track marks, but find nothing. The air smells of moldy earth and motor oil. I spot a tarp in the corner, cross over and lift it. Dust motes flare and a circa 1965 John Deere tractor looms into view.

Disappointment presses into me. I wanted Starkey to be our man. He's a convicted rapist. A pedophile. A man with an appetite for porn and God only knows what else. But his height tells me he's not the man who attacked me in the woods last night. He doesn't fit the profile. He's not organized. Not highly intelligent. As desperately as I want to solve this case, my gut tells me he's not the killer.

I stride toward the men and point rudely at Starkey. "Don't leave town."

"I'm on parole. What do you think I'm going to do? Take a fuckin' Hawaiian vacation?"

I start toward the door. "Let's go."

I reach the Tahoe first and climb in. In the relative warmth of the cab, I suddenly feel as if I haven't slept for a week. A dull ache hammers at the base of my skull.

Tomasetti pulls out of the driveway and heads toward town. I stare out the window at the bleak landscape and try not to let the heat and low hum of the engine lull me to sleep.

"He's not our guy," Tomasetti says without looking at me.

"I know."

"Most serial killers have an above-average IQ."

"Rules out Starkey." I glare at Tomasetti. "Next time you feel like going Dirty Harry, do it on your own time, okay?"

He looks at me as if I offended him. "You're the one who hit him."

"I smacked him upside the head to get his attention."

"You kicked his chair out from under him." Shrugging, he returns his attention to the road. "I was impressed."

I catch myself grinning. Under different circumstances, I might have liked John Tomasetti. I may not agree with his tactics, but I know he had my back in there. Before I can analyze further, he makes a quick turn into the parking lot of McNarie's Bar. It's one of two drinking establishments in Painters Mill, a dive replete with red vinyl barstools, half a dozen booths and a jukebox from 1978 with all the original music selections.

"What the hell are you doing?" I demand.

"I could use a drink." He swings open the door and gets out.

"A *drink*?"

He slams the door.

I shove open my door and slide out. "It's ten o'clock in the morning. We have work to do."

Glancing at his watch, he keeps walking. His stride is so long, I have to jog to keep up. "Damnit, John, we need to get back to the station."

"This won't take long."

I stop beside a rusty Toyota pickup, and watch him disappear inside. I look around the deserted parking lot, too pissed to notice the cold or the clouds gathering in the west.

"Starkey was right," I mutter as I start toward the door. "He's an asshole."

CHAPTER 21

Corina Srinvassen couldn't wait to get on the ice. She'd fantasized about it all through her eighth-grade history class. Through literature class, health class with Mr. Trump where they learned about STDs, lunch with Lori Jones and study hall beneath the watchful eye of Mrs. Filloon aka Scary Bitch.

When the three-twenty bell rang, Cori hit the door running. She planned her routine on the long bus ride home. She was going to try the double twist today. She was alone, after all; no one to laugh at her if she fell on her butt. By four-fifteen she'd changed clothes and slipped out the door before her mother could stop her.

The sky hovered heavy and low as she trudged through the woods toward the pond. The ice would be rough today. That happened when snow fell, melted and refroze. There was no way around Mother Nature's quirks. One of these days Cori was going to have the money to go to an indoor skating rink in some fancy mall. The kind that was surrounded by swanky shops and the Zamboni kept the ice as smooth as glass.

Slinging her skates over her shoulder, Cori crested the hill and Miller's Pond loomed before her like a big tarnished nickel. She ran down the embankment toward the lacing stump and kicked off her boots. Cold snaked through all three pairs of socks, and by the time she'd laced up, she was shivering. Pulling on her mittens, Cori wobbled down the bank, stepped onto the ice and pushed off. The rough surface didn't slow her down. In that instant she was Michelle Kwan. The winter-dead cattails were adoring fans brought to their feet by the grace and beauty of the young skater from Painters Mill, Ohio.

A pang of excitement went through Cori with that first, heady rush of speed. Closing her eyes, she raised her arms like a ballet dancer and took flight. She was one with the ice. A bird in an endless sky, spinning and dipping and free-falling to her heart's delight. She wasn't sure how long she skated. When Cori looked around, the sky had darkened even more. Snow, she thought as her skates bumped along the frozen shore. She was trying to find the best spot to try her double twist when the low rumble of an engine interrupted. Curious, she skated to the north end of the pond and trudged up the earthen dam. A short distance away, she caught a glimpse of a snowmobile disappearing into the woods. Weird, she thought, and wondered why someone would drive all the way out here and then leave so quickly.

She was about to resume skating when something in the snow drew her eye. A garbage bag, she realized. The snowmobile guy had dumped a bag of trash. Stupid litterbug. Then she remembered her friend Jenny telling her about people dumping kittens. She hated animal abusers even more than litterbugs.

Not wanting to take the time to remove her skates, Cori walked awkwardly over the tufts of frozen mud. Her blades clanked against the ground as she made her way across the dam and down the embankment. There was no way her mom would let her keep a whole litter of kittens. She could probably give one to Lori; her mom liked cats.

A few yards from the bag, Cori noticed something red spilled in the snow. It looked like paint, but her stomach suddenly felt funny, like when you woke up at night from a bad dream. That was when she remembered the kids on the bus making up scary stories about a dead woman. Her mom had told her not to go to Miller's Pond today. She'd told her she didn't want her on the ice alone. But Cori knew that wasn't the real reason, and she wished she hadn't sneaked away.

Pulling out her cell phone, Cori started toward the bag. Every now and then she looked toward the woods to see if there was anyone there. She listened for the snowmobile's engine. But no one was there. Twenty feet away, recognition kicked her brain. Horror like she'd never before known in her young life sent a scream pouring from her throat. Seeing a real-life dead body was nothing like in the movies.

Cori stumbled back, tripped on her skates and went down hard on her butt. "Ohmigod!" She scrambled to her feet. Her finger shook when she hit the speed dial button for home. "*Mom!* I'm at the pond! There's a dead lady!"

"*What?*" Somewhere far away, she heard her mother's voice. "Oh God, Cori. Honey, get out of there!"

"I'm scared!"

"Run, honey. Take the path. Stay on the phone. Daddy and I are coming."

Too afraid to stop and remove her skates, Cori took off as fast as her feet would carry her toward the long path home.

I've been in McNarie's Bar more times than I care to admit. When I was sixteen, I had my first taste of Canadian Mist from some biker who was either too stupid or too drunk to realize I was a minor. I smoked my first Marlboro in the ladies' room with Cindy Wilhelm that same year. Had my first kiss from Rick Funderburk in the back seat of his Mustang in the parking lot when I was seventeen. I probably would have had sex that night had my father not shown up in the buggy and dragged me home. It doesn't take long for a determined Amish girl in full self-destruct mode to unlearn the values her parents had so painstakingly instilled.

As an adult, I've stopped in a time or two. The bartender, a gorilla-size, red-haired man I know only as McNarie, is a good listener. He has a decent sense of humor and makes one hell of a vodka and tonic.

I push open the door and wait for my eyes to adjust to the dim interior. I smell cigarette smoke and that old-beer reek common to bars. I spot Tomasetti slouched in a booth. An empty shot glass and two full ones sit on the table in front of him. I'm not surprised.

A stout woman behind the bar eyes me like a dog watching some stray slink into its yard. I give her a nod and start toward the booth.

Tomasetti looks up when I approach. "Glad you could make it, Chief. Have a seat."

"What the hell do you think you're doing?"

"Having a drink. I ordered one for you, too."

"We don't have time for this." I look down at the shot glass and resist the temptation to splash it in his face. "Take me back to the station."

"We need to talk."

"We can talk at the station."

"More private here."

"Goddamn you, Tomasetti."

"Sit down. You're drawing attention to yourself."

Despite my efforts not to, I've raised my voice. A combination of stress, lack of sleep, and a subtle, crawling fear have gotten the best of me. "Take me back to the station. Right fucking now."

He picks up the shot glass and hands it to me.

I ignore it. "I swear to God I'll call your superiors. I'll file a complaint. You and your bad attitude will be out the door so fast you won't know which end is up."

"Calm down," he says, "I ordered a couple of sandwiches. If you want to get them to go, that's fine."

I walk to the bar and lean toward the saloon doors that lead to the kitchen. "We'd like those sandwiches to go!" I call out.

A young man who looks too dirty to be anywhere near food comes out and gives me a nod. I go back to the booth and slide in across from Tomasetti.

"You like riddles, Chief?"

"Not particularly."

"I've got one I could use your help with."

I look at my watch.

"There's this cop," he says. "Pete."

I ignore him.

"Pete's a good cop. Experienced. Smart. Anyway, there's this killer loose in the town where he's a cop. This killer has already murdered two people. Pete knows he's going to do it again."

I glare at him. "Are you going somewhere with this?"

"I'm getting to the riddle part." He picks up the shot glass, drinks it down, and eyes me over the rim. "The twist is that sixteen years ago there were four murders with exactly the same MO committed in this town. And then, *bam!* the killer disappeared off the face of the earth. Why would this cop, Pete, refuse to believe the killer from sixteen years ago is back? He's a reasonable guy. What are the odds that two killers with exactly the same MO would haunt this same town? Why would Pete be reluctant to ask for assistance from other law enforcement?"

I want to give him a smart-assed reply, but for the life of me I can't think of one. "Maybe Pete thinks the killer is a copycat."

He nods as if considering, but I know he's not. "When I tell this riddle, most people think Pete's hiding something."

"Like what?"

"That's what makes this such a good riddle." He shrugs. "I was hoping you could help me get inside his head and figure it out."

I feel my pulse throbbing at my temples. I remind myself there's no way he could know what happened, but the reassurance is little comfort. I've underestimated John Tomasetti. He isn't just a figurehead with a badge. He's a cop with a cop's suspicions and the resolve to get to the bottom of those suspicions no matter what it takes.

"I'm not very good at riddles," I say.

"I think Pete's hiding something." He shrugs. "I thought he might come clean if the right person asked."

All I can think is *How does he know?* "You're full of shit, Tomasetti."

He smiles, but it's the cunning smile of a shark. A big one with bottomless black eyes, sharp teeth and an unfailing killer instinct. Leaning back in the booth, he studies me as if I'm some lab experiment gone wrong. "So how did you go from being an Amish farm girl to a cop? That's one hell of a leap."

The quick change of topic throws me, but only for an instant. "Just trying to buck the system, I guess."

"Anything in particular inspire you?"

I'm saved from having to answer when my phone chirps. "I gotta take this," I say and hit the Talk button.

"We-got-another-body!" Lois's voice blasts over the line like a foghorn.

I stand so abruptly, I bump the table and knock over a glass. "Where?"

"Miller's Pond. Petra Srinvassen's girl was skating out there and found it."

I'm out of the booth and running toward the door. I hear Tomasetti behind me, his boots heavy against the floor.

"Are they still at the pond?" I hit the door with both hands. I barely notice the dark sky or the cold as I run toward the Tahoe.

"I think so."

"Tell them to be careful. Tell them not to touch anything or disturb any tracks. I'm on my way."

CHAPTER 22

John had always been a suspicious son of a bitch. Once upon a time that was one of the traits that made him a good cop. He didn't give a damn where those suspicions took him. He'd arrest his own grandmother if she crossed the line. He supposed that was why it came as a shock to realize he didn't like the suspicions creeping over him when it came to Kate Burkholder.

Experience had taught him that people let you see only what they wanted you to. Whether they succeeded in that all too human art of deception depended on a couple of things. How good an actor they were. And how good you were at judging character. John had always considered himself a damn good judge of character.

By all accounts, Kate Burkholder seemed like a straight shooter with just enough edge to make the hard choices when the chips were down. But John sensed a thin layer of ambiguity beneath that girl-next-door exterior. She might project an air of moral resolve, but his gut was telling him there was more to the formerly Amish chief than met the eye. If it hadn't been for the note, he might have let it go. Now, he couldn't. He was pretty sure she was hiding something. But what? The question rolled around inside his head like a lone die as he jacked the speedometer to eighty.

"Right at the stop sign," she said.

He braked hard and made the turn, tossing a sidelong glance at Kate. "You might want to get on the horn and get some of your guys out there," he said. "Our man might still be in the vicinity."

Shaking herself as if from a dream, she hit her lapel mike and quickly set up a perimeter. "Turn left." She directed him to a narrow back road that had yet to see a snowplow. John drove too fast and the Tahoe obliged by fishtailing around a curve.

"Slow down."

"I got it."

"I don't want to end up in the ditch," she said testily.

"I don't do ditches." The Tahoe bumped over a snowdrift. John slowed for a turn, caught sight of the Dead End sign ahead and let off the gas.

"Here. Stop."

The Tahoe skidded to a halt two feet from the weathered wood guardrail. Tomasetti scanned the area. No cars. No tracks. "How far to the scene?"

"Quarter mile." She pointed. "There's a path through the woods."

"We've got to hoof it?"

"Shortest route."

"Shit."

They disembarked, both pausing to look for tire tracks. "Doesn't look like anyone's been here," he said.

"There's another road on the other side of the field." She fumbled the radio on her lapel. "Glock. I'm 10-23. Hogpath Road. Use Folkerth. If this guy's still around you might be able to cut him off there. Watch for tracks."

Kate led him to the mouth of a path cut into the trees.

"There's another way in?" he asked.

"If you have a snowmobile and wire-cutters, you could go in from any direction and not be seen."

With Kate in the lead, they set off at a jog. At one time in his life, John had been in good physical condition. He'd lifted weights and run ten miles a week. But the self-destructive lifestyle he'd indulged in for the last two years had taken a toll. A hundred yards in, he was breathing hard. Another fifty and he got a stitch in his side that felt more like a heart attack. Kate, on the other hand, seemed to be in her element. Long strides. Good form. Arms pumping in perfect cadence with her feet. *A runner,* he thought. He noticed something else about her, too. The tempo of her footfalls actually increased the closer they got to the scene.

Around them, the trees and snow cast them into a weird black-and-white twilight. John tried to listen for their quarry, but all he heard was the roar of blood in his ears and his own labored breathing. Just when he thought he was going to have to stop, the trees opened to a clearing. Beyond, a large frozen pond reflected a slate sky. Three people huddled a few feet from the bank. A man in a denim jacket, a woman in a down coat and a girl wearing ice skates.

Kate pointed. "That's them."

"Any reason we should be suspicious of them?"

Shaking her head, she started toward them. "They're a nice family."

John knew even nice families kept secrets.

Kate reached them first. Though everyone seemed to know everyone in this town, she showed them her ID and identified herself. The woman and girl were crying, their cheeks red from the cold. The man stood stone-faced. Despite the temperature, John saw sweat on his forehead.

"Where's the body?" Kate asked.

The girl raised a mittened hand and pointed. "By the c-creek."

"Did you see anyone?" John asked.

"A m-man. On a s-snowmobile."

"Where?"

"Down by the creek. In the trees."

"Can you tell me what he looked like?" Kate asked.

The girl's teeth chattered uncontrollably. "He was too far away."

"Was he wearing a jacket or coat? Do you remember what color it was? Or maybe his helmet? The snowmobile?"

"Blue, maybe. I d-don't know. I only saw him for a second."

Kate's attention went to the girl's parents. "Stay here." Touching the radio at her lapel, she started across the ice. "Be advised the suspect may be on a snowmobile."

Her voice and demeanor were outwardly calm, but John sensed an emotion he couldn't quite put his finger on beneath all that control. Because another body had shown up on her watch? Or was there something else going on? Was he just being paranoid? Or was Kate Burkholder holding out on him?

"Why would he dump the body way out here?" she asked.

"People use this place much? For skating?"

Her gaze met his. "It gets crowded on the weekend this time of year."

201

"Maximum shock value."

They crested the earthen dam. John saw the knife-slash of skate blades in the snow left by the girl as she'd walked down the embankment.

"There." Kate pointed. "Down by the creek. In those trees."

John saw what looked like a garbage bag that had been dumped and ripped open by wild dogs.

Kate started down the hill, her arms flailing as she skidded over the frozen peaks of earth. John followed, but he never took his eyes off the object in the snow.

"Watch for tracks," he warned.

They trudged through a deep snowdrift. Then, as if blocked by some invisible force field, they stopped. John had seen a lot of crime scenes in the years he'd been a cop. He'd seen death from natural causes and murders so bloody and horrific that even veteran cops dropped to their knees and vomited. He'd seen the neat and brutal execution-style murders common to drug dealers eager to make their mark. He'd seen innocent children cut down in the crossfire of gangland wars. He'd seen babies murdered and dumped like trash. None of that prepared him for the sight that accosted him now.

The body lay next to a garbage bag. John saw pale flesh streaked with blood. A thatch of brown hair. The dead stare of a taxidermist's glass. A mouth stretched into a silent scream. There was a lot of blood, and it made for a shocking contrast against pristine snow. Several pink objects lay a few feet from the body. At first glance, he thought they were scraps of fabric, and his cop's mind jumped at the thought of possible evidence. Upon closer inspection, he realized these objects were organs that had been removed from the victim's abdominal cavity.

Pieces had been cut from her body. He saw part of what had once been a breast. A finger lay ten feet from her outstretched arm. A length of pink-gray intestine leaked a red-green substance into the snow like a macabre snow cone. She'd been eviscerated.

"Oh my God."

Vaguely, he was aware of Kate beside him, breathing as if she'd run a marathon. A sound that was part gasp, part groan escaped her. John felt that same sound echo inside him. An expression of outrage and shock rolled into a single, awful emotion. He clung to his clinical perspective. But it was a thready clutch, and before he could stop it, his mind took him back to the day he'd found Nancy and the girls. He saw charred, blackened bodies with grotesque, clutching hands. The smell of cooked meat and singed hair . . .

"Any sign of the suspect?"

Kate's voice brought him back. She was speaking into her lapel mike. She looked at Tomasetti, but her eyes seemed slightly unfocused. "Call the sheriff's office. Tell them we need every man they can spare. I want this place surrounded. And get Coblentz. Tell him to drop everything and get out here."

She dropped her hand from the lapel mike and briefly closed her eyes. "Goddamnit."

"Do you recognize her?" he asked.

"No," she said. "My God, it's hard to tell."

He took that first, dangerous step toward the body. The stench of blood hung in the air. The victim had been cut from sternum to pubis. Several organs bulged from the opening. Steam rose from its bloody depths, and John knew that just a short time ago this woman had been alive.

"This is a huge escalation." He could feel his heart pounding, the rush of blood through his veins. He wanted to think it was from the run. But he recognized the primal fear of death coursing through his body. Until this moment, he hadn't known he even possessed such a strong will to live.

Outdoor crime scenes were difficult. The cold and snow and sheer size of this one would make it a nightmare.

"Chief!"

John looked toward the dam twenty yards away to see T.J. sliding down the embankment. In his peripheral vision, he saw Kate physically gather herself. She met the young officer at the base of the dam.

"He got another one," she said.

T.J.'s eyes flicked toward the body, then quickly away. "Aw, man. Aw, Jesus."

John addressed T.J. "I'm going to follow the tracks. I need you two to stay here, secure the scene until I can get a couple of techs out—"

"I'm going with you," Kate cut in, her voice fierce.

"I'd rather—"

"You're wasting time." Drawing her weapon, she started toward the woods.

"Shit." Shaking his head, John gave T.J. a nod and started after her at a jog.

They followed the snowmobile tracks into the woods, careful not to disturb them. The path the killer had taken was narrow with trees on either side. Kate jogged on the right side of the tracks. John took the left, keeping an eye out for anything the killer might have dropped in his haste.

For several minutes the only sounds came from their muffled footfalls against the snow and the rustle of fabric as their arms pumped. The woods seemed hushed. A crow cawed and took flight. In the instant that followed, a distant sound snagged John's attention. Too close to be coming from the road. Too high-pitched for a plane or jet.

He stopped, motioned for Kate to do the same. "Do you hear that?"

She cocked her head. "West of here. There's an open cornfield." She hit the mike. "I'm a mile north of Miller's Pond. Suspect is west of us. See if you can intercept."

She took off running. John followed. He was beyond pain now. The stitch had moved to the center of his chest. It would be just his luck to have a fucking heart attack out in the middle of nowhere.

They ran for what seemed like an eternity. Through deep drifts and the jagged peaks of a plowed field. Kate stopped on the steep bank of a creek, raised her hand in a request for silence. John's breathing was far from silent, but he tried. Putting his hands on his knees, he sucked in air.

"Son of a bitch is gone," she said.

"Yeah, but to where?"

Close fucking call.

He hit the garage door opener from fifteen yards away and punched the throttle. He barreled in fast, skis skidding, cleats scraping concrete. Squeezing the brake, he set his foot against the floor, jammed his ankle. The big machine came to a rest an inch from his workbench. Unfastening the chinstrap, he removed the helmet and tossed it onto the seat. He shook from head to toe. Euphoria and exhilaration pumped through him like some illicit narcotic. The need to ride that razor edge fed something ravenous inside him, reminded him that he was alive and life was good.

He dismounted and stood. His crotch was wet, his underwear sticking uncomfortably. He'd worn the cock ring. In hindsight, it had been a stupid thing to do. Reckless. Indulgent. He'd been so aroused while carrying her from the snowmobile to the place where he'd left her, he'd climaxed in his pants. If he hadn't been so rushed, he would have fucked her cold dead body and not felt a damn thing but gratification.

He thought of all the things he'd done to her and another wave of exhilaration washed over him. She'd been courageous. Challenging. Strong. She'd had attitude and endurance and dignity. The best one yet. He'd done things to her he'd dreamed of for years, but never had the guts. His level of satisfaction had been high. He respected and admired her in a way he hadn't the others.

Over the years, he'd experimented and discovered what he liked. He'd learned how to get the most from the women he took. He knew what type of woman he liked, what to look for. Before, there'd always been an underlying panic that made him jumpy and frightened. That fear had nearly ruined the rush. He was risking a lot to live out his fantasies; he wanted the experience to be worth it. This woman had lived up to his wildest expectations. He'd taken his time and savored every moment.

Already he missed her. He wished he'd kept her longer. The letdown was already encroaching on his high. The descent into disappointment that left him feeling deflated and empty. He'd once been told he had an addictive personality. He was too disciplined to indulge in vices as stupid and self-destructive as cigarettes or booze. But killing, having that ultimate power over another human being, was something else altogether. An addiction more powerful than any narcotic. A high he could not live without.

Bending, he unlaced his snow boots. Working the suspenders of the bib snow pants over his shoulders, he stepped out of them and tossed them over the seat of the snowmobile. Next, he unzipped his fly, removed the cock ring and wiped the semen from his skin. He would have liked to change underwear, but there was no time.

He snagged his keys from the workbench and slid into his vehicle. Opening the garage door, he backed out. By the time he pulled onto the street he was already anticipating his next kill.

CHAPTER 23

"Aw God! Aw Jesus no! *No!*"

I hear the screams from two hundred yards away. It's a terrible sound in the silence of the woods. I glance at Tomasetti. He looks back at me, his expression asking, *Now what?*

A new and terrible fear throws me into a run. A dozen scenarios rush through my mind. Did one of the victim's family members arrive? Did the killer return? I pick up speed and crash over a low-growing bush. I hear Tomasetti behind me, cursing, warning me to be cautious.

I burst into the clearing. To my utter shock, I see Norm Johnston kneeling beside the body. T.J. stands over him, his hands on the councilman's shoulders. I know immediately something's wrong with Norm. He's on his knees, rocking like an autistic child, his head bowed. I approach slowly. "What's Norm doing here?"

"Mrs. Srinvassen called him." T.J. looks at me, his face ashen. "She recognized the vic. It's his daughter."

The words nearly drop me to my knees. Brenda Johnston is twenty years old. Smart. Sweet. And beautiful. A young woman with a bright future. Norm and I aren't exactly friends, but I've heard him speak of his daughter. It's the only time I even came close to liking him because I knew he had at least one redeeming feature: He was a good father. He was crazy about his only child. The knowledge that she is dead makes me feel sick inside.

I turn my attention to Norm. He's looking at me as if this is somehow my fault. His face holds unfathomable pain. Tears stream from his eyes. His cheeks are nearly as red as the bloodstained snow. "It's my little girl," he sobs.

"Norm." I set my hand on his shoulder. It trembles violently beneath my palm. "I'm so sorry."

He remains hunched over the body. Blood stains his coat and slacks, his hands. A smear of crimson streaks his left cheek. He doesn't seem to notice. He's so distraught, he doesn't realize he's contaminating the scene.

"Norm," I say gently. "I need you to come with me."

"I can't leave her like this. Look at her. He . . . gutted her. My little girl. How could someone do that? She was so beautiful."

Tomasetti comes up beside me. I glance sideways at him. His jaw is clamped tight, the muscles working. "Mr. Johnston," he says. "Go with Chief Burkholder. We'll take good care of your daughter for you."

"Can't leave her like this." He rocks back and forth. "Look at what he did to her."

"She's gone, sir."

"Please don't make me leave her."

"You need to let us do our jobs. We've got to protect the scene."

Norm looks at him, his face screwed up. "Why her?"

"I don't know." Tomasetti nudges me aside, and I let him. "But you can bet we're going to get him."

Taking the man's arm, Tomasetti helps him to his feet. "Pull yourself together, Mr. Johnston. Go with Chief Burkholder. She's got some questions for you."

Johnston is like a zombie. I make eye contact with Tomasetti, but I can't read his expression. I don't know what to do with Norm. He's in no condition to be questioned, and I'm not very good at comforting. But he needs a friend and there's no one else to do it so I take his arm and lead him toward the dam. "Let's walk."

"Chief Burkholder!"

An odd sense of relief skitters through me when I see Nathan Detrick and Deputies Hunnaker and Barton come over the crest of the dam. As recently as yesterday, I would have resented his presence. Today, everything else is secondary to stopping this killer.

Detrick reaches us, his eyes flicking from me to the body of the victim. "Holy Mother," he says in a guttural voice.

"I've got officers setting up a perimeter." I hear my own words as if someone else is speaking them. "The killer may still be in the area. Probably on a snowmobile."

Detrick speaks into his radio. "I want every man on a perimeter around Miller's Pond. Rockridge Road. Folkerth Road. County Road Fourteen. Subject may be on a snowmobile." Clipping the radio to his belt, he addresses his deputies. "Get this area cordoned off. Get some tape up." He looks at me and shakes his head. "I got here as quick as I could."

"I appreciate it. We're stretched pretty tight."

His gaze drifts to Johnston, and he raises his brows.

I lower my voice. "His daughter."

"Aw, hell." Detrick sets his hand on the man's shoulder and squeezes. "I'm sorry as hell, Norm." His eyes land on me. "I can take over here, if you want to get him home."

"Thank you." I touch Norm's arm. "We could use a ride to the station."

"No problem." Putting his fingers to his mouth, Detrick whistles for one of his deputies.

I call Norm's wife on the way to the police station and ask her to meet us there. My call frightens her, but I will not relay news of her daughter's murder over the phone. I can only hope she doesn't hear about it elsewhere before she arrives.

On the drive, Norm calms down enough to talk to me. I learn that the last time he saw Brenda was around nine P.M. the night before. He called her earlier today and left a message, but she didn't return his call. Brenda lived alone and worked as an office manager for a doctor in Millersburg. A call to the office tells me she didn't show up for work this morning, which is unusual for the responsible young woman. That tells me the killer may have gotten his hands on her last night. This is the first step in establishing a timeline.

Lois looks up from the switchboard when we enter the police station. Her eyes widen at the sight of the Norm. Tossing me a concerned look, she mouths, *What happened?*

I shake my head and she doesn't press. "Call Reverend Peterson and tell him I need him here. Mrs. Johnston is on her way. Send her right in. We'll be in my office."

She never takes her eyes off Norm. "Sure thing."

Norm heads toward my office without speaking. He's no longer crying, but his agony is palpable. I need a few minutes to gather my composure, but I don't want to leave him alone. I follow him into my office to see him drop into the visitor's chair adjacent to my desk.

Last night's coffee sits like sludge in the pot. I pour a cup, but I wish for something stronger. Sliding behind my desk, I pull out a fresh pad, an incident report form and a witness statement form. "I need to ask you a few questions, Norm."

"I can't believe she's gone." His eyes fall on mine. "She was everything to me. The best thing I ever did."

I have no words to console him. Feeling inept, I pick up my pen and look down at the form. Dread curdles in my gut when the bell on the front door jingles, telling me his wife, Carol, has arrived. I sit there, listening, my heart pounding.

I hear heels against tile and then Carol Johnston appears in the doorway. Her eyes flick from me to Norm, then back to me. She wears a green swing coat with a faux fur collar. She's a petite woman well into her fifties, but she looks a decade younger.

"What happened?" she asks.

I think of their once-lovely daughter, the way she looked lying in the snow, her body cut to pieces, and I feel like crying.

I rise. "I'm afraid I have terrible news."

"What news?" I see the initial rush of fear in her eyes. She looks at her husband. "What is she talking about?"

"Brenda is dead," I say.

"What?" The woman looks at me as if I punched her in the solar plexus. "That's crazy."

Norm rises, like a stooped old man crippled with arthritis. "Carol."

"No!" She puts both hands against her face so quickly, I hear the slap of her palms against her cheeks. She spins, doubles over, and an elongated "Nooooo!" rips from her mouth. "Nooooo!"

I want to put my hands over my ears to block her agonized cries. Because I cannot look at Carol, I train my eyes on Norm. "I'm sorry," I say.

"How?" she keens. *"How?"*

"Murdered," Norm chokes. "The killer got her. Just like the others."

Carol's knees hit the floor. She raises her face and hands skyward, screaming, then buries her face in her hands. "Noooo!"

Norm goes to her, tries to help her to her feet, but she fights him off. "Brenda!" she screams. "Oh, my God, Brenda!"

Lois appears in the doorway, her eyes going to me. "Is there anything I can do?"

"Call Reverend Peterson again," I say. "Tell him it's an emergency."

Nodding, she backs away.

Norm lifts Carol and eases her into the chair, but she doubles over and keens uncontrollably.

Wiping his face, Norm stands opposite my desk, vacillating as if he's just stepped off a roller coaster. But his eyes are sharp when they land on me. "Was she raped?" he manages.

"We don't know yet."

He scrapes a hand over his face, his fingers digging into his eyes. "Why in the name of God hasn't this maniac been caught?"

"We're doing everything we can," I offer.

Carol Johnston raises her head and thrusts a finger at me. "This is *your* fault!"

The words cut with the proficiency of a blade. I try not to react. But my recoil is physical.

Norm's face crumples. "Did she suffer?"

"We don't know." It's a lie; Brenda Johnston suffered plenty before she died. But I spare them the truth, if only for a short while. "They'll need to do an autopsy."

"Aw . . . God." Air rushes between Johnston's teeth. A single sob escapes him before he regains control. "Three people dead. Incomprehensible." His voice rises. "How could this happen?"

"We're working around the clock. Investigating this case aggressively—"

"Aggressively? Is that what you call it, you heartless bitch? You couldn't even be bothered to call in the sheriff's office. I had to call BCI for you. You call that *aggressive*?"

This scene has played out in my head a hundred times in the last two days. A worst-case scenario I knew I would face sooner or later. Even so, I don't know how to respond, and train my eyes on the pad in front of me. "I know this is a bad time, Norm, but I need to ask you some questions."

"I have some questions for you, too," he says ominously. "Like why didn't you call BCI for assistance when you first realized you had a serial killer on your hands? Why haven't you called the FBI? You've mishandled this case from the get-go, you incompetent bitch."

Something inside me curls, like a bug prodded by a cruel child. "I'm doing the best I can."

"My daughter is dead," he snarls. "Evidently, your best isn't good enough."

"Don't go there," I say.

He doesn't relent. "Had you done your job, she might still be here!" Choking out a sound of animal rage, Norm lunges at me. I have time to rise before his hands clench my collar. He shoves me against the wall hard. "I'm going to fucking fry you for this. You got that?"

"Get your hands off me." I pry at his hands. *"Now."*

Carol looks up. Even locked in her own dolor, she knows the situation is about to explode out of control. "Stop it! This isn't helping."

Johnston stares at me as if he wants to tear me apart. I see grief and rage in his eyes, and I wonder how far he's going to take this. "Please try to calm down," I say. "I know you're upset."

"Upset is not the right word!" Grasping my collar, he yanks me toward him, then shoves me against the wall before releasing me.

"Don't do this," I try. "I need your help."

"Pacifist Amish bitch!" He spits the words as if he's bitten into something rotten. "I'll deal with Detrick. Not you."

Carol Johnston looks as if every bone in her body is broken as he takes her arm and they start toward the door.

That's when I notice Tomasetti standing in the hall. He's watching me, but I can't read his expression. He steps aside to let the couple pass.

I stand behind my desk, staring, but seeing nothing. For the first time in the course of my career, I feel incompetent. I've faced intolerance before. But bigotry isn't what churns like shards of glass in my stomach. *Had you done your job, my daughter might still be here.* The truth of those words guts me. Putting my face in my hands, I sink into my chair. Vaguely, I'm aware of Tomasetti entering my office, but I don't look at him. I feel old and as broken as Carol Johnston looked.

Sighing, Tomasetti settles into a chair. "Ugly scene."

I'm so engulfed in my own misery I can't respond.

"The perp got away," he says. "He made it to the road, and we lost him."

Another layer of disappointment settles on top of a hundred others. "Did you get anything useful?"

"Glock and a crime scene tech from BCI are working on footwear impressions and some imprints of the snowmobile's skis. We think it might have been a Yamaha. Won't know for sure until they match treads."

I raise my head and meet his gaze. "I'll get started on a list of people in the area who own Yamaha snowmobiles." But I'm still thinking about the Johnstons. "Doc Coblentz show up?"

"They were moving the body when I left."

"Did someone get photographs?"

"We got it covered."

I sink back into my dark thoughts.

After a moment, he says, "Don't let what he said get to you."

My phone rings, but I ignore it. "Why not? He's right."

His eyes narrow. "About what?"

"I should have called for help."

"Why didn't you?"

The ringing stops. Seconds tick by. "Because I screwed up."

"Why didn't you call for assistance, Kate?"

I stare blindly at my desk blotter, but all I see is Brenda Johnston's torn body lying in the snow. Her organs strewn about like trash.

He tries again. "Talk to me."

I shift my gaze to Tomasetti. "I can't."

"Cops make mistakes, Kate. We're human. It happens."

"It wasn't a mistake."

My response puzzles him. For the span of several minutes, neither of us speaks. My phone rings again, but I don't answer. I'm a vacuum inside, as dark and cold as space. I have nothing left.

"I'm the last person who has the right to lecture anyone on right or wrong," he says.

"Is that some kind of confession?"

"Look, if you know something about this case that you haven't told me, this would be a good time for you to open up."

The temptation to let everything pour out is strong, but I can't do it. I don't trust him. I don't even trust myself.

After a moment, he sighs and rises. "Why don't you let me drive you home so you can get some sleep?"

I try to remember the last time I slept, realize I can't. I don't even know what day it is. The clock on the wall says it's nearly six P.M. and I wonder where the day went. The need to work eats at me even as exhaustion fogs my brain. I'm fast approaching a state in which I'll become completely ineffective. But how can I rest knowing there's a killer out there, stalking my town?

I rise. "I have my own vehicle."

"You're in no condition to drive."

"Yes, I am." Only then do I realize I'm not going home.

CHAPTER 24

The setting sun peaks out from behind a wall of granite clouds as I head for the Explorer. The wind is calm, but I checked the weather report online. We're in for some serious snow tonight. I snatch up my cell phone as I slide behind the wheel. Glock picks up on the first ring. I'm inordinately relieved to hear his voice. "Please tell me you got at least one good impression," I begin.

"Footwear impressions stink. But we got a decent one from the snow-mobile."

Hope flutters in my chest, but I bank it because it makes me realize how desperate I am. "Did the lab give you a time frame?"

"Tomorrow. Late."

"Did anyone get a look at him?"

"One of Detrick's deputies thinks he saw a blue Yamaha. Perp wore a silver or gray helmet."

There are hundreds of snowmobiles in the area. "Tell Skid I want a list of all Yamaha snowmobiles registered in Holmes and Coshocton Counties. Narrow it down by color. Blue. Silver. Gray. I want background checks and alibis on the owners."

Glock clears his throat. "Ah, Detrick already put two of his deputies on that, Chief."

Uneasy surprise quivers inside me. "All right. I'll follow up with Detrick."

"I don't know if you've heard, but the media showed up after you left. Steve Ressler. Crew from Columbus. A couple of radio stations. That fuckin' Detrick prettied up for the cameras and held a press conference right there at the pond."

"How did it go?"

"He didn't say shit, but he looked good doing it."

I sense there's more coming.

"One of the reporters asked about you," he adds. "Detrick made like he didn't know where you were. Like he was covering for you or some shit."

"I was with Johnston. I notified next of kin." I hate it that I feel the need to defend myself.

"You don't have to explain. Watch that fuckin' Detrick, though. He's a glory-grabbing son of a bitch."

This development worries me. I feel the case spiraling out of my control. Detrick raising questions about my credibility. Tomasetti edging closer to the truth. My life hanging in the balance.

"How's the Johnston family?" Glock asks.

I tell him about the scene at the station.

"Norm's got a big mouth. You think he's going to make trouble for you?"

"I don't know. Maybe it was just the grief talking." Ahead, pink-rimmed storm clouds roil on the western horizon. "Thanks for the heads up on Detrick. I'm going to try to get some sleep."

I hit End. I want to call Norm, but I know his wounds are still too fresh. I wonder if he's spoken to Detrick and filed a complaint against me, and I hit the speed dial for the sheriff's number. I get voice mail. A good sign that he's avoiding me. I know Detrick won't hesitate to use me as a fall guy if this case doesn't come together soon. I should be thinking about damage control. About my career and covering my ass. But I've never done my job based on the perceptions of others. I don't intend to start now.

I hit Doc Coblentz's number. "Do you have a prelim yet?"

"I just got her onto the table. My God, Kate. I've never seen anything like it in my life."

"Anything carved onto her abdomen?"

"With the evisceration, I haven't been able to tell yet. There's a lot of damage."

"Throat cut?"

"Like the others." He blows out a breath. "I'm not sure that's what killed her."

"He changed his MO?"

I'm surprised when the doctor's voice quivers. "I believe the evisceration may have been antemortem."

All the blood seems to rush from my head. I've never fainted, but I'm so shaken by the news I have to pull over. For a moment, neither of us speaks. Then I ask, "Do you think he might have medical training?"

"I doubt it. The incisions are crude. He just butchered her."

"Was she raped?"

"I haven't gotten that far."

"Anything else?" I ask.

"A crime scene tech from BCI was here earlier. He took nail scrapings and swabs. We measured the incised wounds and he took some photos. He mentioned he might try to identify the type of chain used from the bruise pattern on her ankles."

A thought occurs to me. "Did anyone find her clothes?"

"Not a shred."

"I think he's keeping the clothes."

"Why would he do that?"

"He's keeping them as trophies."

"That's your area of expertise, not mine."

"When will you do the autopsy?"

"First thing in the morning."

I don't want to wait that long, but it's my desperation talking. People need to eat and sleep and go home to their families. "Will you give me a call? I'd like to be there."

"Kate, I don't know why you do that to yourself."

I wonder if maybe it's one of many ways I choose to punish myself. For what I did. For what I didn't do. "See you in the morning."

I end the call. Around me, dusk hovers low and gray. To my right, a group of plain children wearing traditional Amish garb—black coats and flat-brimmed hats for the boys, headscarves for the girls—play an impromptu game of ice hockey on a pond next to the road. For an instant, the scene sweeps me back to my own childhood. A time when I was never alone and had no concept of loneliness. My life was filled with family, worship, chores—and playtime every chance I got. Before the day Daniel Lapp introduced me to violence, I was a happy and well-adjusted Amish girl. My life was carefree and full of promise. Those simple days seem like a thousand lifetimes ago.

As I drive by the children, a deep ache of loneliness assails me. A longing for what is lost. My parents. My siblings. A part of myself I cannot reclaim. I wave to the kids. Their smiles bolster me. I glance in my rearview mirror as they resume their game, and a powerful need to protect them rises up inside me.

My sister Sarah and her husband live in the last house on a dead-end road. William has cleared the lane of snow, probably with his horse-drawn plow. He's considered a conservative amongst the Amish community. While my brother Jacob uses a tractor, William adheres to traditional horsepower. More than once it has been a point of contention between the two men.

A neat row of blue spruce trees, their boughs laden with snow, runs alongside the lane. The massive barn stands two stories high. Built on a slope, it sits on an angled stone foundation. Half a dozen windows dot the façade. Four cupolas jut from the apex of the tin roof. No one knows for certain, but it's rumored the house and barn date back two hundred years. A time when barns were the center of rural life and architectural works of art. My parents brought Sarah and Jacob and me here many times when we were kids. I chased chickens, played hide-and-seek and bottle-fed newborn calves. Once, on a dare, I jumped from a hay chute and sprained my ankle.

I park behind a sleigh, my headlights reflecting off the slow moving vehicle sign mounted at the rear. Beyond, the windows of the house glow yellow with lantern light. It's a cozy and inviting scene. But as with my brother's home, my welcome will not be warm.

I take the sidewalk to the front door and knock. I barely have time to gather my thoughts when the door swings open. I find myself looking at my older sister. "Katie." She whispers my name as if it's a bad word. Her gaze flicks sideways and I know William is inside. "Come in out of the cold."

The aromas of cooked cabbage and baking yeast bread titillate my appetite as I enter. But I won't be asked for dinner. A kerosene lamp illuminates the living room. I see a large homemade table and bench. On the opposite wall, a framed needlepoint sampler that had belonged to *Mamm* hangs front and center. The initials of our great-grandparents are sewn into the fabric next to locks of their hair. I remember running my fingers over those locks and wondering about the people they came from.

"Come into the kitchen," Sarah says.

I follow her to the kitchen to find her husband at the table, hunched over a bowl of steaming soup.

"Hello, William," I say.

He stands when I enter and bows his head slightly. "Good evening, Katie."

"I'm sorry to interrupt your dinner."

"You are welcome to hot soup."

The invitation surprises me, since I'm under the *bann*, but I shake my head. "I've only got a few minutes." I look at my sister and force a smile. "I wanted to check on you. See how you're feeling."

She places a hand over her distended abdomen, but her gaze slides from mine. "I feel good," she says. "Better than last time."

"You look great."

William smiles. "She eats like a horse."

"She ate us out of house and home when we were kids." I smile, hoping it looks real. "It's good for the baby."

"Bad for my bulging middle!" she exclaims with a little too much enthusiasm.

An uncomfortable silence ensues. I touch her shoulder and make eye contact. "Are you still working on the baby quilt?"

"I'm almost finished."

"Could I see it?"

My request surprises her, but her eyes light up. "Of course." Touching my shoulder, she starts toward the living room. "Come."

The stairs creak beneath our feet as we climb to the second level. I follow her to the bedroom she and William share. It's a large room with two tall windows and an angled ceiling. The furniture is heavy and plain. A dresser that had once belonged to our parents. A chest with steel pulls. And a sleigh bed covered with one of Sarah's quilts.

She crosses to the dresser and lights a glass lamp. Golden light casts shadows on the ceiling and walls. "You look tired, Katie."

"I've been working a lot."

Nodding, she pulls out a partially completed quilt. Curved patches of seafoam green and lavender form a complex pattern. I see the required seven stitches per inch and as always, I'm awed. Quilting is extremely labor intensive; a good quilt will contain over fifty thousand stitches. Most Amish women learn to sew early in life. Most can make a decent quilt. But very few ever become good enough to design a piece of art like this.

Thinking of the baby my sister carries, I touch the soft fabric. I think of the babies she's lost in the past; I think of my own losses and for a moment I have to blink back tears. "It's beautiful."

"Yes." Her smile is real this time. "It is lovely."

I drop my hand and ask the question that's been eating at me since Tomasetti waylaid me in the bar with his riddle about Pete the cop. "Sarah, have you told anyone about Daniel Lapp?"

She brushes a speck of thread off the quilt. "I do not wish to speak of that, Katie."

"Did you tell someone about Lapp?"

Lowering the quilt, she stares at me as if I've just pulled out my pistol and shot her dead-center. "I did what I had to do."

"What does that mean?"

"I prayed to God for guidance. When I woke yesterday morning, I knew I would find peace, that you would find peace, in the truth."

A keen sense of betrayal cuts me. "Who did you tell?"

"I sent a note to Bishop Troyer."

"What did the note say?"

"The truth." She looks down at the quilt. "That you know who the killer is."

The words send a flood of panic through me. The scene at the bar with Tomasetti flashes in my mind's eye. For an instant, I'm so stricken, I can't catch my breath.

"I am sorry if this hurts you, Katie. But I felt very strongly that telling the truth was the right thing to do."

"You don't know the truth!" Turning away from her, I begin to pace. "Sarah, how could you?"

"Your police friends can help you find Daniel now," she offered.

Heart pounding, I rub my hands over my face and try to calm down. "Did you sign the note? Do they know it came from you?"

"I did not sign my name."

I try to think through the ramifications, but my brain is so muddled by exhaustion, I can't think past the panic clenching my chest.

"Katie, what happened?"

I stop pacing and look at her. "Bishop Troyer took the note to the town council. Maybe the mayor. Now, they're suspicious of me. Are you happy now?"

"I am not happy to see you hurting. All I want is for Daniel Lapp to be caught."

"We don't know that he's the killer!" I shout.

She glances nervously toward the door. "Please do not shout."

Trying hard to fend off the fingers of panic crawling all over me, I draw a deep breath. "Sarah, I need to talk to you about what happened that day."

She starts to turn away, but I set my hands on her shoulders and force her to face me. "I need you to remember. Think back to that day. Is it really possible Daniel Lapp survived?"

"If he's back, then he must have survived." Her fingers flutter at the neckline of her plain dress. "You saw him, too."

The human mind is a powerful thing. Like the body, it possesses protective mechanisms to safeguard it against trauma. The abject horror of what happened that day was branded into my brain and will remain there forever. But I remember few details of the rape, even less of the shooting. The one thing I do recall with vivid clarity is the blood. On the curtains. On my hands. An ocean of it glistening on the floor.

Too much blood for anyone to have survived.

"There was too much blood," I whisper.

"What?"

I look hard at my sister. "Did you go with *Datt* and Jacob to the grain elevator?"

She stares back, her expression stricken. "No."

"How do you know they buried the body?"

"I heard *Mamm* and *Datt* talking. In the barn. A few days after it happened."

"What did they say?"

"*Datt* told *Mamm* he put Daniel in the hole where no one would ever find him."

"In the hole?" My heart tap dances against my ribs. "What does that mean? What hole?"

"I do not know. A well, maybe. I did not ask."

In the hole . . .

The words tumble in my head like sea glass in a kaleidoscope. "I have to go."

Sarah looks alarmed. "Where?"

"To find Daniel Lapp," I say, and hit the stairs running.

CHAPTER 25

Following the chief of police on some half-baked hunch probably wasn't a very good idea. With the temperature dropping fast and the snow coming down in earnest, John figured it fell into the downright stupid category. He was reaching for the ignition key when headlights cut through the darkness, telling him a vehicle was coming down the lane. "Shit," he muttered.

He'd parked a dozen yards from the mouth of the lane, but he'd be lucky if she didn't spot him. If she looked hard enough before turning onto the road, she'd see him. He might be a good liar, but he'd have one hell of a time explaining this. Leaning against the seat back, he watched the Explorer barrel down the driveway. It hit the road with enough speed to fishtail and then sped toward town.

Relieved, John started the engine, turned up the heat and put the Tahoe in gear. He wasn't exactly sure why he was following her. Kate Burkholder hadn't done anything wrong. Aside from not calling in the feds or the state for help, she was investigating the murders much the same way he would have had he been in her shoes.

It was the appearance of the mysterious note that had aroused his suspicions. Mayor Brock had delivered it just that morning. Had it come from anyone other than an Amish bishop, John might have written it off as a hoax. It was, after all, ludicrous to believe Kate knew the identity of the killer as the note had claimed.

But over the years John had learned to trust his gut. Right now it was telling him she was hiding something. Did she know the killer? Was he a relative? A lover? Was he Amish? Was she protecting him?

The questions gnawed at him as he followed her toward town. It was after nine P.M.; she was probably going to call it a night. That was fine by him. He could use a hot shower and some food. Not to mention a drink . . .

But Kate didn't turn onto Main Street. Instead she headed south on the highway, a little too fast considering the road conditions. Curious, John fell back to a discreet distance and followed her into Coshocton County.

"Where the hell are you going?" He punched off the headlights as she turned onto a little-used road. Surprise rippled through him when she pulled into an abandoned grain facility. Intrigued, he watched the Explorer disappear behind the building. John parked a hundred yards away and shut down the engine.

"What are you up to, Kate?" he muttered.

The only answer he got was the tinkle of snow pellets against the windshield and the nagging insistence of his own suspicions.

I know coming here is a mistake. Chances are, I'll dig until I'm exhausted, frostbitten and disheartened, and still not find what I'm looking for. In some twisted way, I want to believe proof of Daniel Lapp's death will exonerate me for not telling anyone he could be a suspect in these murders.

Gathering the shovel, the pickax and my Mag-Lite, I enter the structure through the rear door. The place seems different now that I'm alone. The wind tears at the loose sheet metal outside and whistles through every crack, filling the place with the ghostly moans and groans of some Halloweenesque haunted house.

Cold nips at my face as I walk the length of the building. Though I was raised in farm country, I've always been foggy on the mechanical workings of the grain elevator. After that night with Jacob, however, I hit a couple of Web sites and learned the basics. Fifty years ago, trucks loaded with wheat or corn drove through the overhead door and onto the platform to be weighed. Once the truck was weighed, the driver pulled forward and dumped the load of grain into the "boot pit." The empty vehicle was weighed again and the driver was paid per pound for the weight difference.

"So where the hell is the boot pit?" I say aloud.

The overhead door shudders with a gust of wind. I hear snow pinging against steel. Picking up the Mag-Lite, I shine it around the weigh platform. The boot pit grate should be nearby. I set down the flashlight and ram the tip of the shovel into the ground where I think the truck drive-through aisle might have been—and a hollow thud sounds.

Using the shovel like an oar, I scrape away dry earth and spot a rotting piece of plywood. Dropping to my knees, I use my hands and tear at the ground like a crazy woman. I hear gasping sounds echoing off the walls. It scares me when I realize those sounds are coming from me. Unearthing the plywood, I drag it aside. Hope leaps through me when I see the rusty grate. The boot pit is about eight feet square and twelve feet deep. The elevator leg has long since been removed, but the hole was never filled. Grabbing the flashlight, I shine the beam into the pit. I see chunks of broken concrete, loose dirt, gravel and a pile of broken boards.

I use the shovel to pry at the grate, but the heavy piece of steel doesn't budge. I keep a cable in my vehicle during the winter months and use it for hauling stranded cars out of snow. It strikes me that I can use it to move the grate. Grabbing my keys, I run to the Explorer and back it up to the grate. When the vehicle is in position, I snatch up the cable and secure the hooked end to the Explorer's undercarriage. I clip the other end to the grate. Sliding behind the wheel, I jam the Explorer into four-wheel drive and give it gas. The cable goes taut. The engine revs. The tires spin and grab. Steel screeches against steel as the grate is pulled from its ancient nest.

I drag it about three feet, then kill the engine and get out. Snatching up the Mag-Lite, I shine it into the hole. It's too deep for me to jump; the last thing I need is a broken ankle. Realizing I can use the cable to rappel down, I unhook the end from the Explorer and drop it into the pit. I toss the shovel in next. Finally, I sit on the edge, grasp the cable and lower myself into darkness. The air smells of earth and dust and decay. The instant my feet touch the ground, I swing the flashlight beam around the pit. A rat skitters across a pile of weathered boards.

The shovel lies on the ground a few feet away. I pick it up and use it to tap on the pile of wood. I'm not unduly frightened of rodents, but I don't want one jumping on me. Propping my flashlight on a cinder block, I start dragging boards aside. Dust curls up to irritate my nose and eyes, but I don't slow down. I lift a length of sheet metal and toss it aside. A rotting two-by-six crumples in my hands. I look down and find myself staring at several small pale objects in the dirt.

I snag the flashlight. My blood freezes in my veins when I realize the objects are teeth. Nearby, I discern a tattered scrap of fabric. Is this what's left of Daniel Lapp? Squatting for a closer look, I identify several ribs still attached to a length of spine. Then I spot the skull and I know. Daniel Lapp is dead. The knowledge fills me with a bizarre mix of relief and dread. I'd been certain he was the killer. But if not Daniel, then who?

I don't know how long I stand there. It's as if this revelation has paralyzed me. The logical side of my brain tells me to bury this part of my past and go home. Forget about Lapp and concentrate on finding the killer. Salvage what's left of my career. I begin dragging wood over the remains. When that's done I go to the cable and proceed to climb out of the pit. I'm in good shape, but it's not easy. I'm nearly to the top when I catch a glimpse of movement above. Too large to be a dog or raccoon. Someone's there. Shock jolts me with such force that I nearly lose my grip. I freeze, my body shaking, my thoughts reeling.

Did someone follow me?

I look up, but see nothing. I hear myself breathing hard. My hands ache from clutching the cable. I'm aware of my gun against my side. But even armed, I'm in a vulnerable position. If someone wanted to harm me, this would be a prime opportunity.

I begin a frantic climb to the top. The toes of my boots dig into the walls. Loose dirt crumbles. My breaths echo off the walls. I slide my hands up the cable, pulling until my muscles quiver with exertion.

Finally, at the mouth of the pit, I drag myself out. Shaking and gasping for breath, I look around and get the shock of my life. John Tomasetti stands ten feet away, his flashlight in one hand, a sleek Sig Sauer semiautomatic in the other. His eyes burn into mine and then he blinds me with the light.

"Looking for something?" he asks.

My mind scrambles for a lie. My pulse roars like a jet engine on takeoff. I can only imagine how bizarre this must seem to him. I'm covered with dirt and probably look as strung out as a junkie on a three-week binge. Lucky for me I'm pretty fast on my feet. "I'm following up on a lead." I make a show of brushing dust from my pants. "What are you doing here?"

He ignores my question, his flashlight beam moving from me to the pit. "Lead on what?"

I don't want him near the pit. I'm not sure how well I covered those bones. I want to slide the grate back into place and get the hell out of there. "An anonymous call about illegal dumping. Guy claiming someone dumped paint and some type of solvent."

It's a viable lie. An ordinary person would believe it. But John Tomasetti is no ordinary schmuck. I can tell by his expression he doesn't believe me.

"Did you find anything?" he asks.

"Not a thing." I pull the cable from the pit and start toward the Explorer. "Crank call, probably. Teenagers. We get that here."

"Maybe I'll have a look for myself."

"There's nothing down there but rats." It strikes me then that it's no coincidence Tomasetti is here. He didn't drive by and see my headlights. The son of a bitch followed me.

The realization rattles me further as I slide behind the wheel. Tomasetti circles the pit as I move the Explorer into position. I need to get that grate over the pit before he decides to act on all that suspicion I see in his eyes.

I back the Explorer to the grate and slide out. My hands shake so badly now I can barely get the hook around the undercarriage.

"You nervous about something, Chief?"

"Just cold."

"You're in an awful big hurry to cover that hole."

"I just want to get home."

He pauses. "Kate, what the fuck are you really doing?"

I don't look at him. I can't. I'm too close to some precipitous edge. Once I go over the brink, I may not be able to drag myself out. "Look, this is the second complaint I've taken about dumping here," I snap. "I didn't feel like going home, so I'm following up."

"Is that why you're shaking?"

I finish with the hook and straighten, meeting his gaze. "In case you haven't noticed, it's cold."

"You're fucking sweating. Covered with dirt. Look at you. Now what the fuck is going on?"

"I don't know what you think you know, but I don't appreciate you following me around, spying on me. Whatever it is you're doing, I want it to stop. You got it?"

"You're lying to me and I want to know why."

I laugh. "You need to talk to someone about all that paranoia, Tomasetti."

"You didn't go into that pit because you were following up on a complaint."

"Like you know."

Abruptly, he strides toward me, shines the light in my eyes. "You want to know what I know, Chief? I know that someone in this town believes you know who the killer is. I think you're hiding something." He thrusts a finger at the pit. "And I know you didn't go into that goddamn hole because of some anonymous tip." He circles the boot pit, shining his light into the darkness. "If I go down there, what am I going to find?"

"What do you want from me? Did Detrick tell you to follow me? Or was it the town council? Are you their new lapdog?"

One side of his mouth lifts. I can't tell if he's smiling or snarling. "You know better than that."

"Do I?" I start toward the Explorer. I'm close to pulling this off. All I have to do is slide the grate back into place and leave. I don't think he'll go to the trouble of moving it again.

I climb behind the wheel and twist the key. The engine turns over. I reach for the shifter. The next thing I know the door flies open. I gasp when Tomasetti reaches in, turns off the ignition and takes my keys.

"What the hell do you think you're doing?" Jumping out, I make a wild grab for the keys.

He drops them into his pocket. "Let's just say I'm following up on a hunch."

"This is ridiculous. Give me my keys. Now."

Removing the cable from the grate, he tosses one end into the pit.

Panic ignites in my chest. I can't let him find those bones. "You're over-stepping."

"Not the first time I've been accused of that."

"I swear to God I'll have your job for this."

Taking hold of the cable, he braces his legs against the side and drops into the hole like a rock climber.

"Tomasetti, damn it, stop playing games. I want to leave."

No answer.

"Damn it! There's nothing there!" I look around wildly. For a crazy instant I actually consider pulling out the cable and stranding him. Of course, I can't do that. I'm going to have to deal with this. With what I've done. The secrets I've covered up all these years.

My entire life flashes before my eyes. My career will be ruined. My parents' memory, their reputations, will be dragged through the mud right along with the rest of the Amish community. My brother and sister and nephews will suffer. I could find myself facing a grand jury. Worse case scenario, I could be tried and sent to prison for murder . . .

I rush to the pit and look down to see Tomasetti shove a piece of plywood out of the way with his foot. I can see the skull from where I stand. Dizziness descends. I feel sick and terrified. I can't believe this is happening.

"What the fuck?"

Turning away, I press my hand to my stomach. I can't cover this up. It's over. The secrets end here. Nausea seesaws in my gut. I make it ten feet before I throw up. The thud of my knees hitting the ground surprises me. I've been knocked unconscious before, but I've never fainted. The swirl of confusion tells me I'm close now. Somehow I lose time, seconds or maybe even minutes, because the next thing I know Tomasetti is kneeling beside me.

I jolt when his hand touches my shoulder. I'm embarrassed and humiliated, but I'm not sure I'm finished puking so I don't move. I don't acknowledge him. I look down at my gloves in the dirt and I feel like crying.

"You okay?" he asks after a moment.

"What do you think?"

"I think you've got some explaining to do."

I dry heave and spit.

He waits a moment before speaking. "Those remains. Do you know who it is?"

I close my eyes, squeeze them tight. "Yes."

"Who?"

"Daniel Lapp."

"Who's Daniel Lapp?"

"An Amish man."

"How long has he been dead?"

"Sixteen years."

"How did he die?"

"Shotgun blast."

"Do you know who killed him?"

"Yes."

He pauses. "Who?"

"Me," I say and the tears come in a rush.

CHAPTER 26

John had experienced a lot of bizarre moments in his years as a cop. He'd even partaken in a few he didn't like to spend too much time dwelling on. This one took the cake. An admission of murder was the last thing he expected when he followed Kate Burkholder here tonight.

He had pretty good instincts when it came to people. Perhaps to a lesser degree when it came to women, but then who the hell knew. He was too jaded to be shocked by much of anything. Still, this shocked him. Worse, he didn't know what to do about it.

Setting his hands beneath her shoulders, he helped Kate to her feet. "Come on. Up and at 'em."

She seemed almost weightless, and for the first time, he realized there wasn't much to her; most of her bulk was coat and a perception of largeness he attributed to the force of her personality. She hadn't struck him as a crier. Up until this moment, she'd handled the stress like a pro. She'd been tough and focused despite the ugliness of the case. But he knew the dam was breaking. There was no wailing or theatrics, but the look of misery on her face was so profound John could feel it creeping into his own psyche.

Taking her shoulders, he turned her to him. "Kate, what the hell is going on?"

"Johnston was right," she choked. "I . . . blew th-the c-case. Because of . . . this."

He wished he'd never followed her here. He didn't need this. Didn't want to deal with it. Wasn't even sure he cared. His life was complicated enough without throwing a dead body into the mix.

"Pull yourself together," he snapped.

She met his gaze, jerked her head.

"We need to talk about this."

"I know." She wiped frantically at her cheeks, and he wondered how long it took for tears to freeze on skin.

"Is there someplace warm we can go?" he asked.

"The bar. My place." She shrugged. "Or you could just speed things along and take me right to jail."

"Your place." He looked around, wishing he were anywhere but here. "I have a feeling we're going to need some privacy for this."

"You have no idea."

As he handed her the keys, the possibility that she might make a run for it crossed his mind. "You wouldn't do anything stupid, would you?"

She gave him a sage look. "I've already used up my quota for stupid," she said and started toward the Explorer.

She lived in a modest brick ranch on the edge of town. There was no glowing porch light to welcome her. The driveway had yet to be shoveled. He parked curbside and watched Kate pull into the driveway. She started toward the front door without waiting for him.

The thought that his being here could get the tongues wagging drifted through his mind, but John didn't have a better idea. Besides, it wasn't as if the chief of police and the investigating field agent didn't have anything to talk about while they were in the midst of a serial murder case.

He got out and cut across the yard. She'd left the door open, so he stepped inside and closed it behind him. The living room was furnished with an eclectic mix of furniture. A brown contemporary sofa contrasted nicely with a cream-colored chair. An antique cabinet in need of refinishing held an assortment of vases and bowls. The house smelled faintly of candle wax and coffee.

Kate stood at the coat closet and hung her parka. She wore a navy police uniform that was badly wrinkled from wear, as opposed to a lack of pressing.

Bending, she began unlacing her boots with small, competent hands. The uniform wasn't tight, but he could see enough of her to know she was put together nicely. He guessed her to be about five feet six inches tall. Athletic. Maybe a hundred and fifteen pounds. She was wide at the hip, but it was the kind of wide that made his male interest flare.

Crossing to the closet, he hung his own coat, but his focus was on Kate. Her dark brown hair was tousled, as if she'd gone the entire day without brushing it. Her complexion was splotched from crying and pale against the dark curtain of hair.

Once her boots were off, she went through the living room and disappeared down a hall. John wandered into the kitchen. It was surprisingly homey, with light ash cupboards and a contrasting Corian countertop. A stack of bills lay on the built-in desk. A half-burned candle sat in the center of the small dining room table. A normal kitchen except for the fact that its owner had just confessed to murder . . .

Kate emerged a few minutes later. She'd changed into jeans and an oversized gray sweatshirt with *Columbus Police Department* emblazoned on the front. She'd washed the dirt smudges from her face and run a comb through her hair.

"Nice place," he commented.

She brushed past him without responding. Walking to the refrigerator, she stood on her tiptoes and retrieved a bottle from the cabinet above. "The cabinets need updating."

"Unless you're going for some quaint country look." He frowned at the bottle of Absolut in her hand.

"I hate country." She gave him a sagacious look. "Don't bother telling me alcohol isn't going to help."

"That would be hypocritical of me."

"By the time I finish telling you about those remains, you're going to need it."

Setting two glasses and the bottle on the table, she went to the back door and opened it. A ratty-looking orange tabby darted in, hissed at John, and then disappeared to the living room.

"He likes me," he said.

She choked out a sound that was part laugh, part sob, pulled out a chair and collapsed into it. "You're not going to like this, John."

"I figured that out when I saw the skull." He took the chair across from her.

She uncapped the vodka and poured. For a moment they stared at the glasses, unspeaking. Then she reached for hers, drank it down without stopping and poured another. That was when John knew she was a hell of a lot more cop than she was Amish.

He asked the question that had been pounding at his brain since he'd spotted the bones. "Does the body have anything to do with the serial killer operating in Painters Mill?"

"I've been operating under that assumption." She looked into her glass and shrugged. "Until tonight."

"Maybe you ought to start at the beginning."

I feel as if my life has been building to this moment. Still, I'm not prepared for it. How in the name of God does one prepare for complete and utter ruination? Worst-case scenario, Tomasetti walks out of here, goes straight to the suits at BCI who will proceed to destroy my life. If that happens, I've already resolved to protect Jacob and Sarah. Not because they're any less guilty than me, but because they have children; I don't want my nephews or Sarah's unborn child dragged into this. I don't want the Amish community tarnished; they don't deserve that.

I look at Tomasetti, taking in the cold eyes and harsh mouth. He might walk a thin line, but I have a terrible feeling that ambiguity won't help me tonight. "Regardless of what I tell you, I want to see this case through. You have to promise me."

"You know I can't promise that."

I take another drink, force it down. Alcohol, the temporary cure for misery. The words I need to say tumble inside my head, a tangle of memories and secrets and the dead weight of my own conscience.

"Kate," he presses. "Talk to me."

"Daniel Lapp lived on a farm down the road from us," I begin. "He came over sometimes to help with baling hay and chores. He was eighteen years old."

Tomasetti listens, his cop's eyes watchful and assessing. "What happened?"

"I was fourteen years old that summer." I barely remember the young Amish girl I'd been, and I wonder how I had ever been that innocent. "*Mamm* and *Datt* went to a funeral in Coshocton County. My brother, Jacob, was in the field cutting hay. Sarah was delivering quilts in town. I stayed home to bake bread."

I pause, but Tomasetti doesn't give me respite. "Go on."

"Daniel came to the door. He'd been helping Jacob in the field and cut his hand." Even now, a lifetime later, recalling that day disturbs me so profoundly my chest goes tight. "He attacked me from behind. Took me to the floor. I screamed when I saw the knife, but he hit me and he kept hitting me." I feel breathless and lightheaded. Vaguely, I'm aware of my breaths coming too quick, too shallow. "He raped me."

I can't look at Tomasetti, but I hear the scrape of whiskers as he runs his hand over his jaw. "The Amish like to believe we're a separate society," I say, "but that's not always the case. We knew about the murders that had occurred in the last few months. *Datt* told us it was an English matter, the deaths were of no concern to us. But we were scared. We kept our doors locked. We prayed for the families. *Mamm* took food to them." I shrug. "We didn't get the newspaper, but I'd been to the tourist shops in town and read the stories. I knew the victims had been raped. I thought Daniel Lapp was going to kill me."

"What did you do, Kate?"

"I grabbed *Datt*'s shotgun and shot him in the chest."

He stares at me, unblinking. "Did you call the police?"

"I might have if we'd had a phone. But we didn't. I was hysterical. There was blood everywhere." A breath shudders out of me. "My sister came home. She saw the body on the floor and ran out screaming. She ran for over a mile and got Jacob."

"No one called the police?"

I shake my head.

"What about your parents?"

"It was dark by the time they got home. Jacob explained to *Datt* what happened. I think if Lapp had been English, *Datt* would have called the police. But Daniel was one of us. My father told us this was an Amish matter and would be dealt with his way." I take another breath, but I can't get enough air. "He and Jacob wrapped the body in burlap feed bags and put it in the buggy. They drove to the grain elevator and buried it." I look at Tomasetti. "When they came home, *Datt* told us never to speak of it."

"Didn't people wonder what happened to Lapp?" he asks.

"His parents spent weeks looking for him. But after a while most of the Amish came to believe he'd fled because he could not abide by the *Ordnung*. Eventually, his parents believed it, too."

"So the crime was never reported," he says.

"No."

"Tough thing for a fourteen-year-old kid to handle."

"You mean the rape or the fact that I killed a man?"

"Both." He grimaces. "And the fact that you could never talk about it."

"I started acting out after that. I hooked up with some English kids. I started smoking, drinking. Got into trouble a few times. I suppose it was my way of dealing with it. The murders stopped after that. Until tonight, I thought Lapp might be the killer."

"So when the first body showed up, you thought what? That he'd survived?"

I stare down at my hands, find them shaking, so I clasp them together. "Yes."

Silence ensues. My mind scrolls through the repercussions of what I've done. I have no idea how Tomasetti will react. One thing I'm certain of is that my law enforcement career is over. But that's a best-case scenario. If the media gets wind of this, they'll descend like vultures and rip me apart as if I were carrion.

"Evidently, Lapp isn't our man," he says after a moment.

"I killed the wrong man."

"He was a rapist," he says.

"But not a serial murderer."

"He had a weapon. You acted in self-defense."

"Taking a life is against God's laws."

"So is raping a minor child."

"Covering up a murder is against our laws."

"You were fourteen years old. You trusted your father to do the right thing."

"I was old enough to know killing a man is wrong." I force myself to look at him. The house is so quiet I hear snow pinging against the window. The hum of the refrigerator. The hiss of heated air through the vents. "Now that you know my deep, dark secret, what are you going to do about it?"

"If you confess publicly, you can kiss it all good-bye. Your career. Your reputation. Whatever financial security you've got. Not to mention peace of mind."

"Haven't had much of that, anyway."

"Look, Kate, I've done some things that aren't exactly aboveboard." He shrugs. "I'm in no position to judge you."

"Aside from my family, you're the only one who knows."

He refills our glasses. I don't want any more; the vodka is fuzzing up my head. But I pick up the glass anyway. "I don't understand why the murders stopped after that day."

"Maybe what Lapp did to you is completely separate from the murders."

I know sixty to seventy percent of sexual assaults go unreported. I suspect that percentage is higher in the Amish community. For the first time, I wonder if I was Lapp's only victim.

"Kate, this leaves us with a big fucking problem."

"You mean me, don't you?"

John leans forward. "Your fate as a cop aside, let's say we get this guy and the case goes to trial. If someone finds out you were involved in a crime that was covered up, some hotshot defense attorney could use that to discredit both of us and blow the case to hell and back. Maybe even put this guy back on the street."

"No one has to find out about Lapp," I say.

He gives a harsh laugh. "Who else knows?"

"My brother, Jacob. My sister, Sarah."

"What if they decide to talk?"

"They're Amish. They won't."

"Who sent the note to the bishop?"

"My sister." My laugh is dry. "She thought I should share that with my counterparts."

"How are you going to explain it?"

"An obvious hoax."

He picks up his glass and downs the drink. I do the same, and we set our glasses down simultaneously. He gives me a grim, unhappy look. "I don't know you very well, but I think you're a good cop. I think you care. That alone makes you a better cop than me. But you know as well as I do secrets have a way of getting exposed."

"Kind of like old bones." I stare hard at him. "Unless you bury them really deep."

"If I found out, someone else can."

"I don't want my family brought into this. I don't want the Amish community to pay for something I did."

"Look, Kate, you've got a few things going for you on this. There were extenuating circumstances. There's the self-defense angle. Your age at the time of the shooting."

"So what are you going to do?"

"I don't know."

I stare at him, my heart pounding. I want to know if he's going to turn me in, but I'm afraid to ask. Tears burn behind my eyes, but I hold them at bay. The last thing I want to do is break down in front of the man who's probably going to destroy my life.

"I have to go." His chair scrapes across the floor as he rises. "Try to get some sleep."

He leaves the kitchen. A little voice inside my head screams for me to go after him, plead with him to keep his mouth shut, at least until this case is solved. But I can't make myself move. The slamming of the door is like a death knell in my ears. As I reach for the bottle, I know there's not a damn thing I can do but wait for the hammer to fall.

CHAPTER 27

I arrive at the police station a few minutes before seven. Mona sits at the switchboard, her feet on the desk, eating an apple and reading her usual fare.

"Hey, Chief." Her feet hit the floor. Her eyes widen slightly when she looks at me. "Tough night?"

I didn't sleep much after Tomasetti left, and I wonder if I look as wrung out as I feel. "Nothing a cup of whatever you're brewing won't cure."

"It's cinnamon hazelnut." She passes messages to me. "Doc Coblentz probably won't get to the autopsy until midmorning."

The news suits me just fine. Now that I know for a fact Daniel Lapp isn't the killer, I plan to spend the morning working the relocation angle.

"Weatherman says we got more snow coming," she says.

"He's been saying that for a week."

"I think he's right this time."

I snag coffee on the way to my office. Sliding behind my desk, I pull out the Slaughterhouse Killer file and a fresh legal pad. While my computer boots, I hit Skid's cell number. "Did DRC give you anyone besides Starkey?"

"He was the only one."

"Did you check with hospitals?" I ask. "Institutions?"

"I struck out, Chief. Sorry."

"It was worth a shot."

"You got anything new?"

"I'm working on it. See you in a few."

I disconnect and spend a few minutes Googling moving companies within a thirty-mile radius of Painters Mill. There are none with a Painters Mill address, but a Web site pops up for a moving company in Millersburg along with a U-Haul franchise. Grabbing the legal pad, I jot contact information. I know the angle I'm pursuing is a long shot, but it's all I've got. I dial Great Midwest Movers, where I'm put on hold and transferred.

"This is Jerry Golan, how can I help you?"

I identify myself and get right to the point. "I'm working on a case and need the names of people who moved out of the area from 1993 to 1995. Do you guys keep records that long?"

"This about them murders up there?"

"I'm not at liberty to get into details." I lower my voice. "But just between you and me it could be related. I'd appreciate if you'd keep it under your hat."

"My lips are sealed." He lowers his voice as if we now share a secret, and I hear the tap of a keyboard on the other end of the line. "The good news is we've kept all our records since we opened in 1989. The bad news is, they're all over the place. We moved back in '04. Everything got boxed up. Some of it's in storage and some's here at the office."

"All I need is the names and contact information."

Another whistle sails through fiber optic cable. "Might take a while."

"Any way you can expedite that for the chief of police?"

"Well, jeez, I guess I could call in a temp."

"Would it help if I told you to send the bill to me?"

He brightens. "Yes, ma'am. That'd help a lot."

A temp isn't in the budget, but I'll cover it somehow. After hanging up, I go to the Coshocton County Auditor Web site. I stumble through a few pages before finding what I'm looking for. The site offers public access to tax records for real estate sales and transfers. I click on the link and go to the Advanced Search. "Bingo," I whisper and enter the dates I'm looking for.

Unfortunately, the database only goes back ten years. I click on the "Contact" button and request a listing of sales for the county between January 1, 1993 and December 31, 1995.

Next, I go to the Holmes County Auditor Web site. I'm pleased to find that the site offers a "sales search" by property district. There are dozens of districts, broken down by township and village.

My phone buzzes. I see Glock's cell number on the display and pick up. "Hey."

"Something's going on," he says without preamble. "Auggie Brock called a few minutes ago and asked me to meet him at the police station. Said it was urgent."

"What?" Alarm shoots through me. "Did he say why?"

"No, but I thought you might want a heads-up. I'm on my way."

The line goes dead.

Troubled, I stare at the phone. It surprises me by buzzing again. Mona's number pops up on the display and I pick up. "Auggie and his entourage just walked in," she whispers. "They're coming your way."

I look up to see Auggie Brock at my door. I hang up. Behind Auggie, I see Janine Fourman. A tremor of uneasiness goes through me when I see Detrick and John Tomasetti bringing up the rear.

My heart rolls into a hard staccato. "What's wrong?"

No one answers. At first I think there's been another murder. Then the truth hits me, like a fist rammed into my solar plexus. John told them about Lapp. About what I did. They're here to fire me. Maybe even arrest me. The thought paralyzes me with fear. With shame and a keen sense of betrayal. With the knowledge that I'm in very big trouble.

I stare at John. He stares back with those cold cop's eyes. Bastard, I think. *Bastard.*

"We'd like a word with you," Auggie begins.

I rise, my uneasiness growing into a wild and unwieldy panic. "What's going on?"

Auggie clears his throat. "Chief Burkholder, effective immediately, based on just cause, we are terminating your employment contract with the Village of Painters Mill."

I feel as if I've been Tased. I stare at him, speechless, my mind reeling. "On what grounds?"

Bristling with impatience, Janine speaks up. "We've received a complaint about the way you're investigating these murders."

"A complaint? From who?" But I already know.

"Finger-pointing isn't important at this juncture," she says.

"The hell it's not." I look at John. He returns my gaze levelly, and I wonder if he knew about this and didn't tell me. I shift my attention to the mayor. "You had better start talking."

"We held a closed-door session this morning," says Auggie.

"Who?"

He motions toward the group. "All of us. It was decided."

I see Glock standing behind John and feel the knife sink in a little deeper. Did he know about this?

Janine Fourman looks at me like a mother admonishing a badly behaved child. "This is not personal, Kate. We're acting in the best interest of Painters Mill."

Auggie produces a sheet of paper and hands it to me. "You're being relieved of your duties for just cause. It is the opinion of the council that your lack of experience has prevented you from pursuing this case in the proper manner."

I cut in. "Lack of experience?"

Ignoring me, Auggie continues. "That finding is based upon your delay in calling for assistance from other law enforcement agencies, namely the FBI, BCI and the Holmes County Sheriff's Department. There was an official complaint filed. We reviewed it in depth. And it is the consensus of the council that you be removed from your position until all the facts are known. In the interim, Sheriff Detrick will be the acting chief until the situation is resolved."

Relief flits though me that there was no mention of human remains. "Sounds like you stayed up all night rehearsing, Auggie."

He has the audacity to blush. "This is not a reflection on you, but your lack of experience and the difficult circumstances of these murders."

"I'm doing everything humanly possible to solve this case." I hate the desperation ringing in my voice. "We're working practically around the clock."

Janine grimaces, the first show of anything but smug satisfaction. "We know you've worked hard. We know you care. That's not in question here. It's just that we don't feel you have the *experience* to work on a case of this magnitude."

"Don't do this," I say to Auggie.

The mayor averts his gaze. "The decision has been made."

I look from face to face, but it's like staring at a brick wall. They've made up their minds. I know it's more political than personal, but that doesn't keep it from hurting. I have a personal stake in this case. I want to see it through. "You're making a mistake."

Auggie nods at Glock. "Officer Maddox, if you could relieve the chief of her badge and sidearm. Kate, you can take a few minutes to pack your things if you want. I'm afraid you'll have to leave the Explorer here, since it's a city vehicle. Officer Maddox will drop you off at your house."

Glock gives him the best fuck-you look I've ever seen and holds his place at the door.

I look down at my desk. My computer screen still displays the Holmes County Auditor Web site. I can't imagine packing my things and walking away. This job may be my life. But this case has become an obsession.

Shaking his head, Auggie leaves my office. Janine gives me a wolverine smile and follows him. I glance toward the hall, but Tomasetti is gone. I feel abandoned and betrayed by all of them.

I look at Glock. "Are you going to make sure I don't steal any paper clips on my way out?"

He holds my gaze. "Fuckers waylaid me with this, Chief."

The loyalty behind his words should console me, but they don't. I sink into my chair, trying to put things into perspective.

Glock drops into the visitor chair. "Fuckin' Johnston."

I rub my eyes. "Was Tomasetti involved?"

"I don't know."

I scan the papers spread out on my desk. My notes and theories and reports. The Slaughterhouse Killer file. The crime scene photos. Dozens of calls that need to be returned. How can I walk away when things are so damn unfinished?

"Chief, if it wasn't for the baby coming I would have walked," he says. "Fuckin' health insurance."

I can't imagine never sitting behind this desk again. In some small corner of my mind I think if I do walk out that door, I'll just keep on going and never come back. But I know better than most that you can't run from your past.

"I guess I need to pack."

Glock looks miserable.

I hit the speaker button on my phone and dial Mona. "Can you bring me a box?"

A cautious pause. "Why?"

"Just do it, Mona, okay?"

I hang up. A moment later she appears at the door with an empty copy paper box. Her eyes flick from me to Glock and back to me. "What'd they do?"

I don't answer, but I see the knowledge in her eyes. "Chief? Did they . . ." She lets the words trail.

"Yeah," I say.

"They can't do that." She looks from me to Glock and back to me. "Can they do that?"

"It's in my contract."

"But you're the best police chief this town ever had."

"It's politics," Glock growls.

Blindly, I begin tossing items into the box. A couple of framed photos. A brass paperweight Mona gave me for Christmas. My diploma and certificates hanging on the wall. What I really want I'm pretty sure I won't be walking out with: my goddamn case.

For several minutes both Glock and Mona watch me pack. The switchboard rings and Mona shakes her head. "I don't believe this," she says and rushes out to grab the call.

Humiliation sets in when Detrick enters. He looks from me to Glock to the box on my desk, his eyes finally landing on me. "I'm sorry things worked out this way."

I want to vent some of the anger pumping through me. I want to call him an ass-kissing, limelight-grabbing, case-stealing son of a bitch. Instead, I toss a scented candle into the box and frown at him. "You call in the feds?"

"SAC'll be here tomorrow," Detrick answers.

I nod, wondering if John knew and didn't see fit to tell me. "Good luck with the case."

Detrick says nothing.

I pick up the box and walk out the door.

CHAPTER 28

I feel like a wounded animal that's gone to its cave to lick fatal wounds as I carry my box of belongings through the door. Around me, the house is silent and cold and reminds me of how empty my life will be without my job. The repercussions of my termination have started to sink in.

When I was eighteen years old and announced I would not be joining the church, the Amish bishop put me under the *bann*. My family wouldn't take meals with me. It wasn't done to injure, but in the hope I would come to my senses and live the life God had planned for me. I felt banished and alone. Neither of those things were enough to sway my decision to leave, but it had hurt.

Today, I feel much the same way. Abandoned. Betrayed. I should be worried about more practical matters like the loss of income and health insurance. I should be concerned by the fact that my career has taken a major hit and there are no job prospects within fifty miles. I'll be forced to sell the house and move. All of these concerns are dwarfed by my growing obsession with this case.

I set the box on the kitchen table. I spot my legal pad lying on top and resist the urge to pull it out. I want to continue working the relocation angle, but it's going to be tough without resources.

A scratch at the window above the sink interrupts my thoughts. I look up to see the orange tabby glaring at me from the sill. I try not to think about the parallels between the unwanted stray and myself as I cross to the door and open it. The cat bursts in with a waft of cold air and a confetti swirl of snow. I go to the refrigerator, pour milk into a bowl and pop it in the microwave. "I know." I set the bowl on the floor. "We're fucked."

I consider having my first drink of the day, but I know getting shitfaced before noon will only make things worse. Instead I walk to the bedroom, exchange my uniform for jeans and a sweatshirt, and grab my laptop off the dresser. Settling at the kitchen table, I fire up the computer and start with the Holmes County Auditor Web site. It's tedious work that will probably net nothing more than eyestrain and a stiff neck. But at least it will keep me occupied. The last thing I want to do is sit around and wallow in self-pity or, God forbid, go into full self-destruct mode.

By noon I'm frothing at the mouth with frustration. When I can stand the silence of the house no longer, I turn on the television to some mindless afternoon fare and return to my computer. At one o'clock, I pour myself a double shot of Absolut and drink it down like lemonade on a hot day.

I call Skid, but get voice mail. I had assigned him the task of checking snowmobile registrations for the two-county area. I wonder if he's gotten wind of my termination and decided he doesn't have to answer my calls. I'm in the process of dialing his home number when Pickles calls.

"I can't believe those goddamn pencil-pushers," he begins without preface.

"What's going on there?"

"Detrick is making hisself right at home in your office. Mona says if he starts bringing in those fuckin' animal heads from the taxidermist and mounting them on the walls, she's going to quit."

"FBI there?"

"SAC arrived a few minutes ago. Some wet-behind-the-ears dipshit with a master's degree in ass-kissing and the common sense of a beagle. Detrick is practically sucking his dick."

I get a good belly laugh out of that despite my dark mood.

"I'm glad one of us thinks this is funny," Pickles grumbles.

"I'm just glad you're mad for me."

"Department ain't going to be the same without you, Kate. You gonna fight it?"

"I don't know. Probably not." I think of Tomasetti, but I don't ask about him. I can't help but wonder if he had a hand in this. "How's Glock holding up?"

"He hates this shit, but he's hanging in there. I swear if his wife wasn't about to spit out a baby he'd tell those pencil necks to go fuck themselves."

"How about you?"

"I'm thinking after this I might retire for good. Nothing I hate more than having to answer to a bunch of suits."

I pause. "Can I ask you for a favor?"

"Hell yes, you can."

"Go to Skid's cube. See if you can find the list of snowmobiles registered in the two-county area. Scan it and fax it to me, will you?"

"I can do that."

It's a comfort knowing I have someone inside the department I can count on. In the back of my mind I wonder if Mona will copy the file for me. "What else is going on?"

"Glock is sending everyone out to recanvass. It's a good call, but they're batting zero, Chief."

I want to remind him I'm no longer chief, but it feels inordinately good to be called that right now. "Thanks, Pickles."

"My pleasure."

I hang up and go back to my laptop. To my surprise, the Coshocton County clerk has e-mailed me the names of people who sold property from 1993 through 1995. There are seventeen names. I want to run the entire list through OHLEG for a cross-check. I wonder if my OHLEG account has been disabled. Curious, I pull up the site and enter my user name and password. I let out the breath I'd been holding when the law enforcement main menu appears. I go directly to OHLEG-SE, the search engine, and enter the names. I do the same with SORN, Ohio's Sex Offender Registration and Notification database. It's a long shot, but you never know when you might catch a break.

Knowing I'm in for a long wait on my inquiries, I go to the Holmes County Auditor Web site and begin the tedious process of searching for people who sold or transferred property from 1993 through 1995. It's probably a waste of time; even if my suspicions are correct and the killer changed locales, he could have rented an apartment. He could have owned property in another county. Or the property could be listed under the name of a family member. The variables are seemingly endless. That's not to mention the small problem that I'm no longer a cop. Even if I do find some connection, I'm going to have a hard time doing anything about it.

I stumble through the Web site, netting a total of four names. A knock at the door startles me. In the living room, I put my eye to the peephole to see John Tomasetti standing on the porch with his collar turned up against the cold. White specks of snow cover his shoulders. His expression is grim. Taking a deep breath, I open the door.

His eyes meet mine, then skim the length of me. "I'd ask how you're doing, but that glass in your hand gives it away."

"How much did you have to do with it?" I ask.

"I'm not that big a hypocrite."

"The timing is just coincidence, huh?"

"That's right."

"Here's a newsflash for you, *Agent* Tomasetti. I don't believe you."

He frowns, shifts his weight from one foot to the other. "Can I come in?"

"I think the smartest thing you can do is leave."

"No one's ever accused me of being smart."

I give him a withering look.

"Look," he says, "I'm not the enemy here."

"You stabbed me in the back."

"Someone filed a complaint against you. Considering that scene in your office yesterday, I'd say Johnston is a pretty good guess."

He's right; Glock told me as much. But it's not enough to quell my anger. I don't feel like being reasonable and I don't know who to trust.

"If I had spilled your secret to the town council," John says, "you can bet your ass you'd be in some interview room surrounded by a bunch of gnarly cops asking nasty questions about the whereabouts of a missing Amish man."

I step back and open the door. "Why are you here?"

He enters the foyer and closes the door behind him. "I wanted to make sure you're all right."

I look down at my glass. It's empty. I want to refill it, but I don't want him to know my frame of mind has deteriorated to that low point. "You could have used the phone."

"I'm sorry about the job."

"Do me a favor and don't apologize, okay?"

Nodding, he shrugs off his coat. He expects me to take it, but I don't, so he carries it to the sofa and tosses it over the arm. "You can fight the termination, you know. There's an appeal process."

"Probably not worth it."

He starts toward the kitchen and I realize he's spotted my laptop and notes. I follow, wishing I'd put things away before letting him in. I don't want him to know I'm still working the case.

His eyes take in the scene and he frowns. "You're not one of those obsessive cops who can't let go, are you?"

"I just like to finish what I start."

"And maybe I'm a well-adjusted, middle-aged man." Shaking his head, Tomasetti goes to the cupboard and pulls out a glass.

"Why don't you make yourself at home?" I say.

Holding my gaze, he crosses to me, invading my space slightly, and takes my glass from my hand. At first I think he's going to take it away. Instead he sets both glasses on the table. I watch, fascinated, as he pours three fingers of vodka into each glass, then passes mine back to me. "So, are you okay, or what?"

"I'd feel better if you kept me in the loop."

"I've got a penchant for breaking the rules, anyway."

"No one has to know."

"The truth usually comes out sooner or later." He raises his glass. "Believe me, I know."

I clink my glass to his and down the drink. The vodka burns all the way to my stomach. My already fuzzy head goes fuzzier. I look at Tomasetti, really look at him, and a weird quiver of attraction goes through me. I'm not sure if it's because he's my best link to this case or if it's something a hell of a lot more complicated.

He's not a handsome man. Not in the traditional sense. But the package as a whole is appealing in a dangerous and unconventional way. I could take any one facet of his face and call it ordinary. But when you put all of them together, there's nothing ordinary about him. He's all dark shadows and sharp angles and secrets as taboo as my own.

"I plugged the crime signature data into VICAP," he says, "but nothing viable has come back."

"VICAP wasn't widely used, particularly by small towns, until recently."

"I know that."

"So maybe you could broaden the search criteria. I'd like to have a look at what comes back myself."

"And I thought you let me in because you're starting to like me."

"Now you know I have an agenda."

His laugher is a deep, musical sound and I realize it's the first time I've heard it. "I guess it's a good thing I don't have a fragile male ego."

"Will you do it?"

"We could probably work something out."

"That kind of answer could be construed as sexual harassment."

"It could be. But you're no longer on the payroll."

My heart rate is up. I feel light-headed. I want to blame both of those things on the vodka, but I'm honest enough with myself to admit it has more to do with the man.

He finishes his drink and starts toward me. He has the most unnerving stare of anyone I've ever met. Only when my rear presses against the counter do I realize I'm backing up. That I'm filled with an edgy anticipation that's part cognitive, part physical. I stop analyzing when he reaches me. Setting his hands on the counter on either side of me, he locks me in.

"What are you doing?" I manage.

"Screwing things up, probably."

"You're good at that, right?"

"You have no idea." Dipping his head, he leans close and presses his mouth to mine. Shock and pleasure vibrate through my body on contact. His lips are firm and warm. I feel his quickened breaths against my cheek. I'm tempted to open and take this to the next level, but some ingrained protective instinct I've developed over the years won't let me. In terms of passion, the kiss doesn't amount to much. But with regard to impact, I feel as if I've just been hit with a burst of machine gun fire.

I don't remember reaching for him, but my arms find their way around his shoulders. Tension quivers in the hard mass of muscle beneath my hands. He deepens the kiss, his tongue probing, sliding between my lips. I take him in and revel in his taste. I smell the pine and musk scent of his aftershave. Need coils and flexes inside me. I'm keenly aware of the hard length of his penis against my pelvis, and I go wet between my legs.

I'm not totally inexperienced when it comes to intimacy. When I lived in Columbus I had a couple of tepid relationships and one serious, ill-fated affair. But it's been a while and I'm more than a little rusty. He doesn't seem to notice.

He slides his hands to the sides of my face. I open my eyes to find him staring at me. His expression is a mix of surprise and perplexity. His calloused palms cradle my cheeks. We're breathing hard, as if we've both just finished a marathon.

He runs his knuckles down my cheek, a touch so feather-soft that I shiver. "That was unexpected," he says.

"But nice."

"Better than nice."

Reaching up, I take his hands from my face, but I can't stop looking at him. My mouth still tingles from his kiss. "The timing could be better."

"I'll have to work on that."

A knock on the door interrupts the moment. Tomasetti steps quickly back. "Expecting company?"

"No."

Leaving the kitchen, I cross to the front door and check the peephole. Surprise ripples through me when I see Glock on the porch, his hat pulled low against the wind. My first thought is that they've discovered another body. I open the door. "What happened?" I ask, motioning him inside.

"Chief." Glock's eyes widen when he spots Tomasetti. "Detrick just made an arrest."

"What?" I say. "Who?"

"Jonas Hershberger."

Disbelief rears inside me. I know Jonas. I went to school with him. Up until the eighth grade, anyway, when the Amish stop going to school. He lives in a ramshackle pig farm a few miles from where Amanda Horner's body was found.

"He's one of the most gentle people I've ever known," I say.

"We've got evidence, Chief."

"What evidence?" Tomasetti chimes in.

"Blood. At Hershberger's farm."

"How did the arrest come about?" I ask.

"We were canvassing the area. Detrick saw a suspicious stain. He did a field test for blood, got a positive. He asked for permission to search and Jonas agreed." Glock shrugs. "One of Detrick's deputies found a piece of clothing that might have belonged to one of the vics. Detrick has the whole place cordoned off and they're looking for more. There's a BCI crime scene tech out there right now. Detrick and the SAC have Hershberger in the interrogation room. It looks like he's our guy."

John looks at me. "I've got to get down there."

I desperately want to go with him. That need is an agony that goes beyond physical. I begin to pace, every nerve in my body jumping. I'm aware of Tomasetti pulling on his coat. "Goddamnit," I mutter.

He crosses to me and sets his hand on my shoulder. "I'll call you as soon as I know something."

I'm too upset to speak, so I nod.

Glock is already out the door. Giving me a final look over his shoulder, Tomasetti follows. I trail them as far as the front porch. I barely feel the cold as I watch both men climb into their vehicles and pull away.

"Damnit," I whisper.

And I wonder if, after all these years, God has finally seen fit to punish me for what I did. And for what I did not.

CHAPTER 29

Some nights are darker and colder and longer than others. This is one of those nights. It's only eight P.M., but it feels like midnight. I'm hungover and so unsettled I can't stand being in my own skin. After Tomasetti and Glock left earlier, I had another drink. Not to mention a good old-fashioned cry. But crying and drinking myself into a stupor aren't my style. I'm more proactive than that. Yet here I am, pacing the house, bawling like some high school girl, doing the one thing I swore I wouldn't: feeling sorry for myself.

I should be relieved a suspect has been arrested. I should be elated knowing no more women will die. My career might be in the toilet, but there are worse fates. So why the hell do I feel like someone has just ripped out my guts?

It's not until I'm in my Mustang and heading toward the Hershberger farm that I identify the core of my disquiet: Jonas is not a viable suspect.

I've always made a conscious effort to keep my prejudices and preconceived notions removed from my job. I know, perhaps better than anyone, that the Amish are not perfect. They're human. They make mistakes. They break rules and traditions. Sometimes they even break the law. Some have strayed from basic Amish values, going so far as to drive cars and use electricity. But not Jonas. I know for a fact he doesn't drive. Not a vehicle. He doesn't even use a motorized tractor for his farm. There's no way in hell he drove that snowmobile.

That's not to mention the fact that he doesn't even come close to matching the profile of this killer. I've known Jonas most of my life; he doesn't have a mean bone in his body. When I was a kid, *Mamm* and *Datt* bought pork from the Hershberger family. Once, while *Datt* and Jonas's father were talking, Jonas took me to the barn to see their new kittens. The mama cat, a pretty little calico, had already birthed four kittens. Jonas was so wrapped up in the new babies, he didn't notice that the cat was in distress. Lying on her side, she was panting, her pink tongue hanging out. I could see her little body straining to expel another kitten. We didn't know how to help her, so Jonas ran to his father and begged him to take the cat to the English veterinarian in town. I knew that wasn't going to happen. Jonas cried like a baby. I'd been embarrassed for him and upset that the cat was suffering and would probably die right along with her kittens. I learned later that after the mama cat passed, Jonas bottle-fed the four babies, and they survived.

Such a small thing in the scope of a lifetime. I know people change. I know life can take a toll, and time has a way of turning innocence to cynicism, sweet to bitter, kindness to cruelty. But I also know that most serial murderers are sociopaths from birth. As children, many begin their dark journey with animals. Few are made later in life.

It's been years since I spoke to Jonas, and I know he's changed. I've heard the rumors. After his wife's passing five years ago, he became somewhat of an eccentric. He lives alone and has been known to carry on conversations with people who aren't there, including his dead wife. His farm is run-down. He doesn't exercise good manure management and the smell is terrible. He keeps to himself, and no one seems to know much about him anymore. That doesn't keep them from talking.

I want to speak with Jonas, but I know Detrick won't let me. I settle for the next best thing and drive to his brother's farm. James Hershberger's place is almost as decrepit as Jonas's. I pray I don't run into law enforcement as I pull into the driveway. The last thing I need is for someone to figure out I'm not as gone as they'd like me to be. A buggy is parked at the rear of the house. A Percheron gelding stands quietly with its rear leg cocked, its coat covered with snow. I park behind the buggy and take the sidewalk to the porch.

The door opens before I knock. James Hershberger stands just inside, his expression telling me I'm not welcome.

"I just heard what happened to Jonas," I say in Pennsylvania Dutch.

"I do not wish to speak with you, Katie."

Quickly, I explain that I've been fired.

He looks surprised, but doesn't open the door to let me in. "I do not understand why the English police have arrested my brother for these terrible deeds."

"Does he have an alibi?" I ask.

The Amish man shakes his head. "Jonas is a solitary man. I try to be a good brother, but I do not see him often. He leads a simple life. For days in a row, he does not leave the farm."

"Do you know what kind of evidence the police have?"

"The policeman claims to have found blood on the porch." James fingers his full beard. "Katie, my brother is a butcher. There is often blood. But it does not belong to any of the women."

"Have you been to see him?"

"The police will not allow it." He shoves his hands into his pockets. "He did not do these things. I stake my life on that."

"I know he lost his wife a few years ago. How did he handle her death? Did it change him in any way?"

"He was deeply saddened, of course, but neither bitter nor angry. Her death only served to bring him closer to God."

"Does he drive a vehicle?" I ask.

"Never. He still uses the horses to farm." He looks at me, his expression beseeching. "Katie, he would not go against God's will. It is not in his nature."

Once again I'm reminded of the kittens. Reaching out, I touch James's arm. "I know," I say and start toward the Mustang.

I don't want to go home, but I have nowhere else to go. I consider driving to Jonas's farm, but if the police are still processing the scene they won't let me on the property. I wonder what forensic testing on the blood will reveal. Is it possible the shy Amish boy I once knew transformed into a monster in the span of twenty years?

I spot John Tomasetti's Tahoe parked in front of my house, and a small rise of anticipation runs the length of me. As much as I don't want to admit it, I'm looking forward to seeing him. I want to believe it's because of the case. I don't let myself analyze it any more closely than that.

We meet on the front porch. "What does Detrick have on Hershberger?" I ask as I open the door.

"I sent the blood to the lab." He's got snow in his hair and on his shoulders. He's staring at me with those intense eyes and I realize I like being the focus of his attention. "It's human."

The news puts a chink in my hope for a quick exoneration for Jonas. I hang John's coat in the closet. "Have they typed it?"

"The blood is O negative. Hershberger is A positive," he says. "Brenda Johnston was O negative. DNA will tell us if it's hers."

"When do you expect results?"

"Five days. Seven max."

None of this is good news for Jonas. I'm keenly aware of John behind me as I walk toward the kitchen. Flipping on the light, I go to the stove, fill the teakettle with water and set it on the flame. "You think he did it?" I ask.

"If the blood is from one of the vics, it's a slam dunk."

I turn to Tomasetti. "I've known Jonas since we were kids. He's not a violent man."

"People change, Kate."

"Have you interviewed him?"

John nods.

"What do you think?"

He makes the hand sign for crazy. "I think he's a fuckin' loon."

"Emotional problems don't make him a killer."

"Doesn't vindicate him, either."

"What about an alibi?"

"He rarely leaves the farm."

"Tell me about the evidence."

"In addition to the blood evidence, a BCI tech found a shoe believed to have belonged to one of the victims. A bloody length of baling wire. A knife that fits the specs of the murder weapon."

The news shocks me. "Don't you think that's just a little too neat? Think about it. He hasn't left a single clue behind and all of a sudden he leaves all this stuff at his own property?"

"Kate." Surprise ripples through me when he wraps his fingers around my upper arms. "Stop. It's over. We got him."

I meet his gaze. "Jonas didn't do it."

"Because he's Amish?"

"For God's sake, John, he doesn't drive. He couldn't have been driving that snowmobile."

"Or so he says."

"He doesn't fit the profile."

"Profiling isn't an exact science."

I sigh, wishing I could be satisfied the way everyone else seems to be. "Did you run the modified MO criteria through VICAP?"

He groans in exasperation. "Anyone ever tell you you have a hard time letting go?"

"I want to look at the reports."

"Look, I told the analyst not to bother, since we made an arrest."

"John, please."

He sighs. "You're wasting your time, but I'll call her back and ask her to e-mail them to you."

"Thank you." Raising up on my tiptoes, I kiss his cheek.

"They want me back in Columbus, Kate. I came to say good-bye."

This shouldn't come as a surprise, but it does. "When are you leaving?"

"I'm packed. I was going to take off tonight."

In the last couple of days John has become an unlikely ally. He's been a source of support and information. I realize he's been a friend, too. "I'm glad you came by," I say.

One side of his mouth hikes into a half-smile. "You just wanted to pump me for information about the case."

"That, too." I like his sense of humor. I wonder what it would be like to have him in my life. "I was just getting used to having you around."

"Most people just want to get rid of me."

I laugh outright, but I'm suddenly uncomfortable. I'm not very good at farewells. I can't meet his gaze. I start to turn away, but he reaches out and stops me.

"We left something unfinished earlier," he says.

"You mean the kiss?"

"For starters."

He leans into me until his body is flush against mine. My heart pounds like a metronome run amok. For the first time in days, thoughts of the case leave my head, and my entire focus shifts to John. Lowering his head, he brushes his mouth against mine. His breath smells of peppermint. The kiss is gentle, but not tentative. Pulling away, he slides his hands to my face. "I've been wondering what might have happened if we hadn't been interrupted."

"I probably would have chickened out."

"Or I would have said something inappropriate and pissed you off."

"Maybe we're just a little out of practice."

"You think maybe we could stumble through the basics?"

"If we put our minds to it and stay focused we could give it a shot. See what happens."

We grin stupidly at each other. I don't want this moment to be awkward, but it is. I realize neither of us are good at this kind of intimacy.

"You want a drink?" he asks.

"Will it help with the butterflies?"

"Helps with all sorts of things." Stepping back, he goes to the cupboard above the refrigerator and pulls out the bottle of vodka. I turn off the stove, gather glasses and set them on the counter.

Scratching at the window draws my attention and I see the orange tabby, his face covered with a frosting of snow.

"Cold night for that little guy." John crosses to the door and opens it. The cat darts inside, hisses at John, then disappears into the living room.

"He's warming up to you," I say.

"I've got that stray cat thing going." He pours into our glasses and raises his to mine. "Here's to the end of a long and difficult case."

I clink my glass to his, and try not to wonder if the case is really over. We knock back our drinks without breaking eye contact. I know what's going to happen next. I can't remember the last time I felt this way. I can't believe I'm actually thinking about acting on the reckless impulses running hot in my blood.

He takes my glass and sets in on the counter. The next thing I know I'm being swept into his arms. "What are you doing?"

"I was thinking about trying to get you into bed."

"Funny, I was just thinking the same thing about you."

He kisses me, but this time it's not tentative. It's the kiss of a man who knows what he wants and isn't afraid to take it. "So are you okay with this?" he whispers.

He's asking about the rape, I realize. "At one point in my life, I would have run away from this moment and never looked back. Or maybe I would have sabotaged whatever relationship we'd begun."

"I thought I had the market cornered on the relationship-busting thing," he says.

"You don't."

"Is that a warning?"

"Probably."

He looks at me with those dark, intense eyes. "No pretenses, Kate. It's just us. You and me."

"And our baggage."

Laughing outright, he carries me down the hall and starts into the first bedroom.

"Wrong room," I say.

"Sorry." He backs into the hall and carries me into my bedroom.

He puts me down next to the bed. His eyes go to the old kerosene lamp on my night table. "Does that thing work?"

"It belonged to my *mamm*." One of the few things I have of hers. "Matches are in the night table."

"Don't go anywhere." He softens the words with a smile.

My nerves are snapping now. I watch as he removes the globe from the lamp. A match flares, then flickering light fills the room. He crosses to me, sets his hands on my shoulders and gazes into my eyes. "It's been a long time for me." He glances away, then back. "Not since Nancy."

"Two years is a long time to be alone."

"Plenty of demons to keep me company."

I think about everything I've read or heard about him, and I wonder if the stories are true. If he went rogue after his wife and kids were murdered. I wonder if he would tell me the truth if I asked. I wonder if I really want to know.

He slides his hands to the hem of my sweatshirt. I lift my arms and he pulls it over my head. His gaze flicks to my bra, skims down my belly, lower. He runs his hands through my hair, mussing it. His fingers linger on either side of my face, then he snags the straps of my bra with his thumbs and tugs them over my shoulders.

Cool air washes over my breasts, and I shiver. I'm keenly aware of his hands going to the fly of my jeans. His fingers tremble as he unfastens the button, then tugs down the zipper. Self-consciousness creeps over me. Needing something to do with my hands, I reach for the buttons of his shirt. But my fingers are shaking and I fumble them.

John takes my hands in his and kisses my knuckles. "How is it that you can chase a madman into the woods in the dead of night and not even break a sweat, but when it comes to this, you're shaking so hard you can't even manage the buttons on my shirt?"

"I think if push came to shove, I could probably kick your ass, Tomasetti."

He grins. "I think you probably could, too."

I try to smile, end up flushing hotly. "I'm not very good at this."

"Yes you are." He touches his mouth to my forehead. "Don't be nervous. It's only me."

He unbuttons his shirt and it opens to a solid chest covered with a thatch of dark hair. He's muscular, but not buff. Thin, but it's a long-distance-runner kind of thin. My thoughts evaporate when he tugs my jeans down my hips. I step out of them, then watch as he kicks his own slacks aside.

His touch is electric, positive and negative charges skittering over every nerve ending in my body. Slowly, he backs me to the bed, pushes me back and comes down on top of me. Arousal comes in a flash flood. It courses through me with every hammer strike beat of my heart. I arch, wanting him, wanting this moment, wanting too much.

As John eases his body into mine, I feel as if we're the center of the universe and a kind God has blessed two imperfect people with a perfect moment.

CHAPTER 30

John lay on the bed and listened to the wind drive snow against the windows. Next to him, Kate slept with the quiet motionlessness of an exhausted child. This wasn't the right time for him to be thinking about Nancy, but he was. For a long time after her murder, he'd been able to feel her. Not a physical presence, but more of an imprint on his psyche. At some point in the last months, he'd lost that. He could no longer conjure her face or the scent of her perfume. She'd become a memory.

He wasn't sure how he felt about that. For two years, living had been about grief and misery and rage. It had been about wallowing and self-loathing. It had been about punishment. And then it had been about revenge. He'd stopped caring. About his job. His friends and relationships. He stopped caring about himself. Then along came this last-chance case, and Kate with her troubled eyes and pretty smile and secrets nearly as dark as his own. Somehow, he'd been thrust back into the land of the living. Not an easy transition for a man teetering on the brink of self-destruction. He still had a long road ahead, but this was a start.

He should have known there would be guilt. There always was. Because he was alive and Nancy and the girls were dead. Because life went on without them. Because *he'd* moved on. Sleeping with Kate would bring complications, too. He was in no frame of mind to be taking on a relationship with a woman. He wasn't very good at making people happy. Eventually, expectations would come into play. He knew they were expectations he couldn't or wouldn't meet.

Sliding from the bed, he stepped into his jeans and left the bedroom. He grabbed his coat and keys, then headed for the Tahoe. He didn't know why he was running away. Maybe because being close to someone took a hell of a lot more guts than being alone.

Around him the night was so quiet he could hear the patter of falling snow. He hadn't smoked in almost six months, but at this moment he needed a cigarette with the intensity of an addict looking for a fix. Opening the passenger door, he plucked a pack of Marlboros from the glove compartment and lit up. He'd just taken that first heady puff when the front door squeaked open.

"You going to smoke that all by yourself?"

He turned to see Kate standing on the porch in a fuzzy robe and wool-lined mocks. She shouldn't have looked sexy with her hair mussed and her body lost in the robe, but she did.

"I didn't want to smell up the house," he said.

"I could crack a window."

She did and they sat at the kitchen table and passed the cigarette back and forth until it was gone.

"I feel like I've corrupted you," John said.

"I hate to ruin whatever image you've drawn of me in your head, but that wasn't my first smoke."

He studied her, liking the way her hair fell into her eyes, and the way she swept it back with her hand. At that moment, he figured he liked just about everything about her. "So who *did* corrupt you?"

She grinned. "I have this friend by the name of Gina Colorosa. We went through the academy together."

"Ah, those wild academy days." Suddenly, he wanted to know everything about her. "How did Gina manage to corrupt a nice Amish girl?"

"If I tell you everything, you'll have to arrest me."

"I like Gina already."

As if remembering, she smiled, then sobered. "I didn't fit in here, especially after the bishop put me under the *bann*." She shrugged. "I was young enough to convince myself it didn't matter. I was angry and defiant. I saved enough money for a bus ride and moved to Columbus when I turned eighteen."

"That had to have been a tough transition."

She gave a self-deprecating laugh. "Talk about a fish out of water. All I had to my name was two hundred dollars. I wore the dresses my mother made. I cut the hem, but . . ." She shook her head. "You can imagine. Anyway, I was broke. No job. No place to live. Didn't know a soul. I was basically living on the street when I met Gina."

"How did you meet her?"

"It wasn't love at first sight." Her eyes flicked down, then went back to his. "It was cold. I needed a place to sleep. She didn't lock her car."

"You slept in her car?"

"She got in to go to work the next morning and there I was." Her lips curved into a wry smile. "I've never told anyone that before."

"So did she call the cops, or what?"

"Threatened to. But I must have looked pretty harmless because she took me into her apartment. Fed me. The next thing I know, I have a place to live." Another smile, amused this time. "Gina did all the bad things I'd been warned about. Smoking. Drinking. Cussing. She seemed very worldly to me. I don't know how or why, but we hit it off."

"How did you get into law enforcement?"

"Gina was a dispatcher with the Columbus PD. I finally landed a job waiting tables at a pancake house. At night, she'd come home and tell me about her day. I thought she had the most exciting job in the world. I wanted a job like hers. So I went back to school, earned my GED. A month later, she got me a job as a dispatcher at a substation near downtown. That fall, we enrolled in a criminal justice program at the community college. A year later, we were in the academy."

He stared at her, realizing he was getting caught up in this. Getting caught up in her. Not a good frame of mind for a man who would be leaving in a few hours.

"What about you, Tomasetti?"

"I came out of the womb corrupted."

Laughing, she reached for the pack of cigarettes. John wasn't sure why it pleased him when she lit up. Maybe because it made her more human, a little less perfect and a tad closer to his own tarnished soul.

"So what did you do before you were a cop?" she asked.

"I was always a cop." He rolled his shoulders to ease some of the tension creeping up the back of his neck. "I think this is where you're supposed to ask me about what happened in Cleveland."

"I figured if you wanted to talk about it, you would."

She didn't look away. That impressed him. Probably more than he would ever be able to tell her. "How much do you know?" he asked.

"The media version. I know they usually don't get it right."

"It's an ugly story, Kate."

"You don't have to talk about it if you don't want to."

For the first time in his life, he did. Kate had given him something he hadn't had for a long time: hope. Made him realize he might not need the alcohol and pills to get through the day. The time had come to lance the boil, let the demons out, start the healing process. "Do you know who Con Vespian is?"

"Every cop in the state knows about Vespian. Cleveland's version of John Gotti."

"With a little Charles Manson mixed in."

"Narcotics. Prostitution. Gambling."

"He had his fingers in a lot of pies, but he dealt mostly in heroin. Big time stuff, including murder when it was convenient. Worse when he wanted to make a point. Vespian and I go way back to when I was a street cop. I busted him twice. He got off both times. Every narc in the city had a hard-on for him. But he was one lucky son of a bitch. Dangerous, too, because he was half fucking crazy."

"Bad combination."

"He got off on beating the system. I wanted to be the one to bring him down. Somewhere along the line, it got personal."

Her expression sobered, and John could tell she knew the story was about to take a dark twist. "My partner was an old-timer by the name of Vic Niswander. Great guy. Good cop. Funny as hell in a politically incorrect way. Just became a grandpa. Four months away from retirement. We used to kid around about it, but he wanted to get Vespian before he left."

Remembering, John smiled. But as his mind took him through the nightmare that followed, the smile made him feel as if he'd just bitten into a rotten piece of meat. "Vic and I had a snitch inside Vespian's operation. I don't remember where we found this guy. Just some dipshit junkie by the name of Manny Newkirk. Couldn't think his way out of a bag. He'd spill his guts for twenty bucks. One night I set up a routine meeting with him, but I got side-lined. Kid stuff—frickin' basketball or something—and I couldn't make it. Niswander went in my place." He blew out a breath to ease the pressure in his chest. "Someone ambushed them. Sons of bitches doused both of them with gasoline and burned them alive."

John didn't look at her. He couldn't. Not with those ugly images running through his mind. "Everyone knew Vespian was responsible, but we couldn't prove it."

"But why burn a cop like that?" she asked.

"Vespian wanted information. And he got it."

"What information?"

"My home address."

Her recoil was minute, but John saw it. She knew what came next. "He went after your family."

He nodded. "They broke into my house when I wasn't there. Vespian and a couple of thugs. They raped my wife, raped my little girls, then murdered all of them. Burned them alive the same way they had Vic."

Reaching across the table, she laid her hand over his. "I can't imagine how horrific that must have been."

"Some of the details never made the papers. The bodies were so burned, there was little evidence left. I didn't find out about the rapes until I got my hands on Vespian."

He couldn't talk about what he'd seen when he broke through the line the fire department had set up. He wasn't a strong enough man to voluntarily re-call those horrific images. "The brass put me on sick leave. Somehow I got checked into a hospital. Fuckin' psycho ward." He tried to smile, but didn't manage. "To tell you the truth, I barely remember."

"I don't understand why the cops didn't go after Vespian."

"Oh, they did. You know how cops are. They pulled together. Went after him. But the son of a bitch was *untouchable.*"

"I can't imagine what that did to you," she whispered.

"Well, while all that is going down, I'm in the hospital drooling all over myself. One morning I'm in this *One Flew Over the Cuckoo's Nest* group therapy shit, and some crazy guy tells me all I need to get myself cured is a mission. I got to thinking about that, and realized he wasn't as crazy as everyone thought." He looked at Kate. "So I found a mission."

"You went after Vespian."

"A cop can make a pretty good criminal when he puts his mind to it." John stared hard at her. "Do you want to hear the rest?"

She nodded. "If you want to tell me."

"I started following Vespian, got to know his routine. Where he went. Who he spent time with. Every other facet of my life went by the wayside. I didn't eat. Didn't sleep. But I was never hungry or tired. That crazy guy was right. I fixated on Vespian and it cured me.

"He played poker every Wednesday night. Like clockwork he drove to this mansion in Avon Lake. He usually left around three or four A.M. One morning when he walked out to his Lexus, I was waiting."

Kate stared at him, her expression braced. She knew what he was going to tell her next. It was like watching a train mow down a stalled car.

"I hit him with the taser. When he went down, I cuffed him, threw him in the trunk and took him to a warehouse I'd rented. Bad neighborhood on the waterfront. I tied him to a chair, and by God I got a confession. Got all the gory fuckin' details on tape. Torture. Rape. Not just my wife, but my kids. Little girls."

"Oh, John—"

He cut her off. "I knew that tape would be deemed inadmissible." He blew out a breath, wiped his wet palms on his slacks. "I didn't plan to kill him, Kate. All I wanted was the confession. But when he told me what he did to them . . . it was like I stepped out of my body. I watched while someone else doused that sick motherfucker with gas and burned him alive."

John could feel the tremors wracking his body. His breaths shuddered out like stifled sobs. The sound was inordinately loud in the silence of the house. When he held out his hands, they shook uncontrollably, so he set them on the table in front of him, looked Kate square in the eye and told her what he'd never told another human being. "I watched Vespian burn, and I didn't feel a goddamn thing but satisfaction."

She blinked rapidly, but it wasn't enough to stanch the flow of tears. Her hand shook when she wiped them away.

"Now you know what kind of man you slept with tonight," he said. "You know what I did. Why I did it." He shrugged. "Poetic justice? Cop gone bad? Or just plain murder in the first degree?"

For the span of several heartbeats, the only sound came from his quickened breathing and the howl of the wind around the eaves. After a moment, Kate cleared her throat. "Did the cops know you did it?"

"They suspected me from the get-go. It didn't take a rocket scientist to connect the dots. It didn't take long for the cops to start sniffing around." He forced a smile. "But I was careful. I didn't leave them anything to work with. All they had was circumstantial crap."

"Enough to put you before a grand jury."

"Yeah, but it took that jury less than an hour to hand down a no bill." He smiled. "You see, the real evidence was against Vespian's partner. I know because I planted it. That wasn't in the papers."

"Vespian's partner was eventually tried and convicted."

"He's serving a life sentence in the federal pen in Terre Haute." He smiled. "Now that *is* poetic justice."

"What did you do after that?"

"Got my old job back. Deskwork because they thought I was a menace to society. I'd crossed a line, Kate. Big fuckin' line. Once you do that, you can't go back. The brass wanted me gone. They made life tough. Eventually, they got their wish."

"How did you end up at BCI?"

"Technically, I had a clean record. I think the commander was so glad to wash his hands of me, he pulled some strings, got me hired. What the hell else are you going to do with a psycho, corrupt, highly decorated police detective?"

"Ship him off to a place where he can't cause any problems."

"Exactly." He looked away, grimaced. "But we both know problems have a way of following you around. I'm pretty much washed up at BCI. That stigma thing. Too much baggage . . ." He lifts a shoulder, lets it drop. "Not to mention the booze and drugs."

"John." She said his name with sympathy. "How bad?"

"Shrinks handed out prescriptions like candy, trying to figure out how to fix me. I was more than happy to oblige."

He hated the disappointment he saw in her eyes. But Kate wasn't the first person he'd disappointed in the last year. He'd disappointed just about everyone he knew, including himself.

"Are you going to be okay?" she asked.

"Let's just say I'm a work in progress." John rose. Her eyes widened when he stepped close. Wrapping his fingers around her biceps, he eased her to her feet and looked down at her.

"Being with you," he said. "Like this. Working with you. It helped, Kate. It made me feel things I haven't felt in a long time. I want you to know that."

"I do," she said. "I know."

CHAPTER 31

The blast of the phone wrenches me from a fitful slumber. Rolling, I reach for it before I'm fully awake. "Yeah."

"Is this Chief Kate Burkholder?"

For a fraction of a second, I'm still the chief of police, and someone is calling with a break in the case. But it's only the remnants of sleep tickling my fancy. In the next instant I remember I was fired. I remember Jonas Hershberger was arrested. I remember sleeping with John Tomasetti.

I sit up. "Yes, I'm Kate Burkholder."

"This is Teresa Cardona. I'm a crime analyst with BCI. John Tomasetti asked me to forward the VICAP summary report to you."

I sense John's absence. The house has that empty feel I'm so accustomed to. Swinging my legs over the side of the bed, I reach for my robe. "Yes, I'm anxious to see it."

"I don't have your e-mail address."

I rattle off the address. "How quickly can you send it?"

"How about right now?"

"That would be great. Thanks." I hang up feeling both excited and deflated. The good news is I'll finally have the crime-matching information I need. I don't want to examine too closely the cause of the latter. It would be easier, simpler, to believe the pang in my chest is from the loss of my job and the probable end of my law enforcement career. But I'm honest enough with myself to admit it has more to do with John's departure without so much as a good-bye. I resolve not to dwell. I've got enough on my plate this morning without adding a heap of morning-after jitters.

Ten minutes later, armed with a cup of coffee, I'm at my desk in the spare bedroom, opening my e-mail program. Sure enough, I find an e-mail from T. Cardona. I click on the attachment and download a pdf file named: paintm-lOH_inquiry53367vsumrpt.pdf. One hundred and thirty-five pages of detail fills my screen. An endless stream of *Victim Information, Types of Trauma Inflicted on Victim, Offender's Sexual Interaction, Weapon Information,* and dozens of other criteria. It's going to take a lot of coffee to get me through all that information.

I start with *Types of Trauma Inflicted on Victim.* By noon, I'm wired on coffee, information overload, and a growing case of cabin fever. I try to stay focused on the case, but my thoughts stray repeatedly to John. Last night was an anomaly for me. Maybe it's a remnant of my Amish upbringing, but sleeping with a man is a big deal to me. I can't stop thinking about him. About everything we shared. And everything that was said.

Most people would condemn him for doling out vigilante justice. Though I've walked that fine line myself, I believe it's wrong to take a life. But I know some anguish is too horrendous for the human heart to bear. Some crimes are too unspeakable for the mind to accept. For John's sake, I hope he can find some semblance of peace.

At two-thirty a knock at the door yanks me from my work. I'm inordinately happy to find Glock on my back porch. "You know things are bad when visitors come to your back door," I say.

"Don't want to get those tongues wagging." He steps inside, brushing snow from his coat. "Nasty out there."

"Weather guy is calling for six to eight inches by morning."

"Fuckin' winter." But his eyes are on my laptop humming on the kitchen table and the reams of paper surrounding it. "You look like you could use a break."

I close the door behind him. "Anything new on the case?"

"We're still at Hershberger's farm, looking for evidence."

"What do you think?

"Hershberger is fucked."

At the counter I pour two cups of coffee. "You think he did it?"

"Evidence is overwhelming. The shoe we found belongs to Amanda Horner. Her mom identified it this morning. We've got underwear with DNA. We're waiting to hear back from the lab."

"Don't you think all of that is kind of convenient?"

"There's no way he could have possession of the shoe or underwear unless he had contact with the victim."

"You guys check CODIS?" CODIS stands for combined DNA database system. Administered by the FBI, it's a searchable database of authorized DNA files.

"Still waiting."

I hand him a cup. "How are Pickles and Skid holding up?"

"Detrick has them out in the cold, digging around in pig shit."

No pun, but I hate the idea of Detrick assigning the shit jobs to my officers, especially Pickles, who's getting up in years. "Detrick pushing his weight around?"

"Strutting around like he just arrested Jack the fuckin' Ripper. Says he's going to take all of us on some big hunting excursion if we tie this thing up nice and tight."

"Nice incentive if you like plugging deer."

"Most of his guys are into it. I guess Detrick used to be some big shot hunting guide in Alaska."

"Detrick, the great white hunter."

Glock doesn't look impressed. "How are you holding up, Chief?"

Thoughts of Tomasetti flash in my mind, but I quickly ban them. "I know this is going to sound crazy, but I'm absolutely certain Jonas Hershberger is innocent."

Glock blinks at me, clearly surprised. "He's a strange bird."

"So is Terry Bradshaw, but that doesn't make him a psychopath."

"We've got a shitload of evidence."

"I know Jonas, Glock. He doesn't drive. Doesn't have access to a snowmobile. There's no way he did those murders." I think about that a moment. "Did you check to see if he relocated during that sixteen-year period?"

"He's been in the same house since he was a kid. Inherited it when his parents were killed in a buggy accident eight years ago." He pauses. "We did find a couple of fifty-gallon drums he used to burn trash. We sent ash samples to the lab to see if he burned the clothes."

"Did you find any porn or S&M videos? Sex toys? Instruments of torture? Anything like that?"

"No, but he slaughters pigs on site. He's got knives. Knows how to use them."

"A lot of the Amish do their own slaughtering for meat. My dad butchered cattle."

"So how do you explain the evidence?"

"I can't. I know it's damning. It just . . . doesn't feel right. For example, the sixteen-year gap and then three murders within a month. What was the trigger?" I pause. "Have you talked to Jonas?"

He nods. "Detrick and I questioned him for about an hour this morning. At first he wouldn't speak English, just Pennsylvania Dutch. When he finally did start talking, he denied everything. Gets all offended when we ask him about the women. Detrick came down on him pretty hard, but he didn't crack."

"What do you think?"

"He's so damn stoic and reticent. Hard to figure him out."

"He have a lawyer?"

"Hasn't asked for one."

I nod, troubled by the thought of Jonas alone and at the mercy of Nathan Detrick.

Glock rubs his hand over the back of his neck. "Jesus, Chief, we sure miss having you around. I'd feel a hell of a lot better with you in running the show."

Tears threaten so I take a swig of coffee.

"I heard Detrick had a closed-door meeting with Janine Fourman and Auggie Brock the night before you got the axe," Glock says.

"How do you know?"

"Secretary over at the city building called after she heard what happened to you. I'm just reading between the lines, but I'll bet Detrick wasn't there to talk about the fuckin' weather."

Anger fires inside me when I think of all the things that might have been said and everything I stand to lose because of it. "That son of a bitch."

"You heard from Tomasetti?"

The heat of a blush climbs up my cheeks. It's a stupid reaction. Glock doesn't know Tomasetti and I spent the night together. Still, I can't meet his gaze. "I think he left early this morning."

"Really?" He laughs outright, obviously surprised by my reaction. "You and Tomasetti, huh? I'll be damned."

"Probably best if we don't go there."

He clears his throat and focuses his attention on the mess spread out on the kitchen table.

"I'm following up on a couple of things," I say.

"I didn't think you were balancing your checkbook."

"Tomasetti left me with some crime-matching stats. I'm working on the change of locales angle."

"Anything?"

"Not yet. But there's a lot of ground to cover." I pause. "Any word from the Johnstons?"

"Funeral is tomorrow."

I nod. "How's LaShonda?"

"Big as a frickin' house." A grin splits his face at the mention of his very pregnant wife. "Gonna be any day now."

"Give her my best, will you?"

"Will do, Chief. I gotta git." He starts toward the door, opens it and steps outside. "Gonna get slammed with snow."

"Yeah."

"Give me a call if you need anything."

He disappears around the corner, and I'm suddenly engulfed by an overwhelming sense of loneliness. I feel isolated and cut off, as if I'm the only person left on earth. As the snow swirls down from a cast iron sky, I'm reminded of how much my life here in Painters Mill means to me—and how much I stand to lose if I don't fight for reinstatement.

I go back to the VICAP report. It makes for grim, monotonous reading. Murder. Rape. Serial crimes with all the disturbing details that go along with them. By six o'clock the words begin to blur. My eyes feel as if they've been filled with sand. I've been on the phone so much my ear aches. Still, I've got nothing. Doubt begins to gnaw at my earlier resolve. Maybe I'm wrong. Maybe Jonas Hershberger is guilty. Twenty years have passed since I knew him. I know firsthand that time and events can change the course of a person's life. Look at me.

Stymied, I go to the cabinet above the fridge and pull out the bottle of Absolut. I pour too much into a tumbler and take that first dangerous sip. Back at my laptop, I try to log in to OHLEG to check on my earlier inquiries only to find my account has been disabled.

"Damn it." My last law enforcement tool is gone. I stare at the screen, frustrated and angry, with no idea where to go from here.

On impulse, I pull up a popular search engine and type "carving," "abdomen" and "exsanguination" and hit enter. I don't expect much in the way of useful information. Too much weird crap on the Internet. I get links to excerpts from novels, some bizarre short story, a college thesis on the media and violence. I'm shocked when I see a link to the *Fairbanks Daily News-Miner*. I click and read.

THIRD BODY WASHES UP ON THE TANANA RIVER

Alaska State Troopers say the body of an unidentified woman was found late Tuesday by a group of hunters. The woman is Caucasian and appears to be in her late twenties. According to Trooper Robert Mays, "her throat was cut" and she had "ritualistic carvings on her abdomen." This is the third body discovered along the bank of the remote Tanana River in the past six months and valley residents are alarmed. "We're keeping our doors locked," says Marty West, a Dot Lake resident. "I don't go anywhere without my gun." The body has been sent to Anchorage for an autopsy.

I stare at the screen, my heart pounding. The similarities are too striking to ignore. Nothing had come up on VICAP, but that's not too unusual; the database wasn't widely used by local law enforcement until recently. Some of the older data wasn't entered into the database at all due to lack of manpower.

A glance at the clock above the stove tells me it's nearly eight P.M. Alaska is in the Alaskan Time Zone, which is four hours earlier. I google the Fairbanks

PD for a phone number and dial. After being transferred twice, I'm told Detective George "Gus" Ogusawara retired seven years ago. I ask if he knows where Gus is living. He refuses to give me a number, but tells me to try Portland or Seattle.

I go back to the Internet. Lucky for me, Ogusawara isn't a common name. I start dialing and get the right man on my second try. "Is this George Ogusawara?" I begin.

"Who want to know?" A tenor voice with a strong Asian accent.

Quickly, I identify myself as chief of police. "Were you an investigator in Fairbanks?"

"I was a detective in Fairbanks, ma'am. I retire as Detective Lieutenant seven years ago. Now that you know you have the right fellow, what you want to know?"

"I'm investigating a series of murders similar to the ones that happened in Fairbanks back in the early 1980s."

"Bad medicine, those murders. Give everyone nightmares, including me. What you want to know?"

"I understand the killer carved something on each victim's abdomen."

"Before he torture and kill them, yes. Guy a sick motherfucker, let me tell you."

"The report I'm looking at doesn't say what he carved. I was wondering if you recall what it was."

"Even a hard-assed cop like me don't forget something like that. He carve numbers. You know. Roman numerals. One. Two. Three. Like that."

"Was the killer caught?"

"He the only reason I don't retire until I'm too old to enjoy myself." He pauses. "You think you got him down there?"

I don't want to tell him too much. Already, I've crossed a line by telling him I'm chief of police. "I'm not sure. Is there anything else you can tell me about these murders?"

"They the worse thing I ever see. Real bad guy, this killer."

"You've been very helpful. Thank you."

He starts to say something, but I hang up. My mind races with the information I've just been given. Three similar murders in Alaska, over three thousand miles away. Is there a connection? Could it be the same killer? If so, what took the killer from Ohio to Alaska and then back to Ohio?

I go back to the search engine and pull up everything I can find on the Tanana River Killer. I'm reading a small article from the *Tanana Leader* when a name stops me cold.

Nate Detrick, a guide for Yukon Hunting Tours, discovered the
body and contacted police . . .

I almost can't believe my eyes. What are the odds of similar murders that happened thousands of miles apart touching the same man's life twice? In some small corner of my mind, a memory pings my brain. A statement Glock made earlier.

Detrick used to be some big-shot hunting guide in Alaska.

That's when I remember this isn't the only place the sheriff's name has come up in the course of my research. Curious, I go to the Holmes County Auditor's Web site. An honest-to-God chill sweeps through me when I see that in September 1994, Nathan Detrick and his wife, Grace, sold their 2,500 square foot home in Millersburg.

I don't dare acknowledge the connection my mind has just made. This has to be a coincidence. Nathan Detrick is a cop. To suspect him would go beyond ridiculous. He's above reproach. Above suspicion.

Or is he?

Detrick is one of a handful of people who moved away from Painters Mill during the sixteen-year period. I now know he lived in Alaska where three similar murders occurred. I've been a cop long enough to realize this warrants follow-up.

I look down at my hands to find them shaking. I know I'm wrong about this. Coincidences *do* occur, and I'm an idiot for looking at Detrick. But the sheriff fits the profile far better than Jonas. My cop's gut tells me to keep digging.

Remembering the list of snowmobile registrations I asked Pickles for yesterday, I quickly rifle through the papers on the table until I find it. It's a typed list of names of people who own blue or silver snowmobiles registered in

Coshocton and Holmes Counties. Midway down, Detrick's name appears. He owns a blue Yamaha.

"No way," I whisper. "No way."

I go back to the computer and start looking at Detrick in earnest. Half an hour into my search, I discover a newspaper story in the *Dayton Daily News* from June 1986 about a bright young police officer who recently relocated from Fairbanks, Alaska, to join the Dayton Police Department. Donning full dress uniform, flanked by his wife, a handsome young Detrick smiles for the camera. The story is dated two months after the last murder in Alaska.

I begin looking for similar murders in and around Dayton during the time Detrick was there. I hit a dozen Web sites, one leading to the other— newspaper, television and radio Web sites, a few nonrestricted law enforce- ment sites, even a Crime Stoppers—but I find nothing. Only when I expand my search to the surrounding states do I hit pay dirt. A story in the archive section of *The Kentucky Post* from March 1989 snags my eye.

BODY FOUND ON RIVERBANK IDENTIFIED

The nude body of a woman found last week by a jogger on the bank of the Ohio River has been identified as twenty-year-old Jessie Watkins. According to Kenton County Coroner Jim Magnus, the woman's throat was cut. Covington Police and the Kenton County Sheriff's Office are "aggressively seeking the perpetrator," said an unnamed law enforcement source on Monday. Watkins, a known prostitute, was last seen leaving a bar in Cincinnati. Investigators have no suspects at this time.

I pull up a map Web site and plug in the cities of Dayton, Ohio, and Cov- ington, Kentucky. Covington is about an hour's drive from Dayton. Doable in one evening with time to spare.

Next, I do a random search for similar crimes in Michigan, but I strike out. Undeterred, I try Indiana. For an hour, I go from site to site to site. Just when I'm about to give up, I find a buried story on the murder of a young migrant worker, whose body was found in a cornfield between Indianapolis and Rich- mond.

MIGRANT WORKER FOUND MURDERED

Police have few clues in the murder of thirty-one-year-old Lucinda Ramos, whose body was found in a cornfield not far from Interstate 70 near New Castle on Monday. "I've never seen anything
like it in my life," said Dick Welbaum, the farmer who nearly ran
over the body with his tractor. An anonymous source with the
Henry County Coroner's office said there were "ritualistic carvings"
on the victim's body. When asked about the possibility of a cult,
Mick Barber with the Henry County Sheriff's Office offered no
comment. He did say that the sheriff's office is working in conjunction with the New Castle PD as well as the State Police to find
the person or persons responsible.

The term *ritualistic carving* sticks in my mind. A check of the map site
tells me New Castle, Indiana, is an hour and twenty minutes from Dayton. I
pull up the Indiana State Police Web site and dial the main number. Within
minutes I'm on the phone with Ronald Duff in the Criminal Investigation
Division.

I identify myself as the chief of police and cut right to the chase. "I'm wondering about a murder you investigated back in 1988. Vic's name was Lucinda
Ramos."

"I've killed a lot of brain cells since then. Let me pull the file."

He could have refused to talk to me because I'm using my home phone.
Sometimes if a cop isn't certain of who he's talking to, he'll call them back at
the police department. I'm guessing it was the fact that I'm looking at a cold
case that prompts him to speak to me without verifying my credentials.

He comes back on the line a few minutes later. "You think you got a lead
on this case?" he asks.

"We've had three murders here in Painters Mill. I'm looking at cold cases
in surrounding states for a signature match."

"Anything I can do to help. What do you need specifically?"

"The report I'm looking at mentions a ritualistic carving on the victim. I'm
wondering if you can tell me anything about the carving."

Papers rattle on the other end. "I've got the coroner's report here. Says, and

I quote 'carving in the skin is superficial and is located eight centimeters above the navel.'"

"What is the carving of?"

More papers rattle. "I don't see any notes, but I got a crime scene photo here. Let me get my glasses." He pauses. "It kinda looks like a capital I and a V."

"Like a Roman numeral?"

"Could be."

I can't believe what I'm hearing. "Was there any reason this data wasn't entered into VICAP?"

"We didn't start using VICAP here until 2001. Nothing in the archive has been entered yet. Lack of manpower and budget. You know how that goes."

"Can you scan and e-mail that photo to me?"

"Sure thing. What's your e-mail address there?"

I rattle off my e-mail address and hang up. My first impulse is to call John, but I hesitate. All I have are some vaguely suspicious circumstances. My looking at Detrick as a suspect could be perceived as an embittered and disgruntled former chief lashing out at the person who took her case. I need more before I involve anyone else. I'm not even convinced I'm right about Detrick. If I move prematurely, the whole thing could blow up in my face like a stick of dynamite.

Back at my laptop, I pull up a spreadsheet and start a timeline, filling in the blanks with information gleaned by phone or the Internet. Detrick was a wilderness guide for Yukon Hunting Tours from February 1980 to December 1985. All three Fairbanks murders occurred during that period. In early 1986 he moved to Dayton, Ohio, where he began his law enforcement career with the police department, working as a patrol officer until 1990. The murders in Kentucky and Indiana happened while he lived in Dayton. If I'm correct, Lucinda Ramos was victim four. Jessie Watkins was victim number five. In 1990, he landed a job with the Holmes County Sheriff's office as a deputy and moved to Millersburg, which is when the Slaughterhouse Murders began. He killed four women during that time, victims six through nine. He sold his house in 1994 and moved to Columbus where he made detective and stayed until 2005. No similar murders that I know of occurred during that time frame, but then I haven't researched it thoroughly. He returned to Painters Mill in 2006, ran for sheriff and won by a landslide. The most recent murders began with victim number twenty-two. I'm missing ten victims during the time he lived and worked in Columbus. Other than that discrepancy, the timeline fits like O.J.'s glove.

I jump when the phone rings. "Hello?"

"Chief." Mona whispers my name with urgency. "You better get down here."

It's nearly midnight. Judging from her tone, I know the news isn't good. "What happened?"

"Jonas Hershberger just tried to hang himself."

CHAPTER 32

The worm dieth not and the fire is not quenched.

Or so says the Bible with regard to hell.

Had I not had those conservative moral values branded into my brain at a young age, I might have believed Jonas Hershberger tried to commit suicide. But I don't. The Amish believe in living their lives the way Jesus lived His life. Forgiveness and humility are part of that undertaking. Suicide happens, but it is rare. And it is the one sin for which no forgiveness is granted.

My wipers wage a losing war with the snow as I park next to Mona's Escort. I spot Pickles's old Chrysler along with a city car. Glock's vehicle is glaringly absent. I hit the ground running and enter the reception area with a swirl of snow. Mona stands near the switchboard with her headset on. "What happened?" I ask.

"Jonas tried to hang himself. Detrick and Pickles are in the basement with him now."

"He okay?"

"I think so. He's conscious."

"Call an ambulance." I rush to the rear hall, and take the steps two at a time to the basement. The jail is outdated and small with two six-by-six cells and a tiny jailer area. I emerge from the staircase to see both Detrick and Pickles standing over Jonas, who is sitting on the bench.

"What happened?" I ask.

Both men swing around to look at me, obviously surprised by my presence.

"You are not authorized to be here, Burkholder." Detrick's face is red. His bald head gleams with a sheen of sweat.

I step closer for a better look at Jonas. His hands are cuffed behind his back. Shoestrings from his boots are tangled around his neck. I see bright red abrasions just below his jaw line.

"Idiot tried to hang hisself," Pickles says between pants. "Sheriff got here just in time to stop it."

Considering what I've discovered recently about Detrick, I have a terrible feeling that's not the way things really went down.

The sheriff starts toward me. "What are you doing here?"

A ripple of uneasiness goes through me. I have a sinking suspicion he's going to throw me out. I look at Jonas. "What happened?" I ask quickly in Pennsylvania Dutch.

Jonas looks at me, his expression shaken and afraid. "I was sleeping and the English policeman attacked me." He motions toward Detrick. "He choked me with the shoestrings from my boots."

Detrick reaches me, moving in close enough to invade my space. "I asked you a question."

I meet his gaze. "I thought I might be able to help with the language barrier."

"If I need your help, I'll ask for it."

All I can think is that Jonas is in danger. "He needs to go to the hospital. Get checked out."

"Looks fine to me." Detrick's eyes narrow. I see cunning and wariness in their depths. He knows I'm lying, but he doesn't know why. "You need to leave, Kate. Now."

Leaning close, he makes a show of sniffing me. "Have you been *drinking*?"

"No."

"You're lying. I smell it on your breath." He gives Pickles an incredulous look, but he addresses me. "She's drunk. What the hell are you thinking, drinking and driving on a night like this? Coming over here when we already have enough to deal with?"

"I haven't been drinking." I have, but I'm not going to admit it. Detrick is trying to discredit me in front of Pickles.

"Burkholder, you need to go home," he says. "Right now."

"Make sure Jonas gets to the hospital," I say to Pickles.

Detrick grabs my arm. "I'll escort you out myself."

Pickles comes out of the cell. "Get your hands off her."

Detrick jabs a finger at him. "Shut the fuck up, old man."

Pickles holds his ground, but looks at me. "Maybe you ought to just go, Chief."

"Don't let anything happen to—" The next thing I know, Detrick's hand clamps around the back of my neck. He shoves me hard against the bars. "Give me your hands."

"I'm leaving," I say.

"You had your chance. Now give me your goddamn hands!"

Every instinct in my body screams for me to resist. Knowing that will only escalate the situation, I offer my wrists. "I didn't do anything wrong."

"You're drunk and disorderly." He tugs handcuffs from the compartment on his belt. He's breathing hard. His palms are slick with sweat as he pulls my hands behind my back and snaps the cuffs onto my wrists, cranking them down hard enough to hurt.

Pickles crosses to us. "Sheriff, that's not necessary."

Ignoring him, Detrick glares at me as if he wants to take me apart with his bare hands. "I don't know what you think you're doing, but you just bought yourself a lot of trouble."

"I was trying to help. That's all."

"Bullshit. You got juiced up and came here to start problems."

My heart is beating so hard I can barely catch my breath. I try not to think of the murders this man may have committed. I'm handcuffed and defenseless. If he decided to pull out his sidearm and kill all of us, there wouldn't be a damn thing I could do to stop him.

"I thought Jonas might respond to someone who speaks Pennsylvania Dutch," I say. "That's all."

"In the middle of a blizzard? After midnight? You're half drunk and you decide to mosey down here to *help*? Burkholder, I wasn't born yesterday!"

"Mona called her," Pickles puts in, obviously trying to defuse the situation. "That's why she came. Come on. She's a cop. Cut her some slack."

Detrick jams his finger at Jonas, but addresses Pickles. "Do you realize her talking to this suspect could cost us this case! She's not a cop! Some lawyer gets ahold of this, and that piece of shit in there could get off. Is that what you want?"

For the first time, Pickles looks uncertain.

"Let me go or I swear you'll find yourself in court." I try to make my voice strong, but it's breathless and high.

"You are in no position to threaten me." Grabbing my arm, he shoves me toward the staircase.

When we enter the reception area, Mona gasps and stands, gaping at me as if I'm on my way to the gallows. "What happened?"

"It's okay," I say.

"But why did he—"

"She's drunk." Detrick forces me to the desk, then spins me roughly around so he can unlock the cuffs.

I look at Mona. "I'm not drunk."

Detrick sighs. "I'm going to do you a big favor, Burkholder, and cut you loose. But if you show up again drunk or sober or in a fuckin' spaceship, you're going to jail. You got it?"

The cuffs snap open. "I understand."

"Chief, what's going on?" Mona asks.

"I'll explain later," I say, rubbing my wrists.

Detrick points at the door, as if I'm a stray dog that's wandered in off the street. "Get out before I change my mind and throw you in the drunk tank the rest of the night."

"Keep an eye on Jonas," I say to Mona.

"I called an ambulance," she says.

"Cancel it," Detrick snaps. "That murdering piece of shit is fine."

Shaking her head, Mona grabs the phone and dials.

Detrick glares at me, something darker than contempt glittering in his eyes. "Get the hell out of here."

I leave without looking back.

Mona Kurtz had always prided herself on her ability to stay calm during stressful situations. Mainly because she was really into the whole cop thing. She liked the excitement. She admired the way they kept their cool when all hell was breaking loose. She didn't feel very calm tonight.

She used to love her job at the police department. She was a night bird by nature, and working the graveyard shift was perfect. The phones and dispatch radio were relatively quiet, so she could read or catch up on homework from the criminal justice course she was taking at the community college, and the guys always gave her the scoop on all the good gossip around town.

Unfortunately, the job had pretty much gone to shit since the murders began. Everyone was on edge. The guys needed reports typed or data entered into the computer. The phones rang off the hook until the wee hours. People were getting downright weird. To top things off, Nathan Detrick had set up shop in the chief's office. The sheriff might have some charm—if you liked bald old guys, anyway—but there was something about him that gave Mona the freaking willies.

The job really started sucking after the chief got fired. Mona still didn't know all the details. But she knew a lot more than people realized. Phone people, no matter how low on the totem pole, could figure out almost anything from who called whom and the messages they left. As far as she was concerned, Chief Burkholder had been royally screwed over.

She couldn't believe the chief had just about gotten herself arrested. It wasn't like Kate to cause problems. What the hell was she thinking? Mona had always put the chief on a pedestal of sorts. In fact, Kate was one of her role models. Well, the chief and Stephanie Plum, anyway. Detrick handcuffing her and threatening to arrest her was downright freaky.

"Strange stuff going on tonight."

Mona looked up to see Pickles approach. "Tell me about it."

Craning her neck, she glanced toward the hall leading to the basement. "Where's Baldy?"

Pickles leaned against her desk. "In the chief's office."

Mona lowered her voice. "Was the chief really drunk?"

"She's been under a lot of stress with these murders." He sighed. "Ain't the first time a cop turned to booze."

Mona doodled on her message pad. "I wish she was still chief."

"You and me both."

"I hate all this weird shit. Working for Detrick sucks."

The switchboard trilled. Turning her radio down, Mona slid the headset over her ears and hit Talk. "Painters Mill PD."

"This is Ronald Duff with the Indiana State Police calling for Chief of Police Kate Burkholder."

"Chief Burkholder isn't in." Mona still couldn't bring herself to tell people Kate was no longer chief. Breaking that kind of news to the public wasn't her responsibility. She supposed she was hoping everything would get straightened out and Kate would return. After tonight, it sure didn't look that way.

"You know how to reach her?" the man asked.

"Sheriff Detrick is here. Can he help you?" She'd been instructed by the sheriff to pass all the chief's calls to him, which Mona had been doing.

"That would be fine. Thanks."

"Can I tell him what it's regarding?"

"I found a better image of the victim here in Indiana, and I wondered if he wanted me to fax it."

Satisfied Detrick was the correct person this man should speak to, Mona transferred the call.

Wind and snow buffet me as I slide into the Mustang and slam the door. I can't believe what just happened. I'm shaking so hard I can barely get the key in the ignition. I know it sounds crazy, but I think Detrick is the killer. All the evidence points to him, and after what Jonas just told me . . . Detrick must have planted the evidence found at Jonas's farm. If he gets the chance, he'll kill Jonas to cover his tracks.

That's when I realize I'm in over my head. I can't handle this on my own. Not only am I no longer a cop, but my integrity has come into question. Detrick has done everything in his power to discredit me—and quite effectively. If I start making accusations, people will think I'm disgruntled over losing my job.

I didn't want to call John until I had rock-solid proof implicating Detrick, but I can't put it off any longer. Jonas is in real danger. It's going to be a hard sell, but I need John's help. I dial his number as I head out of town.

Though it's after midnight, he picks up on the second ring. "You okay?" he asks.

"I'm in trouble."

"Now there's a surprise. What happened?"

"Promise me you're not going to call me crazy and hang up."

"You know I have a soft spot for the mentally disturbed."

I choke out a laugh that sounds more like a sob. "I think I know who the killer is."

"I'm listening."

"Nathan Detrick."

The silence that follows is so profound that for a second I think I lost the connection. Then he sighs. "You came to this stunning conclusion how, exactly?"

Quickly, I tell him about the murders in Fairbanks that occurred while Detrick worked there as a hunting guide. That he actually "found" one of the bodies. I tell him about the murders in Kentucky and Indiana and their proximity to Dayton where Detrick was a cop. I tell him Detrick owns a blue snowmobile. I lay out the timeline. "I know it's circumstantial, but you have to admit, if you put it all together, it's compelling."

"Kate, goddamnit."

I close my eyes. "John, listen to me. I think Detrick framed Hershberger. I think he's going to murder him to shut him up." Quickly, I explain what happened at the station.

"Detrick's a fucking cop. A husband with three teenaged girls. He coaches the football team."

"I know who he is! And I know how this sounds!" I snap. "Look, he's in the middle of a messy divorce. Maybe that was the trigger for this escalation."

"Kate . . ."

"I don't like this any more than you do. But I can't ignore what I've found."

He sighs, and I get a bad feeling in the pit of my stomach. The kind of feeling when I know someone whose opinion I value is about to say something I don't want to hear. Because that person is John, it hurts. And it scares me because without him, I'm on my own.

"It fits," I say, trying to sound calm. "He lived in every city where the murders occurred. The signatures are almost exact. He actually 'found' one of the bodies. We both know these kinds of killers have been known to get involved with the police investigation. He's a cop so he knows how to cover his ass. He worked at the slaughterhouse as a teenager. He shaves his head, John. Did you ever wonder why the lab never found a single hair at any of the crime scenes? I'll bet he shaves all of his body hair."

"That sounds paranoid as hell."

"Then help me disprove it."

"Does Detrick know you suspect him?"

"No."

"Keep it that way." His curse burns through the line. "Give me a few hours to get there."

The drive from Columbus to Painters Mill would normally take a couple of hours. But with the storm dumping snow at about an inch an hour, I know it could be morning before he arrives. "Okay."

"I want you to go home. Get your facts in order. I'll be there as soon as I can."

"Thank you."

"Whatever you do, don't let Detrick know you're looking at him. And do me a favor, will you?"

"Depends."

"Watch your back."

He disconnects without saying good-bye.

The doubt I heard in his voice weighs on me. Being formerly Amish and a woman, I've had to work hard to earn the reputation I have. Credibility is important to me. I hate it that both of those things have come into question.

Turning the Mustang around, I start toward home. Visibility is so poor I can barely see the streetlights along Main. The county has sent out snowplows, but there aren't enough to keep up with the deluge. I'm two blocks from my house when I see the flash of police lights in my rearview mirror. At first I think it's Pickles, wanting to speak with me about what happened back at the station.

That theory is dashed when I glance in my side mirror and see a sheriff's office Suburban. Even in the heavily falling snow, I recognize Detrick's silhouette when he gets out. For a crazy instant, I consider jamming the Mustang into gear and making a run for it, but I know fleeing will only make things worse. All I have to do is stay cool. After all, he doesn't know I suspect him.

I had to relinquish my service revolver when I was fired, but I possess a concealed firearm license and own a nice little Kimber .45. Quickly, I snatch the firearm out of the console and drop it into my coat pocket.

Detrick taps on the driver's window. I hit the down button. "What's the problem?"

"Turn off the engine."

"What?"

"Do it, Burkholder. Get out of the vehicle. Right now."

"I haven't done anything wrong."

"You've been drinking. I smelled it back at the police station. I smell it now. Get the fuck out of the car."

My heart begins to pound. I hadn't expected this. A dozen responses scroll through my brain, but none of my options are good. "I'm not comfortable doing that, Detrick. I'll follow you back to the station and submit to a Breathalyzer there."

"Not comfortable?" He glares at me through the six-inch opening of the window. "Open the door. Now."

I keep my voice level and unemotional. "Call another officer out here and I'll comply."

"Get out of that fucking vehicle!" he roars. "Now!"

I think of the horrific things this man might have done. I can't imagine him believing he can get away with harming me. But there's no way I'm getting out of my vehicle. I hit the automatic door locks.

"Don't make this harder than it has to be," he says.

"Get Pickles out here and I'll comply." Snow swirls in through the six-inch open window.

He leans closer. "You make me drag another cop out here and I'll throw the book at you. DUI. Resisting. Whatever else I can think of. I'll ruin you, Burkholder. You'll be lucky to get a job as a parking lot attendant."

I say nothing.

"Have it your way." As if resigned, he straightens and reaches for the radio. "This is 247—"

The window shatters. Glass pelts me. I catch a glimpse of Detrick's gloved fist as it flies toward my face. I see something dark in his hand. I ram the shifter into gear, but before I can stomp the gas, I hear the sickening *crack!* of the stun gun. Five hundred thousand volts of electricity jump from the electrodes into my neck.

It's like being hit by a baseball bat. I feel the jolt all the way to my bones. I'm aware of the Mustang rolling forward, but I can't make my foot hit the gas. The charge has paralyzed me. Confusion swirls in my head. As Detrick reaches in and turns off the ignition, I know I've made a fatal mistake.

CHAPTER 33

It took John an hour to get out of the city. Not only were the roads hazardous, but multiple accidents had many streets blocked. The driving wouldn't have been so bad, but at some point he'd started to worry about Kate. Her suspicions about Detrick might sound outrageous, but she had a good head on her shoulders. More importantly, she was a good cop. If her suspicions were correct, there could be a serial murderer with a badge on the prowl in Painters Mill.

While waiting for an accident to clear on Highway 16 out of Newark, he tried her cell, but got voice mail. He left a message, then tried her home phone. Something darker than worry gripped him when he got her machine.

"Where the hell are you?" he muttered and disconnected.

He still had Glock's number on his cell, so John tried him next. To his relief, he answered. "Have you seen Kate?"

"Not since earlier today. What's up?"

He debated on how much to tell. "I was wondering if you could swing by her house and check on her."

"I can go by there right now." He paused. "You going to tell me what's going on?"

John inched past a jackknifed eighteen wheeler where EMTs pulled the driver from a mangled cab. "I can't get into it, Glock."

"I'm officially fuckin' worried now, Tomasetti."

"Check on her. I'll fill you in when I get there." Squinting through the snow flying at his windshield, he jacked the speedometer to forty and hoped like hell Kate was wrong.

I'm aware of being dragged from my vehicle. Snow on my face. In my hair. Spilling down my collar. I'm in terrible trouble, but I'm in no shape to do anything about it.

Another *crack!* sounds.

Pain rocks my body, jumbles my brain. My muscles lock up. I'm face-down in the snow. It's in my mouth and eyes. Cold against my face. I sense Detrick kneeling beside me. My hands being yanked behind my back. I try to fight, end up flopping around like a fish.

"You should have let it go, Kate."

I try to scream, but my mouth is full of snow and I manage only a sputter. I try to shake off the disorientation. But it's as if I'm locked in a fog.

He hits me with the stun gun again. Pain wrenches a groan from me. My muscles go rigid. I feel my eyes roll back. Consciousness slips and the world goes monochrome. I'm aware of him tromping through the snow. Moving around. But I'm too dazed to determine what he's doing. I tug on the bindings at my wrists, but they remain tight. Rolling, I raise my head and look around. Snow swirls down from a black sky. I see headlights. And then Detrick is standing over me.

"You're not quite so smart now, are you?"

The next thing I know his hands are beneath my arms and he's dragging me. I try to kick, realize my feet are bound. He opens the trunk of my Mustang, lifts me as if I weigh nothing, and throws me inside. I land hard on my shoulder. I feel his hands at my ankles, yanking them up and behind me, and I realize he's hog-tying me.

"Help me!" I scream as loud as I can. *"Help!"*

"Shut up."

"Help me *please*!"

Grasping my hair, he yanks my head back and shoves a wad of fabric into my mouth. Before I can spit it out, he wraps a length of tape over my mouth and around my head.

Reaching into the trunk, he yanks the emergency trunk release cable, disabling it. "So you don't get any ideas about climbing out."

The trunk slams and I'm engulfed in darkness. I hear myself breathing hard through my nose. My pulse roars in my ears. I hear the engine start. Not my vehicle, but his. A moment later the Mustang moves, and I realize he's towing my car. In that moment, I'm more scared than I've ever been in my life. I know Detrick is going to kill me. I've seen his bloody handiwork. Panic rears inside me and I begin to struggle mindlessly. Animalistic grunts tear from my throat only to be trapped by the gag. I writhe and buck until my entire body trembles with exhaustion and adrenaline.

After what seems like an eternity, I force myself to calm down. I take deep breaths. I focus on relaxing my arms, then my legs. After a few moments my head clears and I can think. He disabled the emergency trunk release, but I know there's a hatch between the trunk and the back seat. If I can find it, I might be able to escape.

Maneuvering around in the trunk is awkward and agonizingly slow. I feel for the seat latch with my face. It takes several minutes, but I finally find it in the forward right corner. I need my teeth, but my mouth is taped. Pressing my face against the latch, I use it to peel away the tape. I feel the sharp edge cutting my lip, but I don't care. Slowly, the tape peels back. Clamping down with my teeth, I pull hard on the latch, and the mechanism clicks. I butt the seatback with my head. A muffled sob of relief escapes me when the seat folds down.

It takes every ounce of strength I possess to squirm from the trunk to the back seat. Using my shoulders and hips and head, I push myself to the floor, then worm forward until I'm wedged between the front seats. I'm nearly to the driver's seat when the vehicle stops.

Panic descends. I squirm frantically, somehow make it over the console, and roll onto the driver's seat. Using my forehead, I hit the automatic door locks. Then I press my chin against the horn. Relief flits through me at the sound. I think of the Kimber in my pocket, and try to think of a way to get to it. I see my cell phone on the passenger seat. Without thinking, I writhe toward it, grab it with my teeth. Can't get it to my pocket, so I duck my head, drop it down my shirt.

A hand reaches through the broken window. An instant later, the door swings open. Grinning, Detrick thrusts the stun gun at me.

Crack!

Vivid pain explodes through my body. My muscles seize. I catch a glimpse of his face as he reaches for me. I lean my weight against the horn, reveling in the blare of it, praying someone hears it. Rough hands yank me from the vehicle. I land in the snow. The next thing I know I'm being dragged by my hair. Pain zings across my scalp. I hear hair being torn from its roots. Snow goes down my collar. I twist, try to get my bearings. We're in a clearing, surrounded by trees. Ahead, I see the dark silhouette of a farmhouse. A silo beyond. A drooping barn.

All thoughts leave my head as I'm dragged up the steps. I flounder, trying desperately to free my hands and feet. My head strikes the top step hard enough to send a scatter of stars across my vision. My coat scrapes against wood as I'm hauled across the porch. Detrick lets go of me, shoves open the door. I smell mildew and cold, dirty air. He lugs me over the threshold as if I were a sack of grain. Claustrophobia threatens when the door slams. All I can think is that the monster has taken me to its lair.

Terror leaches into my brain, drop by terrible drop. I'm paralyzed with it. I think of Amanda Horner, Ellen Augspurger and Brenda Johnston. In my mind's eye I see their brutalized bodies. I wonder if this is part of what they endured before he killed them. I wonder if I'll perish the same way.

The door opens and then slams. I'm alone, but I know he'll be back. The wood floor is cold and rough against my cheek. I lay on my side, breathing as if I've just run a mile. My back aches from the uncomfortable position, but I know the worse is yet to come.

My pulse is in the red zone. I can't stop shaking. I need to think. Fight. Escape. Kill the son of a bitch if I get the chance. Raising my head, I look around. I'm in an old house. There's no furniture. Probably abandoned. Vaguely, I wonder if this is one of the properties on the list, and then I remember I'd put Detrick in charge of checking them out. Chances are, it never got done.

He returns carrying a kerosene heater and a toolbox. A shudder moves through me when he makes eye contact. "I'll bet you're wondering how I knew you figured out my little secret."

I stare at him.

"Your buddy with the Indiana State Police called for you. He wanted to talk to you about a cold case in Indiana. For some reason, he thought you were still the chief. You wouldn't know anything about that, though, would you?"

He sets down the heater and kneels next to it. I work at the bindings at my wrists as he lights it. I don't know what he used to tie me up with, but it's soft and not easily undone.

Yellow light floods the room when the heater is lit. Straightening, he crosses to me and rips the remaining tape from my mouth. I spit out the wad of fabric and for several seconds all I can do is gulp air and choke back sobs. I spot the knife in his hand. A scream pours from my throat when he leans close, but he only cuts the rope binding my wrists to my ankles.

My hands and feet are still bound, but at least I'm no longer hog-tied. Straightening, I roll onto my side and look up at him. "You can't possibly get away with this."

Setting his left hand on my shoulder, he pats me down with his right. "You packin' heat tonight, Kate?"

"No."

He finds the Kimber in my coat pocket and pulls it out. "Nice piece." Holding up the gun by its grip, he grins at me. "Expensive, too." Assuming a shooter's stance, he aims it at my forehead. "How does she shoot? Accurate? Much recoil?"

"Tomasetti knows everything," I say.

"That drunk doesn't know shit."

"I told him everything. He's on his way. It's over."

"What exactly do you think you know?"

"I know about the murders in Alaska. In Kentucky and Indiana. The four murders here in Painters Mill sixteen years ago."

"Figured all that out by yourself, huh?"

"The people at BCI know, too. It's over, Detrick. You can either give it up, or you can run. You could be in Canada by morning if you go now."

"And what? Spend the rest of my life looking over my shoulder? Not my style."

"You'll go to prison if you stay."

I see arrogance in his eyes. He doesn't believe me. He's not taking me seriously. "There's only one problem with your assertions, Kate."

My throat is so tight I can't speak.

"You don't have any proof. No DNA. No fingerprints." He shrugs with the nonchalance of a man dismissing a mildly annoying child.

"The circumstantial evidence is enough to get them looking. They look hard enough and they'll find proof. It's just a matter of time and you know it."

A grin spreads across his face. "You're forgetting I already have a suspect in jail. Do you have any idea how much physical evidence I have against Jonas Hershberger?"

"You mean the evidence you planted?"

"I have blood. Fibers. Hair. We're talking DNA, Kate. Personal effects from the vics. Clothes belonging to the victims are buried out by the barn. Your officers just haven't found the right place yet, but they will. Hershberger's gonna fuckin' fry."

"Tomasetti's got a search warrant. He's probably at your house right now." The lie flies off my tongue with the vehemence of brimstone and fire from a preacher.

His smile falters. The look that emerges chills me to the bone. "You're a lying cunt."

"You kill me and every cop in the state is going to be all over you."

His lips peel back. The transformation from charming to psychopath happens so quickly I'm not prepared. He lunges at me, yanks me to my feet with so much force that my head snaps back. "You think you can rattle me with your lies? You think I'm stupid?"

"I think you're a pathetic freak."

"Let me tell you how this is going to go down." He says between clenched teeth.

I try to twist away, but he's got a vise grip on the sleeves of my coat and gives me another hard shake. "You're so distraught over losing your job and your complete and utter failure with regard to this case, you couldn't take it anymore. So you get yourself juiced up. You drive to this deserted farmhouse. Have yourself a few more drinks. Then you sit down on the floor, pick up that pretty little

Kimber, stick it in your mouth and pull the trigger. How's that for a happy ending?"

"No one will believe that." The words are a scream inside my head, but they come out evenly.

"You wouldn't be the first cop to eat a bullet because of the job."

"Here's a reality check for you, Detrick. Tomasetti knows what you did. He's going to take you down. Your problems are just beginning."

Moving with the speed of a striking snake, he grasps both sides of my face with his hands and pulls me close. "I'd sell my soul right now to cut you," he whispers. "I'd slice you open and pull out your intestines the way I did the Johnston girl. Then I'd turn you over and stick it in places where you good girls don't like it stuck in."

I steel myself against his closeness, against the horror of the words. I stare at him, hating him, hating everything he is. "You do that and the cops will know I didn't commit suicide. How are you going to put these murders on Jonas if another body turns up while he's in jail?"

"You think you're real smart, don't you? Let me tell you something. There are a lot of things I can do to you the cops won't be able to detect if this place burns down with you in it." He motions toward the heater. "You put that thing too close to those curtains and this dump will go up like it was the Fourth of July."

I shudder when he runs his tongue down my cheek. I smell garlic on his breath. The musk of drugstore cologne. The warmth of his breath against my face. The wetness of his spit on my skin.

"As long as I don't break any bones, the fire will take care of any evidence. I wear a condom, you know." He pats his coat pocket. "Got a whole box right here just for you."

I head-butt him in the face as hard as I can. I hear his nose crack. He shoves me, cursing, and clutches his face. I catch a glimpse of blood between his fingers an instant before I land hard on my backside. I don't wait for him to come after me. I roll toward the Kimber he dropped, wiggle like a worm until my right hand brushes the grip. If I can get my fingers around it . . .

Detrick kicks the weapon away. I look up to see him slide the knife from his pocket. He leans over me. I roll onto my back. Raising both legs, I mule kick him. He reels backward, arms flailing. I hear glass shatter, realize I nearly sent him through the window. I flip onto my side and look wildly for the gun. My last chance. My only chance of getting out of this alive.

But the Kimber is nowhere in sight. I squirm frantically in the direction he kicked it. Detrick's hands come down hard on my shoulders. I twist, try to get into position to kick him again. I see his arm come toward me.

Crack!

Five hundred thousand volts of electricity ignite every nerve ending in my body. Pain wrenches a scream from my throat. My muscles contract. Light explodes inside my head. The next thing I know my cheek is against the floor. Another *crack!* and my body goes rigid. I feel my eyes roll back. I hear my teeth snap together. I taste blood at the back of my throat. My bladder releases.

Crack!

And the world fades to gray.

CHAPTER 34

LaShonda wasn't happy about him going out in the storm. Glock didn't like it either, but he didn't have a choice. He'd tried Kate's home phone and her cell and gotten voice mail both times. Considering the weather and Tomasetti's cryptic call, he was worried.

He knew Kate was despondent about the murders and the loss of her job. Best case scenario, he'd find her at home snuggled up with a bottle of something eighty proof. It wouldn't be the first time a cop had turned to alcohol for comfort or escape. It was the other possibilities that had him concerned.

He parked on the street in front of her house and squinted through the swirling snow. Usually, she parked in the driveway. Tonight, the driveway stood vacant. He told himself the Mustang was probably in the garage due to the storm. But Glock had been a cop long enough to know when he needed to listen to his gut. This was one of those times.

Wind and snow pelted him as he walked to the garage and looked in the window. Uneasiness rippled through him when he found it empty. At the back door, Glock tried the knob, found it locked. Using his gloved hand, he broke the pane nearest the knob, reached inside and unlocked the door. The house was warm and smelled of coffee. He flipped on the light. "Chief? It's Glock. You here?"

The wind whipping around the eaves seemed to mock him.

Glock set his hand against the coffeemaker, found it cold. Papers and files and a laptop covered the kitchen table. He glanced down to see handwritten notes. The state police in Indiana. A former detective from Alaska. A newspaper story.

Quickly, he cleared the rest of the house, but Kate was not there. Back in the kitchen, he called Tomasetti. "She's not home," he said without preamble.

"I'm twenty minutes away," Tomasetti said. "Meet me at the station."

"What the hell's going on? Where's Kate?"

"I'll explain when I get there. Do me a favor and see if you can get Detrick on the line. See where he's at, what he's doing. Don't let on that you're suspicious about anything."

"What does Detrick have to do with this?"

"I think he might be . . . involved."

"Involved in what?"

"The murders."

"*What?* You gotta be fuckin' kidding me. Detrick?"

"Look, I don't know for sure. Just call him, okay?"

"What if he's at the station?"

"If he is, that'll be the best news I had all day. If he's not, then I'm pretty sure Kate's in trouble."

Awareness returns slowly. The first thing I become aware of is the cry of the wind. I hear snow battering the windows. I lay on my side with my knees drawn up to my chest. My wrists are bound behind my back. The arm I'm lying on is numb. My ankles are still bound. I'm shivering with cold. The crotch of my jeans is wet, and I remember peeing when Detrick hit me with the stun gun.

I open my eyes. Yellow light from the heater dances on the ceiling. I feel cold air flowing over me, and I remember the window is broken. I look around. My heart jigs when I spot Detrick, standing in the doorway. At some point, he removed his coat. He wears a denim shirt over a turtleneck and a nicely cut pair of trousers.

"You broke my nose," he says.

I notice the blood on the turtleneck. "How are going to explain that?"

"People fall when the sidewalks are icy." His eyes run over me. His smile chills me. "You're shivering. Cold?"

I say nothing.

"You shouldn't have broken that window. Heater would have had it comfortable in here by now."

The hopelessness of the situation is like a dark hole and I'm about to get sucked into it. This man is going to kill me. It's just a matter of when. And how. Time is on my side, but I know it's running out.

"You going to behave yourself if I cut the rope on your ankles?"

"Probably not."

He laughs. "You try anything stupid, and I'll hurt you bad this time, you understand?"

He looks at me the way a starving dog looks at a piece of meat before devouring it. He's going to rape me. I see it in his eyes. The thought repels me, but I remind myself I've already survived it once. I can survive it again. I want to live. That interminable will pulses through me with every rapid-fire beat of my heart.

He starts toward me. I notice the stun gun in his hand. "Don't use the gun," I say.

"You going to cooperate?"

Unless I get the chance to kill you. "I'll do whatever you want."

He kneels next to me. The knife glints like quicksilver in the light from the kerosene heater. The scrap of fabric binding my ankles falls away. I feel his eyes on me, but I can't bring myself to look at him. I know he'll see my fear. I know he feeds on that.

My heart cartwheels in my chest when he begins unlacing my left boot. I stare at his fingers. The manicured nails. The rock-steady hands. He's so utterly normal-looking I can almost convince myself this isn't happening.

But the man unlacing my boot is incapable of feeling any emotion other than the gnawing compulsion of his dark hunger. Tonight, that hunger is focused on me—and minutes away from spiraling out of control.

The clock on the dash reads three-thirty A.M. when John parked the Tahoe outside the Painters Mill police department. Snow swirled in when he pushed open the front door. Mona sat at the dispatch station, a lollipop in her mouth, both feet propped next to her monitor. A lilting Red Hot Chili Peppers tune floated from a radio on the credenza. She looked up from her book when John entered. Her feet hit the floor and she stood.

"I thought you left."

"I'm back." He headed toward Kate's office. "You seen the chief?"

"Not since Detrick just about arrested her."

"Any idea where she is?"

"I figured she went home."

"How long ago did she leave?"

"A couple of hours, I think."

"Where's Detrick?"

"I assumed he went home, too." He brows snapped together. "Is there something going on?"

The bell on the front door jingled. Glock blew in looking as grim as John had ever seen him. Mona yanked the sucker out of her mouth. "What's going on, you guys?"

Ignoring her, John turned to Glock. "Were you able to get Detrick?"

"I tried his cell, but he didn't pick up."

"Try him at home."

He expected the former Marine to question the wisdom of calling the sheriff at three-thirty in the morning. Instead he slid his cell from its nest and hit two buttons. "Lora? Hey, it's Rupert Maddox." He looked at John as he spoke. "Yeah, everything's fine. I was just wondering if you could put Nathan on the line for a sec." Glock's brows go up. "He's not there? Really? Do you know where he is?" He nods. "Well, that's dedication for you. I'll get him on the radio. Sorry to have bothered you."

His grim expression fell on John with the same levity of the words that followed. "Housekeeper says he's on patrol."

"Try him at the sheriff's office." John turned his attention to Mona. "See if you can get him on the radio."

Sliding the headset over her ears, she hit a couple of buttons and spoke into the mouthpiece. "This is dispatch hailing 247. Sheriff Detrick, do you read?"

"Try his cell phone again," John said to Glock.

The former Marine lowered his cell. "Voice mail."

"Shit." John's mind skittered through his options. "Detrick own any property around here?"

Glock shook his head. "I don't know."

"What about abandoned farms or—"

"I have a list!"

Both men looked at Mona. She looked excited by the prospect of helping. "I have a copy of the one I gave Detrick." Grabbing the mouse next to her computer, she clicked and the printer spit out two pages. Mona handed them to John. "I broke it down by homes, farms, and businesses within a fifty mile radius."

"We need manpower," John said.

"What about Pickles?" asked Glock.

"He's on tonight," Mona put in. "Took a call about fifteen minutes ago. Guy skidded off the road down by Clark. He's trying to get a wrecker out there."

John looked at the list. "Call Pickles. Tell him it's urgent. Tell him to start checking these locations."

"What's he looking for?" she asked.

John struggled with how much information to reveal. "We're looking for Kate. Her vehicle. We think she might be in trouble."

"What kind of trouble?" She looked from man to man.

John lowered his voice. "We just want to find her."

"Tell Pickles to stay off the radio," Glock added. "Cell phone only."

"I got it."

"Call Skid, too," Glock put in. "If they find Kate, tell them to call John or me only."

John swung his attention to Glock. "I'll call SHP and have them put out an APB on her vehicle as well as Detrick's."

"Roger that."

Turning, John started toward the door. "We'll cover more ground if we split up. You take the first property on the list."

Glock came up beside him. "Where are you going?"

"I'm going to stir the beehive and see what flies out."

Detrick lived in a two-story Tudor on the south side of Millersburg. John pulled curbside to find the house totally dark. He knew he was about to cross a line. But there was no way around this. Kate was missing. If she was right about Detrick, she would be dead by morning. There was no time for protocol. For all intents and purposes, his career was already over, anyway. May as well go out with a bang.

He trudged through deep snow to the front door and hit the doorbell a dozen times. When that didn't rouse anyone, he pounded with his fist. After a few minutes, a middle-aged woman in a pink robe and matching slippers opened the door, leaving the security chain in place. "Do you have any idea what time it is?" she snapped.

"Mrs. Detrick?"

"I'm Lora Faulkor, the housekeeper. Grace and the kids moved out about a month ago."

John showed his badge. "Is Sheriff Detrick here, ma'am?"

"I assumed he's on patrol. Working on those murders." Her expression transformed from annoyed to worried. "Has something happened?"

"I have reason to believe he could be in trouble, ma'am. May I come in?"

Closing the door for an instant, she unfastened the chain and swung it open. "What's happened?"

"All we know is that he's missing."

"Missing? Oh my." She began wringing her hands. "I told him not to go out in this weather. He probably had a wreck."

John entered a large living room furnished with early American oak furniture. Modular sofa. A coordinating plaid chair. A hint of wood smoke in the air from an earlier fire.

"Why did Mrs. Detrick move out?" he asked.

"I assumed it was because of the divorce. There was a lot of tension, of course. Mr. Detrick works a lot of hours and has no time to cook or clean, so he kept me on."

"I see." The timing of Detrick's marital situation didn't elude John. "Does he have a study or home office?"

She blinked, clearly surprised by the question. "Why on earth do you need to see his office?"

"I need to ascertain his whereabouts. It might help me figure out where to look. If he keeps a record of his patrol grid."

"Wouldn't he keep that at the sheriff's office?"

"Time is of the essence, ma'am. If you could just show me to his office."

"Oh. Well. I guess you could take a look. I just don't see how that will help." Pressing her hand to her stomach, she started down the hall. "Are the rest of the deputies out looking for him?"

"Every available man."

"How long has he been missing?"

"About two hours now. We can't get him on the radio or cell."

"Oh, no. My goodness. That's not good."

He followed her down a hall, the walls of which were adorned with dozens of framed photos. Detrick's kids, he thought, and wondered how a father, a *cop,* could lead such a dark double life.

She entered a room and turned on the light. A study, John thought, taking in the desk topped with a banker's lamp. Beyond, a floor-to-ceiling bookcase was filled with books and knickknacks that weren't quite pretty enough for the rest of the house. Several law enforcement plaques adorned the walls.

"What exactly do you need to see?" Lora asked.

Ignoring her, John went directly to the desk. Locked. He'd reached the point of no return. He gave the housekeeper a hard look. "Where's the key?"

"I don't understand why you need to go through his desk. This doesn't make sense. Why are you doing this?"

Picking up a letter opener, he knelt behind the desk and rammed the point into the lock, breaking it.

"What are you doing?" she cried.

He rifled the drawers. Within minutes, he'd searched the entire desk, but found nothing. "Where else would he keep personal papers and things?"

"What's really going on here?" she asked. "Who are you?"

"We're trying to ascertain his whereabouts." John put his hands on his hips and looked around. "Where does he keep his personal effects?"

"I think you should leave."

"I'm afraid I can't do that."

"I'm calling the police."

"The police are out looking for Detrick, ma'am."

That stopped her, but John knew it wouldn't last. "I need to know where he keeps his personal effects."

When she didn't answer, he crossed to her, grabbed her arms and shook her. *"Where, goddamnit!"* he shouted.

She gaped at him, her mouth quivering. "He keeps some things in the attic."

Leaving her, he took the steps two at a time to the second level. All he could think about now was Kate. The time they'd spent together. The note of utter certainty in her voice when she'd told him about Detrick.

He found the attic door at the end of the hall. He heard the housekeeper behind him. "I want you to stop right now and tell me what's going on!" she cried.

John went up a narrow stairwell, opened the door and hit the light switch. A bare bulb dangled from a rafter, illuminating a small attic crowded with boxes, an old metal file cabinet, a half dozen folding chairs, a collapsed patio table umbrella.

"I'm calling Deputy Jerry Hunnaker right now," Lora said.

John looked up to see her standing at the door with a phone in her hand. "You do what you have to do." Spotting a beat-up file cabinet, he crossed to it and yanked on the drawer, but it was locked. "Where's the key?"

"I don't know." She punched numbers into her cell phone.

John looked around for something to break the lock with. Finding an old umbrella, he rammed the metal tip into the lock.

"What are you doing?" she screamed.

He hammered away at the lock until the top drawer rolled open. He saw files near the front. At the rear he found several Tupperware containers and a shoebox. He started with the files. Bank statements. Utility bills. Meaningless forms and warranties. Finding nothing of interest, he pulled out the shoebox and found photos. He knew immediately they were police file photos. Hundreds of them. Dead bodies. Homicides. Suicides. Horrific accidents. The one thing they had in common was that all were violent.

John reached for one of the Tupperware containers, opened it. He found a pair of women's panties. He went to the next, found a black bra. A sheer *kapp*, the kind worn by an Amish woman. Souvenirs, he realized. "Christ." The one thing he hadn't found was something that would lead him to Kate.

He started toward the door, nearly running over Lora, who stood in the doorway. "I called Nathan's office," she said. "They don't know anything about him being missing. I told them what you were doing. They're on their way."

"If Detrick was in trouble, where would he go?"

"I have nothing to say to you."

Before he could stop himself John grabbed her shoulders, put her hard against the wall. "If I don't find him, he's going to kill someone! Now where the fuck is he?"

"Kill someone?" She stared at him, her mouth agape and quivering. "You're crazy! Nate wouldn't hurt anyone! He's a police officer! He wouldn't do that!"

"He already has!" John shouted. "Is there someplace private he goes to be alone?"

"H-he never mentioned a place!"

"Does he have a cabin? Anything like that?"

"I don't know!"

Struggling for control, he released her and stumbled back. For several seconds they stared at each other, then John turned and took the stairs two at a time to the ground floor. He went through the door and ran to the Tahoe. By the time he climbed behind the wheel he was shaking. Snatching up the phone, he called Glock. "Detrick's our man."

"How do you—"

"I just left his house. I went through his office. He's got souvenirs."

"Jesus, Tomasetti."

"Where are you?"

"North side of Painters Mill. I've checked two farms on the list, but I'm batting zero."

"They could be anywhere." John grabbed the list of abandoned properties off the console. "We gotta find her, Glock. She's in trouble." Starting the engine, he pulled onto the street. "Where do I look?"

"There's an abandoned motel off of Route 62 out of Millersburg. I'm heading that way now. You're closer to Killbuck. There's a house there that's on this list."

John squinted down at his list, frustrated because he wasn't familiar with the area. "Goddamnit, we need more manpower."

"Pickles and Skid are out looking. We'll find her."

John ended the call and made the turn onto State Route 754. The township of Killbuck was ahead, the abandoned house just beyond. The snow made for agonizingly slow travel. Visibility had dwindled, making it difficult to see the road. Even the telephone poles and road signs were invisible. In a few hours travel would be impossible.

He squinted through the windshield at the swirling maelstrom beyond. "Where are you, Kate?" he whispered.

The only answer was the steady beat of the wipers and the echo of his own fear.

CHAPTER 35

I watch him remove my boots. Around me, the old house creaks and moans against the storm raging outside. Even with the heater turned on high, the room is cold. My legs and arms shake uncontrollably. I can no longer tell if it's from the cold or from the endless stream of terror coursing through me. I recall my last conversation with John, and I wonder if he believed me about Detrick. I wonder of he's looking for me. If *anyone's* looking for me. Or if I'll end up like the others.

Detrick sets my boots aside and looks at me. Even in the dim light, I see the hunger burning bright and hot in his eyes. I'm so repulsed my stomach threatens to rebel.

"You're shaking," he says. "I like that. I like it a lot."

I look at him dead-on, trying to conjure anger, anything but this fear that's beating me down. "It was you that night in the woods, wasn't it?"

"I'd dropped her panties. Fell right out of my pocket." He grins. "Close call, wasn't it?"

"Why do you it?"

He looks amused by the question. "My mommy wasn't mean to me and my daddy didn't rape me, if that's what you're asking."

"I just want to know why."

"I like it. I always have. It's pretty much textbook with me. Started with animals when I was a kid. I killed a kitten when I was eight, gave me a boner like I'd never had before."

As he speaks, I take a mental inventory of my physical condition. My toes are numb with cold. My ankles are stiff from the rope. My hands are still bound, but my legs are free. I can fight. I can run.

"I want to rip you open," he says. "I want to hear you scream and grunt. I want to see your eyes bug out." He grips his penis through his trousers and massages himself. "See what I mean? It's like fuckin' Pavlov's dogs. I think of cutting you, and then I gotta do it. I got to hurt you, and then I gotta get off. My cock ain't gonna quit until it's done."

I suppress a shudder. "If I die tonight, the cops are going to be all over this. They'll figure it out. They'll know Jonas Hershberger isn't the killer."

"Keep talking, Kate. I like the sound of your voice."

My breaths rush between my teeth. Too fast. Too shallow. I'm scared. So damn scared.

Kneeling, he moves toward me. I recoil, but he snags my hair in his fist and yanks me toward him. "I'm going to take off your pants. You're going to lay there like a good little bitch and let me. Or I'll hit you with the stun gun. You got that?"

He pushes me onto my back. My elbows and hands grind into the floor beneath me, but I don't fight him. Not yet. Let him get distracted. Let him think I'm going to be easy.

I cringe when he moves my coat aside and unfastens my jeans. His hands are rough. For the first time they tremble. His breathing is elevated. Despite the cold, I see a sheen of sweat on his forehead.

"I'm going to hurt you. It's going to be bad, Kate. Worse than anything you could ever imagine. You're going to scream."

He yanks my jeans down my hips, past my knees, then rips them from my ankles. The air is brutally cold against my bare legs. I sit up, trying to cover myself. The blow catches me off guard. Open-handed across my cheek. Hard enough to make me see stars. I fall back, then turn onto my side to keep the weight off my arms.

Snarling something I don't understand, he yanks me up by my hair. Pain screeches across my scalp. The second blow is like a stick of dynamite going off in my head. I fall back, and lay still, my cheekbone aching.

Above me, Detrick unfastens his pants and jams them down to his knees.

He's looking down at me, his mouth pulled into a perpetual snarl. "You're going to be the best one yet," he whispers.

His erect penis bobs in front of him, purple-red and bulbous. Reaching into the breast pocket of his shirt, he removes a condom, rips it open. His hands shake as he covers himself. The sight of his clean-shaven groin shocks me, though it shouldn't. I was right; that's why the lab techs never found hairs. I see the lubricant glistening on the condom, and I think of the other women who suffered the same fate I face now.

Terror sits like a cold stone in my chest. Nausea seesaws in my gut. The rape will be bad, but I know it's not the worst thing that will happen to me tonight. I try to think like a cop. I need to go on the offensive. Find his vulnerable point. But at this moment, I feel as if I'm fourteen years old again and paralyzed with terror.

Stuffing the condom wrapper into his shirt pocket, he kneels in front of me. He's going to hit me again; I see it in his eyes. Wild thoughts rampage my brain. A thousand screams of outrage clog my throat. His pants sag at his ankles. A vulnerability. My legs are free. My quads are the strongest muscles I have. I have an instant to react.

I draw both legs back and kick him in the chest as hard as I can. An animalistic bellow bursts from his mouth. He reels backward, lands hard on his backside. His back strikes the kerosene heater, knocking it over. Hope flares inside me when kerosene and flames spill onto the hardwood floor.

Then I'm on my feet. I kick his coat into the flames. Two yards away, Detrick jumps to his feet. His face is a mask of fury as he yanks up his pants. His eyes flick from me to the fire. A hysterical laugh bubbles up when I realize he doesn't know which is the bigger threat.

He lunges at me. I turn to run. I try to recall where I last saw the Kimber. On the floor? The mantel? No time to find it. I streak to the front door, turn, twist the knob with my bound hands.

A scream tears from my throat when his hands slam down on my shoulders. He yanks me back, throws me to the ground. All I can think is that I should have hurled myself through the window.

I kick at him wildly, legs pumping, not aiming. I land several blows. He screams a curse. Punches at my legs with his fists. But the pain doesn't register. If I stop kicking, I'm going to die.

I fight like I've never fought before. Vaguely, I'm aware of the fire a few feet away. I smell smoke and kerosene. His coat burns next to the heater. The floor is catching, flames leaping three feet into the air. Hope soars at the thought of a passerby noticing the light.

All hope evaporates when he comes down on top of me. The first blow glances off my chin. I try to twist, roll away. But his weight crushes me. I kick with my right leg, but the angle is bad. A second blow slams into my left temple. My head bounces against the floor. White light explodes behind my eyes. He hits me again and I hear my cheekbone crack. Pain zings up my sinuses. Darkness crowds my vision, and I struggle to stay conscious.

Stay conscious! Fight him!

My brain chants the words like a mantra. I try to head-butt him, but he's ready this time. Hissing a curse, he drives his fist into my solar plexus. The breath rushes from my lungs. I hear myself retch. I try to suck in a breath, but my lungs seize.

The next thing I know his hand is around my throat. He's incredibly strong. I open my mouth for air, but my airway is crushed. Panic descends in a rush. I buck and writhe beneath him. Stars fly in my peripheral vision. I feel my tongue protrude. My eyes bulge. I wonder if this is what it's like to die.

Dark fingers encroach on my vision. Vaguely, I'm aware of him speaking, but I don't understand. Consciousness ebbs. All I can think is that I want to live. *I want to live!* And then the darkness reaches out and pulls me into the abyss.

John would have missed the house if it hadn't been for the yellow glow in the window. At first he thought he was imagining things. That maybe the dash lights were playing tricks on him. Then he saw it again. A flicker of yellow through the seemingly impenetrable wall of snow.

Headlights? Flashlight? Or fire?

Cutting the headlights, he stopped the Tahoe in the middle of the road. He tugged the Sig from his shoulder holster, pulled back the slide to chamber a bullet. Snow and wind bombarded him when he opened the door. Visibility was down to a few yards. He fought his way toward the house. Thirty feet in, he caught another glimpse of light. He nearly ran into the vehicle sitting in the driveway. Detrick's Suburban, he realized. Immediately behind it, Kate's Mustang was attached with some type of tow mechanism.

John slid his cell phone from his coat and dialed Glock. "I found them." He could barely hear his voice above the scream of the wind. "The abandoned house near Killdeer."

"I'm on my way."

John dropped the phone into his pocket. He had no idea what to expect inside. But he had two things going for him. First, he knew Detrick kept his victims alive for quite some time. Second, the storm was the perfect cover.

CHAPTER 36

The first thing I'm aware of is that I can breathe. My mouth sags open. My tongue feels like a dry sock, but I suck in air by the mouthful. I smell smoke and kerosene. I'm laying on my back, my arms locked beneath me. I hear the wind outside, tearing around the house, a beast on a rampage.

I open my eyes to find Detrick over me. I see blood beneath his nose. The dark stain of it on his shirt. Everything that happened rushes back. The fight. The fire.

I raise my head and see that the fire is out. I feel the cold floor beneath my backside, and I realize my panties are gone. Detrick stands a few feet away. He's removed his slacks, completely this time.

"Scream for me, Kate." Crossing to me, he kneels and comes down on top of me. "Scream for me."

I do the only thing I can manage and spit.

He stiffens, then his tongue snakes out and licks the spittle from the side of his mouth. I stare into his awful face. A face etched with unfathomable cruelty. I can't believe my life is going to end this way. I can't accept that. I won't. The will to live rages inside me. Too powerful to be snuffed out. Too hot to be cooled. All I can think is that I'm not going to let him do this.

But hope is quickly dwindling. That precious lifeline has been severed. I'm alone in a raging sea with no chance of rescue.

Closing my eyes, I throw my head back and scream.

* * *

Blinded by snow and wind, John felt his way to the rear of the house. Twice he lost his footing and fell, but he never let go of the Sig or lost his sense of direction. The wind tore at his clothes as he went around to the back. He saw a porch, the screen flapping like laundry in the wind. Keeping low, he ascended the concrete steps and approached the door.

Dim light floated through the grimy glass. John peered inside, saw a dilapidated kitchen. He twisted the knob and the door creaked open. Praying Detrick didn't hear him, he crept inside.

Kate's scream raised the hairs at the back of his neck. His heart rate spiked. John had seen a lot of terrible things in his years as a cop. He'd seen the inhumanity man can inflict; he'd seen his own family murdered. Still, the anguish echoing in that scream went through him like a switchblade.

He sidled through the kitchen. Pressing his back to the wall, he peered into the next room. Dim light from a heater illuminated Detrick kneeling over Kate. He was nude from the waist down. John couldn't see her face, just a partial silhouette as she lay on the floor.

A second scream rent the air. Gun leading the way, John rounded the corner. Detrick must have sensed his presence, because he turned his head. His eyes widened. He jumped to his feet, looked wildly around.

"Get your hands where I can see them!" John shouted.

Detrick lunged toward the mantel.

Kate raised her head. *"Gun!"* she screamed.

John fired twice. Center mass. The first shot hit Detrick in the side just below his armpit. His body went rigid, then he went to his knees. The second shot penetrated his right cheek, snapping his head around as if he'd been punched. He fell on his side and lay still.

John didn't remember holstering his weapon or crossing to Kate. He saw her shattered expression. Bare legs covered with specks of blood. Hurt, he thought, but alive.

A sob tore from her mouth when he knelt beside her. "I'm here," he rasped. "It's okay. You're going to be okay."

"He was going to kill me," she choked.

"I know, honey. I know. It's over. You're okay."

She was bare from the waist down. He didn't let himself think about what might have happened as he worked his coat from his shoulders and covered her. All that mattered was that she was alive. He hadn't been too late. Not this time.

"How bad are you hurt?" he asked.

She was sobbing now, shaking uncontrollably, unable to speak.

John wanted to pump another round into Detrick. "I'm going to untie your hands, okay?"

Gently, he helped her sit up. He used his pocketknife to cut the cloth binding her wrists. When they were free, he took her hands between his and rubbed. "Are you hurt?"

"I'm okay."

"Kate, did he . . ."

Tears streamed from her eyes when she looked at him. "No."

Relief struck a hard blow. John could feel his own emotions winding up. "Come here," he whispered.

She reached for him.

"Everything's going to be all right," he said.

"Promise me," she whispered.

"I promise." When he wrapped his arms around her, she broke into a thousand pieces.

CHAPTER 37

Snow glitters beneath a brilliant January sky. Around me, the citizens of Painters Mill emerge from their homes and businesses like cautious animals after a long hibernation. Sidewalks are shoveled and windshields are scraped. A big John Deere tractor clears snow from the traffic circle. I can smell the doughnuts from the Butterhorn Bakery down the street.

Three cars are parked in the spaces in front of the police department. I recognize all of them. My reserved spot is empty, as if they're expecting me. I pull in and shut down the engine. It's the first time I've been back since being reinstated as chief of police. I'm unduly pleased to be here. But that's not to say I don't have mixed emotions about what I face inside.

Two days have passed since the terrible ordeal I went through with Nathan Detrick in that farmhouse. I've relived every horror a thousand times since. But I know it could have been worse. I know I'm lucky to be alive.

Nathan Detrick survived his gunshot wounds. He was transferred to a Columbus Hospital yesterday where he underwent surgery and as of this morning was listed in stable condition. The doctors say he's going to make it. I should take some consolation in the fact that he'll live to see his trial and prison. But I don't think the world is a better place with him in it.

The FBI and BCI have started looking into cold cases, beginning with the Tanana River Murders in Alaska. I spoke to the SAC this morning, a veteran agent by the name of Dave Davis, who will also be checking similar crimes and missing persons reports for the time period when Detrick was a police officer in Dayton. No one knows if it's true, but so far Detrick has confessed to having killed as many as thirty women in the last twenty-five years.

Aside from some deep bruises and lacerations, I was given a clean bill of health by the emergency room resident at Pomerene Hospital. It's the other, not-so-visible injuries that are still giving me problems. The flashbacks are bad. The nightmares are worse. The doctor assured me they are a normal psychological response to the kind of trauma I went through. He recommended a therapist in Millersburg and assured me the nightmares would fade with time. I hope he's right.

John Tomasetti stayed with me that first day. I spent most of the time sedated and fighting sleep. He fixed soup and coffee, refused to give me vodka when I asked for it, and talked to me when I needed it. When I tried to thank him for saving my life, he told me I was just experiencing a case of hero worship and it would probably wear off in a few days. I have no idea where our relationship will go from here. One thing I do know for certain is that I will always consider him a friend.

I reach the front door of the police station and hesitate. I'm not inordinately vain, but the bruises on my face and neck are bad. I did my best to cover them, but I'm pretty inept when it comes to makeup. All that jazz in a jar can only do so much. My lip needed three stitches and is swollen to twice its normal size. I try not to think about that as I open the door and step inside.

Mona mans the dispatch station, the headset over her ears, her eyes on the computer monitor in front of her. She looks up when the bell on the door jingles and offers me a big smile. "Chief!"

"I didn't actually catch you working, did I?" I ask.

Flushing, she rises, comes around the desk. "Homework, actually. Sorry." I try not to wince when she throws her arms around me. "Boy, are we glad to see you. Welcome back."

"Media been around?" I ask.

"Took a couple of calls this morning. Most of them are calling for an interview with you. I've been telling them you're not allowed to talk about the case."

"Keep up the good work."

I look over her shoulder to see Glock emerge from his cubicle. He's not big on smiles, but I see the grin in his eyes as he approaches. "How you feeling, Chief?"

"Better," I manage.

Pickles surfaces from behind Glock. "Well, I'll be go to hell. Ain't you a sight for sore eyes. No pun on the word *sore*, Chief."

"Don't make me smile," I say. "Pulls my stitches."

"Not gonna be easy, seein' how everyone's so damn glad to have you back," Pickles says.

I shake both men's hands and then Mona's. "It's good to be back."

The familiarity is balm for my soul and I take a moment to soak it in, hoping my emotions don't choose this moment to betray me.

"We heard about what happened at the farmhouse," Glock says.

"If you need anything," Mona adds quickly.

"Just let us know," Pickles finishes for her.

I smile at them. "Just don't treat me like I'm some kind of invalid, okay?"

"Hell no." Pickles laughs. "Sure as hell ain't going to do that."

Glock finally breaches the subject no one wanted to raise. "So how did you know to look at Detrick?"

"I didn't, at first. One thing I was utterly certain of was that Jonas Hershberger wasn't the killer."

"How did you know it wasn't him?" Mona asks.

"Kittens."

"Kittens?"

I tell them about the litter Jonas saved when we were kids. "I think most sociopaths are born, not made. Very few are created by life events."

"Detrick matched Tomasetti's profile to a T," Pickles says.

"There's some wisdom in there somewhere," I reply.

"If it hadn't been for you—" Mona begins, but I cut her off.

"Don't give me too much credit, okay?" I think of Daniel Lapp's remains in the grain elevator. "I don't deserve it."

I'm saved from having to explain when the switchboard beeps. Mona rushes toward her desk to take the call, and I head toward my office. I flip on the light, and I'm surprised to see that my desktop is neat. The last time I was here, it was covered with papers from the Slaughterhouse Killer file. I realize Mona or Lois must have tidied it up for me.

I've barely made it to my desk when the phone rings. I look down, see Mona's extension on the display and hit speaker.

"Chief, I just got a call from some guy out on Dog Leg Road. Says there're loose cows on the road."

I think of the last time we got the call about Stutz's livestock, and I smile. "Dispatch Skid, will you? Tell him to cite Stutz this time. He's had ample time to get that fence fixed."

"Roger that."

I end the call and lean back in my chair. From where I sit, I can hear Glock and Pickles arguing the pros and cons of criminal profiling. I hear the drone of the switchboard. The scratch of Mona's radio. Being here, in this place, feels right. This is where I belong. Here, with my officers. In this town.

I'll continue to live with my secrets. I know there are worse fates. I think of my nephews, Elam and James. I think of Sarah and the baby she's carrying. I think of Jacob and the ugliness that has passed between us. I think of my own isolation, my inability to connect, and I realize the time has come for me to reach out. They are my family, and I want them to be part of my life.

I think of John for the dozenth time today, and I wonder where he is and what he's doing. I wonder if he thinks of me as often as I think of him.

My phone buzzes again. I look down and see a 614 area code with "BCI" on the display. I pick up, already anticipating the sound of his voice. "I was wondering when you were going to call," I say.

"I hear you got yourself reinstated."

"They came begging yesterday."

"I hope you weren't too easy."

"I held out for a raise."

"Good for you." He pauses. "I was in the neighborhood and was wondering if you'd like to go to lunch."

"Columbus is a hundred miles away, Tomasetti. How can you just be in the neighborhood?"

"I told the brass I needed to handle some case-related paperwork down there."

"We could probably hustle up a report or two."

"I told them it would be an overnight trip." He lowers his voice. "Just between us, I've got a big crush on the chief of police."

My lip hurts, but I smile anyway. "I hear the diner's got a pretty decent pot roast."

"In that case I'll pick you up at the station in fifteen minutes."

"I'll be here," I say, and disconnect.